STRIPPED

STRIPPED

Racy Lee

iUniverse, Inc.
New York Lincoln Shanghai

Stripped

iUniverse books may be ordered through booksellers or by contacting:

iUniverse
2021 Pine Lake Road, Suite 100
Lincoln, NE 68512
www.iuniverse.com
1-800-Authors (1-800-288-4677)

This is a work of fiction. All of the characters, names, incidents, organizations and dialogue in this novel are either the products of the author's imagination or are used fictitiously.

ISBN-13: 978-0-595-40020-1 (pbk)
ISBN-13: 978-0-595-84405-0 (ebk)
ISBN-10: 0-595-40020-5 (pbk)
ISBN-10: 0-595-84405-7 (ebk)

Printed in the United States of America

To my sister. No one in the world could be closer than identical twins. In a sense, we are the same person, even though at birth I was fat and bald while you were skinny with lots of hair! We have our own language and share a bond that no one else can comprehend. We both are passionate about tacos, reading, and recognizing things in the background that no one else notices. Thank you for being one of my biggest cheerleaders. I love you.

Acknowledgement

Firstly, I give many thanks to God for continuing to bless me each and every day.

To my intelligent and beautiful daughter, thank you for your patience and understanding for the times when I needed to stay focus. I hope that I have shown you how to fulfill your dreams and never give up on your passion! Carpe Diem! Cool…mommy wrote a book!

To Mommy and Pretty, words cannot express my sincere appreciation for the ongoing support and unconditional love that you have given. If I can be half the mother that you both are, I will be highly successful. You have taught me to stay humble, hard-working and hungry.

To the best little sister and little brother in the world, I love you guys!

Thank you to my family and friends for all of your love and support as I drove you crazy through this process.

Lastly, JD thank you for creating my very first deadline, and encouraging me to pursue my lifelong dream.

Introduction

I know it's evil to speak ill of the dead, but I hate John more than words. When the prison warden called to tell us that he had been stabbed to death by another inmate I didn't cry, I didn't feel anything. I was silent, relieved, and grateful.

My mom married John when I was 11 years old, after my real daddy had walked out on us. He said he was going to his boy's house to watch a fight, and he never came back. My mom thought that maybe he was too drunk to drive, or his car broke down when he didn't come home. She called him a dozen times, and when he finally picked up his cell phone, he told my mom that he was in love with someone else, and he would be by to get his shit in a day or two. My mother fell like a sack of potatoes. She cried for days, she didn't eat, and she gave up on raising me. My beloved daddy had ripped my mother's heart out, and left me orphaned with a million unanswered questions. The cocksucker snuck in the house to get his stuff when I was at school. I was so confused because I still missed him even though he had treated me like shit. I hated him as much as I loved him.

My mom used to be the kind of woman that grabbed men's attention wherever we went, but she began to let herself go both physically and emotionally. It was painful to watch her turn into somebody that I didn't know. My mother was always energetic and full of life, but she started to fade before my eyes. Her spirit had been smothered, and I watched her grow weaker as weeks turned into months. Her identity was attached to being married, so when he left she fell apart.

After he was gone, I realized that they hadn't been very happy in the last few weeks before he left. They were yelling at each other all the time, and my dad started coming home really late or not at all. He wasn't spending a lot of time with us, and my mom made excuses for him. I remembered hearing my mom complaining and making threats, but I know she didn't expect him to leave.

She started fucking up at her job at the bank making account errors, calling in sick, and coming in late. As a child, I remember trying to get my mom out of bed, so that she could start getting ready for work before I left for school. When all of the other kids were playing at recess, I was wondering if my mom had got up and went to work, or if she was still lying on the bed in her dark room with the curtains pulled tight. She had been working at the bank for a couple of years, so they gave her warnings, and then they wrote her up, but it got so bad they had no choice but to fire her. I was so disappointed in my mom, but I never said anything because I didn't want to make her feel any worse than she already did. Our lives changed overnight after that.

My mom dragged me to the welfare office, and we got hooked up with the total package: welfare, food stamps, and Medi-Cal. Money was tight, and my mom suffered. As we stood in line at the grocery store, I looked around to make sure none of my friends were around because I was so embarrassed when my mom pulled out the food stamps. I felt poor, like my mom wasn't really trying, and everybody in the world had a better life than I did. I wanted to crawl under the counter when we had more groceries than we could afford, and my mom started grabbing things out of the plastic bags, handing it to the checker to take off of the bill. The people standing in line behind us would breathe hard, roll their eyes, and whisper to each other about the pathetic welfare case and her poor little girl.

After my dad walked out of the door to go watch the heavyweight match, I never saw him again. For years, I kept thinking that he would show up because we never moved, and I just knew that he was missing me as much as I was missing him, but I finally realized that he didn't. Every year, I made a Father's Day card from construction paper in the shape of a shirt and tie, but after I held onto them for about a week, I ended up giving them to my uncles or cousins.

All through middle school, I got perfect grades because I thought my daddy would hear about my perfect report cards and perfect behavior, and he would fall all over himself to congratulate me, hold me in his arms, and apologize for leaving, but he never did. I also had to be strong for my mom. She was a fucking mess after my dad left, and I ended up being the parent as I microwaved frozen food, cleaned up the house, and reminded her to brush her teeth. She left pitiful voicemails on my dad's phone, begging him to come home until he finally changed his number. After awhile, I didn't care about myself anymore; I wanted my dad to come home for my mom. He was the only person that could make her whole again, and I began to miss my mom more than I missed him. I was too young to understand relationships, breaking up and betrayal, but I knew that I would never let a man have that much power or control over me *ever*.

Mom met John after her friend dragged her to a bar about six months after daddy left. She was starved for attention and affection, but her desperation blinded her judgment. Right away, John started hanging out and making himself real comfortable in our house. I remember him throwing chump change at my mom every now and then, and the money hypnotized her. She had been having a hard time paying bills and keeping food on the table, and John swooped in like Superman. The more money he gave my mom, the more she let him hang around. John introduced us to his relatives and we had family night every Saturday. He took us to places that we hadn't been since daddy was home.

After a couple of months of him posting up and spending the night, they announced that they were getting married. I never liked John. I couldn't figure out why exactly, but he made me feel uncomfortable. I tried to tell my mom, but she always made excuses for him. Even after I told her that her husband kept "accidentally" walking in the bathroom after I took a shower or walking in my bedroom without knocking, she didn't put his ass out. She told me that I was imagining things, John was a good man, and I had misunderstood his intentions. He was just trying to be a father to me. I wasn't crazy, and I knew what I was feeling wasn't wrong. I never trusted him.

We didn't really see it until after the wedding, but John was an alcoholic. He took his ass to work everyday, but he would start drinking as soon as he came home. He was a mean drunk; he would yell at my mom and me about things that he didn't see. All I did was homework and chores because I didn't want him to say anything to me. I wanted to be invisible. When he started hitting on my mom, I wanted to move with my grandma, but she convinced me that he would change. I hated seeing my mother as a helpless victim. Her survival had been based on men, what they could provide for her, and the power they had over her. I didn't know if she married John because she loved him, or because he could provide for us. The bottom line was that I couldn't trust her anymore because she didn't protect me the way a mother should.

One night after John had been drinking all day, he crept into my dark room and placed his dirty hand over my mouth. I woke up to a fear that I had never known before. The smell of stale liquor made me dizzy. He pulled my nightgown up, and stuck his finger up my pussy. I cried and begged him to stop as he moved that nasty finger in and out. The pain was killing me, and I was crying so hard that I couldn't breathe. I started praying for God to tell my father to come save me, and John finally pulled his finger out.

I thought my prayers were answered until he climbed on top of me and whispered in my ear to be quiet or he would kill me. He tried to shove his nasty dick in my innocent pussy, and I bit my lip so hard that I could taste the warm blood in my mouth. His hand started slipping from my lips, and I yelled as hard as I could. My mom bust in the room, turned on the light, and put a gun to John's head. I had never seen the gun before, but I was relieved to watch him turn into a bug-eyed frozen bitch when he felt that cold, black pistol at his temple. The police came, and John ended up getting sent to prison.

My mother apologized over and over for every time that she didn't believe me when I told her that he wasn't shit. It wasn't until years later that I realized that she must have believed some of what I was telling her because she came in my room that night with a loaded gun. She hadn't been there for me before that, but she was right on time that night. It would take years for us to mend our relationship because I had so much resentment built up for the way she just checked out after my dad left. I always thought my mother was strong and independent, but even when my reality changed I never stopped loving her.

I made a vow to myself that I would never let money make a victim out of me the way that it had turned my mother out. I was never going to put myself in a position where I was broke and embarrassed like I was when I was a child. A child should never have to worry about whether or not the lights would be on when she got home from school. I worried about bills, food, and my mother's well-being when that wasn't my job. My childhood was taken from me before I was ready to leave it. Playing outside and fucking up in school weren't options for me.

I decided that I would never be willing to trade in my soul out of desperation and helplessness like my mom did. Money is a necessary evil, and my twisted relationship with loot started when I was just a kid. I learned at a very young age that money had the ability to design a person's decisions, their happiness, and ultimately their life.

CHAPTER 1

I was running late, so I had to dip through thick traffic on the 405. I pulled up to Hypnotiq's spot and called her cell. She said she would be right out. While I waited, I pulled my visor down to look in the lighted mirror. I pooched my lips together, applied a little more lip gloss, and poked at my hair. I was slapping R. Kelly's *Feeling On Your Booty* when my stomach growled, and I remembered that I had a Snickers in my bag. I surrendered to my hunger, and got out to grab my emergency chocolate from the trunk.

It was a little windy when I got out of the car, and my hair blew across my face. Several pieces of hair locked onto my sticky lip gloss, I carefully pulled the long, honey-blonde strands off of my lips. When I was leaning over my trunk, two Mexican guys in a Nissan Sentra covered with primer paint honked and yelled out of their car. I was used to the honking, the stares, and cats basically loosing their minds when they saw my fine ass pushing a brand new silver, 3 series convertible BMW on 22s. My shit was tight.

With skin the color of coffee with two creams, almond-shaped eyes, dimples, and a body from another planet, I was as bad as my car. I smiled as I got back in the car, and tore open the candy bar while I waited for Hypnotiq to come down. I wasn't doing too badly for a 23-year-old that barely held a high school diploma.

Finally, I saw her walking toward the car. Hypnotiq was fine enough to make a rainbow-flag-waving fairy switch teams. Her real name was Renee, but her stage name truly expressed the spell that she unknowingly cast on her many fans. She was caramel-colored with long, black flat-ironed hair. Her engaging, brown eyes could light up a room, and her flirtatious smile gave you butterflies when she aimed it at you. She was tall with a banging body: big ass, tits the size of small cantaloupes, and a tiny waist. She was one of the finest girls at the club. Not only was she was in high demand for table dances, parties, and the stage, but the guys and the girls adored her. Hypnotiq knew that she looked good. She appreciated the compliments, but she never took it too seriously, or made a big deal about the constant attention she got from men.

Hypnotiq had been at the club for three years, so she had seen and heard it all. I had only been there for two, so she shared her knowledge about the strip game, and helped me out when I first started. She was cool to hang out with because she was real. She was one of the only girls from the club that I even fucked with because there was always drama with those gossiping, hating-ass bitches.

"Hey girl!" I walked over to her side of the car and gave her a hug.

"Sorry it took me so long. Jason called just as I was getting ready. You know how he gets right before parties, especially this one!"

Jason was Hypnotiq's boyfriend. They had been together for two years, and he worshiped her. He was more of a square than the guys that we were used to seeing at the club; he was faithful, loving, and honest. Jason was a handsome, hard-working man who made a decent living delivering packages for UPS. Even though they were in a committed relationship it seemed like he never felt secure. It seemed as if he wasn't sure if he truly deserved to be with her, so he constantly went out of his way to prove that he was worthy of her love. They took frequent trips to Vegas, he bought her gifts just because, and was there for her anytime she needed anything. Jason treated her like she was the only chick in the world, and he better had because there were a million other niggas *and* females standing in line to get at her if he was ever caught slipping.

I popped the trunk, and she put her stuff in and closed it. After she stepped into the car, we headed toward the 405 North to the 10 East.

Big D was one of Hypnotiq's biggest customers, and he was throwing a party at his house. She only met him a couple of months ago, but he had been breaking her off ever since. They had never fucked, but he loved to watch her breathe. He would come in the club a couple of times a month, and would give her no less than $500 every time. Big D was a business manager for a couple of singers and rappers. He was balling, and being married didn't seem to get in the way of him trying to get at Hypnotiq. His wife knew about Hypnotiq because she had busted his secretary trying to set up a Vegas trip for two, and she wasn't invited. The poor secretary thought she was going to get fired, but it wasn't her fault that Big D's wife was snooping around on her desk while she went to the bathroom. The trip was canceled, but Big D didn't stop chasing Hypnotiq.

The house was in Baldwin Hills, so we drove down Crenshaw, past the mall, and up the winding hills. We passed some phat-ass houses on the way to Big D's, but his was the tightest. It was a white, two-story house with a red door, and ivy growing all over the front and sides. The yard was neatly manicured, and there were several cars parked in the driveway and on the street. There was a Mercedes G500, S600, and the Maybach, a Bentley coupe, and a Phantom. *This* was a party!

"Hypnotiq, are you for real?"

"Hey, I told you Big D said he was inviting ballers only. We're getting paid tonight!"

"Good looking! I owe you one!"

I pulled the car in the driveway behind Big D's black Range Rover with black Giovanni 22s. Hypnotiq told me that was his run-around car; the Bentley was parked in the garage.

"Where's wifey? I know she's gotta be out of town."

"Yeah, Big D isn't crazy. She's in New York shopping."

"It must be nice."

"Must be."

We grabbed our bags out of the trunk, and walked to the door. Before we reached the doorbell, the aroma of fine cigars caught our attention as we walked past the side gate. Hypnotiq rang the doorbell, and Big D showed up with a fat cigar in his mouth. He was in his early 40s with perfect, medium-brown skin. He had pretty eyes with eyelashes as long as my fake ones, but he had a big nose that looked more like a parrot's beak. Big D was attractive though, and his beak didn't get in the way. He was tall with a little beer belly. With the paper that he had, he didn't need to work out. He had on an LRG sweatsuit with fresh Pumas, and a tight fade. He looked good. I would fuck him. He snatched the important cigar out of his mouth, and greeted us as if we were the last two females on the face of the earth.

He gave Hypnotiq a big hug and kissed her on the cheek. He hugged me too, but not like Hypnotiq. He led us in the house, and I was easily impressed by everything my eyes absorbed. We walked through the lavish den to the park-like backyard, and he introduced us to his boys. I quickly counted six of them. They were businessmen too, and they looked like money: expensive clothes, shoes, diamond jewelry, casually smoking Cuban cigars on the patio with a breathtaking view of Los Angeles. They couldn't hold back their excitement as they stared at the two stallions standing in front of them. They smiled at us like a couple of teenaged boys looking at Playboy for the first time; they had to be married. A rich, single cat never got that juiced because they had the ability to pull bitches like us any day of the week.

Married cats had fat, boring, nagging wives at home, and they weren't used to looking at fine, sexy females on a regular. Big D offered us Caramel Apple Martinis, and told us to make ourselves comfortable in the downstairs bedroom. We took our drinks with us, and found the bedroom. It had its own bathroom with a large fish tank that covered the whole wall behind the sink from the ceiling to the floor. There were dozens of exotic fish in all colors and sizes swimming around *in* the wall. It was the prettiest thing I had ever seen.

"This shit is tight. I can't believe you never fucked him! He has it going on!"

"Believe me I want to, but the timing is always off. He travels a lot with business and his wife stays on his line, but she's not here tonight!"

We laughed and finished our drinks. The caramel was sweet and buttery, and the Grey Goose hit the spot. Hypnotiq went to get us two more, and I started to take my clothes off. She walked in with the drinks, and I was putting my costume on.

"So wassup for tonight? What do they want?"

"Big D said they want us to dance for a little bit, but they wanted to see us get down. You cool with that?"

Hypnotiq was fine, and I secretly had a little crush on her. I wasn't into females, but there was something about her that made you want to just be around her. She was top shelf and so down to earth. We had tongue-kissed and touched each other at other parties, but that was it. I couldn't get down with just any female, but I could fuck with Hypnotiq.

"That's cool. How are we going to do it?"

"Just follow my lead."

Hypnotiq had fucked other girls before, so it wasn't a big deal to her. She was going to be my first. I had never met a female that made me even think about eating pussy, but Hypnotiq was sexy and her body was out of control. I sipped on my second glass of courage, and finished getting dressed. As Hypnotiq took her clothes off, I really looked at her body now that I knew I was going to be on it, in it, and tasting it.

Hypnotiq's body looked good. Her titties were perfect, a full C in a teardrop shape; they were perky and she had big, dark brown nipples. Her stomach was flat, and she had a big ass. Her hips were big enough to let you know she was a woman, and they made her waist look itty bitty. Hypnotiq was thick. She had nice legs with big, tight thighs. She had a belly button piercing with a diamond stud and chain. She caught me looking at her.

"What? Do I have a tag?"

"No, you're cool. I was just looking at your outfit."

"Thanks, it's new."

Niggas told me I was fine too, but I was intimidated by her beauty. Not jealous. I just appreciated her.

When Hypnotiq finished getting dressed, she threw on her robe to tell Big D that we were ready. She gave him the CDs, and he put the music on. His friends moved into the den, and he dimmed the lights. Hypnotiq came back in the room, dropped her robe, and we walked out together. We looked good. When we walked out of the bedroom, we went over to the men in our 6" heels, her French maid costume, and my sexy, Catholic schoolgirl outfit. We came out to the R. Kelly that I was listening to in the car. I loved that song because it made me feel sexy. I was feeling the Grey Goose on an empty stomach, very light and easy.

I went up to the finest one in the group while Hypnotiq focused on Big D. I slowly walked up to him, leaned in, and seductively rubbed my titties on his face. The other men started yelling, and I blew in his ear and watched him squirm. I grabbed his hands and put them on my hips while I moved them around. I turned around and bent down to touch my toes. I slowly shook my ass from side to side right in front of his face. I could feel him stroking my ass with the bills, and I saw a few of them hit the ground. All 20s. This was going to be a good night.

I sat my ass on his lap, and moved it around until I felt his hard dick. I began to grind on his lap to the beat as I lay back and rest my back on his chest. He kissed the back of my neck. His hands were traveling from my thighs to my pussy, so I snatched his hands and yanked them to his sides. I whispered in his ear, "Bad boy!" I stood up in front of him, looked him dead in the eye, and slowly unbuttoned my blouse. I teased him by holding onto the last button, but after I unhooked my bra it was over. I let my double D's go wild, and the men got louder. I let him rub my titties, but when his tongue grazed my nipple, I moved on to the next man leaving him wanting more.

I looked over at Hypnotiq and Big D. He was trying to be cool, laying back in his chair with a cigar in one hand, and his martini in the other. He had a big smile on his face, but you would've thought she was cleaning his carpet instead of taking him to ecstasy. She had straddled his lap, like she was riding his dick with clothes on. She was slowly moving up and down, and he was just sitting there not giving anything back. If his boys weren't watching, he would've been holding her waist, and pushing her down harder on his dick as she moved around on his lap. He would've been rubbing and sucking on her titties, and sweating like a pig. Right then, he showed me how much he really was feeling her because he felt like he needed to hide it.

I walked to the middle of the den, and spread my legs into the splits. Bouncing my pussy up and down drove the men crazy. I lay on my back, and opened my legs wide until my feet were pointed near my ears, then I stretched them towards my shoulders to form a big letter "A" with my body. After I did a somersault and landed on my hands and knees, I popped my ass until they couldn't take it.

I stood up, and put my hands on my knees so they could see my pussy pop. Money was flying everywhere, and the floor was covered with former President Jackson's face. All that loot made me feel sexy as hell. I danced harder and faster, pulling out tricks that I didn't even know I had. I grabbed my titties hard, and pulled them up close to slide my tongue between my cleavage, then I licked my left nipple, and then the right. I ran my hand from my stomach to my pussy, and I used my index and middle finger to caress my lips and clit.

I closed my eyes, threw my head back, and rolled my hips in a wide circle. With my other hand, I put my middle finger in my mouth, sliding it in and out so slowly. I slid completely out of my costume, and lay on the floor again. This time I lay on my side, rested my head on my bent elbow, and stretched my top leg to the ceiling to form an "L." I pointed my toes, and kept moving my leg around like an X rated ballerina. I rolled onto my stomach, and hiked my ass up in the air while my head stayed low. I slowly spread my legs so they could see my pussy, and when one of them moved closer, I quickly shut my legs. The men groaned until I opened my legs again. This time I left them open, and one cat got so close I could feel the heat from his breath on my thighs.

I could see Hypnotiq and Big D from the corner of my eye, and Mr. Cool had left the room. He stopped denying his pleasure; he looked like a kid sitting in front of a loaded Christmas tree. The song finally ended, and I started to get up as the men started clapping. Yeah, they were gentlemen; most niggas just sat there and watched you get up off the ground in silence. I gathered up all the money and my costume, thanked them, and slid into the bedroom.

Hypnotiq came in a few minutes later. She wasn't as hot and sweaty as me because she basically stayed on Big D for the whole song.

"Girl, you keep all those tips you got. Big D broke me off."

I was thankful, but that was fair since I held it down for the six of them on my own, and I handled it.

"Thanks girl. I haven't counted it yet, but I know it's cool."

"Cool. So, now let's go do our thing. You ready?"

"Yeah, just let me wash up a little. I got hot doing all that gymnastic shit!"

"I saw you working it out!"

I walked in the bathroom, and ran the hot water. I grabbed my body wash, and rubbed it into a washcloth until it was lathered up. I ran the towel over my armpits, my pussy, and my ass. I rinsed the soap out and ran the clean towel over my body. I sprinkled a little baby powder, and sprayed Victoria's Secret "Love Spell" all over my body. I retouched my makeup, and went back into the bedroom. Hypnotiq went into the bathroom, and I lay down on the bed butt naked. I just wanted to get off my feet for a minute, and lay in that classy, expensive bed.

Hypnotiq and I walked back into the den completely naked with 6" platform clear sandals. The music was playing, and we stood facing each other in the middle of the den. She gently grabbed my face, and kissed one cheek, then the other, and then my lips. She sucked on my bottom lip, and then gently parted my lips with her tongue. She slowly slid her sweet, juicy tongue in my mouth until she found mine. Our tongues danced together, and our mouths became wet. I could hear the men loudly whispering to each other, but I tried to block them out so that I could fully enjoy the moment.

Hypnotiq started grabbing and rubbing on my titties, and I scooped hers up. She pulled on my nipples, and pinched them. It stung so badly that I smacked her ass in retaliation. She looked surprised, but she smiled and grabbed my ass and pulled me closer. I backed up and started sucking on her nipples, and she ran her fingers through my hair, gently at first, then she pulled it until my lips were off of her tits. She forced me down to the ground, and lay on top of me. She wrapped her thick legs around mine, and touched my cheek with the back of her hand. I responded by moving my face to meet her hand. She had a soft touch, and she made me feel beautifully sexy.

She stuck her slippery tongue in my mouth again, moved it slowly around my neck, and down my body. She stuck her tongue in my belly button, and gently bit my skin on a trail down to my lower body. She spread my legs, and sucked my inner thighs. With her hand, she rubbed my clit with her three middle fingers until I was moist. Finally, she ran her tongue over my clean-shaven pussy until she reached my clit. Hypnotiq's tongue flicked like a snake, and went around like a puppy, it drove me up the wall. I felt like I would go crazy if she didn't stop, and crazy if she did stop. She sucked all over my pussy in a hypnotic rhythm. I was in a trance.

Hypnotiq brought her hand back up and started finger-fucking me, first with one finger and then two. I closed my eyes, and forgot about the party, the men, and the performance; all I could focus on was this gorgeous female bringing me pleasure like I had never known.

I had always heard that women knew how to do it better because they knew how they liked it, but I was completely unprepared for what came next. She used her tongue to make large, slow circles around my clit until I felt all of my nerves standing at attention. Hypnotiq's tongue moved faster and faster, and just before the flood was unleashed, she slowed down, and then stopped. I thought I was loosing my mind, but I opened my eyes, and Hypnotiq was on all fours backing up towards me. She slowly began to lower her body near my mouth. I ate her pussy like a homeless man at the shelter on Thanksgiving.

I grabbed her ass, and pushed it down on my face. I stuck my tongue out and massaged her clit like I was sucking a dick. She started sucking on my pussy again while she was grinding her clit on my firm tongue. We both began to move around to the same beat until *we* were about to cum. Our hips rotated wildly, and we both whispered that we were cumming when all of a sudden I closed my eyes tight and felt Summer, ice cream, and my birthday all at once. We both let out a loud moan, and our hips started to move slow and stiff. The feel of her tongue on my clit made me jerk and I jumped away from her mouth. If she would've licked it again, I would've died.

CHAPTER 2

When Hypnotiq and I drove home that night, we talked about everything that had happened at Big D's house. She fucked Big D in his wife's bed, and his dick was about 9 or 10 inches long. She said that he knew how to work that big thing, which was different because most niggas that were hung like a horse didn't have much skill, they didn't have to. She said he sucked her pussy, and she came in just a few minutes. She was riding him, he was riding her, he hit it from the back, and she came again when he was on top. If a man could make a woman cum when he was on top he was clearly the man. He had to know how to lean in her pussy, and rub his dick lightly, but firmly on her clit until she came.

She said the dick was more than cool, but her pussy was hella sore. She probably wouldn't be able to walk straight the next day, and we laughed loud and hard at her silliness. Big D wanted them to hook up again, and she told him to make it happen. In other words, he was the married one, so he had to free himself up for her. Hypnotiq would have it made fucking with a cat like that.

She asked me if I kicked it with one of his boys, and I told her that one of them *tried* to fuck me. He was so excited, but his little dick wouldn't stay hard, so I told him to stop because what I really wanted was to suck that pretty dick. His stupid ass believed me, I blew the whistle, and he broke me off $500. Hypnotiq made $2800 that night, and I made $1900; rent was paid for two months after working for three hours in a mini-mansion for some ballers.

I wondered if Hypnotiq would mention what had happened between us. I didn't want to be the first one to say anything because I didn't want her to think that I thought it was a big deal. I pretended to be listening to her, but I really wasn't paying attention. I couldn't stop thinking about how she made me feel; it was better than any man ever had.

From the first time I saw Hypnotiq, there was something that drew me to her. I wasn't jealous of her, I just wanted to be around her. I didn't want what she had, I appreciated what she had. She was a stunner, but it wasn't just her looks; her personality was cool, and she brought electricity to a room. She was positive, and cool with everybody. Hypnotiq was an intelligent, classy ho. She was on a paper chase too, but she handled her business in a "professional" way. She kept her dirt to herself, and if a wife or girlfriend called her, she told them that they had the wrong number. Some of the girls at the club were messy and they got off on drama, but Hypnotiq tried her best to avoid it. I never heard her gossip or talk shit about the other girls. Even though I thought she was above the strip game, she never looked down on anybody. Hypnotiq was the kind of female that other females wish they were. She had her share of haters, but anybody that got to know her knew that she was special.

I wondered if things would be the same between us, or would one of us feel awkward around the other? I tried as hard as I could to act the same, but deep down, I was looking at her with different eyes, listening to her with different ears, and casual touching was no longer casual. Now, everything meant something. When she brushed past me to grab her bag out of the bedroom, I wondered if she was giving me a sign that she wanted to kick it again. When she called her boyfriend to say that she would be home soon, I wondered if I should be jealous. When she dressed in front of me after the party, I wondered if I should hide my eyes. I was confused but excited all at once. I had discovered something that I had never experienced before, and I didn't know what that feeling meant. I didn't know if I should act on it anymore, or just deny the strong connection that I had to her. I didn't know if I should allow myself to adore her.

Before she got out of the car that night, I decided that I probably wasn't gay. Hypnotiq was the only female that made me feel like this, but there were a lot of guys that I had been attracted to or wanted to kick it with. Maybe the emotion that I felt for Hypnotiq crossed all boundaries; I was feeling her the way that I would feel a man, but that was a once in a lifetime experience.

Hypnotiq had a party lined up almost every weekend, and she asked me if I wanted to go with her on Friday. Of course I told her yes; Hypnotiq always attracted men with lots of money that were more than willing to share with her. We hugged, and she got out of the car. I watched her walk up to her apartment, and then I drove off. I went home, threw the money in the freezer and took a shower.

CHAPTER 3

I felt like shit. I stared in the bathroom mirror, and looked at my tired face. My body felt warm all over, and my eyes were heavy. I was not in the mood, but I knew that I had to handle my business. I splashed a little cold water on my face, pulled my g-string up, straightened my weave, and opened the bathroom door to join Hypnotiq. She was fixing herself up too, but I was ready to do the damn thing before I said fuck it, and lay my worn-out body on the king size bed in front of me.

"Hypnotiq, you ready to get this money?"

"Are you okay? You don't look too hot."

"Hell nah, but I'm not about to fuck this loot off either! I'll be fine."

"Yeah I hear you. Let's do this, but let me know if you're not feeling it, and I'll take over."

Hypnotiq was always so supportive and giving. If nothing good came out of stripping, at least I had met a friend for life. We walked out of the bedroom to the large suite that was completely filled with suits. Hypnotiq said they were lawyers, so I really had to do extra, and show these uptight niggas how we got down. I strutted across the room, making sure all eyes were on me. Yeah, I'll give them their props, they looked like money, but I couldn't let them know that I was impressed because they paid to see me, and it was my job to make them forget about their perfect wives they left at home.

These parties were usually pretty cool, drunken nights where squares turned into freaks. A few of them, married or not, were always guaranteed to offer the girls $200–$500 for anything from a hand-job to fucking. Some girls took them up on it; I did what I felt like, when I felt like it. It really depended on the mood I was in, how they looked, and what I had seen in the mall recently. These professional types were nothing to be afraid of because they had too much to lose: job, family, reputation. The girls didn't have to worry about them getting physical, forcing them to do anything they didn't want to do, or run out without paying.

The ones to worry about were the gangster parties where niggas didn't have shit to lose, and had to prove how tough they were by calling females bitches and getting rough with them. They loved to pull out heat, making threats, and telling bitches to do this and that. Some of the girls had been robbed, and others were forced to give head or get their pussy snatched. It didn't happen all the time, but it was more likely to happen with the corner boys versus the professional types. The drama usually went down in house parties, or cheap motels where the management had a policy about minding their own business. That's why I only did parties in hotels where there was an actual lobby, a front desk clerk that spoke English, and security just in case anything popped off.

As Hypnotiq and I strolled over to the man of the hour, I began to feel dizzy, but I refused to give up the $250 plus tips that I was getting for this party, so I walked as sexy as I could to the other side of the room. Trick Daddy's southern slang over a tight beat prepared me for what came next. I stood in front of the groom in my caramel-colored g-string, matching lace bra, chaps, cowboy hat and boots. He looked up at me as if surrendering, and I rolled my hips, licked my lips, and tossed my weave over my shoulder. I had him, and although he may have had Sally Homemaker at home, he was mine for the night.

I leaned in real close to his ear and whispered, "You want this pussy Daddy?" After he allowed the right words to be released from his lips, I unleashed the freak that they paid to see.

I turned around, bent down, and stuck my ass right in his face. Their oohs and ahhs gave me the rush that I needed a few minutes ago when I was dragging my tired ass from the bathroom. I put my hands on my knees, and popped my ass on his lap as hard as the chair could stand while Hypnotiq danced for the rest of them. I threw my bra across the room, and seductively rubbed my titties on the groom's chest. He grabbed them hella hard, and pinched my nipples so hard that I pulled away. He pulled me back closer, and I could feel his hard dick on my thigh. He turned me around so that my back was to his face, and I began to grind on his lap, slower at first, then faster and harder. The music got louder, the lights grew brighter, and I began to feel like I was in a fish tank as sounds echoed off the walls.

Sweat began to bead at my forehead, then a feeling of darkness came over me, but this time I didn't fight it. I gave in, and I heard my body hit the floor, but I didn't feel any pain when my head hit the wall on my way down. I heard the groom shouting at me, and then he yelled for Hypnotiq. I heard her yell across the room, "Alizé! Alizé!" I wanted to tell her that I was okay, but I couldn't speak. I could hear all of the drama going on around me, but I couldn't move or speak. Everyone was fussing over me, and arguing about whether I needed ice or a hot towel. Just as suddenly as light turned to dark, my eyes began to open, and I was able to talk again.

"I'm cool. What happened?"

"Girl, don't scare me like that again! You were giving Michael a dance, and then you just passed out! Girl, we didn't know what happened. For a second I thought you were dead!"

"I must have fainted. I started feeling hot and then it was a wrap! I could hear you guys talking, but I just couldn't say anything. I'm sorry if I scared you. This was supposed to be a bachelor's party, not the damn E.R!"

The suits were forgiving, and after Hypnotiq and I went to the bathroom to splash cold water on my face, the show was back on. After a few minutes into the second act, they forgot all about the faint stripper that lay in the middle of the floor a few minutes before and enjoyed the second act of the performance.

After Hypnotiq dropped me at home, I allowed the thoughts to get in my head that I tried to ignore as I sat in her car pretending to be listening while she talked about one of the suit's forcing his phone number on her.

Was I pregnant? My period was supposed to have started yesterday, but nothing yet. How did I let this shit happen? My game was tighter than this, and even though I had fucked two niggas last month, it could only be one person...Tony.

By now my body was wore out, and I started feeling irritated about the possibility of dealing with another fucking abortion. Hypnotiq must have been reading my mind because she started a conversation about my fainting episode.

"So do you feel? I can't believe you passed out like that."

"I know. That was a trip. I'm okay, I just feel really tired."

"Maybe you need to get some rest. We've been staying out a lot lately with all these parties."

"Yeah, but it's not just that."

Hypnotiq was my girl, and I needed to talk to someone about my fucked up situation. Even though a part of me didn't want to put it in the universe, leaving it in my head was driving me crazy.

"I might be pregnant."

I didn't waste any time beating around the bush, but spitting it out like that caught Hypnotiq by surprise.

"Shut up! Tony?"

"Yup!"

"What are you going to do? Have you told him?"

"Hell no! I need to find out for sure before I call him and get cursed out for nothing! Of course he's going to put the check down, but I'm not tripping. I need a baby like I need a hole in the head!"

"Damn girl! Well let me know if you need a ride to the clinic. I got you!"

I knew that if I needed her she would be there for me, and it felt good to get that off my chest. Hypnotiq pulled up to my apartment and I went up the stairs very slowly and carefully. I still felt a little lightheaded and I didn't want to end the night by tumbling down the stairs.

I lived in an upgraded eight-apartment complex in Hollywood that was built in the 1940s. The bedrooms, living room, and kitchen were huge like in all old apartments, and I had hardwood floors throughout and marble countertops. My brown leather couches, trees, and modern art on the wall were banging, and the canopy bed in my bedroom was tight. The rent was cool and it was close to Sunset Boulevard, so I really liked it. I wish I had a washer and dryer in the apartment, but you can't have everything.

After I got inside, I took my clothes off and got in the shower. When I got out it was 1:25 am, and I wondered if Tony was out. I didn't even know what I was going to say, but I called his cell phone, and the voicemail came on right away.

"Hey, this is Tony. Leave a message." Beeep!

His phone was usually turned off when he was at home so I hung up, and got in the bed because as soon as I opened my eyes, I was running to the drug store to get a pregnancy test. If I was pregnant, I had to get rid of it as soon as possible; I didn't want to start throwing up, gaining weight, and getting nasty stretch marks.

CHAPTER 4

As I drove down Centinela Boulevard I called Brandy to tell her about a pregnant stripper that passed out at a bachelor party. I had been sharing my life with her for over 5 years, and I trusted her with my life. We had been through a lot, and I knew she would always have my back. I didn't call my mom because she never did like my lifestyle, and I wasn't in the mood for a lecture. There was no way I was having this baby. Tony wasn't having that, and I didn't need a kid right now anyway. I had no choice but to get an abortion. On my way to get the test, I thought about him, how we met, and why I was going to the clinic for the second time in two years.

Tony had played with the Los Angeles Sunshine for the last two years of his six-year pro basketball career, and he lived with his wife and two kids. I could always spot an athlete, so when he came in the club I made sure to prance my ass in front of him. He was 6'9", built, and Hershey chocolate bar fine. Tony had a body out of this world, and I couldn't wait to mount his ass from the first time I met him. I asked him if he wanted a lap dance, and I ended up giving him four, but he gave me a $100 which meant I got a $20 tip. The dances were different than what I was used to giving because I was seriously trying to work it out, and he kept whispering funny things in my ear, and tickling me. He had a big personality, and he made me laugh.

I could tell that he didn't take himself that seriously because he didn't act all arrogant like some of the athletes that came into the club. He was cracking jokes, telling basketball stories, and kept the waitresses busy all night. I ended up sitting at the table with him and a couple of his boys for about two hours, and we had a good time. After we talked by ourselves for a little while, he asked me if I wanted to kick it sometime. When I asked him what he meant, he said that he just wanted to hang out and have some fun. I was trying to act cool, but I was happy that he finally put it out there.

We exchanged numbers, and he said that he was going to call me the next day. I didn't even bother asking if he was married because I saw the platinum and diamond bling on his finger when he paid for his lap dances. I just wanted to kick it, so I didn't trip off the fact that he was married because I knew how it was going down regardless. Before he left, Tony gave me another $50 "tip" and told me to walk him to his car. I told him that I couldn't leave the club, but in reality, I thought he wanted me to boss him up; everything had been so cool that I didn't want to ruin it the first night. He said that he just wanted to go outside for a minute, so that we didn't have to holler over the music, but I wasn't born yesterday.

Guys like him came into strip clubs, and looked for females to fulfill their fantasies, freaks that would perform the porno tricks they would never ask their classy wives to do. They loved hitting it in the ass, getting their booty holes licked, and having orgies. We were the ones they invited on trips and hooked up with hotel rooms, so they would have guaranteed pussy, instead of getting caught up with groupies that woke up the next morning with money and a lawsuit on their mind.

These niggas liked to come in the clubs like Big Willy buying drinks and lap dances for their boys, but then scurry back to their wives and kids in the suburbs. The most ironic part of this entire situation was the fact that these ballers didn't even fuck that good. They would lie on the bed, and let you go to work. They wouldn't even hold your hips or slap your ass while you were riding them, they just laid there so quietly to the point that you wondered if you should check for a pulse.

They didn't kiss, eat pussy, or even get on top most of the time. They loved head, and they wanted it in the bed, in the car, and while they were watching the game on t.v. The only other thing they would bring themselves to do was hit it from behind, but there definitely wasn't a lot of variety. Some of them had big dicks, but they didn't do much with them. It was all about the girl, and what she could do for them. I had been in hotel rooms where my girl and I would fuck two cats side by side, and we were the show. We were riding those two niggas like jockeys in a race while they looked like two dead horses. It would be way too intimate for them to touch, lick, or put in any effort at all for that matter, so they lay there like mummies getting served.

I never planned a serious future for Tony and me, so I didn't care that he never took me out for the whole eight months we had been dealing with each other. Of course, he had to keep me a secret, so we didn't go out to dinner, movies, or anything else in public. If he was taking his wife to a club, he would call and tell me not to show up. If we happened to show up at the same spot when he was with his wife, he wouldn't acknowledge me at all, and then he would send one of his boys over to tell me to quietly leave. His wife was #1, and I was what we called "work" in the hood.

Work came from the saying "putting' in work", and it was used to describe the women that men kept around for sex with no strings attached. Work couldn't make any demands, or have any expectations of a relationship. When you got a call, you had to make yourself available, or a call was placed to the next female. Work was called for wild parties and barbecues when the wives were out of town. Typically, work didn't receive money or gifts, and if one of the guys heard that their work was fucking somebody else, they couldn't trip because that wasn't their "girl." No one could "stake claim" or "catch feelings" for work. No one *ever* left their #1 for work; that was grounds for being shamed out of the clique.

Outsiders wondered why any self-respecting female would put up with that kind of bullshit, but it was simple. These cats were ballers: professional athletes, club owners, dealers, and hustlers. It didn't matter what they looked like; to be in the company of these men was exciting because they were shot-callers with bigger-than-life personalities. There was always the possibility that you could come up by hanging out. The connections alone were worth it. They knew somebody in every business, and if you were cool and treated them right they would hook you up in their network. The truth is that everybody wanted to be around people with money, niggas too.

Even though the guys would never put money in the girls' hand for shopping, hair or nails, they would buy food and drinks for the barbecues and parties, and they paid for hotel rooms and plane tickets. They loved to play dominoes and card games, betting hundreds of dollars for the fun of it. The females dressed the part, but most of the time they were broke as fuck sitting in fine homes, surrounded by millionaires when they couldn't even pay their $50 electric bill because they spent their last getting their hair done. Ballers never asked their work if they were okay with money or bills for the month, and the females never wanted to look needy, so they never asked for help.

Attractive females used their looks to get what they wanted. Even though they were only considered work, they had access to million dollar homes, they sat shot-gun in expensive cars, and were exposed to things that they may not have ordinarily experienced. Work was flown in for short out of town visits in vacation homes with beautiful grounds and swimming pools, perfect for parties and getaways while the wives were at home with the kids. These guys had money, cars, houses, clothes, jewelry, and loved to do it big, but the two worlds never collided; they were family men that also enjoyed the company of other females when they kicked it with their boys. They were like little boys competing over who's chick looked the best, or what girl gave the best head. They wouldn't dare show up to a gathering by themselves, so they would wait until they got in touch with someone before they left the house. These cats would never bring a girl to the party with them. They would give them directions, and tell them to meet them there.

A lot of times, you couldn't even tell who came with who because most of the guys were playing cards or dominoes, and the girls were just sitting around talking. Plus, the guys didn't want to look like they were cupcaking, so they stayed with the guys talking shit and drinking. The females got involved when the drinking games started. It was a cheap attempt for the guys to show off their work in front of their boys.

Crazy as it may seem, other women envied work because it was a position of privilege that not all females were qualified for. Work had to have a certain look: yellow to light-brown skin, hella fine, tight body, designer or fashionable clothes and shoes, naturally curly or permed hair, and nice jewelry or accessories. They couldn't look sloppy or raggedy *ever*, they had to represent at all times, house parties, clubbing, or just hanging out at the house. The guys were high maintenance, and their females had to be too. The guys got in quiet competitions about who had the finest chick, biggest titties and fattest ass. Work was basically a trophy, another thing for the guys to pull rank with.

It was a complete package, but the main ingredient that work had to have along with fine ass looks was personality; you had to be discreet and cool as fuck. When outsiders asked if you fucked with one of the ballers, you had to say no to protect him and his family. If a female got off on drama, she couldn't be work. Calling or having confrontations with the wife was completely unacceptable and grounds for termination. If you ran your mouth, you couldn't be work. The guys could brag about what they do at parties with their work, but they better not hear anything about the female telling their business. If you had an attitude or got your feelings hurt easily, you couldn't be work. They didn't want to have serious talks, deal with issues of jealousy, or a developed sense of entitlement. No matter how long the "couple" got along, work had no right to expect anything from their dude. You had to be able to laugh, take a joke, and act like one of the guys because they just wanted to have fun.

You had to be available, understanding, patient, and flexible. The guys would call work at all times of the day and night for head, pussy, or just to keep them company. Most of the time they would call at the last minute to hook up, and they were known to cancel without much notice. Work was considered dispensable; they were there for casual fun without obligation or responsibility. Ballers didn't accept whining, complaining or heavy demands; they got enough of that at home.

There was one other position that an outside female could hold…number two. Wifey was #1, work was #3, but the in-between was #2. Any female outside of your relationship was first considered #3 because there was a woman at home, but occasionally a relationship could go from work to more of an affectionate association, but that only happened if the man was unmarried. If one of the fellas was married, he could only have his wife and work (#1 and #3), but if they only had a girlfriend or baby mama, they could have a girlfriend, a number two, and work (#1, #2, and #3).

Number two status was actually a pretty rare category. It didn't happen a lot because most of the men were either married or in long-term relationship, but mostly because a female had to be skin tight to go from a three to a two. Twos had certain privileges that threes did not, such as no longer holding the marked title of "work".

Twos were treated more favorably than work; they were invited to movies, lunch, and spent more quality time with the man, more than just wild parties and flossing at clubs. Twos were generally taken care of with money and gifts, and the relationship wasn't as open to the clique as the dealings with the work. This woman gained more respect and status, and she was the closest thing to a girlfriend if the guy didn't already have one. The two's relationship was more private, and the guy genuinely cared about the girl and how she was doing. I could never be a two because Tony was married, but it didn't stop him from raw-dogging me that night he was feeling Remy Martin, and forgot to pull out.

When I got home, I ran up the stairs, and barely noticed my nosey-ass neighbor waving at me from her porch. She was an older black woman that always seemed to be peeking her head out of her door whenever there was any excitement going on. Her name was Mabel and she lived there alone. I never really talked to her, but I'm sure she knew more about me than I knew about her. Old Mabel had seen dudes coming in and out all times of the night, she saw me staggering up the stairs drunk as hell, and she heard the banging on the wall when I was getting my fuck on. I gave her a fake wave, and made a mad dash through my apartment to the bathroom. I had been holding it since I woke up because I knew that the first piss is the best one for the test.

I ran in the bathroom, hopping around from side to side, and dropped the paper bag near the sink. I fumbled with the box until I found the test stick, unwrapped it and straddled the toilet. I stuck my arm under my ass, and let the pee flow onto it. I felt relieved, but a little nervous as I stood up and put the stick on the counter. It only took 5 minutes for me to realize that I was pregnant with Tony's baby.

CHAPTER 5

I called Tony, but he had somebody on the other line. I wanted to hurry up and have this conversation, get the money, and get this shit over with, but I had to wait for him to call me back. He had to be with one of his boys because if he was with his wife, he wouldn't have answered the phone at all. He always kept his phone on vibrate, so that if a female called him, he would just ignore it, and his wife wouldn't trip wondering why he was avoiding the call because she never heard it. I never understand why the wives tripped anyway. They had all of the luxuries of having a millionaire for a husband, so what if they were fucking other bitches? They were living the life, and if that was me, I wouldn't give a fuck. Most of them knew how their husbands were getting down, they just didn't want the shit in their face. My phone rang about an hour later.

"What you doing later?"

"Working out."

"We need to talk."

"About what?" I paused because I hadn't expected to tell him over the phone.

"Tony, I'm pregnant." There was a long silence, and then the shock quickly disappeared as reality began to creep in.

"What?! How?"

"Tony, it had to be that night you got real faded. You were fucking me skin to skin, and you didn't pull out."

"Yeah, but why didn't you go get that morning after pill?!"

"Now it's my fault?"

"No, it's just—so what happens next?"

"That's why I wanted you to come through, so we could talk about it."

"I'll be there around 8."

We hung up, and I already knew that he was probably going to say some stupid shit, and piss me off when he got to my apartment. I counted to 10, and called Brandy to update her on my life. Brandy didn't strip, so she was the person I went to when my life got to be too much, even for me. I loved the fact that she was on the outside of all the bullshit. I could talk to her, and she could give me advice about the shit that all the girls at the club thought was normal. I had been dancing for two years, and Hypnotiq was the only dancer that I thought was cool enough to kick it, so her and Brandy was the only ones that I actually talked to about my personal life.

Brandy and I met the year after high school while we worked in the accessory department at Bloomingdales in the Beverly Center. When I told her that I wanted to go to the Amateur Night contest at the all-black *Aces* strip club, she thought I was kidding. I told her that I was tired of selling belts, hats, and not making any money; I needed a new gig. Ever since I was in high school I had heard about how cute and thick I was: ass, tits, legs, and small waist, so I knew I could make bank. I had known a couple of girls in the strip game, and they used to tell me how much money they made, and the thought of all that loot for dancing around in panties and a bra sounded right on time to me. I loved going out to clubs, so the thought of dancing around in front of rich men *and* getting paid sounded like easy money. I was tired of my boss breathing down my neck, and working for bullshit. I was sick of customers asking me stupid ass questions and having so many demands.

Do you have any more of these in the back? Can you call another store? Why isn't it on sale? I got it from the clearance rack.

At first, Brandy tried to talk me out of it. She was so naïve and sweet that the idea of a strip club scared her to death.

"Mia, are you sure you know what you're doing? I've heard so many horror stories about strippers, and the things that happen to them in the clubs."

"Like what?"

"Drinking, drugs, fights, lesbians…sleeping around."

"I'm not worried about all of that. I want to make some money and maybe meet a baller. No offense, but I'm too cute to be selling belts for the rest of my life."

"None taken. That's exactly why I'm taking classes. I don't want to work at the mall forever either."

"You worry too much. Nothing is going to happen to me. I'm going to be the same old Mia, just making more money."

"I don't think you're being realistic. How are you going to be around all of that, but it's not going to effect you?"

"Brandy I want the money, the excitement of getting up on stage, and meeting men that can do something for me. I'm tired of these lying, broke ass niggas with baby mama drama."

"You don't think you can meet a good guy *outside* of the club? I just don't want you to run to the club, looking for one thing but finding another."

"I'm going to make the money and not let the money make me."

I tried to convince her, and myself, that I would never get caught up in the bullshit. I just wanted to make some serious money, honestly and easily. She was only trying to protect me, she didn't want to see me get hurt or turned out by the club, the guys, or the dancers.

At the time, I really thought that it was possible to work on the brink of hell yet remain angelic. I thought that I could wear an invisible bulletproof vest, blinders, and walk around with a floating stainless steel wall between myself and the seediness of the club. But I was no different than any other would-be dancer; every girl that walked through the velvet curtains thought that she was going to be special, unaffected by the call of endless money for acts that she would have slapped somebody in the face for merely asking, just an hour before she became a stripper. An enormous amount of denial mixed with the youthful excitement of being adored by many was enough to push any good girl in the wrong direction.

Strip clubs stretched out its ghostly arms, and silently preyed on little girls without daddies, cracked out mothers, and victims of physical, mental, and sexual abuse. True enough, there were a few rebellious, silver-spooned chicks that wanted to walk on the wild side and taste the unsavory lifestyle that their parents worked so hard to keep from them, but the majority of the females that decided to take their clothes off for a living were at the club looking for the soul that they had lost somewhere down the road. I had my own demons, but at the time, I really thought I was going to dance to make more money. I too was one of those damaged girls looking for my missing self-esteem that my mother and father separately robbed me of.

The attention and the adoration of men was sometimes more important than the money. Old men getting dances from girls young enough to be there granddaughters, beautiful birds with broken wings, satisfied a primitive need in both to father and be fathered. Most of the time, the sweet old men spent more money than their younger counterparts, plus they didn't make the girls feel like ho's even though they sat there half naked; they had actual conversations with them and sincerely asked how they were doing. Under the guise of acceptance and pseudo-unconditional love, the ongoing attention and affection from a man was almost enough to make up for all that was missing and not forgotten.

It was harder to convince Brandy than it was to convince my own mom but only because my mom was so far removed from the lifestyle that she had no idea what really went on in those kinds of clubs. Besides, my mom had been so apologetic and guilty ever since her husband tried to rape me that she never had the heart to disagree with me. Like me, Brandy had heard a lot of things about strippers, but I thought that I was dipped in Teflon, and I was going to hold onto my morals with both hands. After I eased Brandy's concerns with a speech that would've made a used car salesman proud, she agreed to go with me, and I set my plan into action for getting ready to win the next contest.

Amateur Night was held every Wednesday night, and once I told Brandy on a Saturday afternoon that I was serious about the contest, I planned to be ready for the following Wednesday. That next day, I dragged Brandy with me to Frederick's of Hollywood to get a couple of outfits, and a pair of sexy high-heeled stripper sandals, the clear plastic ones that had five inch heels and a one inch platform. When I got home, I tried on the costumes, and danced in front of the full-length mirror in my bedroom. As the big day got closer, I went to the shop to get my hair flat-ironed, and proceeded to the nail shop for a manicure and pedicure.

By Wednesday afternoon, my nerves had got the best of me. The thought of dancing half naked in front of a group of hungry men was scarier than the 110 freeway during rush hour. My mind created scenarios that including me slipping, falling, and/or making a fool of myself in some form or fashion. I practiced walking on my brand new stilts around the safe, carpeted floor in my mother's house, but for some reason I never considered walking on the concrete just outside the front door.

Brandy was going to come by and get me because I didn't have wheels back then. Before she got there, I had packed a bag with my outfits, sandals, and the other things that I would need. I threw on some jeans and a top, and put on a little makeup. The contest started at 9, but the girls had to be there by 8. The winner was chosen by the audience, so I called invited a couple of friends and co-workers to come out for support.

When I walked up to the door, I could hear the music, and I started to shake a little as I thought about strange men looking at me and touching themselves in the smoky, dimly lit room. I told the bouncer in the doorway that I was there for the contest, and he told me to go around the back, and enter the building through the kitchen, but Brandy had to walk in the front. It's a good thing she wore a mini skirt because the sign on the door said that all females going in the club had to wear skirts or dresses. I found out later that that was the club owner's way of keeping butches out of the club because they were bad for business; they intimidated some cats and caused drama or fights as the dykes tried to pull females from their men.

Brandy parked on the busy five-lane street, and I walked around the corner, through the parking lot, and knocked on the back door. The mostly industrial neighborhood was primarily Mexican and there were taco shops on every corner. The hustlers stood at the freeway entrance selling oranges, peanuts, and roses. The club was in the perfect place because the factory and warehouse workers dropped in the club at lunch or after work. A sloppy, fat bouncer was sitting on a stool next to the door. He asked if I was there for the contest while he looked me up and down like a barbecue rib dinner. He knocked, and a short, light-skinned girl opened the door, and I stepped in the kitchen. There were about six or seven girls hanging around a desk where I assumed the manager sat. There were in sparkly, brightly-colored outfits with long weaves, and drag queen makeup. Only a couple of them was pretty, and I wondered why the other ones were even there because they weren't that cute, and had bodies like little girls, no boobs or booty. Their laughter and casual conversation ended when they saw me. The manager was a very handsome man in his 50s with beautiful skin and wavy, salt and pepper hair. He stood up, and asked me if I was there for the contest.

"Yes, I am."

"Okay, I just need your driver's license. I need to hold onto it until you leave. The contest starts in an hour. You have two songs, one topless, and your ass has to be covered when you are on the outside of the stage. You can wear a thong when you are in the middle of the stage dancing topless. You need to go to the DJ booth and choose your music. The dressing room is in the back by the bathroom. Oh, and what's your stage name?"

That was the one thing that I forgot...a stage name. I gave him the first thing I thought of, my favorite thug passion.

"Alizé."

"Okay, you'll go up third because two girls got here before you. Any questions?"

"No, I don't think so."

He opened the desk drawer to put my ID away, and I saw disposable razors and tampons next to pens and paperclips. I turned to walk away, and I could feel the other females checking me out, and I knew as soon as I left the room, they were going to chop me up because I was the new fish.

I walked out of the kitchen, behind the bar, and entered the table and chair area. It was only 8:15, and the room was already packed with a gang of horny ass brothas. As I walked through, men stopped talking and drinking to turn their attention towards me. It felt like they were undressing me with their eyes, burning holes through my clothes. I had heard that Wednesdays were big because the guys were always anxious to see fresh meat. Besides Friday and Saturday nights, Amateur Night became the most popular night of the week. It was dark, and I couldn't find Brandy, but when I saw a female sitting alone at the bar, I knew it had to be her. I went over and thanked her again for coming, and that I would come back after I changed into my outfit.

I walked towards the back corner where I found a tiny little room full of lockers; it was not a dressing room. The bathroom was directly across the hall, and the girls opened both doors wide to form a barrier between the audience and the naked ladies. One girl was in the bathroom squatting over the toilet putting a tampon inside of her. She stood up, cut off the string that was dangling between her legs, and flushed the toilet. She wasn't embarrassed at all, but I turned before she saw me looking at her. I walked in the locker room, and found two girls getting dressed. They were naked, and walking around getting their stuff together. I realized then that you couldn't have a shy bone in your body to work in a strip club.

"Hi, are you in the contest too? I'm Miracle, and that's Coco."

"Hi, I'm Mia, well...I guess I'm Alizé for the night."

"You going up third?"

"Yeah, that's what the man in the kitchen said."

"You nervous?"

"No, not really." I had to lie. I didn't want them to think I was a punk.

"Well we are! We have never danced before. Have you?"

"Nah, but it doesn't look too hard though."

"Yeah well, it doesn't look hard from down here, but onstage is totally different when all eyes are on you. These cats have been coming up here for years, and they know what a dancer is supposed to look like. It's not just about being cute and having a nice body. You have to know how to work it!"

Miracle rolled her hips, and threw her booty out with a pop! We all laughed, and continued to get dressed. I had already lied and said I wasn't nervous when

I really was, and now Miracle was reminding me of everything that I had tried to forget, professional strip club customers that were thirsty for new blood, and more treacherous than the audience at the Apollo Theater.

Miracle was the cutest. She had a pretty face and a tight body. Coco was not as cute, but she had nice tits. They put on a gallon of baby oil, and sprayed so much Victoria's Secret body splash spray that I thought I would choke. They were putting deodorant in the crack of their ass and under their titties, they had fake eyelashes and long acrylic nails. Miracle's pussy was hairless, and she was putting foundation makeup on her bikini line to cover up razor bump scars.

They were much more prepared then I was, so I figured they knew dancers that hooked them up with the 411. Several more females came in the locker room, and it was getting crowded in there, so I quickly claimed a locker, and put my things away. I was done, so I went to pick my music, and then join Brandy at the bar.

I still wasn't used to walking on those high heels, so I walked very slowly and carefully because if I fell on my ass in front of all those people, I was liable to run out of the doors in absolute embarrassment. I'm sure people thought I was trying to be extra sexy, but I was just trying to stay on my feet. Everybody was looking at me as I walked to the bar, males and females. I had on a black lace, two-piece boy short and bra outfit with a black thong underneath.

When I reached Brandy she gave me a big hug, and told me how cute I looked. My heart was still beating fast, and I told her to come with me to choose my music. We went to the front corner of the club where the jukebox was. A huge man was sitting there in front of the admission window. He was so massive that he should have had two stools underneath his big ass.

"Hi, I need to choose my music."

"What's your name, and when do you go up?" His mouth was covered with fried chicken crumbs and grease, and I thought I would die if a piece of that food flew on me.

"I'm Alizé, and I'm going up third." I grabbed Brandy's arm, and leaned back as I was talking.

"Most girls choose a fast song first while you're on the outside rectangle, then a slow one when you're topless in the middle of the stage. What do you want?"

"Jay Z *Big Pimpin'* and Jagged Edge *I Gotta Be.*"

"Cool. By the way, I'm Elgin."

"Thanks." I wanted to scream, *"Elgin, wipe your mouth!"*, but I restrained myself.

Brandy and I walked back to the bar, but someone had already snatched her seat, so we stood near the front door, and checked out the crowd. There were men in work uniforms for Department of Water and Power, UPS, and Fed Ex. There were a few suits, but mostly baggy jeans with throwbacks, clean Air Force One's, and lots of bling. Even though this was a black club, I saw several white and Mexican men sitting at the bar just as comfortable as the brothas. There were a couple of females in the audience, but I figured they were doing the same thing that Brandy was doing for me. There were strippers walking around too. Some of them I had seen in the kitchen earlier, but most of them I hadn't seen before.

The dancers were leaning, flirting, and sitting on men's laps while they pretended to be listening to whatever the guys were saying. Their laughs were so fake, and they kept touching the men's arms, legs, and heads while they were talking to them. Some of the girls were painfully made-up, curvy, long acrylic nails, cheap outfits, and tons of makeup unsuccessfully trying to cover up years of Speed and Hennessey. Almost all of them had weaves…curly, straight, blonde, black, medium, and long, but some of the girls were actually pretty cute and dressed as well as they could for being half naked.

Their bodies were all different; most of the chicks had nice-sized tits, but only a few of them had fat asses. I was a little intimidated because my ass was cool, but not as big as a bunch of them. I saw cellulite, stretch marks, and baby fat bellies from the Mommies, but it didn't matter because black men tended to be more forgiving for Mother Nature's remnants, so an all-black club made perfect sense because the white clubs weren't as sympathetic.

Miracle went on stage, then Coco, and then it was my turn. They were okay, but I'm glad that I wasn't first because I learned a couple of things just from watching them on stage, like how to come out from behind the curtain, where to face when I was dancing, and who to pay attention to in the audience.

"Coming to the stage is Alizé! Put your hands together for her, and make her feel welcome!"

I stood behind the curtain backstage while the two-stool DJ announced my name. I was shaking as the music started, and then I heard Jay-Z over the speakers. I closed my eyes, took a deep breath, and opened the curtain. The multi-colored lights were bright, and there were over a hundred eyes staring at me, and for a minute, I almost forgot everything that I had practiced.

I walked out at a snail's pace, and then I began to awkwardly wiggle my hips, stiffly running my hands up my thighs and around my stomach like a defective robot. I had to catch the beat because my rhythm was completely off. I didn't want to look in anybody's eyes; I just danced around the stage pretending to be sexy because I wasn't feeling it at all. I noticed a bit of pity money scattered on the stage, but I felt like a fraud that was soon to be bum-rushed from the stage. I prayed for the song to end so that I could make my speedy exit before the barrage of boo's began. Then I heard Brandy's voice near the stage.

"Work it out girl!"

Those three words gave me the confidence I needed to snap out of my self-induced pity party. My energy and drive was restored; I squatted with my legs wide open, hands on my knees, and rolled my hips about a foot in front of a suit sitting right in front of the stage. His eyes looked like they were about to pop out of his head as he threw a dub on the stage. I immediately learned two things: get grimy, and *always* look them in the eye.

By the end of the first song, I had reintroduced myself to my goal of becoming a dancer. I walked backstage, and slipped behind the curtain to catch my breath. The next song was topless, and naturally scarier than the first trip on stage. I heard the beginning of Jagged Edge, and it reminded me of my ex, Bernie. I opened the curtain, and walked inside of the rectangle. The lights were darker onstage this time, and it was harder to see faces.

I seductively walked to the front of the rectangle like a pro after just one song under my belt, and I slowly began to dance very erotically, touching my shoulders and arms. I leaned my head back, and closed my eyes. I turned to face the mirror on the back wall of the stage, and I began to unfasten my bra. I slipped out of it, and flung it across the floor until it reached the curtain, and halfway slid under the opening. I covered my tits with my hands, and slowly turned back around to face the crowd.

I caught the eye of a horny, old man in front of the stage, and he became my focal point. I opened my fingers enough to expose my nipples, and then gradually released my fingers, and jiggled my double D's in his direction. I was extra after he threw a dub on the stage. As I began feeling the song, and re-mixing memories of Bernie and the nicest dick I had ever had, I lowered my body to the ground, lay on my back, then raised and rocked my hips back and forth. I rubbed my legs together until my clit woke up, and ran my hands along the inside of my thighs near my pussy. The music started to fade, and when the fat DJ shouted, "Give it up for Alizé!" I snapped out of the temporary trance that I had been under. I was almost embarrassed because I had transformed myself from *Aces* to Bernie's bedroom, and I was just leaving his bed as the audience clapped.

There were six girls in the contest that night, and I walked out as the winner. I got $100 and the chance to work at the club if I wanted to *and* I made $140 in tips! I knew that I would be back because I had never made such easy money so fast in my entire life. I was 20, and the thought of making over $200 a day turned me on. I got excited about playing dress up, having men adore me, and being able to buy anything that I wanted. The money was so easy, and I got it so quickly that I thought I was invincible to any bullshit. I was going to go to work, keep it professional, and get every dime that I could out of the club, but little did I know that the lifestyle would eat me up, and spit me out just as easily.

CHAPTER 6

Tony called at 7:45 that night to say that he was running late, but he was still coming. I went in the bathroom, and checked my hair, makeup, and fit before I even hung up with him. He liked me to look good whenever he came over, and I always made sure that I did just that. Most women got a man, and just let their looks go to shit. If only they took the time to please their men, they wouldn't be running to women like me that looked fierce every time we saw them. I had on some tight, pink BEBE warm-up pants, and a white BEBE shirt with rhinestones. I always made sure my apartment was clean, and stocked with the foods and drinks that he liked. This was where we spent most of our time, so I always made sure he was comfortable.

Tony rang the doorbell at 8:30, and I instantly started to feel a little nervous. I opened the door to let him in, and I could tell by the look on his face that he was as worried as I was. We gave each other a questionable hug, and he went to sit down on the couch.

"You want something to drink?"

"Nah, I'm cool. So what's going on?"

"Well, I was supposed to start my period two days ago, and it didn't come, so I took a home pregnancy test today, and it was positive."

"So you're sure?"

"Pretty much."

"How much does the abortion cost?"

"It's $325, but damn, you can act like you give a fuck!"

Tony stood up, and I had never seen him so serious. He was known as a jokester, but this was a side of him that I had never seen.

"What do you want me to say? I fucked up, but we got to get this shit taken care of. I can't have the press, the team, or my wife finding out about this."

"I'm glad to see that you give a fuck about everybody but me!"

"It's not that I don't care Mia, but you knew what the deal was when we hooked up. My family and job come first."

"I don't give a fuck! If you loved your wife so much, you wouldn't have been over here fucking me every chance you got! Run me my money and get the fuck out of my house!"

He reached in his pocket, and laid four crisp $100 bills on the coffee table, and walked towards the door. Just as he was about to turn the doorknob, he turned to face me.

"Call me when it's done."

"You got me fucked up!!"

After I slammed the door behind him, I had to admit that the talk didn't go the way that I had hoped it would. I expected him to be apologetic and sympathetic, yet he was arrogant and inconsiderate of my feelings. He was acting like I was trying to trap his ass when he nutted in me! I thought he would apologize for putting me in that position, and ask what I wanted to do. I'm realistic, and I knew there was only one option for a pregnancy outside of his marriage, but he could've finessed the situation a little instead of making me feel cheap and dirty. Brandy came over to calm me down.

❧   ❧   ❧

"Do you believe these niggas?!"

"Mia, you know I'm your girl, but what did you expect? He's married with kids, and he plays in the NBA. He's not going to risk any of that for a fling."

"I don't give a fuck about any of that bullshit! I have to have a fucking operation because this motherfucker nuts in me, and he's acting like *I'm* the one that fucked up!"

"Okay, you're right, but now what?"

"I don't appreciate being treated like this is my fault! He had no apologies or sympathies for me, it was all about protecting his family and his career!"

"Mia, listen to yourself. What did you expect him to do or say?"

"Are you listening to me? He was an asshole!"

"I'm sure he's just upset. What are you going to do now?"

"I think his wife needs to know what her *husband* has been up to!"

"Girl, what are you talking about?!"

"I'm calling that stupid bitch and telling her what the fuck is going on!! I'm gonna tell her that nigga hit it raw! They got life twisted!"

"Are you serious? You know if you do this your relationship with him will be over forever."

"I don't give a—" Rrrrrring...

It was Tony. I snatched the phone off the hook.

"WHAT?!"

"Mia, I'm sorry if you thought I was being shitty. I was just shocked about this whole situation. We've been cool...look, I don't want any problems. I'm on my way back over." I paused...mad as fuck.

"Regardless, you need to fucking respect me Tony!"

"You're right, and we'll talk when I get there."

I didn't say anything, not sure if I should let him come back over, or stand my angry ground and see him in a day or two after my anger had subsided. In a move that wasn't atypical of our relationship, I gave in to Tony's expectations.

"Okay."

All of my resentment floated up to the ceiling, lingered, and disappeared like smoke from a Swisher Sweet. Dumbfounded, I lay the phone on the table, and sat back on the couch.

"Mia, what did he say?"

"He apologized, and now he's on his way back over."

"What are you going to do? A minute ago you were ready to call his wife!"

"I'm going to let him talk, but when he leaves I will have more than $400!"

"Girl, be careful okay? I'm leaving, but call me if you need anything."

"Don't worry girl, I got this."

We hugged, and Brandy left before Tony appeared at my door for the second time. After she left, I took a minute to really think about what I wanted to happen next. I knew that Tony and I were just kicking it, but I wasn't going to let him treat me like a whore on the street either. This wasn't the first time that I had dealt with a cat like him, so I wasn't new to the game. Working in a strip club, I saw all types of ballers, hustlers, celebrities, and athletes. They flashed big money, and thought they could buy anything, pussy, head...your soul. I was going to let him know that he had me fucked up if he thought he was going to treat me like I was walking up and down Western in a come-fuck-me dress in front of the Snooty Fox.

When the doorbell rang, I slowly sauntered to the door still trying to choose the words I wanted to use for this ridiculous situation. I was hot as fish grease before he called back to apologize, but lucky for him he had called back before

I put his wife on to what's been going on. He would never know how close he came to the front page of *The Enquirer.*

I opened the door, and Tony staggered in like a kid accused of stealing candy from the corner store. I looked at him standing there like a schoolboy, and for the first time I saw his vulnerability; he was no longer the shot-caller. I was pregnant, and if I *really* wanted to keep it, there was nothing he could do about it *but* be mad. Suddenly, I felt powerful, and my anger slid out the door like a played-out houseguest. My anger melted, and I felt a smile grow across my lips. I stood up straight, puffed my chest out a little, and gently shut the door as Tony stepped in the living room. I spoke first.

"What did you want to say?"

"It wasn't cool the way things ended, so I wanted to come back and apologize."

"You got that right."

He had rehearsed quite well. He was trying to make sure I was cool, so that I didn't make trouble for him. Tony was scared that I was going to tell his wife, the team, and the rag magazines! He thought he was slick, but I had one better. I was going to flip it on him, and make him kiss my ass. I was calling the shots now, and he was going to do whatever I wanted for fear of a scandal that could cost him the comfortable lifestyle that he was accustomed to.

"So?"

"Well, I thought about it, and I know that you're probably tripping too. We need to work this out together, without the arguing and placing blame. I didn't mean to offend you; I was just in shock."

"Tony, you caused this situation, I'm the one that has to go to the clinic, and *you're* in shock?"

"Yeah, you're right, and I'm sorry about that. I was on one that night, and I was caught slipping."

He was a soft ass nigga now. First, he was trying to come at me foul, standing up for his wife, his career, and his reputation. Then he realized he was in no position to be talking shit to me. I had him by the balls, and he knew it.

"You have absolutely no reason to be shitty with me. You don't think I've thought about the fact that I have to get an abortion? You need to be cool. I don't appreciate you talking to me like I caused this situation. I'm not stupid. I know you're married, and I know what has to be done."

"I apologize, I was wrong for yelling and not being mindful of your feelings."

"I appreciate that."

"So, what do you need from me?"

That was his non-disrespectful way of asking how much money I needed for the abortion. I wasn't going to get mad and yell again, I was going to take my anger out on his wallet.

"Look Tony, you gave me the $400, but I need more so that I can get some things that I need after the surgery."

The word *surgery* stressed the danger and importance of the situation.

"What do you need?"

I had to hold back my laughter as he stood there looking as nervous as a ho in church.

"How about an even thousand? I need to get pads and stuff, medicine, and a heating pad. Plus I'll probably have to take a cab because Brandy can't take me to the clinic..."

"A thousand dollars huh? Well, I only have another $200 on me, but I'll shoot you the rest tomorrow. So, are you going to call and make the appointment?"

We were playing tit for tat. I asked for more money than I could possibly need, and he agreed to it, so he was free to ask exactly what he wanted to know. He handed me the $200, and I knew right then that he would've given me anything to get that baby up out of my stomach.

"Yeah, I'll call tomorrow."

"Ok, well let me get out of here. I'll call you after practice so that we can hook up some time tomorrow. Maybe I can bring us some lunch."

"That's cool."

"Look, I really am sorry. Forgive me?"

Tony made a sad face, and I couldn't believe how easily he could change my mood from spitting fire to smelling daisies.

"Yeah, I forgive you."

Tony kissed me on the lips, and gave me a thank-you-for-not-fucking-up-my-life hug. It was a long, tight, grateful hug. His hands slowly moved from my back down to my ass. My pussy started to heat up as he cupped my ass, and squeezed it with both hands. I knew that I couldn't fuck for a couple of weeks after the abortion, I wanted some dick, so I had to get out of my own way.

I could feel his dick on my leg, and I pressed my body closer to his. I started kissing on his neck, and he pulled down my warm-up pants. He lifted my top up, and sucked on my nipples. When he removed his mouth from my chest, he left my nipples wet, and they stuck out about an inch. He took my hand, and led me into the bedroom. He took off his clothes, and lay on my bed. I took off my own clothes, climbed on top of him, and laid across my bed next to his statuesque body.

Tony pulled me closer to him, and I started grabbing on his dick. I slid between his legs, licked his balls, and sucked his dick while he finger-fucked me, slowly pulling his finger in and out of my pussy. I climbed on top of his dick, and he didn't reach for a condom. I guess he figured I was already pregnant, so what was the point. I started riding him slow at first, and then faster. Tony lifted his hips, and thrust his dick inside of me. I rocked my hips back and forth harder and harder, let out a little scream, and finally came like a firework show at the beach on the 4th of July.

"Let me hit it from the back."

I got off of Tony's dick, and scooted to the edge of the bed. He got off the bed, and stood on the side. He stuck his dick in my pussy, and hit it a couple of times. He pulled out, and when I turned around, he was reaching for a condom and the lube in my nightstand. He squeezed some in his hand, and rubbed it on my asshole. I held my butt cheeks open, and he slowly stuck his finger in my ass, and tried to massage it open. I felt another finger slide in, and after a few minutes, he took them out. He grabbed his dick and went to work.

It always took a long time to get it in because the asshole was tough, and as hard as a dick was, it couldn't get in there because the hole stayed so tight. Once the hole was massaged and stretched, it was easier to get in. He had to keep adding lube because the ass didn't have natural lube like a pussy, and if his dick got dry, it hurt like hell when he tried to force it in there!

Tony finally got in, and I felt a wave rush over my nerves as his dick entered me. He slowly pulled his dick in and out, but I didn't need to move with him like I would if he was fucking me from behind, there was enough rubbing

The sensation was so different from pussy-fucking. The feeling was deeper and more intense. I felt like I was at his mercy because if he really started fucking the shit out of me, he could kill me. That made it dangerous, risky, yet sexy. Sodomy went against the Bible, the law, and some people thought that a brotha was a fag if he wanted to fuck a girl in the ass. Maybe it was gay if he was fucking another cat, but he was fucking me, and I have a pussy underneath my ass. I have hips, curves, titties, and I smell like a female. Men are much bigger, stronger, and hairier than women. My body was soft, smooth, and much smaller than Tony's.

The booty hole was also very delicate, and Tony was always very careful with me, except once before. There was a little blood after he was too rough after a night of drinking too much at the club. It was uncomfortable when he first started trying to get it in, but once it was in, and I got into it. Tony started going a little harder, and I knew he was getting ready to cum. He came much quicker this way because of all of the friction. I gripped my comforter moaning and groaning, and braced myself for the finale. His dick was as deep as it could go, and I could feel that shit. We both were sweating, wildin' out, and I let out a deep sigh when he finally came.

Tony slapped my ass, and then slowly pulled his dick out. He walked into the bathroom, flushed his rubber down the toilet, and turned the faucet on. He grabbed the small towel on the sink, and began to wash up. I went in behind him, and carefully sat on the toilet. While I peed, my pussy and my asshole were farting! Tony and I laughed at all the sounds coming from my body, and he walked back into the bedroom. My booty hole felt a little wet, and I could feel some thick liquid trickling out. I stood up, wiped, and looked in the toilet.

My shit was a light tan color, thin like tissue paper, and I had to hurry up and sit back down because I could feel something coming out. It was like I had diarrhea, but it wasn't. It was just a little lube mixed up with a little shit. I wiped again and flushed the toilet. I grabbed my baby wipes from the bottom drawer, and wiped my ass. After I used a second one, I threw both of them in the trash, and washed my hands. The smell was tough, so I lit the candle on my counter.

"You okay?"

"Yeah, I'm cool. I just had to clean up."

I grabbed my robe out of my closet, and slid my feet into some slippers.

"You want something to drink?"

"Yeah, give me some juice."

I walked into the kitchen while he was getting dressed. I poured him some juice, and took my ice cream out of the freezer, so that it would soften. I walked back in the room, and handed Tony his juice, and sat on my bed while he put on his shoes.

"I needed that. You always know how to take care of me."

"Yeah and don't forget it!"

"I won't, so I'll call you tomorrow before I come through."

"That's cool."

Tony hugged me, and I walked him to the door. I grabbed my ice cream from the kitchen, turned on the t.v., and plopped down on the couch. I called Brandy while I was flipping channels.

"Hey girl. The Man just left. I told him that I need a "G" to help with my little situation."

"A thousand dollars? What did he say?"

"Girl, he was just happy that I was going the clinic. I really think I could have got more. He only had another $200 on him, but he's supposed to give me the rest tomorrow. He even said he would bring me lunch, and I just cursed him out an hour ago! Shit, I was about to call wifey just before he called!"

"You were just talking shit. You didn't mean it."

"Maybe, but I'm just sick of these niggas thinking they can just use a bitch!"

"Do you even have his home number?"

"Girl, I got the number! After we fucked one night he went to the bathroom, and I looked in his cell phone. I got the house number and her cell number!"

"Wow! You weren't scared he was going to catch you?"

"Before he goes home to wifey, he's always in the bathroom for like 10 minutes. He has a routine. He can't use soap because she would smell it, and wonder why he smelled so fresh at two in the morning, so he washes with plain water. He has to look in the mirror to make sure he doesn't have any marks or lipstick on his body, and he has the same brand of lotion and cologne at my house so that he smells exactly the same when he gets home."

"Do you think his wife knows that he's fucking someone else?"

"If you ask me, I think they all know, but it's like the gay military 'don't ask don't tell' situation because the subject is never brought up on either side. If that was me, I wouldn't give a fuck, just pay me. All men cheat, rich or not so you may as well get that bag."

"I guess, but do you think Lorenzo would cheat on me?"

"Naw, probably not."

Brandy had been with her boyfriend for two years, and I had to admit that he was one of the good guys. He was sweet, and he became the only reason that I hadn't completely swept men under the carpet. He was hard-working, and even though he didn't make a lot of money, he would give Brandy his last dollar. One time her car broke down, and he let her drop him off at work for a week. That was when she had just got her office job on the Miracle Mile, and he didn't want her to have any problems getting there.

Lorenzo had a close family that got together all the time at his mom's house, and Brandy was always invited. They were inseparable. Brandy said they had talked about marriage, it was obvious that they were genuinely in love with each other. At times I got a little jealous when I compared my life to Brandy's. A pregnant stripper fucking with a married, basketball star wasn't the way I thought my life would turn out. I had a lot of shit that I had to deal with on a daily, and I began to think about how my life had gotten to this point. I wondered how differently my life would've turned out if my daddy never left me. I told Brandy I would holler at her the next day, and I hung up the phone secretly wishing that my life looked a little more like hers.

CHAPTER 7

My life used to look a lot like Brandy's, but over the 2 years that I had been stripping, inevitably I had changed dramatically. No female can work in a titty bar for that long, and not be affected by the life. I walked through those velvet red doors as Mia, and walked out as Alizé. The game swallows you up, and you are sucked in before you even know what hits you. I remember the night I won the Amateur Night Contest, I was so naïve and had no idea what I was getting myself into. The money whispers in your ear, and gets louder and louder until it outtalks your morals and principles. Money convinces you that it will make your sins go away. Money is what drives the strip game, and like a crack fiend chasing a hit of smoke, you need more and more. After a while, getting that money is your only motivation.

Money always meant a lot to me because as a child, I remembered feeling inadequate or *less than* the rest of the little girls in my class. Their clothes and shoes were nicer and more expensive than mine. It was enough for me to show up to school bathed and wearing clean clothes. They had better lunches with bologna or salami sandwiches and Cheetos when I had mayonnaise or sardine sandwiches. Most of the girls had spare money in their cute little purses, and I remember thinking that maybe they had to pick up groceries after school like I did. I was taking care of myself most of the time, and I didn't have much to do it with. As I grew older, I became obsessed with money, clothes, and eating good, as if I was somehow making up for my childhood.

After the night of the contest, my monetary high carried me back the next day for a job, and I began my education at the *University of Aces*. The club was owned by Margaret, a white woman who looked more like somebody's grand-mother rather than a notorious den mother. I never understood how she got into the strip game, but she was paid a million times over. There were three different managers that worked for Margaret because she was basically in and out. She usually showed up for a couple of hours in the daytime, but we never saw her at night. I figured it was because she was living her real life with her real family and grandkids.

The rules of the house weren't that complicated. The tip-out was $50, and you could pay it in the beginning of your shift, or at the end of the night. That fee basically covered a dancer paying the cost to perform. If you wanted to work in the day, you had to be at work by 1pm, and for the night shift you had to be there by 8pm. You had to work at least 4 hours when you came in, so you couldn't just walk in, dance onstage once, give a couple of table dances and leave. Margaret wanted to make sure that if the customers wanted to see you on stage again, you would be there.

When you walked around the club, you had to have a top on, and your bottoms had to cover your cheeks, but especially the crack of your ass. If you were onstage, and Margaret saw too much pussy hair, she had a razor waiting and you had to shave in the bathroom before you could go back up. Some of the customers told me they thought it was kind of sexy to see a little hair, but Margaret wasn't having that. That had to be a white thing because she didn't seem to care when dancers got fat, needed their weaves tightened, or needed to stumble around a little less when they were high off liquor or something worse.

Strip clubs were like a meeting place for every vice known to man: sex, drugs, and alcohol. Drug dealers hung around and made deals in the parking lot and the bathroom. They had uppers, downers, weed, coke, Ecstasy, speed, and anything else the strippers and customers wanted. Females did drugs in the locker room, the bathroom, and back in the kitchen. A couple of times the ambulance was called when girls started squirming around on the ground, sweating, tearing their clothes off or had passed out altogether. The first couple of times that I saw it I was scared they were dead or dying, but after a while, I got used to it. Before I began stripping, I never really was a drinker, but I started on my first night at the club after the contest.

Alcohol was a necessary evil at the *Aces* strip club. Dancers needed liquor to get up on stage, to deal with cats pulling and grabbing on your shit as you walked through the club, and to help ease the pain after the lifestyle had eaten up any chance you had of a normal life. Girls that never even drank before became lightweight alcoholics after they started dancing. Stripping was like acting; you had to be a fantasy for your entire shift, and it was tiresome and exhausting. Customers didn't want to hear about your past due bills, your son getting suspended from school for fighting, or your baby daddy getting locked up for the second time this year. You had to smile, flirt, and act like you were everything they thought you were: sexy, beautiful, and problem-free. Customers came in the club to escape nagging, fat wives for a couple of hours, so if you wanted them to stay in the club you had to bring them the happiness they were hard pressed to find at home.

I never figured out why there was so much dyking at the club. I didn't know if girls got turned on by seeing naked female bodies night after night, or if they were already on pussy when they started working at the club. Either way, most of the girls had at least one lesbian experience after dancing, including me. I had sucked some titties before, finger-fucked a few chicks, kissed them in the mouth, and a couple of girls ate my pussy during parties, but it's not that I was gay, cats paid more for girl on girl. Being a lesbian or bisexual was interchangeable. Some girls really got into other chicks, some fooled with girls to try something new and different, and some did it for the money.

Shit got real messy sometimes because bitches would cheat with other girls from the club, and there was always gossip, rumors, and fights. Margaret and the other managers tried to limit the drama, but they couldn't control it and sometimes they were a part of it. One of the managers was a lesbian, and she was fucking one of the dancers so everybody was in their business. Professionalism and best business practices were foreign to the club. Dancers were fucking security guards, DJs, bartenders, waitresses, and each other. The only guys they weren't fucking were the bar backs because they were Mexican, and they didn't speak much English, so they couldn't really communicate with anyone besides themselves. If they tried to holler at a dancer, they could probably hit though because for the right price, it wasn't hard.

Lap dances were $20. Most dancers went to the lap dance area, but you could give one anywhere. You could grind your ass on the man's lap, but you couldn't straddle him from the front. You could rub your tits on his chest, and near his face, but he couldn't suck them. You could not touch the customer's dick, or let him touch your pussy. Most girls followed the rules out in the open, but in the darkness of the table dance area in the corner of the club, it was on and cracking. The security guards shined their flashlights when they saw too much going on, but they still kept finding used condoms underneath the stools.

Some females gave hand-jobs, head, and even fucked customers over there. It would look like they were just bouncing their ass up and down on the customer's lap, but they were actually pulling their panties to the side, and riding dick that was peeking out of a zipper. The table dance area was dark, hot, and funky. It was because of all that fucking that the club got raided by LAPD on a regular. Sometimes the chicks with warrants were hauled off to jail on the nights when there was a lot going on, and the cops wanted to make an example.

To most females, there was a fine line between being a dancer and being a ho. Dancers were propositioned all the time. A whole lot of fucking and sucking went down when money was flowing like Dom Perignon. Brothas paid for hand-jobs, head, fucking and threesomes with other dancers. They were paying anything from $200 all the way up to a couple of G's. Sometimes they would offer to get a room, but a lot of that shit went down right in the parking lot. When dancers walked to their cars late at night, we all had a habit of just looking straight ahead because you were liable to see anything if you started looking in cars as you walked by. And if you in the car the next night, you didn't want people looking in on you either, so it was like a courtesy.

I had kicked it with a couple of regulars to the club, but I never felt like a ho because I knew them, and I wasn't walking up and down Crenshaw Boulevard. I remember the first time one of my customers asked me to get down. I was so nervous, and a million thoughts ran through my head as soon as the proposition left his lips. After I had convinced Brandy and my mom that stripping didn't mean fucking, I really was surprised when the situation popped up. A guy had asked me to fuck him for $500. I had only been dancing for a couple of weeks, and at that time I was spending more than I was making, buying clothes and shit. I was behind on some bills, but I didn't want to ask my mom for money because in the back of my mind, I didn't think I could depend on her. My heart was beating fast, and my armpits were getting sweaty, but I tried to play cool as the word *yes* came out of my mouth.

After the club closed that night, we went to the Ramada Inn by the airport. His name was Thomas and he was a fine, married man that had been buying dances from me ever since my first night. Part of me felt like a whore as he laid the money in my hand as soon as we walked in the hotel room but I assured myself that he wasn't a stranger, even though I didn't know his last name and he only knew me by the name of an alcoholic beverage. I didn't feel sexy, I was hella stiff and scared to death. I basically laid there and let him handle his business, no head, no moaning, and I didn't even get on top. Thomas was respectful and he treated me like a gentleman, even though the fuck wasn't worth $5, let alone $500.

The first time was the hardest, it was a lot easier after that. Some of the girls literally turned into porno stars, but I was never down for that. They didn't use condoms in the movies, and even though they got AIDS tests every 3 months, I thought that shit was off the hook. Everybody knew that the actors were getting down with each other *and* everybody else in L.A. and it was just too much. There were rumors that some of the guys in the movies were gay and there was no way I was going to get caught up in that shit; that was where I drew the line. All money wasn't good money.

Most people had a tendency to believe that athletes and celebrities were paying in the club, but the fact is that the working man spent bread too. Sometimes they tricked off more money than the ballas because a lot of rich cats were stingy with their loot. The working man would break his check in the club when they got addicted to the fantasy. They usually spent most of their money on one girl, and all the dancers knew which regulars belonged to which girls, but that didn't stop them from trying to steal that money if a regular showed up and his dancer wasn't there. That didn't happen much anyway because regulars usually called their dancer to ask when they were going to work, or the dancer would call the regular before she went to work to let him know that she was leaving for the club.

I had gotten to the point with my regulars that they would call and tell me they were going to the club, and I would get dressed and go to work for them specifically. Tommy, one of my regulars, would call me to the club, break me off a couple of hundred for a couple of dances, and leave. The longer you danced, the longer your list of regulars became, but you had to treat them right or they would move on to the next bitch that was scheming and giving him the attention that you weren't. And when you were at the club, you had to juggle all your regulars, and give them equal face time, well…according to bank roll.

Most people thought the customers grabbing your ass, and irritating the fuck out of you was the worst part of the strip game, but it was the females that created the most drama. The competition for customers was vicious, and I peeped that shit right away. When I went in the locker room on my first real night, I really looked at the dancers. A lot of them had nice bodies. Some had big tits, some had a big ass, and a few of those lucky bitches had both, and you could tell that most of them took pride in their bodies and their job by working out on a regular basis.

More and more of the dancers were getting fake tits than when I first started working there. A few of them had had liposuction, and other surgeries to make them look close to perfect. Something had changed over the last two years or so because the black dancers were starting to look a lot like the white dancers. Black girls had always tried to dance at white clubs because they knew rich, white men would pay to see that big, black ass, but they were almost always turned down by the managers and owners.

Supposedly, white managers thought white customers wanted to look at skinny Barbie dolls with blonde hair, blue eyes, silicone tits, and no ass. Thick, country-fed black girls didn't exactly fit that mold, so they weren't hired at those clubs very often. So, that's how the all-black club was created, by a white woman no less. Our club was always filled with all kinds of men, including white men; turns out that a lot of them actually liked that exotic brown skin, thick lips, ass, and thighs.

Black men have always embraced the black woman's thickness, and it was cool because black women had a place to feel proud of their voluptuous figures, but then things started to shift. The black girls with tight, slim bodies looked down on the thicker girls with dimples in their booties and cellulite in their thighs. They talked a lot of shit, and tried to make them feel ashamed of their weight. Some girls were cool with their fullness, and didn't give a fuck what anybody said, but others felt the pressure to get thinner. Some girls used coke and speed to lose weight, but instead of just dropping pounds, they began to look sickly and hollow. I never got caught up in that shit, I liked to eat too much.

All of the girls had piercings and tattoos to draw attention to their bodies. I started getting my adornments a couple of months after I started working at the club. My virgin body screamed "new girl" without ornaments, so I got my tongue, belly button and nose pierced. Then I got a tribal tattoo on the small of my back, a heart tattoo right above my left pelvic bone, and a dollar sign on my ankle.

I had seen every kind of piercing in the club like eyebrow, chin, lip, nipples, and clit. Sunshine had her clit pierced, and had a chain hanging from the bar. One night after closing, she hopped up on the pool table to show everyone under the bright light. Some girls had tats saying "R.I.P. Little Man", "Only God can judge me", "Trust no man" etc., and there were sloppy roses on tits, asses, arms, stomachs, and ankles covering up the name of an ex nigga or two. A few chicks had scars from being stabbed or shot at. The body was a billboard sign that people could read and figure out the kind of life each dancer had or was currently living. The silent marks may have held secrets, but they never lied.

The money in the strip game was notorious, and the only reality of the so-called glamorous life. Brothas didn't mind breaking bread with familiar faces, girls they sat down and had conversations with, but new girls didn't make money for the obvious reasons; they didn't know anybody, so they had to work harder than the OGs. Every dollar they earned was hard to come by, so they couldn't cop a seat at the tables drinking all night like the OGs, they had to shake hands, meet people, and stay in character by prancing around the club teasing customers with the booty clap and titty-shaking.

One truism is that when the money flowed, everybody got paid. If a man was big tipping the waitress and bartender, he was paying for dancers and vice versa. A man's clothes and jewelry were never an indicator of his spending hab-its. Ballers would walk in, buy a few drinks, and never tip anybody but the waitress. In their minds, only tricks would break bread with strippers, and they weren't paying for pussy, so those tight-fisted cats kept their money in their pockets. A lot of times, the Fed Ex man was more generous than the baller dripped in diamonds. The man with construction worker steel toe boots and plaid shirt might spend more than the business man in the pin-striped suit with Kenneth Cole lace-ups. Smart dancers learned to be cool with everybody because you never knew who was holding what.

I was an equal opportunity stripper; anybody that walked through those doors was fair game. Right off the bat, I could never tell who was spending, so it was better to be safe than sorry. Giving a man your full attention and relent-less flirting were the most effective ways of getting that bag. I once sat with an old white grandpa that the other girls laughed at, but I walked away with $320 after an hour and a half.

As far as the government was concerned, I was unemployed, so I had to keep up with their expectations of me. Getting paid under the table meant that I hadn't paid taxes or contributed to my Social Security fund for a few years, so I couldn't buy property without a *real* job. Strippers, drug dealers, and hustlas all went to the same car dealerships that catered to independent contractors such as ourselves. They didn't need paystubs and bank statements, and the finance guy looked the other way when the salesmen were handed $9,000 in cash. Cars were both registered and non-registered, stolen, and some had chopped parts. My BMW came from a car broker that somebody in the club referred me to. It was almost brand new and beautiful, so I didn't ask any ques-tions.

Some of the girls in the club wanted to look like a million bucks, but in real-ity they were a lap dance away from being broke. They would wear expensive clothes, but wouldn't even have an apartment or a car. They would live in motels, and take cabs to work. They spent money faster than they could make it; taking trips, shopping, and staying in the nail and beauty shops.

One thing that strippers were not known for was being smart with money. The ones that lived in raggedy apartments still pushed Mercedes, BMW, or SUV. A lot of times, the cars got repo'd because the chick couldn't keep up with the payments. Some of them dressed in Christian Dior and Versaci clothes with shoes from the Slauson Swap Meet. It was true that strippers could make a lot of money, but that didn't mean they had class. Strippers used the term *hood rich* because most of them were from the hood, and they liked to look rich with the hair, nails, clothes, shoes, and cars, but it was a façade.

They weren't rich, they weren't even well-off; they were poor little rich girls that wanted to look like they had money, but were never taught the proper way to spend and save money. Most of the dancers made a lot of fast money but they lived day to day without thinking about the future.

To the outside world, strippers were hookers, disgusting whores that were too stupid or too lazy to get a real job. They wandered around dark, musty clubs because they weren't smart enough to get an office job, but in reality, dancers were the ultimate hustlers. It was hella hard to run around in six inch heels with your ass out, selling a fantasy than it was for the chicks who sat behind a desk all day. Legitimate jobs ended at 5 o'clock, but hustling never ends. Strippers were always on the grind, coming up on as much loot as they could from every stiff that waltzed through the curtains at the front door.

Dollar signs were everywhere: a group of college guys walking in the door, Friday nights, the 1st and 15th, bachelor parties, playoff games, and pissy-drunk customers begging to be taken advantage of. A dancer's mind never switched into the off position, she was always working, like if somebody asked one of them who the dope man was, she wanted a finder's fee. Strippers were always grinding. In the mind of a stripper, sitting behind a desk making bullshit was a waste of time. The old saying goes *No honor among thieves*, and it rang true in the strip club just as much as it did on the street. There was nobody to run to if one of the other girls stole your regular customer, if your weed sack was short, or if a dancer got raped at a bachelor party. It's like risk versus reward. There was always the possibility of danger but the big payoff was usually worth the risk.

I spent money like everybody else, but I saved more. Because the IRS required paperwork for bank deposits over $10,000, I kept most of my money in the house. It probably wasn't the safest thing to do, but I kept my business to myself so nobody really knew what I was holding, plus I kept some of it in the freezer in t.v. dinner boxes and bags of frozen veggies. The other part of it was in tampon boxes underneath my sink. In an average week, I brought home anywhere from $1400–$2000, and over 2 years, I had saved over $12,000. I wasn't trying to make a career out of stripping, so I was smart enough to put something up for a rainy day. That money was going to sustain me after the club had served its purpose.

CHAPTER 8

I was knocked out when Tony called my phone at 9 the next morning. I was sleeping so hard that the ring scared the shit out of me, and my heart leapt out of my chest. My throat was dry, and my doo rag had slipped off my head during the night, and now it was covering my eyes. I snatched it off, and answered the phone.

"Hey Mia, did I wake you up?"

"I was up. What's going on?"

"I'm at practice, but we get a break at 12. I could come over with Fatburger, and give you the rest of that loot. Did you make that call yet?"

"No, I'll call as soon as we hang up. I think the office is open now. Yeah, you can come through with the food. Tell them to make my burger on the grill, no relish, and I want chili on it. Can you bring me a Napoleon shake too?"

"You mean Neopolitan?" I felt like a fucking idiot. I must have still been half-sleep, but I played it off like I knew what I was saying.

"Whatever, nigga! I'm playing. What time will you be here?"

"I should be there by 12:30 or so. We get a 2 hour break."

"Okay, I'll be here."

We hung up, and I lay back down to think about the dream that I had last night. It was crazy because Tony and I had a baby boy, and we lived in a fat house with a maid, a cook, and an elevator. In the dream I was fitted, my hair was tight, and I had a big ass rock on my finger. Tony was playing with the baby, and I was reading a book with a white cover. Our clothes were all white, and everything in the house was white. Right before the phone interrupted my dream, Tony had said, "I love you, Mia, and I thank you for our beautiful son." I never even thought about keeping the baby before the dream.

Suddenly, I began to really think about the baby that was growing inside of me. I never considered keeping the baby since my baby daddy had a wife, but now I thought about the baby. I was probably only a couple of weeks pregnant, so I wasn't showing, but I wondered what the baby would look like. Tony was tall and hella fine, and I had the dimples and pretty face.

I thought about how my life would change with a baby. I would stop stripping, drinking, and popping E's. And since my baby's daddy is a basketball player, I could stay home with the baby all day. I could drive around in my brand new Range Rover and shop on Rodeo Drive with the rest of the wives. Finally, I would be respected, and not looked down on as a hooker shaking her ass for money. I would go by the club every now and then to remind the haters that they couldn't get on my level.

My fantasy was interrupted by a twinge in both sides of my jaw. Saliva started to slowly form in the corners of my mouth, and I felt light-headed like the other night at the party. I ran to the bathroom just in time to throw up in the sink. I moved to the toilet when I had a break, and I threw up two more times. After I sat on my hands and knees over the toilet for a few more minutes, I thought it was safe to get up. I carefully stood up, and leaned on the sink. I looked in the mirror, and my face was red and sweaty, and my hair was damp. My stomach still felt queasy, so I moved very carefully.

I turned on the faucet, and rinsed the puke out of the sink. Then I cupped my hands underneath the water to rinse my mouth out. I grabbed my towel off of the hook, wet it, and put in on my forehead. I rinsed the towel under the water, and wiped my face. I pulled a ponytail holder out of the drawer, and tied my hair up off of my face. All of a sudden, I felt something going on with my ass, so I ran and sat on the toilet. Liquid poop drizzled out of my ass again. I sat there for awhile, so that I didn't have to come back. My booty hole was a little tender, but coupled with the fact that I was throwing up, it was too much to handle all at once. I rested my chin on my fists that were propped up on my knees. Nothing came out, so I got up, grabbed a baby wipe, and gently rubbed the crack of my ass. After I washed my hands, I carefully walked to the room, and lay in the bed. I called Hypnotiq, but her voicemail picked up immediately. She must have been with Big D, and turned her phone off, so I called Brandy.

"Man, I feel like shit! I just threw up three times!"

"Wow! You have morning sickness. Are you okay?"

"I'm back in bed now. What am I supposed to do?"

"My sister had that real bad for months. You just have to take it easy, eat plain crackers, and drink 7 Up to settle your stomach. Want me to bring you some?"

"Would you? I don't want to throw up on the way to the store!"

"Okay, give me a minute. I'll tell my boss I have to run an errand."

"Thank you girl."

I lay in the bed waiting for Brandy, and fell back to sleep. She rang the doorbell, and I wished that I had given her a key to my place before then. I sat on the edge of the bed for a few seconds, and then I slowly got up and walked to the door. Brandy came in with a bag, and hugged me tight.

"Are you feeling better?"

"I fell back asleep, but I didn't throw up again."

"Well, I brought you the crackers and soda. You want it now?"

"I'm scared I might throw up again. Maybe in a little bit."

"I can hang out with you for a little bit, and then I have to get back to work. I told my boss that I had to get my brakes done."

"Thank you so much for taking care of me. I guess I really am pregnant hun?"

I managed to give her a slight smile, but I was so nauseous and dizzy that it probably wasn't very noticeable. I was so hot that I wanted to rip my clothes off, but I felt a chill at the same time. My booty hurt, my throat was burning from the throw-up, and my stomach ached from the heaving.

"Okay? First you fainted at the party, and now you have morning sickness. It's official."

"Girl, I had the craziest dream last night. I had the baby, and Tony and I lived in a big house with our son. His wife was gone, and it was just the three of us."

"Yeah, that is crazy. You know he would never leave his wife."

Brandy didn't mean to, but she crushed my dream before I could even wipe the sleep out of my eyes, and I regretted ever opening my mouth. Reality hit me like a junky coming down off a high. I sounded more like a schoolgirl with a crush on the boy next door, and less like a stripper that was catching feelings for an NBA player. With that one line, and without her ever knowing it, Brandy had set me straight, and got me back on track. She was right, there was no way Tony would ever leave his respectable wife for me.

Brandy stayed for a little while, but then she took off for work. I ate a few crackers, and drank half of glass of soda. My stomach had settled, but I was nowhere ready for a chili burger from Fatburger, so I had to stop Tony before he brought the food. The smell alone could make me puke all over again.

"Hey, I'm not feeling too good, so you don't have to bring me any food."

"I just talked to you a little while ago. What's wrong?"

"After I hung up with you, I threw up."

"Wow, you cool?"

"I feel better. Brandy came and brought me stuff."

"Well, do you still want me to come over?" I hope he didn't think puking made me lose my mind. Of course I wanted him to still come over. I needed him to run me the rest of the money.

"Yeah, you can still come, but why don't you come after practice so I can rest, and get cleaned up?"

"That's cool…umm…okay…well…I guess I'll call you later then."

It was killing him not to ask me if I had called the clinic. He wanted to ask, but he knew I got sick after we talked earlier, and he didn't want to seem uncaring by asking me to call at that very moment. I let him suffer.

I called the clinic, and the next available appointment was for Wednesday. I hoped that I wasn't going to throw up for the next two days. I lay back down, and slept for a few more hours. Tony came through later, and brought me the rest of the money, plus a 2 liter bottle of ginger ale and a box of Saltine crackers. That was cool, so I ended his suffering, and told him my appointment was for Wednesday. He seemed relieved, but not too excited. I'm sure he knew that too much happiness would look inconsiderate, and terribly selfish. I was irritated, nauseated, and bothered, so I think Tony knew that he had better walk lightly around me. Plus, he's not stupid, he knew that he had to be on his P's and Q's at least until I had walked out of the clinic childless.

CHAPTER 9

One of the nurses called my name, and I got up and followed her to the admission desk. I gave her the money, and she went over all the paperwork, and gave me birth control pills, condoms, and antibiotics. No douching, tampons, or sex for two weeks…blah blah blah…I knew the whole routine. I was just ready to get it over with because I had felt like shit since I threw up two days ago, and I knew I would be back to normal by the next day.

I walked down the cold, generic hallway until I found the dressing room. I picked a locker in the back corner, and started to take my clothes off. I had to remove my sweats, shirt, bra, panties, piercings, and all jewelry. I wrapped myself in the flimsy hospital gown that opened in the back, locked my things up, and stuck the safety pin with the key on my gown. I stretched the hospital bonnet over my head, and put the matching baby blue slippers over my socks.

I walked to the waiting room with the rest of the tramps, and looked at their faces. I wondered how many of them were there because of a married man, or a man with a girlfriend. Maybe I was the only fool. One teenaged black girl looked like she had been crying. Her eyes were red and puffy and she kept sniffing every few minutes. She was about 16 or 17 and in love, but her mama made her get an abortion. There was a white woman about 35 that already had a couple of kids, but didn't want anymore. There were only a few other women in the waiting area, but they kept their heads down because they were nervous, guilty or trying to stay anonymous.

When it was my turn, I walked into the sterile surgery room, and a nurse helped me climb onto the operating table. The lights were extra bright, it was cold, and several people stood around with hospital scrubs and masks over their faces. There was a sheet covering the metal table that held the tools that the doctor would need for the abortion. I guess they didn't want the patients to see them because they may get up, and run out of there. It didn't scare me because I didn't have any other choice, plus this was my fourth trip to the clinic. When I did settle down, I didn't even know if I would be able to have kids.

I had to lie on my back, raise my knees, and open my legs. As a courtesy, they draped a sheet over my knees and between my legs, but I knew as soon as I was knocked out, they would raise the sheet and everybody would be in my shit. The doctor asked me if I was okay, and if I had any questions. A nurse rubbed the top of my left hand with alcohol. Before she stuck me with the needle, she tried to explain her mistreatment of me before the damage was done.

"You're going to feel a little pinch, and then a slight burning sensation as the medicine is released into your hand. You'll be fine."

She carefully poked the needle into the top of my hand, and I squeezed my eyes tight because I knew that burn was a bitch. Shit! I felt fire shoot through my veins when the nurse said, "Okay Mia, we need you to count backwards from 10."

"10...9...8..." I was out.

When I woke up, I was in the recovery room with a couple of other girls, and I felt hella dizzy. For a minute, I forgot where I was, but then I had an itch, and almost scratched the taped cotton ball off the top of my hand. I tried to sit up, but I was still too drowsy, so I lay back down.

A nurse walked in, "How are you feeling, Mia?"

"Sleepy."

"That's normal as the anesthesia wears off. You should feel pretty normal in about 20 to 30 minutes or so. Can I check your pad for blood flow?"

"Yeah."

What was I supposed to say? Everyone that was in the surgery room had already seen everything under my gown, so I agreed, and she helped lift my gown up. Between my legs I had on an old school, long ass, surfboard maxi pad attached to a sanitary belt. I couldn't see the pad, but she said my flow and the blood clots were normal. I thought about how they must have got all that stuff on me while I was knocked out. Pulling me, twisting and turning my body to get me positioned.

"You can lie down as long as you need to, and then you can walk back to the dressing room, and get dressed. Who is coming to pick you up?"

"My friend Brandy."

"Okay, let me know if you need anything else. There is a bathroom at the end of the last bed."

"Thanks."

The entire procedure took most of the day, but it took less than 15 minutes to suck the baby out of my uterus. I called Brandy and she came immediately to pick me up. We stopped for her to get some Popeye's chicken and red beans and rice, and then she helped me up the stairs. All I wanted to do was go to sleep, so I told her she didn't have to stay. Brandy wanted to stay and eat since it was her lunch break, and I told her it was cool. I hobbled in the bedroom, gently laid on top of the comforter, and quickly fell asleep. After Brandy finished eating, she locked the door from the inside, and let herself out. Despite her strong opinions and unsolicited advice, she was a truly good friend. When I needed her, she was there without question.

I woke up to my phone ringing off the hook. I looked at the caller ID and it was Tony, but I didn't answer. He called again about a half hour later, and I knew what he wanted. He wanted to make sure the problem was taken care of, but I didn't have the energy to answer the phone, let alone speak. I still felt weak and tired; my body felt wore down and heavy like a hamper full of dirty clothes. I was cramping, and I felt a little gush of blood come down when I switched positions in the bed. I knew that I needed to get up and eat something, so that I could take my medicine, but I felt like I had run the L.A. Marathon. Something would not let me turn over, and sit up on the edge of the bed. I told myself that I would lie down for another 15 minutes, and then I would get up.

An hour later, I was good to go. I wasn't 100%, but I felt much better than I did before I counted backwards from 10. Just as I was walking to the bathroom, the phone rang, but it had to wait. I pulled my panties down, and saw that the blood had leaked from the pad onto my panties and my sweats. I took everything off, and sat down on the toilet. When I finished peeing, I turned on the shower, put a shower cap on my head, and stepped under the massaging shower head. The hot water felt good on my thirsty skin. I stood there for a long time, and let the water baptize me of my sins.

I had just picked up the phone to call Tony when my doorbell rang. I looked through the peephole, and it was Tony. I guess he got tired of calling. I limped over to the mirror above my couch, and figured that I looked somewhat decent for a post-op abortion patient. I fluffed my hair, licked my lips, and opened the door.

"Mia! I've been calling your phone. Why didn't you pick up?? You cool?!"

"Yeah, I was just tired as hell."

At first he had to act like he gave a shit, but then he asked the question that forced him into his car and drove him to my apartment.

"Did everything…go okay?"

I wondered how long it would take for him to get to the real. He should've been able to look at my fucked up appearance and answer that question for himself. I looked like I had been awake for a week, sleep deprived and fragile.

"I have a few cramps, but I'm cool. Everything went fine. I was just dizzy and sleepy when I first got home. All I wanted to do was crash. I saw that you called, but I just got up and took a shower. I was going to call when I got out."

I didn't want him to think that I was all emotional, crying and shit. That wasn't my first trip to hell, but he didn't need to know all that.

"I just came over because I started getting worried. You weren't picking up your cell or your home phone, and I knew that you should've been done by now."

"Thanks for checking on me, but I'm cool. They pump you with so many drugs that it takes a while to wear off."

"Are you hungry? I could go get you something to eat. What do you want?"

His obvious guilt was busting through his weak smile, but I knew he was human.

"I think I can do Fatburger now, but no chili. Thanks."

Tony left, and I washed a load of clothes and made my bed. When he got back, we ate and tried to act normal, but we both thought about what had just happened, I *was* the pregnant mistress of a star basketball player just a few hours ago, and then I wasn't.

Tony came back with the food, and it smelled so good. I was starving and I couldn't even remember the last time that I ate real food. Because of the surgery, I couldn't eat or drink 24 hours before my appointment, and even before that I was throwing up so I wasn't eating much of anything. I guess my stomach shrank because I couldn't finish my burger. It was made just the way I like it: char-grilled with grilled onions and the works, but my stomach gave up before my heart.

I was envious of Tony as he was able to finish a double burger with chili and fries. He stayed over longer than he ever had. We watched *Scarface* and he stayed with me until I fell asleep. He took care of me that night when I didn't even know that I needed it. I was grateful to him, but I would have never told him. No matter how sweet he was, no matter how much he made me laugh, and no matter how much I liked kicking it with him, I could never forget that he had a wife and kids at home. He would never be mine.

We were cool, but I never treated him like he was my man. I didn't leave him sweet voicemails in the middle of the day, I didn't cook his favorite meals, and I didn't let him really get to know me. This wasn't the first baller that I had dealt with, so I had a normal routine,suck them, fuck them, and leave them wanting more.

Some females in my situation would get all emotional, questioning them about their marriage, and crying all the time because they don't spend enough time with them. I didn't worry the fuck out of them or nag them like the woman they had at home; I was cool. Cats liked hanging out with me because I liked to kick it, but I never pressured or tried to handcuff them. Tony and I hung out at the club, my house, or with his boys, but we didn't have a lot of serious talks, and I liked it that way. You can't miss what you never had.

Tony and I were never as close as we were that night. He was gentle and caring, and for one night, that night, I let my guard down. I guess I was feeling the loss, and he felt responsible, so we leaned on each other. I don't know if he looked different, or I just saw him differently, but that night I saw a side of him that I had never seen before. I was his only focus, and he was attentive to my every need. His cell phone rang, but he put it on vibrate and let it ring. Tony helped me walk to the bathroom, and he stood outside the door until I was done. He went in my room, took the comforter off the bed, and covered me with it as I lay on the couch falling asleep. He cradled my head and rested it on his lap.

Without words being said, Tony was apologizing for forcing me into the situation, both by getting me pregnant, and then by being hostile out of his own frustration and desperation. I didn't let myself think about how things would be when I felt better, and his guilt went home, but I let him take care of me that night.

CHAPTER 10

❀

The next morning, I got up early to find myself in the bed, but not remembering how. Tony must have carried me in the room, and tucked me in. The last thing that I remembered was dozing off on *Scarface* as I laid on the couch after eating a glorious burger. My appetite was back and I decided to make a big breakfast. I felt refreshed, like my old self. I wanted to make sausage, scrambled eggs with cheese, smothered potatoes, toast, and orange juice. I threw on some jeans, a top, sandals, and drove to the store. When I was standing in line to pay for the food, my phone rang. Tony was calling to check on me, and I told him that I was at the store getting stuff for breakfast.

We had never sat on the phone and had such a serious conversation. We usually talked a lot of shit, clowning and laughing, but this exchange was focused and humorless. I appreciated Tony's concern, but I hoped that he would be able to move past his guilt and make me laugh like he used to. I had come to depend on his twisted humor to get me past some of the other bullshit in my life.

"What you making?"

"Scrambled eggs, potatoes, and sausage."

"Damn, that sounds good. You making enough food for me to come through?"

"Yeah, come on."

"I have to take my daughter to her ballet class, and then I'll be over. How long is it going to take you to cook?"

"About an hour from now."

"Okay, I'll call you."

I had to hide my surprise because I was arguing with myself just before he called; I wanted to invite him to breakfast as a way of saying thank you for taking care of me when I was down, but I figured he was with his family, and I couldn't stand being rejected after last night.

He was taking his daughter to ballet class on a perfect Saturday morning when he had just killed our baby 24 hours earlier. After I hung up the phone, I decided that that fact hurt my feelings and he could've saved that bit of information, but I would never mention it to him. I wasn't needy, and I wouldn't dare give him the impression that I was, even for a minute.

Tony said he would be over in about an hour, so I went home and started cooking as soon as I walked in the door. After I cut up the potatoes and onions, I threw them in a large pot with a little bit of oil over medium-low heat. I browned the sausage, and beat the eggs, I went and took a shower. I put on my Baby Phat mini skirt and pink wife beater, makeup, and fixed my hair. I checked on the food, and turned on *My Good Luck Charm* from the Jagged Edge CD.

The doorbell rang, and I went to let Tony in. I opened the door, and he had a Coldstone bag. That was my favorite ice cream, and I couldn't help but smile from ear to ear.

"What is that?"

"I just wanted to bring you a little something. You had a rough day yesterday."

"Yeah I did!"

"I thought so." I let him in the house and gave him a big hug.

"Thank you so much. That was very sweet."

"You're welcome. You were a little out of it yesterday."

"Yeah, I was real sleepy, but I'm cool now."

"The food smells good. Is it almost done because it's been more than an hour! I'm starving!"

He started walking towards the kitchen, but I stepped in front of him. My silly Tony was back, and I welcomed his reappearance. I could only take so much sadness and regret. What's done was done, and it was time to move on.

"You'll see in a minute. Go sit down!"

Before he sat down, he hugged me again, and this time he held me longer. I started to pull back a little, but he looked me in my eyes, cupped his hands around my face, and pulled me in to kiss him. He kissed my lips very softly and gently, but I ended it.

"Let me check the food."

I walked away quickly, and pretended to be caught up with the food, but in reality I was just getting away from him. What was he doing? We had never been this touchy feely before. He mostly came over late at night, we chilled for a minute so that I didn't feel like a complete hooker, fucked, and he went home. There wasn't a lot of cuddling, talking, and we never kissed.

I figured that he was still feeling guilty, and didn't want to look like a complete asshole by treating me anything less than a lady the day after an abortion. He was just caught up in the moment, but after a few days, he was going to be relieved of his sins, and things would be back to normal.

I grabbed the butter out of the fridge, scooped some into the pot, and poured the scrambled eggs in. I poured our juice in two glasses, and put them in the freezer. I liked my drinks really cold, but I hated ice because it just watered it down. I had already set the table, and the eggs were the only thing I was waiting on. I threw the sausage in the microwave for a minute, and then I slipped the bread in the toaster, and leaned on the counter waiting for them to pop up.

"Mia, can I help you with anything?"

"No, I got it."

What I really wanted was for him to stop fucking with me. I finished the eggs, and helped our plates. I brought the two plates to the table, and told Tony to come and sit down. He walked to the table, kissed my cheek, and thanked me for breakfast. We ate, laughed, and talked. After we were full, and couldn't eat another bite, we cleaned off the table, and sat down on the couch. There was an awkward silence that lasted for a few minutes, and then he asked what I was doing the next day.

"Nothing. Why?"

"We're playing in Arizona, and I want you to come."

"I'm still bleeding, and we can't fuck for two weeks anyway."

"That's cool. I still want you to come. We don't have to do anything."

He was off the chain. We didn't go anywhere together unless we were fucking. The abortion was verified, he couldn't fuck, and he still wanted to kick it? I didn't get it.

"Well, let me see how I feel by tonight. When are you leaving?"

"Tomorrow morning. You can leave a little later if you want, and go right to the game."

"Okay, well I'll call you later on tonight."

We chilled on the couch a little longer, and then he said he had some things to take care of before he went out of town. I walked him to the door, and told him that I would call him by tonight to let him know if I felt cool enough to travel. We hugged again, and he left. Finally, I was alone with my thoughts, and I tried to figure out what he was up to. I know I wasn't the first girl he had an abortion by, so it was hard for me to believe that he could have been that racked with guilt.

I cleaned up the kitchen, and lay down on my bed for a nap, but first I had to tell Hypnotiq about my morning, including my invitation to go out of town.

"Damn girl, you going?"

"I'm still bleeding and cramping. I doubt it."

"That would've been fun though. So he's still simping? Ha ha ha! You better milk that cow for as long as you can! That would've been cool for you to get out of town though."

"I know, but I'm really not in the mood. I'll see him when he gets back."

"You want me to come over before I go to the club tonight?"

"Thanks, but I think I'm going to lay it down for a little while. I'll call you later."

"Call me if you need anything."

Brandy had called while I was cleaning up the kitchen, so I called her back.

She had always said that messing around with a married man wasn't smart because someone would get hurt. I told her that I never let feelings get involved, but she said that no one could control real emotions, and if you hang around someone long enough emotions take over regardless of what you *said* you would do. Brandy said that shit because she was romantic, and she was in love.

She thought relationships were black and white, either you were committed or you weren't. She never cheated on her man, and I didn't think he ever did either. I'm not mad at her; it's just that it wasn't my life. My shit was complicated. I hadn't had a boyfriend since I really started stripping, and since then I usually ended up with married men, or men that had a girlfriend, and there was no way I was catching feelings for any of those niggas that came in the club. I didn't fall in love because I knew how it was going down. I didn't even allow myself to get comfortable with that idea. Men looked at strippers, and they wanted the fantasy but not a girlfriend, so I didn't even set myself up for that disaster.

I was very disciplined, and my game was tight. I met these brothas with fat pockets and I fucked them. I didn't want them to leave their girl, and I didn't want them to get a divorce. Shit, wifey can have his cheating, lying, greedy ass. Even though these men were fine, had loot, and were fun to kick it with, the truth is that they could never be trusted, and I wouldn't have any of them for my man even if they wanted a serious relationship *after* they left their woman. Some of these cats got caught up in the fantasy; they thought I was fine, sexy as hell, and ran around half naked all the time. That was a role that I played; it wasn't reality. These corny ass squares tricked off their whole paycheck on a character that I was playing. After two years at the club, my whole view of men had changed. Basically, I thought they were hella stupid for breaking bread with a female that would never mean shit to them.

The money made them feel powerful, like they were in control, but in reality the strippers had the power. If we wanted their money, we knew what to do to get it. When I did table dances, I always grinded on their dick like I was fucking them, and rubbed my tits in their face just as the song was ending, so they would buy another dance. I liked to do table dances to fast songs because they were shorter, and didn't make my legs burn as much. If a long song came on, I made the tricks wait unless they pushed the issue. And while we waited, the guys better be buying drinks, or I moved the fuck on.

I wasn't really drinking when I first started stripping, so the O.G.'s put me up on game. I used to order a Rum and Coke, but the waitress would bring me just Coke, and charge the trick $7 (plus tip), and she would split it with me. That worked until I became a lush, and craved every single drink that was purchased for me. It got to the point that it was hard for me to be in the building without a crutch. Learning how to function in a strip club was easy, most of us dealt with all of our issues from the bottom of a bottle.

Any time I spent time with anybody from the club anywhere outside of the club, they had to pay for my time. When I went to lunch and the movies with regulars, I told them they needed to break bread for the loot I was missing at the club, and they always did it. They paid for beauty shop appointments, manicures and pedicures, clothes, shoes, bills, CDs, and DVDs, anything I wanted. And most of the time, you could get all of this stuff without fucking. The possibility of fucking was the fantasy. To fuck them would make you as real as their burned-out wife, so they kept you in an untouchable status, and that shit worked for both of us.

After my nap, I ate some of the Coldstone ice cream that Tony had brought over. He knew that strawberry cheesecake was my favorite because I talked about it all the time. I ate a big bowl in front of the t.v., and decided it was time to call him. His voicemail came on, so I left a message saying that I wasn't ready to get on a plane yet, and I would talk to him when he got back. Tony called back a little while later.

"Mia, wassup? You can't make it? I thought you were feeling better?"

"Well, I'm feeling better, but I don't think I should push it. If I do too much, the bleeding will get heavier."

I thought that maybe if I was really blunt with him I would scare him away, but it didn't work. He persisted.

"All you're going to do is sit on the plane, and sit in the stands at the game. You could get out of town for a day, and get some rest."

That was just what I needed, to get away from the club for a little while and just kick it, but I wasn't going to feed into whatever Tony was going through.

"Maybe next time, but thanks for the invite."

Tony still tried to get me to go, up until I was hanging up the phone. The truth is that I had talked myself out of going to Arizona. I didn't know what Tony was up to, but I wasn't trying to figure it out either. I was going to do my normal shit, and fuck with him when he got his shit together. After his guilt passed, everything would be back to the way it used to be. I knew that all of this extra treatment was him feeling sorry for me, and after I had completely healed, he would feel better about himself. I didn't want to get to deep into the shit just for me to wake up one day and recognize that reality had snuck in.

CHAPTER 11

The next night Hypnotiq wanted to take me to *The Factory*, and since I hadn't been there in a while, I told her it was cool. I called Brandy to see if she felt like watching some oily, half-naked men bumping and grinding on overweight, desperate chicks, and she said she was down. I needed to get out of the house! I had been pretty much house bound for the last few days, and I was starting to get cabin fever. I was ready to venture past my front door.

Tony had called that morning before his flight left. He asked how I was doing, and tried one last time to get me to jump on a plane. I told him that I really needed to take it easy. He sounded disappointed when he hung up the phone, but I didn't change my mind. As much as I fought it, I had to admit that a little part of me missed him because I had gotten used to him being around pampering and fussing over me.

I ran errands for the next couple of hours. I went by the Beverly Center to get a top to go with my new Apple Bottom jeans, and then ran to Target and the beauty supply. Since I had been cooped up for a few days, I had to make several stops. When I got home I flopped on the couch, watched t.v, and ate some more ice cream. It made me think of Tony, and I wondered how he was going to act when he got home. A few days would have passed, and we will have spent a little time apart, so things would probably just go back to the way they used to be. I woke up a couple of hours later when Hypnotiq called me. She wanted to see what I was wearing.

I hung up the phone and dropped my head between my legs as I sat up on the couch. I felt lazy, and now that I had hung the phone up, I didn't even know if I had the energy to get it together. I went in the kitchen, and grabbed a Smirnoff Ice out of the fridge. I needed to wake up because at that point, I didn't feel like going anywhere. I had an hour to get dressed, so I called Brandy first. I told her to be at my apartment by 8 o'clock.

I turned Lil' John on the CD player, threw my clothes on the bed, and turned the water on. I wrapped my hair, and stepped in the shower. I stood under the warm, running water for a few minutes while the blood flowing down my legs turned the water a dirty pink. I watched as a couple of blood clots rinsed down the drain. I waited until the water turned clear again, then I grabbed my wash towel, held it under the shower head, and poured way too much shower gel on it. After I brushed my teeth, and washed my face, I shaved my legs, and scrubbed the bottom of my feet with a pumice stone. I jumped out of the shower, and rubbed baby oil gel all over my body, and sprayed on some Clinique Happy.

I put on some period panties and stuck a thin maxi pad between my legs. I couldn't wear tampons after the surgery, so I had no choice but to walk around like a diapered baby. I learned my lesson after my last abortion. I had gone to Vegas a couple of days after the surgery, and I couldn't wear period panties with my Seven jeans, so I stuck a super tampon up there, and hit the door. Within a few hours, I was cramping as I was on the dance floor at a night club. I pushed and shoved my way through the thick crowd to the bathroom. The blood clots were chunky, dark red blobs that fell to the bottom of the toilet. Not only did I think that I was bleeding to death, but I got a bacterial infection.

I grabbed my bra, cut the tag off my new jeans and top, and got dressed. I put my makeup on, and brushed my hair out. I ran lip gloss over my lips, and grabbed my high-heeled sandals out of the closet. I sat on the couch sipping on my second Smirnoff when the doorbell rang. It was Brandy.

"Hey girl."

"How you feeling?"

"I'm cool now, but I was a mess before I got in the shower."

"Make sure you take it easy tonight. Have you talked to Tony?"

I really didn't want to start the Tony conversation because I knew where Brandy was coming from. Even though she never said it, I knew that she thought that Tony was just using me, his good time girl. I couldn't blame her because honestly, that's all I was. We didn't have deep conversations about my dreams or fears; he didn't discuss his children or his plans after basketball. We talked about bullshit like, how business was at the club, or how one of his boys needed a girl for a bachelor party.

"He called this morning before he left for Arizona."

"Why didn't you just go?"

"I'm not 100% yet. I didn't want to be out of town limping around like a cripple."

I couldn't tell her the real reason, I had to put some space between me and Tony because that would open the flood gates to a conversation that I was not trying to have with her, Hypnotiq yes, but Brandy no.

"You made the right decision. You could've done yourself some damage by being so active so soon after surgery. Did you watch the game?"

"You know what? I fell asleep on the couch."

"I think I hear Hypnotiq's car."

I looked out the window, and I saw Hypnotiq parking her car. We grabbed our purses, and headed out of the door. We caught her just as she had opened her car door.

"Hey girl!"

"Fuck! You guys scared the shit out of me!"

"My bad! We just wanted to catch you before you got all the way to the door."

"Okay let's roll."

Brandy and I jumped in Hypnotiq's ride, and we rolled towards the club. I looked out the window, and watched the thugs on the corner, drunks hanging around the liquor store, and young cats riding by on spinners trying to get our attention, but I didn't even make eye contact. I looked right through them and their flossiness because I was thinking about Tony. I never really worried about where he was and what he was doing, but suddenly I was thinking about it. I figured the game had just started, but what about later. Was he going to the club, and would he meet any groupies? Was he fucking one *or two* of them tonight? I realized that I couldn't torture myself like that, so I tried to forget about him for the night. That was just the thing that I had hoped to avoid by distancing myself from Tony and his nurse maid routine, emotionally sucking me in just to cut the strings when I was sufficiently hooked.

We pulled up to the front, and females were already starting a line outside the club. Hypnotiq grabbed a park, we checked lip gloss and hair, and hopped out. As we walked to the front, we heard somebody say, "Here they go." Probably some haters, but I was in no condition to get with them tonight, so I didn't even ask my girls if they heard it.

We stood at the end of the line, and I quickly noticed some familiar faces. Strippers showed respect for each other by representing at each other's clubs. The men came and broke us off, and in turn we would go to their club and break them off. It's like an unspoken rule, but everybody knew what was up.

We had respect for the strip game, and we showed that by having each other's backs. Of course there were a few strip club boy/girl couples, but there wasn't too much getting down among the two groups. The same way a lot of females were fucking each other, from what we heard the men were getting down too.

Nobody knows for sure, but there were always rumors, and after awhile you believed some of the persistent ones. Like the old saying goes…*where there is smoke, there is fire.* I had always heard that some of the dancers were fucking each other, or other guys outside the club. None of them looked feminine, so it was hard to believe, but just like a lot of female strippers went both ways, it was possible. The only difference was that men never came in the male strip clubs. The only men in the building were working, like the bartender and the DJ, so if they hooked up with men, they did it on their own time. The same way that female strippers would do any and everything when a lot of money was involved, male strippers did the same. If somebody offered them a lot of cheese to dance at an all-male birthday party, some of the dancers took it. There was a fine line between hustling and being gay; money is what drove the strip game, not sexual orientation.

A few months ago, I heard about a dancer that had just got to work on a Saturday night when he heard somebody honking a horn in the back alley. He went out there, and sitting in a black Navigator was one of the biggest dope dealers on the block. The dancer sat in his truck, bossed him up, and then went back in the club to dance for the ladies. From what I heard, the d-boy had been on lock down for like 5 years, and he got used to men blowing him, so when he got out he looked for the same thing, a strong, masculine mouth. The funny, scary thing was that these cats didn't think that shit was gay because they weren't doing anything but receiving, but in my book, if a man ever let another man suck him off, he's gay!

Although a lot of haters thought that all male dancers were gay, that just simply wasn't the case. I guess some people couldn't understand why a *real* man would prance around in a thong wearing a cowboy hat, and a jacket with tassels hanging off of it. Purely by statistics, some of the guys had to be gay; but no one could tell just by looking, they all looked straight. Most of the dancers wanted to model or act, but they danced strictly for the money and the face time. Most of them were cute, but their bodies were what the women came to see. A lot of them lived in the gym, and their beautifully sculpted bodies turned bored housewives into screaming, horny teenagers that lined up to throw their grocery money at the men that unleashed the passion that had been buried down deep below their duties, errands, and obligations.

The females looked at the sweaty, oiled, muscular bodies, and completely lost their minds; they wanted to be overcome and consumed by wild, aggressive sex that was curiously close to rape. The appeal of the strip club is the same whether it was male or female; both sexes wanted to experience the things they didn't get at home. The same way that women gain weight and start wearing faded, baggy sweats around the house, men let themselves go too. They sat their fat asses on the couch, watching football, and ignoring the women in their lives. Brothers loved to hang out and kick it with the fellas, leaving their women alone at the house. After a while, that shit gets old, and women came to the club for the fantasy, and they were never disappointed.

Each dancer had their own groupies, and they would break their paychecks for their dude. Females would go up to the stage to give them a dance, and they would shower them with hundreds, even thousands of dollars. They would buy them clothes, shoes, jewelry...even rims for their rides. A lot of the guys had wives or girlfriends, but it didn't matter. Most of them would fuck the groupies, but not always because it depended on what they looked like. Some of the groupies were 300 pound heavyweights, and the dancer would shove his face between their tits, or ram their big asses from behind, and we all laughed because it was just nasty. But the big girls paid nicely, and the dancers made them feel like they were the sexiest girl in the spot, so paying for the attention was well worth it for them.

There was a lot of competition for the dancers' attention. Sometimes the groupies wore shirts with the dancer's name or face spray-painted on it. They bought electronic wands and belts that had a scrolling billboard with the dancer's name on it. These stupid females would try to outspend each other by bringing more and more cash to the club. It was all game; a lot of times the guys would give their main girls money out of their own pocket just to make other dancers *think* they had it going on. I had seen so many fights inside the club where a girl got busted fucking somebody else's man. Every now and then a wife or girlfriend would show up just to let those bitches know who was boss. Sometimes females would mean-mug each other, trying to figure out who came to see who. It was funny to me because I wasn't in the shit.

I fucked a dancer a couple of years ago before I got in the game, and he was all the fantasy that a woman would think he was. His name was Chocolate Thunder, and he was beautiful, tall, fine, dark, bodied up, and had mad skills. I was at *The Factory* one night, standing at the bar getting a bottled water when he walked up to me. He told me how beautiful I was, and asked me if I wanted a drink. I told him that I didn't drink, and he seemed impressed. He asked me if I had caught him on stage, and I told him that I had just got there. He ended up asking for my number, and even though I really didn't want to start fooling with a stripper, I gave it to him because he was gorgeous.

We hung out a few days, and then I fucked him. He was off the hook! The rumors were true about male strippers, they loved using toys, eating pussy, and leaving women twisted to the point that they would do anything for them. I have to admit I was feeling Mr. Thunder until his baby mama kept calling my phone. He forgot to tell me that they shared an apartment with their two-month old baby. I stopped answering his calls, and eventually he got the point. I wasn't really tripping because I wasn't trying to marry him, but he was cool to hang out with. Chocolate Thunder wasn't dancing at the club anymore, but there were other chocolate desserts to replace him: Chocolate Shake, Chocolate Fudge, and Chocolate Delight.

We walked in the club, and grabbed seats right in the front. It was considered disrespectful to take the seats in the front row if you weren't tipping. The club filled up quickly as the DJ started playing music, and welcoming the crowd to the club. There was a group of women across from us that they were having a bachelorette party; the most energetic woman had a small, white veil on her head. There was a birthday party set-up on the top of the stage with balloons, tablecloths, and colorful streamers. It was about the time when I started to count the balloons that I realized that I had my mind on everything *but* Tony.

Suddenly, the DJ came over the mike.

"You ladies ready to see the infamous…notorious…men of *The Factory*??? I said are you READY??? Coming to the stage is GQ and Black Stallion!!!!"

Women were yelling and screaming, but the three of us were chilling because we knew the best performers wouldn't be out for a minute. The weaker dancers came out first because for one, nobody wanted to be first, and for two because the club wasn't completely filled yet, and the best dancers wanted a packed house before they came out. A couple of dancers came to the stage that I had never seen before. They had matching white furry outfits with furry cowboy hats.

"There you go Mia!" Hypnotiq was playing with me, and Brandy laughed too.

"I'm cool! Only one of us can wear fur!"

"You know you like that!"

"I'll let you take him!"

We all were laughing as we watched the first few acts without breaking a sweat, then the tides turned, and the stars came out. I always felt bad for the first dancers because all of the guys had to take turns picking up money for the other dancers while they were on stage, and the weaker dancers had to watch the crowd's reaction and the money that they never got.

Some of my boys came on stage, so we went to stand in line to get a dance with them. The ladies would stand on the four corners of the stage floor, and the MC would ask them which dancer they wanted, then the MC would tell the dancers where to go. I didn't feel like dancing; I just wanted to throw them some money. When it got to be my turn, I said wassup to my boy Chocolate Fudge and showered him with 20 ones. He was happy, but I had to back him up off of me because he was getting too excited.

Other females got off on all that, men grinding their dicks on their pussy, but these were my boys and I didn't feel like all that. I could feel the blood gush every time I laughed or moved, so I went to the bathroom to check my pad. I was just in time because the pad was covered with blood from edge to edge. As I was squatting over the toilet, leaning into my purse fumbling for a pad, I heard two females talking by the sink.

"Ooh, Diesel looks so good! I'm fucking that nigga tonight!"

"Girl you tripping! Sonia said his chick just walked in."

"Fuck her! I'm slipping him my number. May the best pussy win!"

They laughed, and finished washing their hands. When I flushed the toilet, and walked out of the stall, they both stopped and looked at me. I'm sure they thought they were alone. I could give a fuck, but I'm sure they were wondering who I was. I washed my hands and as I walked out, I could feel their eyes on my back.

I knew Diesel and his girl, and she didn't play. Angie knew her man was a ho, but she loved his dirty drawls. She didn't mind fighting for her love either. I had seen her fight a couple of times in the club, and she was no joke. The manager had threatened him about losing his job if she didn't learn how to act. The owner even told Diesel that she was suspended from the club but she kept popping up anyway, and since the owner wasn't always at the club she got away with it. Angie had broken tables and chairs, shattered glasses, sending girls to the emergency room for fucking with her baby daddy. I thought everybody in L.A. County knew her reputation, but apparently the chick in the bathroom hadn't heard a thing because she was determined to fuck Diesel. He was fine as hell with a body that would make a straight man cry, but most girls were smart enough to leave him alone.

I walked from the bathroom and noticed that the club was filled to capacity, sexy bodybuilders dripping with baby oil and glistening with sweat was a major attraction from Thursday through Sunday night. But I was a dancer, and I knew that all of it was an act.

Naturally, the dancers were turned on by a few of the females, but most of the time, their dicks didn't even get hard when they were wrapping their lips around some girl's big tits through her shirt, or grinding their dick on some chick's big ass. They were performing. They packed their thongs with socks to make their dick look huge; it wasn't real, and some of them took it too far with the socks. Some of them looked like they had put a whole six-pack in there and it looked ridiculous. Some of the guys didn't like socks, so they took a couple of whacks at their dick to get it hard, and then they would tie a dress sock or a ring around their dick and balls to make it stay hard for a little while. The sock trick worked just as well as the hard dick trick, but it wasn't as realistic because the guys usually went overboard with the socks.

I didn't watch the show like an amateur; I knew the tricks of the trade. The guys waxed their eyebrows, shaved their chest hair, and cut their pubic hair off. Some of them even wore a little makeup in their pubic area to hide scars from razor bumps. They had S-Curls, bald heads, waves, and perfectly-lined fades. They were high-maintenance, pretty boys that stayed in the mirror longer than females, and took their jobs seriously because the more effort you put in, the more money you made.

Right before the Grand Finale, I heard a crash, and turned around to see the female that was talking that shit in the bathroom lying on her back. Angie had hit her over the head with a Heineken bottle, and she fell over the table, and hit the ground. It was over in the first round. The shit-talker had a deep cut on her forehead covered in blood, and she was lying on the ground like she was dead. She didn't move for a few minutes, but then she opened her eyes. When her friend helped her up, she started acting like she had taken a bullet. Of course Angie was long gone, so she was free to talk shit.

"Where is that bitch? I'm up now! What bitch?"

She was screaming at the air and wiping the blood from her eye like a crazy woman. We heard later that the girl walked right past Angie, and gave Diesel a napkin with her number on it, walked by Angie again, and gave her a fucked up look like she was going to fuck her man. Angie grabbed the full beer bottle sitting in front of her, and cracked her one time over the head. That was all it took, and Angie's friends ran her up out of the club. Diesel was still dancing until he saw the girl lying on the floor by Angie. He knew the routine, and he threw his head back in disgust. He hadn't even fucked that girl, and Angie had jeopardized his job…again. I didn't know if Angie was coming back with gunfire or what, so we got up out of there after the girl went down. Hypnotiq and I were starving, so we decided to get something to eat.

We went to Roscoe's chicken and waffles on La Brea and Pico and waited for a table. Roscoe's was always busy, no matter what time of day or night. There were a lot of popular spots to eat in L.A., but Roscoe's was sho nuff. Their old school soul food was off the hook, and worth waiting an hour for a table. The one little bench in the waiting area was never meant to hold all of the people waiting for a table at any given time. Most people ended up sitting outside on the brick planters along the walkway leading to the entrance of the restaurant. The hustle men always set up shop with bootleg movies and CDs, incense, and remote-control cars. The parking lot was full of tight rides sitting on shiny rims. Guys were always dressed in brand name jeans and shirts, clean tennis shoes, fat jewelry, and a new baseball cap on top of a fresh fade. For starters, girls in L.A. always had their hair and nails done. After that, they wore the perfect clothes and shoes to make the fellas lose their minds. Everybody felt the pressure to look good because Roscoe's was a famous hook-up spot, and there were always a few celebrities or athletes in the house.

It was the one of the only kind of places where the food was more important than the atmosphere. The restaurant was old, the tiny little bathrooms only had two stalls, and the plastic dishes and plain silverware weren't fancy enough for the beautiful food that rested on them. The food spoke for itself. You couldn't go wrong with any dish on the menu. The world famous chicken and waffles brought strangers in the door, but the other breakfast food like grits, eggs, and turkey sausage were unbelievable. The soul food side of the menu created fans in all cultures and racial groups. Everybody was in Roscoe's from the Asian students of USC to the white tourists from Colorado.

After we sat down, the waitress handed everyone menus, but I told her that I already knew what I wanted.

"Can I please have a chicken breast, three wings fried well done, rice and gravy, macaroni and cheese, and greens?"

"Sure, and what would you like to drink?"

"A large Lisa's Delight please."

"Damn girl! You hungry?" Hypnotiq always teased me about how much food I ate. It wasn't like I was going to eat it all right then; I was going to take most of it home for breakfast the next morning.

"Just a little bit!"

"You are crazy!"

"Can you bitches hurry up and order, so we can eat?"

They laughed at me, and even the waitress cracked an embarrassed little smile. Roscoe's always required a two-meal order because I had to eat it for at least two days. Lisa's Delight was my drink. It was a glorious mixture of lemonade and iced tea, but the two didn't actually mix so the tea floated perfectly on top. Some people used their straws to mix the two flavors together, but I left mine the way it was. Hypnotiq ordered three wings and a waffle, and Brandy ordered the chicken sandwich and fries. After they finished cracking on me for forcing them to order prematurely, I looked at my phone and saw that I had a missed call from Tony. He must have called when we were slapping music leaving the club, but I didn't call him back. I loved the fact that he was thinking of me when I knew he was getting out-of-town pussy thrown in his face.

Even though Roscoe's was always packed, and it took nearly an hour to get a table, the food came pretty quickly. We were stuffing our faces, reminiscing and laughing about the dancers, the big girls, and the "fight" between Angie and the big mouth. After we ate more than we should have, we rolled our fat asses out of there with our to-go containers, waddled to the car, and stuffed ourselves inside. On the way home, I thought about waking up the next morning, and eating all over again.

CHAPTER 12

The next day, I didn't feel like getting right up when my eyes first opened. I was lounging around in the bed, still under the covers when Tony called my phone at 11 o'clock.

"I called you when we got back to L.A., but you didn't pick up."

"I went out, and I didn't hear it ring. How was the game?"

"We won. Where did you go? I guess you feel better now?"

I wondered if he was asking because he wanted to fuck, because he really was concerned, or if he was just being shitty because I wouldn't fly out of town with him, but I found my way to the club.

"Yeah, I feel a lot better. I went to *The Factory* with the girls."

"What you got going on today?"

"Nothing really."

I was supposed to go to the nail shop with Brandy, but I didn't want him to think that I was busy because he would say that we could hook up another time.

"I thought maybe we could go to lunch."

I didn't know what to say. I wanted to hang out with him, but a part of me knew that it would be all bad. I said to myself *fuck it!*

"Where?"

"I don't know, probably somewhere in the valley. Can you be ready in 20 minutes?"

"Yeah, I'll be ready."

He loved calling me at the last minute, and I always ended up jumping in the shower, throwing on clothes, and running around grabbing makeup and pulling hair. He had a wife and family, but whenever he got free he tried to hook up, so I never had much warning. At first I felt kind of used, but I guess you could say that I got used to the late night calls and short visits. The reality was that there was no room for whining and pitching tantrums about the way I would like things to be. The truth is, if I didn't get it together, the next bitch would.

I turned the shower on, and went to pull out an outfit and some shoes while the water warmed up. I hopped in, and thought about Tony as I lathered my towel with the shower gel. Honestly, a part of me was mad at myself for being so available every time he called. I never told him no, and he had begun to count on that. It made me feel desperate and weak because I always changed plans, and broke appointments with whomever for whatever, just to meet up with him for an hour or less. I knew that if I was *not* available to him that I could easily be replaced. I fronted like he wasn't fucking me, and that I was fucking him, but the truth is, I felt powerless to him.

In my mind, having an unsatisfactory relationship with a high class guy was better than having a high class relationship with a satisfactory guy. I could've had security, love, and affection with the trash man or a postal worker, but there was no challenge or excitement in that. Dinner at five, family pictures, and school plays didn't turn me on, maybe when I was 30 or 40, but not now.

Tony called 15 minutes later to see if I was ready because he was almost at my apartment. He was always on time because his window of opportunity was always very small, so he had to take full advantage of every free moment that he had. I finished up with my hair and makeup, and took one last look in the mirror before I sat down on the couch. I looked good, but I always wanted to look my best because I knew that was what Tony expected. He loved the way that I paid attention to my appearance, and he complimented me all the time. I watched him sometimes, and he looked like he enjoyed other men staring at me because it secretly boosted his ego. And he loved when his boys made comments about my tits. It made me feel like a piece of meat most of the time, but I didn't mind because I liked showing off, for Tony and myself.

Tony rang the doorbell, and my heart began to beat wildly. I realized right then how much I had truly missed him. We hugged each other like we hadn't seen each other in years when it had only been a matter of days. We got in his Escalade, and hopped on the 405. He was bumping 50 Cent, and I was glad because we didn't have to talk. There was an uncomfortable silence in the car; I just looked out the window, wondering where this day was going. I wasn't sure, but I let Tony take the lead.

I thought…I had an abortion by this married man a few days ago, he helped nurse me back to health. After he came back from his trip, I thought his guilt would've been satisfied by now. But for some reason, he came back home wanting to spend more quality time with me. Since I first started fucking with Tony, we had *never* been to a restaurant or anywhere else in public like the movies or the mall. We got together at *Aces,* my place, or his boy's house for barbeques and parties, so this was something new. A part of me resented the fact that all of these changes came only *after* I told him I was pregnant. Would anything have changed between us if I never got pregnant, and *where* was he taking me?

"What do you feel like eating?" It was as if Tony was reading my mind.

"How about Mexican?"

"I ate that last night before we left Arizona. How about Japanese?"

I knew why he picked Japanese food. He didn't want anyone to see us together, so he picked a far-out place full of people that didn't look like us. I had a bad habit of going to the negative first, but in this situation, I was probably right. The valley was 30 plus minutes north of L.A. in the suburbs. The people that settled in the valley were trying to escape the fast, noisy city life, so the chances of him running into somebody that he or his wife knew were slim to none.

"Yeah, that's cool."

It wasn't cool. I wanted Mexican, but that's the price you pay for kicking it with a rich athlete, they call the shots.

For some reason, it was so much easier for me to get my way, talk shit, and boss around a square ass cat, but when it came to Tony, I lost my nerve. I didn't know if I wanted to please him, or if I was just plain intimidated by him, or even worse…maybe I was just grateful to be around him. Either way, I felt cowardly, and I didn't like how it felt when I gave up my power.

We pulled into the parking lot of Benihana, and I pulled down the visor, so that I could check my hair and makeup. Tony stopped the car, and I was getting ready to open the door when his cell phone rang.

"Hello? Yeah I'm getting ready to leave now. What are the kids doing? Cool. Okay let me call you later. I love you too. Bye."

He didn't look nervous, guilty, or apologetic when he hung up the phone. I don't know what lie he had told her about where he was, but I knew that I was supposed to be quiet when his phone rang. Tony didn't even acknowledge the phone call as he took the key out of the ignition, and opened his door. I was stepping out of the truck when *my* phone rang.

"What you doing?" It was Curious Brandy.

"Getting ready to get something to eat. Can I call you back?"

"Where?"

"Benihana."

"What? You never want to go there with me. Who are you with?"

"Tony."

I had hoped that she wouldn't do too much while Tony was standing right in front of me.

"Oh, okay. Well call me later and give me all the details!"

I was grateful for her mercy. I told her that I would call when I got home, and we hung up. Tony and I sat at our table in front of the grill, and he did all of the ordering. He didn't even ask me what I wanted, but I chalked that up to him either being a gentleman or a snob. Either way, I wouldn't have known what to order anyway. The chef came out, and prepared the shrimp, steak, chicken, and vegetables right in front of us, and I had to admit that I was impressed by the show.

I had never been interested in eating there, but now I wish that I hadn't been so stubborn, and taken Brandy up on her offer. The food was off the hook. While we ate, Tony asked me how I was doing.

"I feel a lot better. How was the game?"

"I got three dunks in the 4th quarter! My teammates gave me shit in the locker room, calling me MJ."

"That's cool. I wish I would've seen it, but I was knocked out."

"After the game, I signed some autographs for the kids. It was cool."

"That's so sweet of you. When we were about to leave the club last night, this girl got smashed with a beer bottle."

"Damn what happened?"

"She gave her phone number to the other girl's baby daddy, and she was doing extra. Everybody knows the girl is crazy, but she tried her anyway and she knocked her ass out."

"Let me ask you a question. What would you do if my wife confronted you?"

"Nothing."

"I mean if she was asking you questions, or trying to fight you, what would you do?"

"I probably wouldn't say shit."

"I didn't think so. That's one of the things that I like about your style, you're not messy like some of these other girls."

It sounded more like a backhanded compliment to me. Nice doggie, you've been trained well to keep your mouth shut.

For the next hour, we talked and laughed like we were the only two people in the restaurant. It felt good, and for a split second, I forgot that he had a family waiting for him at home. As suddenly as I remembered his wife and kids, he looked down at his watch, and said that he needed to get back to L.A. Tony paid the bill, and we walked to the truck. As we walked through the parking lot, he stuck his finger through the belt loop on the back of my jeans, and pulled me closer to him. I was pleasantly surprised by his public display of affection, and I giggled in a coy, lady-like way.

Tony walked me to my side of the truck, and opened the door for me. After I climbed in, he aggressively pulled my legs toward him as he stood outside the truck. With his two fingers, he moved my hair from my eye, cupped his hands around my face, looked me dead in the eyes, and kissed me innocently and softly. His lips were soft and wet, and I realized that my feelings for him were undeniable.

We hadn't fucked since the abortion, and my pussy was on fire from feeling his tongue on mine for the first time. I felt his body heat, smelled his cologne, and I wanted to eat him up. He was fine, tall, sexy, and I wanted him to fuck me right then, even though I knew we couldn't. I think if he tried to take it, I would have let him. It was more than the physical; I had begun to see his sensitive, caring side, and I liked what I saw. I had turned the corner in our relationship, and I was not alone.

When Tony dropped me off that afternoon, I thought about the hot kiss he had given me in the truck, and the fact that he had never really kissed me before. I could tell that he didn't like kissing from the first time that we fucked. I was riding him, and bent down to stick my tongue in his mouth, but he turned his face. If he didn't have a wife, I would've felt like a whore for real. I figured kissing must have been too personal since I wasn't his woman. I was teasing him about it later, and he told me not to take it personally, but he really didn't like to kiss. I didn't believe it because I knew that he had to kiss his wife when he made love to her.

Maybe he convinced himself that he would fuck other females, but he wouldn't kiss them with the same mouth that he kissed his wife and kids with. Kissing made my pussy super wet, but I let it go, just as I had done with so many other issues. In a normal relationship, there is give and take, but when a female was dealing with someone like Tony, she learned to give far more than she ever took.

I saw Brandy's call coming in, but I couldn't answer it. I was buzzing from Tony's kiss and our first real date. I knew that she would bring me back down to earth, and I wanted to float among the clouds for just a little while longer. I put off her phone call until about an hour later.

"What happened?? You were supposed to call me when you got home!" She was way too excited.

"I just walked in. It was cool."

Not only was I purposely keeping some of the joy to myself, but I was lying to my best friend.

"You guys don't usually go out like that, do you? What do you think that means?"

That was exactly what I was trying to avoid by not talking to Brandy right away. The overwhelming questions suddenly overwhelmed my buzz.

"Girl, who knows, but we had fun. What you doing?"

"Well, I was waiting for you to go to the nail shop. Want me to come pick you up?"

I felt bad for semi-standing her up from earlier, so I told her I would pick her up in 15 minutes. On the way to Brandy's, I thought about Tony, and how this situation was going to play out. I didn't know what he wanted from me, but I didn't dare ask because then it would be like I was sweating him. One thing that men like Tony liked about girls like me, was the fact that we were very low-maintenance. We didn't nag, complain, and demand things from them; the relationship was very easy-going and non-committed. Instead of trying to figure these things out for myself, I decided to bend Brandy's ear. I picked her up, and we headed for the nail shop. Before we could clear the doorway, the Asian woman in the front of the shop approached us.

"Hello. What you need today?"

"We both need a fill and pedicures, but I need wax too."

"What you need waxed?"

"Bikini, mustache, and eyebrows."

"Okay, you get wax first. Go back now."

I had been going to the same nail shop for years, and the people that worked there always made me laugh. Their clothes never matched and they wore high heels faithfully, even with sweats and other clothes that didn't warrant fancy shoes. I know they talked behind our backs too, but it was cool. If a girl looked too ghetto sexy for the nail shop, talked loudly on their cell phone, or had a big ass, they would gossip in Vietnamese. Even though none of the customers understood a single word that they said, you could just about figure out what they were saying by their facial expressions and body language. When they had to talk business their English was perfect, but they reserved their own language for shit-talking, like when someone messed up a nail and needed it to be repainted.

"Okay. Pick you color. You wait 5 minute, and we do your nail for you. You go to the back for wax."

Brandy and I giggled as we walked to the nail polish counter. It was as if there was a written script because they always said the same thing. I had figured out the fact that picking your nail polish was a stall tactic because that gave them time to clear a seat, and I they thought that once you had picked a color that you were somehow handcuffed to the shop, and no matter the wait, you wouldn't dare leave after you had spent 4 long minutes looking through all of the varieties.

I walked to the back, and started undressing in the cold, badly decorated room. They always went from the smallest job to the biggest, so I was ready for the bikini wax first. I took off my pants and threw them on the back of the chair, but I left my thong on. Even when customers got a *Playboy* wax, the wax girl still wanted them to keep their thong on while they applied the wax. I guess they didn't want pussy staring them dead in the face, so they ask the girls to pull their thong from one side to the other as they waxed and pulled. I lay on my back, and assumed the position, holding my legs back, so that my feet were back by my ears. After she yanked every piece of hair from my pubic area, she finished with my mustache and eyebrows.

The hot wax, followed by the violent ripping of the paper felt like someone had popped me with a 1,000 rubber bands all at once. The stinging sensation burned like hell for a minute, then led way to a dull pain that remained for a couple of hours. She pulled the stray hairs with her tweezers, and lathered my red, throbbing skin with baby oil. By the time I walked out of that little room, it looked like I had been rescued from a burning building.

Brandy and I sat in the chairs chopping up my lunch date. I was at the point where I needed some serious counseling, but Hypnotiq wasn't there, so I had to deal with Pollyanna.

"So girl, wassup with you guys?"

"I wish I knew."

I learned to keep my answers short and non-descriptive so that Brandy would wave the white the flag, but she didn't get my hint.

"I wonder what's going on with his marriage. You think they're cool?"

"When a man cheats, everything can *not* be cool. If he was happy and satisfied at home, he wouldn't be coming to see me."

"Yeah, but she *is* the wife." That was the shit that I didn't want to hear.

"I'm not tripping. It's whatever."

"How long do you think your relationship will last?"

"I have no idea."

"But I mean, do you ever get sick of feeling like he's just using you?"

"Yeah I feel like that, but I'm using him too."

"For what?"

"We have fun, he makes me laugh. I like hanging out with him."

"I just don't want you to get hurt because at some point, he will have to end it when his wife starts getting suspicious."

"Well I'll have to deal with it when it happens. For now, I'm just having fun. Don't worry about me, I'm not trying to marry the man!"

"I hear you, but that doesn't mean your feelings won't get involved. Just be careful."

"Okay mommy!"

We kept talking, and I told her that I knew that I was taking a risk, but every relationship, physical or mental, committed or non-committed, was a risk. What I didn't tell Brandy was that I knew I was setting myself up for a beautiful disaster, but I couldn't walk away.

CHAPTER 13

What a difference a day makes. Ever since the day that I told Tony I was pregnant with his baby, something changed between us. He sat with me after the abortion, invited me on the road, took me to a restaurant, and then we were hanging out all the time. Tony and I began driving to the Valley to eat and go to the movies. He never said it, but I knew that he was less likely to be seen, or run into anyone he knew way out there.

Honestly, I was a little nervous when we first started going out in public because I never knew what to expect. I didn't want him to get busted either because I knew that would be the end of us hanging out, and I was having fun. Unfortunately though, all of our trips were not to the good.

One day when Tony and I had just left Chili's, he ran into one of the assistant coaches from the team. He never introduced me as he stood there talking to him for what seemed like forever. I was irritated, and I guess it was written all over my face. As we walked to the car, Tony brought the issue up.

"What's the matter?"

"Nothing." I really didn't feel like getting into it, but he wouldn't let it go.

"You look like you have a little attitude. Are you tripping because I didn't introduce you to coach? You know how we get down, but I don't need everyone to know my business."

"Tony, I said I'm not tripping."

I lied because I didn't want to cause any problems, but I felt like a piece of eye candy just standing there while they talked. The coach looked me up and down a couple of times in a real perverted way, and then he would look back at Tony. I could tell that he wanted Tony to introduce us. His nosey ass probably just wanted to know if we were fucking so he could try and hit! If I noticed it, so did Tony but he never said a word.

At other times, I felt invisible, like when wifey would call, and he would be sitting next to me, but say that he was hanging with his boys. Sometimes Tony would tell her that he loved her right in front of me, but I guess what else was he supposed to do? It was times like that that I fell from the clouds, but most of the time, I tried to focus on what we had, and not so much on what we could have.

While Tony was driving me home, I pretended like everything was cool, but I what I really wanted was for him to drive faster. I needed to get out of these clothes, let my hair down, and have a drink. I needed to relax because for some reason, that whole coach thing had really pissed me off. The coach looked at me like he was one of the guys at my club, and I was mad at Tony for not checking him, introducing me, or claiming me!

I knew that he would never let someone disrespect his wife like that, and I was mad at myself for allowing him to treat me like that. When Tony got to my apartment, I gave him a fake ass kiss, and hopped out of the truck. He told me that he might come by later, but I secretly hoped that he wouldn't be able to get back out of the house. I wasn't in the mood, and we needed a break from each other. For the last few weeks, we had been seeing each other a couple times a week when he was in town, and I started having higher expectations of him.

Subconsciously, I think I expected him to treat me more like a girlfriend. After we had hung out a few times, I began to realize that he was treating me more like a #2, rather than work. We were doing more things outside of the house like a real couple, and it wasn't for fucking parties and strip poker, we enjoyed the day by ourselves. It all happened so naturally that I didn't even notice right away, but once I did, instead of being satisfied with the increased attention, I wanted to spend more quality time together, I wanted to be respected more, and made to feel more special than he was already treating me.

Reality had its way of rearing its ugly head, regulating the situation, placing a mirror in front of my face when I shuddered at my reflection. And it wasn't until I kept bumping my head, continuously becoming frustrated and frequently agitated that I began to realize that I was doing too much. Tony was married, and I couldn't and *shouldn't* have any expectations of him for my own sanity.

Tony called a few hours after he dropped me off. I was quick to tell him that I was going to work. I didn't want him to think for a minute that he was sliding by.

"Why are you getting ready for work? I thought I said I was coming through?"

"I haven't left yet, but I didn't think you would be able to get out."

"I can't get back over there tonight, but I'm coming through tomorrow because I'm going out of town after that."

"Call me in the morning."

I was curt and to the point. Without saying anything extra, I wanted him to know that I wasn't cool.

"Mia, I can tell that you have something to say, so why don't you just say it?"

I couldn't reach for the tape fast enough to wrap my mouth up before the words left my lips.

"Tony, why did you let your coach fuck me with his eyes?"

"He didn't mean anything by it. That's the way he is. Why are you tripping off that? Is that why you had your mouth stuck out in the truck?"

"I just didn't appreciate the way he was staring at me like I was a whore that you picked up off the street."

"You're starting to make me think that I made a mistake. We've been hanging out a little bit more, and I thought you could handle it, but now you're starting to expect too much. You have always been cool, but now you're starting to trip off stupid shit."

"Whatever Tony!"

Now I was pissed, but more at myself than Tony. I should've kept my big mouth shut because now I felt like an idiot, a needy idiot no less. I gave up my power by looking helpless and emotional. I actually made him think that he and the coach hurt my feelings!

"I'll talk to you later."

We hung up the phone, and I left for the club. When I pulled into the parking lot, I could tell that I wasn't staying. I had only been to the club once since the abortion, and it had been a good night; I made $800 in five hours.

I walked up to the back door, and Tiny let me in. I hollered at the managers, bartenders, and a few dancers, and then I walked back out within 15 minutes. No need in wasting my time because I recognized the couple of broke ass niggas that were in the club. I went home, put my robe on and fell asleep on the couch watching *Cheaters*.

❦   ❦   ❦

Tony woke me up early the next morning. He was on his way to work out, and he wanted to check on my plans for the day. I told him that I was going to work out, run errands, and hook up with Brandy and Hypnotiq for lunch. He told me that he had some business to handle, and he would be by about 9 or so, but he would call me later. I had calmed down since the day before, so I told him that was cool. Luckily, he didn't bring up my childish tissy fit from last night. I got up, and started my day.

I was looking forward to seeing my girls because I could tell them the things I would never tell Tony. Brandy wanted to meet at her house to eat leftover chicken enchiladas on her lunch break. Brandy's cooking was off the chain, and I couldn't wait to eat. I skipped breakfast because I wanted an empty stomach when I got to her spot.

Brandy opened her front door, and gave me a big hug. She was always so upbeat and cheerful, smiling as if the sun always shone on her side of the street.

We walked into the living room, and sat down on the couch.

"The food is heating up. It'll be ready in a few minutes. So what's going on, where's Hypnotiq?"

"Nothing much. I worked out, and ran some errands. I went to the club last night, but it was empty, so I went home. I called Hypnotiq as I was pulling up but she was stuck at the shop with her car. I asked if she wanted me to come and get her, but she said they were almost done. She'll probably miss lunch though."

"What's up with you and Tony?"

I knew it was coming; I was just waiting for the questions to start.

"We're cool. He's coming over tonight before the team leaves tomorrow."

"You guys have been getting really close huh? He wants some ass before he leaves huh?"

"Damn girl, you sound like me! One of us has to stay right, so you better be cool! No, we haven't fucked, and yes I think that's why he wants to hook up tonight."

"You giving him some?"

Brandy was looking at me like the cat that ate the bird.

"Give *him* some? Shit I'm getting *me* some! I haven't fucked in over 2 weeks!"

"Oh okay!"

"I could've got some last night, but he pissed me off."

"What happened?"

"We ran out to Chili's in the valley, and he ran into one of the assistant coaches. He was looking me up and down like I was naked. Not only did Tony *not* introduce me, he didn't even check him for doing too much. I was hella mad! After he called me later I checked his ass, but he said I was changing."

"What is up with you guys? You're spending a lot of time together, but what do you want from him…realistically?"

That was a good fucking question. That was what I loved about Brandy; she kept it real, and she asked me the hard questions that I didn't want to ask myself, let alone answer.

"I wanted him to treat me with respect. I know that he has a wife, but when he's with me, I deserve the same respect he would give her."

"Sweetie, do you hear yourself? He is married. The *only* woman that he will instinctively respect is his wife. I think if you are going to involve yourself with a married man, you have to accept the realities of your relationship. There are limitations."

"You're right, and I had to check myself. I wish that would've kept my mouth shut after everything happened because I regret looking like I give a fuck. I don't want to look needy or soft, you know?"

"Right. Have fun but be careful."

"Trust me, that is the one thing you don't have to worry about. Fuck that nigga!"

I followed Brandy into the kitchen. I got the sour cream, guacamole, and salsa from the fridge, and she took the enchiladas out of the oven. We laughed and talked until I left her house with a full belly and a band-aid on my heart.

At about 8:30, my phone rang, and the caller ID said "Tony Home", and I tripped for a minute because he never called me from home. When I had snuck the number from his phone, I had programmed it in my stored calls. Tony wanted to pick up a movie and some food, and kick it at my house. I told him that would be cool, even though I was supposed to go bowling with Hypnotiq, Jason, and his friends. She had called me a few days ago to invite me, and I totally forgot about it until she called earlier that night to remind me. I didn't tell her that I couldn't make it just in case Tony called and said that he couldn't come by.

After he called to say that he was coming, I made my routine I-can't-make-it phone call, and started straightening up a bit before I hopped in the shower. Hypnotiq was disappointed because she was going to be the only girl, but normally she didn't trip when I flaked on her because she knew I had to get in where I could fit in with Tony. I put on something cute and tight, tossed my hair, and put on a little eyeliner, and lip gloss. I lit the candles, and waited for him to show up. I thought about my discussion with Brandy, and reminded myself to play it cool.

He got there about 20 minutes later with Chinese food and *Goodfellas*. We hugged at the door, and I immediately started making our plates. Tony walked right in, took off his shoes, and plopped down on the couch. He turned his phone on vibrate, and flipped through the channels until he found a basketball game. When it was obvious that the Rockets were blowing the Warriors out, he put the movie in.

Tony brought shrimp fried rice, chicken chow mein, sweet and sour chicken, and fried prawns. Everything smelled delicious even though I had eaten big at Brandy's. I gave him his plate at the couch, and he started eating right away. If it would've been anyone else, I would have checked him for not waiting for me, but it was Tony. I went back in the kitchen, and poured his drink. I fixed a little plate for myself, and by the time I finally sat down to eat, he was half done with his food.

"Do you want something else?"

"I'm getting full, but you can get me another prawn."

I walked to the kitchen to get Tony another piece of shrimp. I didn't mind waiting on him hand and foot like that. I know a lot of females would have said that I was a fool, but we all are to a point. And besides, if more women made their men feel like a king, they wouldn't be out creeping so much. I didn't care that Tony had a wife at home, when he was with me, he was my man, and I was his woman.

After we finished eating, we were sitting on the couch watching the movie when I felt Tony's hand moving under the comforter that I had thrown over us. He was sliding his hand between my thighs, and I was already gone.

"You cool?" Tony wanted to make sure that I wasn't dropping blood.

"I'm cool baby."

His hands wandered slowly between my legs until he reached my G-string. He pulled it to the side, and began to stroke my pussy. His fingers gently caressed my clit, then in and out of my pussy. I was squirming in my seat until I couldn't take it anymore. I tried to reach for his zipper, but he moved my hand. Tony began kissing my neck and ears, and then my mouth. He slid his tongue between my lips as I moaned like a cat in heat.

Suddenly, he got on his knees, tore off the blanket, and shoved his face between my legs. He pulled my panties off, and rubbed his hot, juicy mouth all over my pussy. I was shocked, and I kept thinking *What does this mean?* I was rocking my hips as his tongue flickered on my clit, but I didn't want to cum yet, so I slowed down. He sensed my hesitation, and began to stand up. He held out his hand, and I grabbed it as he led me to the bedroom.

I started to remove his jeans, shirt, and underwear as he was working on my clothes. He threw my bra to the floor, and started grabbing my titties, and sucking on them like he was a teenager. I let out a little moan, and pulled at his dick. I put my mouth over the whole thing, and went up and down on it while his breathing got louder. My tongue wandered all over the head, and then the length of his dick. I sucked his balls until he was jumping off the bed.

"Let me suck on that pussy."

I quickly moved into a 69 before he changed his mind I was on top bossing him up, and he was underneath putting in work. Heaven! We rolled over, and I was on the bottom, but we kept going. I was sucking his dick upside down, and he was loving it. He transferred his tongue from my pussy to my mouth, and I tasted myself. His warm tongue searched the inside of my mouth while I yanked on his dick. He stopped to grab a rubber, and I climbed on top.

I forced his dick inside me, and rode up and down like a rodeo star. My house phone rang, but I ignored it. I rocked my hips in little circles, and lifted my ass up so that only the head was still inside. After I did that a couple of times, Tony palmed my ass, and squeezed it down hard on his dick. Tony's dick was real long and thick, and it rubbed nicely against my clit. It was a perfect fit, and I rubbed my pussy back and fort until I began to cum. Tony put his long fingers around my neck, and squeezed until I had reached my peak. I was floating on fluffy white clouds until the phone rang again. I didn't answer it.

Tony rolled me over, and slid his dick in from behind. He was grabbing on my ass, and he smacked it so hard, I screamed hella loud. He was ramming my shit hard, I was yelling, and the phone rang again.

"Damn baby, go get that shit! It's fucking up my flow!"

Tony pulled his dick out, and I leaned over the bed to grab the phone. The caller ID said "Tony Home," and I knew right away that it was wifey. At the same time, I noticed his cell phone was buzzing on my living room table. I bet she kept calling his cell phone, and when he didn't answer, she called the last number he called before he left the house. Now this bitch had my home number, no less!

"Tony, your *wife* is calling!"

"What?? How the fuck…"

"Remember, you called me from the house earlier?"

"Aww shit! Don't answer!"

"Hi, this is Mia. You know what to do. Beeeeep!"

We both stared at the phone in complete shock. She didn't leave a message, but the phone rang again.

"What should I do?"

"Answer it, and if she asks about me, tell her that you don't know me. Tell her that it must have been a wrong number." I felt cheap, but I did what he asked of me.

"Hello?"

"Who is this?"

"Who were you trying to call?"

"I asked who *you* were."

"I think you have the wrong number…"

"Do you know Tony?"

"Who?"

"Tony."

"No. I think you have the wrong number."

"Sorry to have bothered you."

She hung up. Tony was staring at me, and I had never seen a man look so frantic. His family, his life, his future was in my hands, and I saved him.

Tony snatched the rubber off his dick as he was getting off the bed, and I went to get him a towel. He jogged into the bathroom, turned the water on, and grabbed the soap from the shower. He never used soap, but I guess his busted ass figured he better do extra in case she wanted to smell him when he strolled in the door. He couldn't walk in the house with his face and dick smelling like pussy. Tony wildly scrubbed his face first and rinsed, then his dick, ass, and inner thighs.

I was watching him thinking *Damn nigga! Why don't you just jump in the shower instead of flicking soap and water all over my sink, floor, and mirror!*

After he finished his ho bath, he quickly looked around for his clothes and shoes. Tony was zipping around my house like a zoo animal released into the wild. He was more than nervous, and so pitiful that I decided to help him get his shit together.

"Here…"

I walked to the side of my bed, picked his boxers up from the floor, and handed them to him. I grabbed his jeans and shirt and walked them over to him. By the look on his face, you would've thought that I had given him a million dollars. He gratefully took his shit from my hands, and quickly threw everything on. Tony didn't know if he was coming or going, and the beads of sweat were starting to form a pattern on his forehead. He was breathing hard, and pacing in circles like a lost puppy.

"What are you looking for?"

I had always looked at Tony as *That Nigga.* He was a shot-caller. He got mad respect from his teammates and all of his dudes, and all the females wanted to get next to him. He was funny, cool, and always in control...until tonight. I had never seen this side of him. At this very moment, Tony was powerless and scared, and it made me nervous. I didn't like this view of him, but I knew that he needed my help to get out of the apartment in one piece.

"Where did I put my key?"

I had remembered hearing the jingle in his jeans pocket when I lifted them off of my dresser. His one Cadillac key was attached to a sterling silver valet key ring. Ballers never kept their house key on their key ring.

"Tony, they're in your jeans."

He rubbed his hands on the outside of both of his pockets, and felt them on the right side. He stuck his hand in, and pulled it out so fast I thought he would rip his jeans.

"Look, I gotta go. If she calls back, just say the same thing...and...thanks. I'll call you tomorrow."

Tony ran around grabbing his shit like the house was on fire while I stood in the roaring flames. He picked up his watch, necklace, and cell phone. As he stuffed his feet into his Jordans, he checked his missed calls, and I guess she did call a hundred times because I heard him curse under his breath. He gave me a half-ass kiss on the cheek, and flew out of the door. I stood there in the ashes with my pride on the floor.

How did I get into this situation? I had always told myself that I was only fucking these cats and having fun while it lasted. Not only did I get pregnant by Tony, but I was catching feelings, and now his messy ass had his wife calling my house. I never wanted to have any dealings with her; I never wanted to put a face or voice to the "other woman." It was easier for me to know that she existed as a figure or a symbol, and not so much as a real person.

I still didn't know her name, or what she looked like, but I assumed that she was one of the most beautiful women in the world. I was sure that she was light-skinned with naturally curly hair flat-ironed down her back like the rest of the professional wives. She was tall with the perfect body, perfect skin and teeth, and perfect hair. She probably worked out five days a week, and her kids never cried. She probably dressed in designer clothes, carried a Hermes bag, pushed a Bentley coupe, and lunched with friends on La Cienega in-between shopping.

I pictured Tony's wife as classy, cultured, and sophisticated. She quietly giggled at the right time, used "please" and "thank you," and treated people kindly, but snobby enough to let them know that she had money. How else could she get someone like Tony to marry her, and invite her into a world of fame, riches, and the luxury of staying at home?

Not only did I work, but I shook my ass and fucked for money, "danced" half-naked in rap videos, and never went to college. Besides being fine with a banging body, I wondered why Tony wanted to kick it with me. I was loud, quick to cuss, and jaded by the world that I had been introduced to. I was a hustler, always looking for the next grind, and I never let my emotions guide me into making decisions that would leave me vulnerable to this kind of bullshit. I covered for my married "boyfriend," and he jumped up out of my bed to save his most important relationship.

CHAPTER 14

The following day was filled with waiting and bullshit. I went to bed, and woke up the next morning thinking of Tony. I wanted to call him because I was tired of waiting to find out if we were finished or not. I imagined that he went home that night full of lies and innocence, and she forgave him of course. Actually, I didn't know if she would accuse him of anything because I had successfully covered for him, and why should he look like a jealous fool for nothing? She had everything she could ever want, and maybe she wouldn't give a fuck even if he was creeping.

I knew that he would never initiate a conversation if she didn't ask any questions, so there was a small chance that there wasn't any drama at all. I called Brandy, and she was grocery shopping. I told her about the phone call, and she agreed that it was probably going to be over between Tony and me. It had gotten too messy, and he would never risk his family for his chick on the side.

Brandy said that it was probably best to end it before somebody got hurt. She said that his wife probably knew he fucked with other females, but she had my actual name and phone number, and it was too close. She said that it was cool while it lasted, but we never had a future anyway, so it had to end at some point. I asked her what I should do if he didn't end it, and she said that I may have to be the one to do it. I talked Brandy's ear off until she had to pay for her groceries at the checkout.

How did he have me so fucking twisted? I tried to keep myself busy by cleaning the bathroom, vacuuming, and cleaning out the junk drawer in the kitchen, but I got tired of looking at my phone waiting for it to ring, so I called Hypnotiq. She wasn't busy, so we decided to go to the Cheesecake Factory in the Marina for an early dinner.

Marina Del Rey was the kind of place that made you feel like you were on vacation when you were only about 15 minutes away from home. The glass high-rise buildings and expensive yachts were a welcome getaway from the drama and bullshit of the mainland. The restaurant was a mix with all types, but the one thing that everybody had in common was being seen. Everybody knew that Cheesecake Factory was popping, so you had to dress because you never knew who might come in.

The restaurant was minutes from the airport, UCLA, USC, Beverly Hills, and the Crenshaw strip. Athletes, celebrities, and actors dropped in all the time with their baseball caps and dark shades. The common people were easy to spot because they wanted attention, while the celebrities tried desperately to blend in with the no-names. The menu was a carefully written 10-page flip book, but most people didn't go there for the food. People felt important when they could say they had eaten there because it was trendy. No one parked their own car, and it was worth it to wait in the long line for valet. Everybody was on their cell phones, setting up meetings, and scheduling power lunches.

Hypnotiq and I had our own style. We didn't think we looked like strippers, and would get offended sometimes if somebody asked, but the truth was that most people could pick a stripper out of a lineup nine times out of ten. Our hair was never our own, our clothes were typically over sexy, and the accessories were usually too much. Lots of color, high heels, and extra makeup with fake eyelashes were dead giveaways.

We had Tex-Mex egg rolls for appetizers, Long Island Ice Teas, pasta with chicken, and cherry cheesecake for dessert. As we ate, we talked about Tony and all of the bullshit.

"Have you talked to him yet?"

"Nope! And I don't know if I will. Wifey may keep his ass on lockdown."

"What are you going to do?"

"Shit wait?"

"Yeah, just see what happens before you start making decisions."

"We were just fucking almost a year ago, and now that we're really starting to kick it, his wife calls my house! How did we get here?"

"I know girl. Nothing is planned, and nobody is trying to catch feelings, but it just happens."

"Exactly! We were supposed to be having fun, and now it's like our relationship is all serious and shit! We have disagreements now when we used to just laugh about everything."

"You moved up in the ranks girl! You used to be work, but you're more than that now! With that comes expectations and feelings."

"I guess you're right. I told you about the stupid shit I said the other night, sounding like a nag!"

"Ugh, don't do that again!"

"Okay?! So what's up with you and Big D?"

"Girl, he wants to get me an apartment."

"What about Jason?"

"He hasn't said anything about him, but I know he wants me to be alone. He wants to spend a lot of time with me, and I have to tell him that Jason is over there. He wants to get me a spot over here in the Marina in a high rise."

"Shut up! What are you going to do you lucky bitch?!"

"I don't know. I really do like him, but if I move I know he's going to have a key. Jason and I argue all the time because he can tell there's someone else. Big D wants to take care of me."

"Damn girl! You got two good men! Well let me know if I can help."

"Thanks girl."

When we noticed guys looking at us, we flirted with them, but when they got the balls to come over, we shot them down. We made up something different every time; we had boyfriends, husbands, or we were dating each other. A few of the guys were fine, but I didn't fuck with any of them. I had enough going on with Tony and his wife. He hadn't called yet, but I couldn't stop thinking about him.

Hypnotiq told me that Jason had been talking about marriage more and more, mostly out of desperation but she wasn't ready for all that. She knew that she wanted to have a monogamous marriage, and she wasn't quite ready to give up her side dick. She and Big D had finally got to take that trip to Vegas, and she said that he treated her like she was his girlfriend. They stayed in a suite, and they went to a spa for massages.

Big D gave Hypnotiq money for gambling, and they ate at the best restaurants. He took her shopping at the Forum shops, and she came up on clothes, shoes, and a $1700 purse. She said that he was very sweet, and he held her hand when they walked down the street.

Holding hands was so elementary school, but that's what made it was so sweet and innocent. No one had held my hand in years. Maybe that was what was missing in my life. If someone would just hold my hand maybe I wouldn't have to be so tough. Maybe I could be vulnerable and naïve for once. Maybe I could be satisfied hooking up with a square, and experiencing a *normal* relationship for once. Maybe I was getting tired of the bullshit that came with sharing men.

Even though Big D was treating Hypnotiq like she was his girl, the fact remained that he still had a wife at home. Hypnotiq liked money, not that she was using him for his paper, but she had Jason at home that treated her the same way, but he just didn't have big money to spend on her. Maybe Big D was just too much of a good thing, dick, money, personality, to just give up. He had held her hand, and I could tell by the way she talked about him that she was catching feelings, and I thought to myself *Join the Club! Strippers and the Married Men They Cheat With*. It sounded like a twisted topic for the Jerry Springer Show except that it was my life.

I hadn't had a man to call my own in awhile, and I almost forgot what it felt like to have someone there for you all the time, not just when he could get away from his wife. My last boyfriend was Bernie, a bartender at a club downtown. We were together for about five or six months, and everything was cool except for his BMD (baby mama drama).

Her name was Kathy, and she was a pain in my ass right from the beginning. He had a baby with her when they were seniors in high school, and even though they were all in love, and thought they would be together forever, they broke up after the stress of the baby and insecurity tore them apart. She was a depressed, crying basket-case most of the time. Bernie said that she was always accusing him of looking at other girls to the point that he couldn't take it anymore.

Bernie told her that he would always be there for their daughter, but he just wasn't happy anymore. He had cheated with a cheerleader, and when Kathy confronted him, he broke up with *her*. From then on, she vowed to make his life hell if she ever even *heard* that he had any other bitches around her daughter. It wasn't the hormones because she meant what she said.

I met Bernie when Jamie was three. Kathy would call the house, and if I was over there, she would say that she was coming to get the baby, and Bernie would end up asking me to leave. I was 19 or 20, so my stupid ass did what he asked. She never did come, but she had a way of manipulating Bernie to get exactly what she wanted. After being asked to scurry out of the house one too many times, I told Bernie that he needed to go ahead and get back with Kathy, and leave me the fuck alone.

It was never going to work anyway because even though Bernie met me in the club, after we started getting more serious, he wanted me to quit. That was typical of most guys; they didn't like the fact that their friends could come in at any time and see their girls damn near naked body. When they first started fucking with you, they had bragging rights for fucking a stripper, but when they decided to call you their girl, shit was supposed to change, and if it didn't they spent most of their time bitching and whining about it.

❦   ❦   ❦

I got home, and checked my caller ID, no calls from Tony. He said he was coming over, but maybe he couldn't get out. Maybe we were over. The phone rang about 9:30, and my heart nearly jumped out of my chest. Either way, I was going to be put out of my misery.

I didn't want to be the first one to ask what happened last night because I didn't want him to know that I had spent every moment thinking about him since he flew out of my door. He said that he would be over in about 15 minutes. Here we go. He was either coming to lay down some rules, or quit me.

I couldn't think of anything else to say. I hung up the phone, and ran to throw some clothes on. I wasn't in the mood to do extra, but I had to keep appearances up like everything was all good. Tony was knocking on my door 17 minutes later, and I quickly wondered if he had just left his house, or if was he already out in the streets. Where did he say that he was going to get out of the house?

I hated the fact that I had begun to analyze everything when I could give a fuck just a few weeks ago. I convinced myself that he was leaving me alone. He had to. His wife actually knows my home number, and talked to me over the phone. Tony had fun with me, but there was no way in the world that he was going to risk his family, his career, his life…for me. I opened the door with a plastic smile on my face.

I opened the door, let Tony in, and shut the door behind him. He hugged me, but it was a quick, nervous hug. My suspicions were correct.

"You want something to drink?"

"Naw, I'm cool."

Tony went and sat on the couch, and I knew we were getting ready to have "the talk."

"Well, when I got home last night, my wife didn't say anything about the phone call, and I sure as fuck wasn't going to bring it up. I wanted to say thanks for being cool. Oh, and like I said before, if for some reason she happens to call again, just do the same thing you did last night. Don't give her attitude or talk shit okay? Just be cool."

This was the part where I was supposed to be thankful that he didn't quit me, and agree to whatever he said just so that we could kick it a few more times until she called again. I thought about the fact that I had given up so much of myself emotionally, and I didn't appreciate the way he was coming at me. *He* called my house from his home phone. I didn't do anything wrong, but I was being treated like I shot the sheriff! His attitude added insult to injury.

"So, you guys didn't talk about anything when you got home? She didn't ask whose number you called from your house phone? Do you know a girl named Mia? Where were you last night? Nothing?"

"Nope, not a word. She probably figured I dialed one of my boy's houses."

"Why did you tell me not to talk shit? Wasn't I cool the other night? Why do I feel like you're blaming me for this shit?" I don't know what came over me, but I said it.

"Listen, I fucked up, but I'm just saying be easy if she calls again. Is that cool?"

"Yeah, I got you."

Well, I said what I wanted to say. Not exactly the way that I would have liked to, but I got it off of my chest. I don't care what he said, his wife knew the deal; she just didn't want to tip her hand before she knew what was really going on. His stupid ass didn't even realize that she was going to be watching his every move for the next few weeks at the very least, and he had better check his game. She could've been thinking about revenge, and how filing for divorce on the grounds that he was fucking around would cost him everything.

As a woman I knew how women thought much more than he ever could. But he's a man, and the pussy was tight, so he was back over here the very next day. All I knew is that she better not be following him to my apartment because she would get her feelings hurt if she ever knocked on my door.

"Now, where were we because I didn't get to nut last night?"

"That's your bad. You were the one running up outta here like a little bitch!"

As soon as the words came out of my mouth, I wanted to reach through the air and grab them back. The look on Tony's face shifted from clowning to serious in two seconds flat, and I realized that I had crossed the line. He looked at me like I had spit in his face.

"What the fuck is that supposed to mean? I had to protect what I have at home!"

"What?! First of all, I was fucking with you, and second of all, I don't need to hear that shit! I know what the fuck you have at home, so you don't need to throw that shit in my face!"

"I just wanna make sure you understand how we're getting down. I'm *not* leaving my wife, and if it gets to the point where I even *think* she knows about this, I'm out. I got too much too lose."

"You know what? Maybe you need to go home to your wife then because I don't need this shit!"

"Look, what are we arguing about? I'm not telling you anything that you didn't already know. I have always been honest with you, and you know how we get down."

I was SO fucking tired of hearing that phrase!

How we get down. How we get down. How we get down. How we get down. How we get down. How we get down. How we get down. How we get down.

What I heard was *Bitch, you know you are nothing but pussy.*

"You know what? A lot has been said, and I think you need to go home, and fuck wifey tonight because I'm not in the mood. That's how *I* get down!"

"Mia, what's up? Just like I said the other night, things used to be cool when I would come through, and we would do our thing. Why are you tripping all of a sudden?"

"You got me fucked up! I don't need a shit from you! Remember, you're over here fucking me when you have a wife at home! You're the one fucking around, not me!"

Tony's phone rang. He looked at it, and then raised one finger to his lips as if to tell me to be quiet!

"Hello?"

"Hey baby! Yeah, I'm getting ready to leave the bar…what kind do you guys want…ok, I'll stop and get it…tell her I love her too…ok, bye…I love you too."

He hung the phone up, and it was painfully obvious that it was his wife.

"Well, I gotta get out of here. Do you want me to call you tomorrow or what?"

I just stood there with my back straight, lips tight, and arms folded. He leaned in to kiss me on my cheek, but I turned my face, so that he would miss.

"It's like that?"

He was trying to be sweet and funny, but I was way past that. He was on some other, and I wasn't feeling him. The whole conversation was about him getting some ass and making sure that I understood my place.

"Why are you still standing there? Isn't the family waiting for you?"

"Look, I'll call you tomorrow. I'm not going to stand here and beg you for a kiss. I don't know what you're tripping off of, but you need to calm the fuck down."

"Tony, I don't appreciate you talking to me like I'm a fucking ho on Sunset Boulevard. You're not going to talk to me any kind of way, come in and out, and get pussy whenever you want it."

"I gotta go."

I had pissed Tony off, and he wasn't trying to argue with me. I'm sure he thought I wasn't worth a fight; that was reserved for his wife. I was supposed to be easy and carefree, but I let my mouth get the best of me. He hung his head, and let himself out of the front door.

My shit was wide open. I broke Rule #1…I fell in love with Tony. I didn't want to be emotional, yelling, and screaming, but there I was, standing there acting like he had hurt my feelings by defending his wife. I didn't even say everything that I wanted to say, but I said more than enough. I lost it. I lost my power. At the time, it felt good to get all of the bullshit off of my chest, but after he left I realized that I was doing too much…again. He was just a fuck, and I had allowed myself to forget that very important fact.

This situation was totally different from all of the rest of the times I fucked with married men. I had kicked it with a few of them, but all we did was fuck. We didn't spend time eating, hanging out, and acting like we had a real relationship.

I felt powerful because I was giving them something their wives or girlfriends could not, or would not give them. They were like dope fiends. They used to sweat me, blowing my phone up, trying to hook up whenever I would allow them to see me. If I told them I had to work, they would either come to the club to break me off, or they would pay me the money I lost by not working to hang out with them. They would give me money for bills, shopping, or hair appointments. Most of the time, they were content to just be in my face because we didn't even fuck all the time. A lot of them just wanted the attention. I had a way of making men feel like a giant. I stroked their egos. I looked them dead in the eye, laughed at their corny jokes, and assured them that they had the best dick in the world.

Men are like babies. Just because they learned to walk and talk doesn't mean that they don't need the constant care, attention, and love they were showered with when they were born. Women are usually considered the needy ones, but men are the ones that yearn for someone to make them feel special, and when their needs are not met in the home, they look for it outside the home. When women begin to take their men for granted, and stop thanking them for the hard work they do in the world, at work, and at home with the kids, they find a woman to make them feel whole.

Women cheat too, but they will accept more bullshit for a longer amount of time before they even *consider* making the decision to start fucking with another man. Women don't usually get caught either because we're not messy, and most of all, we don't want to be caught. Women usually cheat for emotional, not sexual, gratification. Men are messy, and I think subconsciously they want to be caught. They want their wife to know that someone else is doing her job so that she can step her game up.

What they really want is for their wife to do the things that the other woman is doing, but because she is too busy or high-and-mighty to cater to her man, they keep the chick on the side. As long as women keep putting their jobs, kids, and friends in front of their men, females like me will stay in business.

CHAPTER 15

When I woke up the next morning, I decided to work out before I went to work. After I ate a bowl of cereal, I slipped on a cute gym outfit. *The Sport Club* was the baller gym, full of celebrities and money-makers. Most of the females showed up in full makeup and hair hoping to hook one. I wouldn't be out-done, but at the same time, I didn't have to do the most. I just brushed my hair into a cute ponytail, and put on eyeliner and lip gloss. When I got in the car, I called Brandy to tell her about the latest episode of the young and trampy.

"Hey girl, what you doing?"

"Just working. My boss wants me to get a presentation together for a meet-ing tomorrow. What about you?"

"On the way to the gym. Girl, drama last night. You have time to talk?"

"Damn! I really don't. My boss keeps coming in here checking on me. Can I call you on my lunch?"

"That's cool. I'll talk to you later."

We hung up, and I pulled into the parking lot of the gym. I grabbed my stuff, and walked in the front door where I handed my membership card to the girl behind the counter. She scanned the card, and looked at the computer monitor to make sure I paid my monthly dues.

"Have a great work out, Mia!"

"Thank you."

As soon as she said my name, I saw a black woman buying an energy bar and water a few feet ahead of me turn around. She looked dead in my face, and I tried to figure out if I knew her. She didn't look familiar, but then she started walking towards me.

"Hi, did I hear that your name is Mia?" She was half-smiling and trying her best to be polite, but her eyes were tight, and I could tell that her question was in fact very serious. She was looking me up and down, but the way she did it was kind of shitty, like she was accusing me of something. Where did I know her from?

"I'm Mia. Do I know you?"

"No, but I think I called your house last night. My name is Camille. Do you know my husband, Tony?"

Wow! Here we were face to face, and she was nothing like I thought she would be. She wasn't tall, light-skinned, or bodied up like a big booty girl in a rap video. She was the Pillsbury doughboy's younger sister. She was shorter than me with light-brown skin and a pretty face. Her medium length flat-ironed hair was in a ponytail and she didn't have on any makeup. Her workout gear was tight, and she was wearing fat diamond earrings.

"Are you fucking my husband?"

She didn't waste any time. My heart started beating faster, and I didn't know what to say. If I told the truth, Tony and I would be a wrap. I guess she could tell that I was going over my options because she started in on me again before I even had a chance to answer.

"I'm trying to talk to you woman to woman. I need the truth."

She was powerless, and pleading with me to give her an answer. She was relentless. If she could've seen herself, her pride would've pushed her out of my path, but she wouldn't take her eyes off of me. Her body was leaning in towards me, and her face was very close to mine, but not in a threatening way. She had nothing to lose by embarrassing herself. The future of her marriage was in my hands, and she had belittled herself by begging another woman for information about her own husband. She couldn't back down now. She had come too far, and I knew that she wasn't going to just let me walk away without giving her the answer that her intuition had already given her. I couldn't stand there, and watch her suffer anymore. I thought about my mom, and how she probably wished that somebody had told her about my dad's cheating ass.

"Yeah, I know Tony."

A wave of relief rushed over her body, and her posture changed. She softened, and the intensity left her face. She wasn't as focused and desperate, and she was satisfied by finally hearing the truth. She wasn't crazy. The truth validated the fool she had made of herself. The silence between us was so loud.

"Was he over there when I called? Did he tell you to lie to me? How long have you been fucking him? Did he tell you that he has a wife and kids?"

People walking in and out of the gym were looking at us pathetically, so I pointed outside the door with my finger, and she followed me towards the parking lot.

"Yeah, he was there, and he told me to lie…we've been…well, it's been close to a year…I knew about you and the kids."

"I knew it. I had his son 4 months ago. I've gained some weight, and he hasn't really wanted to fuck. I thought it was because of the weight, and I've been so tired with the baby, but now I know it's because he was fucking you!"

"You know what? I answered your questions, but I gotta go."

"That's it? I mean, I appreciate you telling me the truth, but you're just going to walk away? And don't you think you owe me an apology?"

"I'm sorry that your feelings are hurt, but you need an apology from your husband. I don't want to be in the middle of this. I have told you what you needed to know, but I'm not going to sit here, and go over every detail with you. It's too much."

"It's too late for all that. You put yourself in the middle when you started fucking with a married man!"

She started to get upset because I was trying to wriggle out of her grip, but she didn't want to let me go.

"Maybe you're right, but like I said, you need to call Tony. I don't know you. You are not my friend or my sister. I never disrespected you."

"You're right. You didn't know me, but you knew he had a wife. How about respecting the institution of marriage? How about having respecting for another black woman and respect for yourself for that matter? I know that he couldn't have been spending that much time with you. Don't you think you deserve more than a piece of a man?"

"I do respect myself, and I don't need a lecture from you. This conversation isn't going anywhere."

"You think I don't know about the thousands of women lined up to get their hands on an athlete? They throw themselves at Tony, even when he's sitting in a restaurant with me and the kids. They get all dolled up to go to basketball games, and pay ushers to get near the bench. They hang out at hotels, restaurants, and clubs where they know the players will be. A lot of women would die to switch places with me, but let me tell you, it's not all that it's cracked up to be. Most nights I go to bed alone, and the money doesn't make up for the loneliness and the insecurity I feel when beautiful women are competing with me for my husband. You know there are times when I am actually jealous of my sister because her husband is anonymous, he works 9–5, and he sleeps in her bed every night. They may not have all of the luxuries that Tony and I have, but she also doesn't have to deal with the females and the bullshit that I have to put up with on a daily basis. This is not the first time Tony has fucked around on me. At this point, I stay because of the kids. I love my husband, but this is not the way that I thought my life would be. Answer one last thing for me. Do you love him?"

"No...I don't." I couldn't look her in the eye because I didn't want her to know that I was lying.

"Are you going to keep seeing him?"

"No..." Again, I didn't look her in the eye.

I could feel her watching me as I walked through the parking lot. At first I thought she was going to try and follow me, but she didn't. There was no need, she had gotten everything off of her chest. I never thought about her, and how she felt being married to Tony, the professional basketball player. I thought her life was filled with money, shopping, and fame. I never thought about the fact that her life could be stressful, but I guess I understood it. I'm one of the females that she was talking about. I flirt with married men, I go to basketball games looking for a sugar daddy, and I don't care about his situation at home. She was upset, but she didn't cry. I'm sure it's because she knew I wasn't the first or the last.

Working out was over. I got back in my car, and just drove. I didn't know where I was going, but I was waiting for my phone to ring because I knew Tony's wife was calling him at that very moment. After he hung up with her, he was calling to cuss me the fuck out. Oh well. His wife was looking me dead in my eye looking for the truth. I could tell that she already knew what was up, but she needed to hear it. I hadn't planned on snitching, but I could see the agony in her eyes. The truth had set her free.

She was staying with him, and I thought that was so sad. Ballers like him were never satisfied with one woman. I think it was the money and the fame. Once a man had that kind of status, they craved extra everything, custom homes, expensive cars, clothes, jewelry, and bad bitches that did some wild shit. They wanted the good girl at home with the kids, and then they had their side bitches. Even before Tony, I hadn't been anything but a side bitch for the last two years.

I was fucked up behind Tony, but it couldn't come close to how fucked up his wife felt at that moment. She was married to him, and had two kids with him. I felt stupid. I had been stressing over Tony and me, but compared to Tony and his wife, we didn't have shit between us. In reality, I meant nothing.

He used me for physical pleasure, and a holiday from his family and responsibility, but that was it.

Looking at her, I felt small. All this time I felt like I had some kind of power because he was risking his family to fuck with me, but then I realized that I didn't mean shit to him. He made me lie to her to cover his ass. That was hella disrespectful to me, and it clearly showed me which one of us he could live without. Before he even allowed himself to be backed into a corner, he would choose his wife and family all day, and drop me like a bag of rocks. I thought about the fact that he was cheating on his wife while she was pregnant. He fucked around on her when she was the most vulnerable, when she felt like a fat cow. What kind of man was he? How did I expect him to treat me when he could treat his wife like that?

I gave her what she wanted because of the way she came at me. She was cool when she had every right to wild out. I'm sure she knew that she had a better chance of getting me to talk if she held her tongue. If she would've been yelling and calling me all kinds of bitches, I would've said *Fuck you* and kept walking, leaving her to do her own investigative work.

❧   ❧   ❧

Camille walked back into the gym, and walked straight in the women's locker room. People were staring at her because they had heard part of the discussion that had just taken place in the front lobby. She changed her clothes, grabbed her gym bag, and walked back out of the gym with her head held high, and not a tear on her face. Her pride and dignity wouldn't allow her to crumble in front of strangers. When she was in the safety of her own car, a tear traveled from her eye, down her cheek, and landed on her expensive track jacket. She started driving down La Cienega, and picked up the phone to call her husband.

"Hey baby. What you doing?"

"I just finished working out, and talking to your little girlfriend."

"Huh? What are you talking about honey?"

"Don't act stupid. I just saw Mia at the gym, and she told me everything."

"Baby…I…where are you? I'll meet you at home."

"How could you do this to me when I was carrying *your* baby? How could I be so stupid? You haven't wanted to fuck me, and now I see why! I blamed myself for looking like a fat ass, and not being sexy enough for you. So what, do you love her?"

"Come on now! No, I don't love her. She means nothing to me. Honey…I'm sorry…I never wanted to…where are you? I'm on my way home."

"I don't want to see you right now. I can't talk to you."

"Baby…meet me at the house so we can talk."

"No." Click!

❦   ❦   ❦

Work sounded like heaven compared to what had just went down at the gym. Even 20 minutes later, it didn't seem real. I couldn't believe that I was actually standing at the gym talking to Tony's wife. I never gave a fuck about wives, but I surprised myself by being on her side. Just before I pulled up to my apartment, my phone rang, and it was Tony. I took a deep breath, and answered…

"What the fuck did you tell my wife?"

"I don't like your tone. You need to speak to me with respect, or I'm hanging up!"

I think he realized that he needed to probe me for answers, so that he would know just how much he needed to explain to his wife. He wasn't stupid. He didn't want to overshare, or volunteer information that she didn't already know, so he needed a recap of the entire conversation.

"Stop playing fucking games! This is my life! I need to know what was said between you and Camille."

Camille. He had never said her name to me before. I guess it was easier for me to fuck him because he never made her a real person for me. *My wife* was not the same as saying *Camille*. She was the living, breathing woman that he went home to every night after washing his dick off in my sink.

"I went in the gym, and the person behind the counter said my name. She heard it, and came up to me. She was all in my grill asking me if she called my house last night. She already knew what was up. She is not stupid. I only talked to her for a minute."

"Did she ask how long we were fucking? What did you say?"

"Yeah, I told her almost a year."

"Fuck! Why didn't you lie?"

"Tony, stop fucking screaming at me! I didn't go and seek her out; we just happened to bump heads, and I didn't know what to do! It was easier for me to tell the truth instead of standing there trying to make up lies. Besides, it's easier to remember the truth than it is to remember lies. I'm telling you, she was not letting me get away without answering her questions. Me stomping off wouldn't have helped you out much either because that would have been obvious that I had something to hide."

"I don't know what the fuck I'm going to do if she leaves me."

I didn't want to hear that shit. What was I supposed to say? He was professing his undying love and desire to stay with his wife. I hadn't felt that low since…since I was talking to Camille at the gym.

"Why are you telling me this shit? If fucking me was such a mistake, you should've kept your dick in your pants! Go home and handle your business then."

"I'm just talking out loud. I'm not trying to hurt you, but damn, this is some serious shit right here. I'm on my way home now. I'll talk to you later."

"Bye." Pititful.

When I got to my apartment, I checked my mailbox, walked in, and packed my bag for the club. It was Friday night, so I thought it would be filled with brothas that just cashed their paychecks. I hopped in the shower, threw on some clothes, and called Hypnotiq from the car to see if she was going to work.

"You working tonight?"

"Yeah, I'll be there about 1."

"I'll see you then. I'm on the way now. Girl, I got some shit to tell you, so try to get there a little early. We can talk in the parking lot, so the rest of those nosey bitches aren't all in my shit!"

"Damn, it's like that? Okay, let me get ready. I'll see you in a minute."

The club was the perfect distraction because nobody cared what a stripper was going through, if she was having a good day or not. I wasn't going to have to be bothered with customers asking me how I was doing because they didn't care. They wanted to see ass, titties, and a pretty face. I wouldn't have to explain when I stared off into space wondering what was going on at Tony's house. No explanation needed when I began to daydream about me and Tony clowning or wrestling around in my living room, and how much I would miss him. No questions asked when a single tear dropped from my eye as I thought about the confrontation with his wife, and the fact that our relationship was over. I couldn't wait to get to work.

I pulled into the parking lot of *Aces*, and waited for Hypnotiq. I didn't want to leave the car because then I would get caught up talking, and it would be hard for Hypnotiq and I to pull away without others trying to follow us. Brandy hadn't called me on her lunch, so I figured she was busy with her project. I didn't want to call again, and get her in trouble with her boss, but I needed her. Hypnotiq finally pulled into the parking lot, and I was happy that I could finally share my drama with somebody! I hopped out of my car, and ran over to Hypnotiq's car. She unlocked the door, and I sat down in the passenger seat.

"Tell me what happened!"

"Girl, Tony wanted to come over the other night, but he called me from his house phone. He came over, we're fucking, so he ignored his phone, and wifey calls my house!"

"Shut up!"

"Of course Tony tells me to lie, and say that she had the wrong number. She asked me if I knew Tony, and I said no. She was cool, and we hung up. We were in the middle of fucking, and he grabbed his shit, and flew out of there."

"Wow!"

"So, he came over the next day. He said that his wife didn't say anything when he got home, but it's like he was checking me! He was like, if she calls back, just be cool. Don't give her attitude or talk shit, so she wouldn't get suspicious and bust his ass!"

"He was doing a lot!"

"Ok? I was like, 'you fucked up, not me!' We got into it, and he ended up leaving. I was talking mad shit. I was like, 'you're not going to be coming over here talking to me any kind of fucking way, and sliding in and out of my spot, fucking anytime you want to!' I didn't give a fuck! After he left though, I felt like a stupid bitch. I was doing too much over that nigga! You know he thinks my nose is wide open now."

"So, then what?"

"Girl, I went to the gym today, and the person at the counter scanned my card, and told me to have a good workout, then said my name! This female turns around, and starts coming towards me! She asked me if she called my house last night!"

"That was *not* his wife!"

"Why wasn't it? Girl, I ended up telling her everything! She wasn't tripping on me, so shit I told her!"

"Wow! What about Tony?"

"Well, she called him right away because then he called me. I told him I snitched, and he was mad at first, but then he hung up to go meet his wife."

"So, what are you going to do now? Are you and Tony done?"

"Pretty much."

"Damn girl, that's better than the *Real World*!"

"Okay?"

Hypnotiq and I laughed, and it felt good to finally get that shit off of my chest.

"Well, I think you're just mad right now. You really do care about Tony, so you guys aren't done just like that. You gave him your heart, even if it was accidentally, and you're not going to let him go over an argument. Just give yourself some time to think about what you want, and what you will and will not accept. But remember to be realistic girl, he is married."

"Yeah, I hear you girl. This nigga got me fucked up for real! A part of me wants him to just stop fucking with me, just so that I don't have to feel this way anymore. It's like the pleasure pain principal. He gives me both at the same time. I could have any of these niggas in the club, but I always seem to pick the ones that I can't have. I must be a masochist. Is that it? The kind of people that only get turned on when you physically hurt them?"

"Yeah, that's what it's called. It's like that? What kind of freaky shit do y'all be doing?" Hypnotiq was looking at me suspiciously.

"I don't mean sexually. I just seem to like the kind of niggas that bring me drama and hurt my feelings. One of these days I need to go out with one of those square ass niggas that come in the spot, and leave these Big Willy types alone! They're killing me slowly!"

"Who you telling? I got a square ass nigga at home, but I'm fucking with Big D! When will we learn? One of these days, Jason is going to quit my ass! I come home late at night with gifts and shit. Some days, I don't come home at all, and when I say that I was with you, he doesn't look like he believes it for a second, but he never says shit. I don't want to hurt him, but I can't leave Big D alone, not now anyway. I'll probably come home one day, and all of his shit will be gone, and I'll be like damn, I fucked a good one off."

"Girl, Jason's not going anywhere! I would bet all the money I have in my house that he would never leave you! You put a root or something on him because he is a bee to your honey, and you know bees can never be far away from honey!"

"You crazy! Jason is my baby. I love him, and I care about him with everything I have in me, but Big D makes me feel like a woman you know? It's hard to explain, but I think I'm at my best with him. Yeah, Jason loves me, but he won't stay if I keep showing out like I have been, and I don't know if I would stop him if he wanted to leave me."

"Does he ever get jealous, questioning you and shit?"

"He asks questions, but then he accepts whatever I say. He never gets crazy or anything like that."

"Good. I don't want to have to hurt his ass!"

I put my fists up like I was fighting the air, and Hypnotiq laughed at me. She was usually pretty good at checking her game, so I wasn't worried about her. Besides, Jason was a bunny rabbit, and that was the thing that we loved about him the most. He was a sweet, sensitive guy, born and raised in L.A…a priceless oddity.

We got out of her car, and I walked to my car to get my work bag. I couldn't talk to anyone the way that I talked to Hypnotiq, she understood me without a lot of explaining, and I didn't mind looking immature, idiotic, or plain goofy in front of her. I was barenaked when it came to her; she saw me without my armor, and she loved me anyway. I bared my soul to her, and she bared it all with me. She was my friend, my sister. We put our masks back on, and walked in the club, temporarily forgetting the intimate conversation that we had in the car because it was showtime.

CHAPTER 16

As soon as I walked into the club, I saw two of Tony's boys at the bar. At first, I thought they would mean mug me, or talk shit, but it became obvious that Tony hadn't talked to them yet when they stood up to greet me.

"How you doing Mia?"

"Oh, I'm cool. How about you?"

"Good. We just got here. Who's your friend?" They were drooling like a couple of hound dogs.

"This is my girl, Hypnotiq. Hypnotiq this is John and Lou." They shook her hand, and she said hello.

"When ya'll going on stage?"

"I don't know. We just walked in, so we have to get dressed, and put our names on the list. It depends on how many girls are here. You staying?"

"Don't trip, we'll wait!"

They weren't waiting for me because they knew I fucked with Tony; they were waiting for Hypnotiq. As we stood there talking to them, they were looking at her like she was the last beer in the fridge, but she pretended not to notice. Part of Hypnotiq's appeal was that she was never overly impressed by brothas making fools out of themselves simply because she was breathing. When we started walking back towards the dressing room, I turned around, and they were staring at Hypnotiq's big ass with eyes like silver dollars. They were punching each other and giggling like high school boys.

It didn't surprise me that Tony had kept the drama between me and his wife to himself. He wasn't the type to share his business with all of his boys. For the most part, Tony kept his personal issues to himself, and the only person that he completely trusted was Ron.

Tony and Ron had known each other since they played on the high school basketball team together. Tony was offered a scholarship, and left town the summer after graduation, but Ron wasn't as fortunate. Tony said that in all actuality, Ron was a better player than him, but Ron's life was full of complication and personal struggles. His mother had been on crack for the last few years, and Ron had to take care of his two younger brothers. When the scouts came to talk to him about playing ball for schools all over the country, he had no choice but to turn them down.

Ron's mother would leave the house for weeks at a time on a drug-induced binge. Even when she was around, he was afraid to leave the boys with her because she would just get up and leave them alone. Sometimes she would have dealers over the house, and she would cook the dope and smoke it right in front of the boys. Ron's mother would blow her welfare check on crack; she couldn't pay the rent or keep the lights on. Ron was all that his brothers had, and he grew up fast playing the role of father at the age of 17.

Ron's mom died shortly after he graduated from high school, and she didn't even attend the ceremony. Tony told me that Ron has secretly breathed a sigh of relief because she looked like death for the last few months that she was alive. Tony ended up raising the boys, attending the local junior college, and working part-time in a grocery store. Ron married young, and had two kids of his own. Ron continued to work full-time at the grocery store, while his wife, Tina, stayed at home with the kids. Tony never forgot his friend, and they stayed in contact throughout the years. Before Tony was even drafted, he promised Ron that he would help his brothers with college tuition. The youngest one went on to college, but the other one sold dope, and was killed in a shoot-out during a robbery when he was 22. Apparently, he was doing it big, and somebody jacked him one night leaving a club. After Tony signed his first NBA contract, he gave Ron the money to open a dance club, and it was popping from the beginning. Ron and Tina worked like dogs to keep the club packed, so Ron didn't have time to be a member of Tony's entourage that followed him to strip clubs, restaurants, and parties.

Tony's groupies included John, Lou, and a couple of other guys that didn't have a life. Everybody had heard about female groupies that would fall all over themselves trying to meet and hang out with athletes, but nobody ever talked about the male groupies. They usually grew up with the athletes, or met them shortly after they joined the league. They didn't really work or have a specific job. They just sort of hung around, and lived on the benefit of having a friend that played ball. Sometimes the athlete would get them small-time jobs associated with college or professional ball, but a lot of the time they just lived off of scraps thrown at them from their boys. Some females fucked with the groupies just to get next to the baller, but the groupies didn't mind. They took whatever they could get. No self-respecting female would fuck with the help. No woman wanted a tag-along that followed after the next man. They were "yes" men, errand boys, and flunkies, losers.

The two niggas sitting at the bar were the worst kind of groupies. They laughed every time Tony made a joke, funny or not. They fucked the groupies that Tony didn't want. They followed Tony around like kids to the ice cream truck. They had girlfriends, but they never spent time with them because they were too busy sniffing after Tony. They tried to make a competition out of who could fuck the bitches with the biggest asses and the biggest tits, and they did shit just to impress Tony, like the time John threw a barbeque at his house when his girl went out of town. All of the guys brought a girl, but John had to bring two.

The chicks that John brought looked like porno queens with their fake-ass triple D's, extra makeup, and six inch heels. They acted like airheads, but most of the guys were impressed. We played a couple of drinking games, and once most of the girls were fucked up and half-naked, the fucking hour began. As people started leaving the party, John told the girls to fuck with each other, and they ended up eating each other's pussy on the lawn chairs in the backyard. Tony came over there rubbing his hard dick on my shoulder, and we went upstairs with John and the porno chicks.

Barbeques absolutely turned X-rated every single time. The parties were off the chain, and we always played truth or dare, strip poker, and stupid drinking games. I made everybody laugh a couple of months ago at the last get-together. In the middle of one of those "you-lost-so-take-off-some-clothing-or-take-a-drink" game, I stood up, stripped naked, grabbed a bottle of Hennessey, sat down, and took a long drink. They all fell out laughing! I told them that I was cutting out the middle man because the point of all of the games was to get drunk and get naked, so fuck it!

As the four of us were going upstairs, Tony stopped to grab a handful of rubbers from their stash in the garage. As usual, John and Tony wanted their dicks sucked first. Tony and John stood side by side on the bedroom wall, and I got on my knees and started bossing Tony. The two girls followed my lead, and started sucking John's dick at the same time. They were licking and sucking all over his dick and balls, and kissing each other at the same time. I couldn't help but move my head to watch that shit. Tony was staring at the bitches looking like he would've given his left nut to be John, so I locked my jaws, and yanked his dick in a way that made him turn away from the girls.

They were working it out, and honestly I couldn't compete. When they fucked us from behind, side-by-side, John was touching my pussy, and Tony was smacking his chicks' asses. I kept turning around to see what was cracking. John was sliding his dick in and out between the two girls, and I could see it in Tony's face that he wanted to switch. Suddenly, the words elevated from my mind into the air. He leaned towards my ear.

"Can we switch?"

"Hell nah!"

I loudly whispered behind my back. I knew it was coming, but fuck that. I didn't know where those tramps had been, and he wasn't sticking his dick back in me after fucking them!

For some reason, they got off on fucking in the same room. I didn't give a fuck because I always had more skills than the other chicks, and they seemed to lose their swagger when I got loose. I sucked hard and fucked hard like I was shooting a porno flick. Everything I did was extra, screaming, yelling, moaning, moving my body like I never had dick before. One chick gave up before the race even started. A few months ago, we were in a hotel room, and I was sucking Tony's dick while the other chick just lay in the other bed next to John watching us. Tony and I ended up fucking and they just sat there. Shit, I wanted to watch too! I looked at the other bed, and I could see the girl hiding on the other side of him. It was dark, but I could tell that they were just sitting there watching us. Later, John told us that she didn't feel good. I couldn't figure out which one of them was lying, John or the girl. Whatever.

Now John's freaky ass was sitting at the bar, at my club, waiting for Hypnotiq. We walked in the dressing room, and started changing out of our clothes.

"Who were they?"

"Girl, those are Tony's boys."

"You think they know what happened?"

"Tony kicks it with them, but they're not tight like that. I'm sure they'll find out at some point, but he's not calling them from jump."

"Really?"

"I'm sure he'll call his boy, Ron, but that's it. He's really the only one that he'll talk to about this kinda shit."

"You think Tony and his wife are still talking? Think she's leaving?"

"By the way she was talking, it didn't sound like it. She asked me if I was going to leave him alone. If she was leaving, why would she ask?"

"What did you say?"

"I told her yeah."

"Are you?"

"You know what? While I was talking to her, I really felt bad for fucking him. She was cool, and I thought about how greedy men are. They have a beautiful wife, family, money, fame…but it's never enough. They want more and more; they're never satisfied. Their appetite for pussy just seems to grow and grow. I'm sure she never cheated on him, but he's been out there doing the most even before me."

"Yeah, but you still haven't answered!"

"Nah, I'm cool."

I was trying to convince myself that I was done with Tony, but in my heart, I knew it would be hard. I missed him already.

Hypnotiq went to the bathroom, and I pulled out my flat-iron. I went over my whole head, sprayed on some oil sheen, and combed it all out. A new chick walked in, and was asking me which outfit she should put on, and I picked the least cute one because fuck her. I walked in the bathroom to get some toilet tissue, and Remy was in there shaving her pussy. Another chick was squatting over the toilet backwards cutting the string from her tampon. She had dripped blood on the seat and the floor, and I told her to make sure she got that up. Nasty bitches! That's why I never sat on that seat. As I was walking out of the bathroom, I saw a standing by the door.

"Damn, can a bitch have a little privacy?"

"My bad ma, I just wanted to see if Remy was in there. She owes me another dance."

Remy heard him, and walked to the door, pussy out, shaving cream, razor, dripping water, everything. That was the thing about the club, bitches weren't embarrassed for shit.

"I'll be out in a minute baby. The ladies are dressing back here. You need to stay in the front."

"I apologize."

He walked back towards the tables, and I went back in the locker room. I popped a bump on my forehead, and plucked my eyebrows. I pulled out my makeup, and decided on smoky eyes. They made me feel sexy. I put on lots of black glitter eyeshadow, eyeliner, and mascara. I put on my stripper clothes, stripper heels, took a deep breath, and marched into purgatory.

Hypnotiq was still in the dressing room, but it was getting too crowded in there, so I told her that I would meet her outside. She kept getting dressed, and

I walked around talking to other dancers, the bartender, and annoying, horny-looking men. I was sitting down talking to one of them when Tony walked into the club. I was so shocked that I stopped talking in the middle of my sentence, and the guy turned to see what I was looking at. Tony motioned his finger for me to come over, and I excused myself. As I stood up, I wondered what he wanted from me. His wife had busted me out, and now he was in my club? What did he want? I wasn't sure, but now he was standing in front of me.

Tony was clearly stressed out. He looked like he had been up all night, but the shit only went down a few hours ago. Tony looked distressed. My heart was beating out of my chest. I didn't know what he was going to say, and honestly I was a little scared because I had basically served him up on a platter. I could have told his wife that she had it all wrong, my name wasn't Mia, I didn't know Tony, but I didn't. I busted him out, she let him have it, and it was all my fault.

"I just finished talking to my wife."

"What happened?"

"She was heated at first, but then we talked, and she calmed down."

"That's cool. Why are you here?"

"I told my wife that I wouldn't see you anymore."

"I figured that. You didn't need to come to my place of business to tell me that."

"I just wanted you to know that I'm not mad at you for telling. My wife has a way of getting what she wants. I hope we can still be cool."

"Tony, we had fun, but I knew you were married. Eventually, it had to end. I'm not tripping."

"The guys told me you were at work, so I decided to come up here instead of coming to your apartment. I don't think I could be alone with you."

"What does that mean?" I knew what he meant, but I forced him to say it.

"My feelings for you have not disappeared; I am respecting my wife and our family. I like hanging out with you, but I can't risk my family."

"We don't have to go over that again. I feel you. Well, I have to get to work. You staying?"

"No, I have to go home."

Of course he did. He had successfully avoided divorce, so he had to be on his P's and Q's for a minute. No hanging out, and no hoes, he had to walk a straight line.

"Well, take care."

We were standing there, and I didn't know if we should've hugged or what. It was so dramatic, but not, because we were standing in the middle of a strip joint. There was no fireplace, ocean, or sunset, just hookers and tricks. He leaned in, and I gave him a half hug with enough space for another person to get in the middle. He patted my back the way people do when they need to remind you that you're nothing but a friend. We let go, and he gave me a look like he would never see me again, like his eyes were trying to burn my image into his brain. He turned around, and started walking towards his boys at the bar. Thank goodness Hypnotiq came up behind me because I felt like passing out.

"What was that about?"

"Basically, he came to tell me goodbye. They called, and told him I was up here, so he wanted to tell me that he couldn't see me anymore. Wifey is staying, and he has to be a good little boy."

"Wow! Are you okay? Why did he come *here*?"

"He said that he couldn't be alone with me at my place."

"He would want to fuck."

"Pretty much. That's cool though. I knew it would happen. I mean damn, me and wifey were face to face!"

"You going to be okay?"

"I'm cool. I just hope we make some money tonight!"

"After work, wanna go get some burritos?"

"Yeah, I'm gonna drown my sorrows in a fat carne asada burrito with guacamole and extra sour cream!"

"Girl, I got your back!"

Hypnotiq grabbed me, and hugged me tight enough to make up for Tony's pitiful hug. She squeezed me, smoothed my hair, and kissed me on the cheek. Hypnotiq was my friend, and I needed her. Amidst all the loud music, red lights, and half-naked females walking around, nobody knew the drama that had just popped off, my married ball player just dumped me, and now he was laughing and joking with his boys like nothing had happened. I'm sure he didn't even tell them. He got busted for catching feelings for a stripper. His boys would laugh him out of the club. In their eyes, I was work, and he shouldn't have been spending so much time with me, treating me like a girlfriend. I had to get over him.

"Come on girl, Big D just walked in. He'll buy us some drinks."

"Let's go."

Out of the corner of my eye, I saw Tony get up from the bar, and he was moving towards the door. I couldn't watch him walk out, but I wanted to see if he was going to tell me goodbye. I looked at him, but he didn't turn around as he ducked behind the red velvet curtain and out the front door.

"Hey baby!" Hypnotiq gave Big D a big kiss on the cheek.

"Hey sweetness. How's my baby doing?" I was even more jealous than usual because I was alone again.

"I'm good now baby."

Hypnotiq really liked him, and I noticed the way he looked her in the eyes, and not at her body like other cats did.

"Alizé, this is my boy Larry. You know Hypnotiq."

His boy reached out to shake my hand.

"Nice to meet you."

I forced a fake smile on my face. Little did he know that I hated the sight of a man.

"The pleasure is mine."

He seemed nice, but I wasn't in the mood to sit and play blonde all night. I sat down, and they ordered drinks for us. We watched a couple of dancers come on stage, and Larry tried to get to know me a little better, but I wasn't the best company. I tried to be polite, but I wasn't feeling it. I heard the words coming out of Larry's mouth, but I wasn't listening. I was thinking about Tony. Ever since I admitted that my name was Mia, I knew that we were over, but now that it was reality, it was unbelievable. I missed him so much that my heart began to ache. It felt like someone was jumping up and down on my chest. I never thought that I would feel this way about Tony, but I did, and now it was all over.

Hypnotiq and I ended up giving the guys a few dances, and we went on stage together. I felt nice after all the drinks, but the liquor got me in trouble. When I was dancing on stage, I was playing with my pussy and pulled my thong to the side a little bit. The DJ saw it, and cut the music. They did that shit to embarrass the dancers, but my stupid ass just laughed as I wobbled to the back of the stage. I was numb, and there was nothing that the DJ could do to make me feel worse than I already did. Big D and Larry bought us more drinks, and left after about two hours.

I was giving some guy a dance when I heard a slow jam that reminded me of Tony. I had to tell the guy that I felt sick, and ran to the bathroom because I didn't want him to see me crying. I felt like shit. Nobody wanted a real relationship with me; they just wanted to fuck. I was in the bathroom crying like a baby, moaning, and holding my stomach. A couple of the girls were knocking on the door asking me if I was okay, and I couldn't answer because I was crying so hard that I couldn't squeeze a single syllable out of my mouth. Liquid courage convinced me to call Tony, so I pulled my phone out of my money bag.

"Hi, this is Tony. Leave a message at the tone. Beeeep."

"Yeah Tony, this is your ex bitch! Why aren't you picking up your phone? Are you with your WIFE? She'll never fuck you like I did. Tell her to call me, and I'll teach her a couple of things! You know you're not done with me! She can't do what I do. You think you can just use a bitch up, and then throw her out with the trash? Who the fuck do you think you are…"

"You have reached the maximum recording time. You have 10 seconds to complete your message. Beeeep."

I pushed the pound button, and erased the message. I looked in the mirror, and my face was red and puffy. My smoky eyes were running down my cheeks, and I had sweated the edges of my hair. I was drunk and dizzy, pacing back and forth. I blew my nose, and splashed cold water on my face. Hypnotiq was at the door.

"Mia, let me in girl." I opened the door, and she held me so tight that I started to cry all over again.

"I'm cool. The Hennessey called him, not me."

She rubbed my back, and followed me into the dressing room. We threw our clothes on, grabbed our stuff, and got out of there.

Hypnotiq and I went to Benito's, my favorite taco shop. She drove my car, and left hers at the club. We sat down at the spot, and ate like a couple of pigs. I ate a carne asada burrito and an Horchata drink. We talked, and Hypnotiq tried her best to make me feel better, but I knew the only thing that would help me get over Tony was time. She drove me home, and we climbed into my bed and went to sleep. I woke up a couple of hours later to throw up. My bathroom carpet and toilet was full of steak, Hennessey, and rice water. I leaned over the toilet for a few more minutes to make sure everything was out. I was sweaty and exhausted.

The next afternoon, I made breakfast for Hypnotiq and me. My head was banging, so I drank a beer with my eggs and toast. I offered to drive Hypnotiq to her car, but she said Jason's boy dropped him at the club last night so he could drive it home for her. That's what I was missing, and I wondered when I would ever find my Jason, or my Lorenzo. In my eyes, Hypnotiq and Brandy were two of the luckiest bitches in the world. Even the liquor wouldn't allow me to forget that Tony was officially out of my life. I was alone.

A part of me was attracted to men that I knew I could never have. I didn't have to worry about whether the relationship would get serious or not because they were obviously unavailable. The other part of me didn't think that I deserved any better. I was a stripper. Strippers weren't respected, they were used. Brothas didn't trust strippers. We tease, fuck, and suck for bread. Can't turn a ho into a housewife right? What man was going to flaunt a stripper on his arm, and call her his girl? We weren't the type of females that men brought home to their mamas. They were afraid of what we might have on or what we may say. Strippers were known to dress provocatively and speak their minds, and sometimes it wasn't politically correct or decent according to average American standards.

People outside the club thought the life of a stripper was so glamorous, but in reality, it was a pitiful, busted life. The money was hella good, but it didn't make up for the bullshit and the drama. More and more lately, I had been thinking about getting out of the game, but I wasn't doing it with just a high school diploma. No legit job was going to pay me even close to what I was making at the club, so I felt trapped. The rope around my neck got tighter, squeezing the lifeblood through my toughened veins to the point that I was too weak to plan a new life.

CHAPTER 17

A couple of weeks later, I constantly told everybody that I wasn't tripping off Tony's ass, but I was in serious denial. I thought about him every second of the day. I watched his games on t.v., and when I was at work, I patiently waited for him to walk through the velvet curtain. His boys came in, and I always made a point to chop it up with John and them because I didn't want it to look like I was going through it.

I remember the day I realized that they knew the deal because they stopped mentioning Tony's name around me. John always used to ask me if I had talked to Tony, or where Tony was, and then he just stopped. The switch was so obvious that I wanted to politely tell him that I didn't give a fuck, but I kept my cool. After awhile, I grew tired of pretending and keeping up appearances. It was fake, pointless, and exhausting. Nobody cared. I would go over and say hello, but I kept it moving. Up to that point, I had been hanging out with Brandy and Hypnotiq, shopping, working, and going out.

I had started drinking more because the Hennessey allowed me to temporarily forget Tony. Popping E's allowed me to float to another planet. I didn't want to think about Tony, stripping, or my fucked up life. I basically stayed high from the day Tony dumped me. I drank, smoked, and popped anything that would stop the agonizing pain that had found a resting place within me. I was walking through a neverending fog that gripped my body, and left me lost and confused. Hypnotiq could see that I was drowning, and she pulled me aside one night at the club. I was so fucked up at the time that it sounded like she was moving and talking in slow motion.

"Girl, how you doing?"

"I'm cool. Why?"

"Girl, your eyes were barely open when you were on stage. Are you sure that you're okay?"

"Awww…you my girl. Good looking out!"

"Sweetie, I've been watching you for the last few weeks, and you're not cool. I haven't seen you sober since…well, since Tony."

Her words pierced my heart, and all the feelings that I had tried to smother bubbled to the surface. The pain was still so fresh, and my heart was in my throat. The tears just fell out of my face. I was thankful, but pissed off that she had awaken my nightmare.

"What am I supposed to do? I love him and he—"

I said it, and I hated myself for thinking it, let alone saying it out loud.

"Alizé, how did you let yourself fall in love with him? He's married. Baby, you broke all the rules, but I knew it because you haven't been the same since that day. Please don't let these niggas get you down. You know what you need to do? You need to stop delaying the grief. Let your heart break so that you can move on. Stop running. All the liquor in this bar can't prevent the inevitable. You can't skip this part…pain before pleasure."

Her words spoke to me, and I hugged her as the relentless tears wet my entire face. I cried out loud. I sobbed like somebody stole my big wheel. I let it all out. Hypnotiq held me tight, and smoothed the hair from my face. I don't know how long I stood there, but when I pulled myself from Hypnotiq's embrace, the heaviness that had been weighing on me drifted into the cloud of purple haze near the table dance area.

"Girl, you need a change of scenery. Michael called me to dance at *The Fish Bowl* tomorrow night, and they want me to bring somebody. You feel like popping it for some females?"

"I'm down. How much?"

"$200 at the door, and tips. You know bitches know how to tip."

"You ain't never lied! Okay, I'm going in the bathroom to get it together, and I'll be back out. Really and truly, I can leave this bitch tonight. I need to sleep it off."

"Whenever you're ready, I can drive you home."

"You have really had my back, and I appreciate it." I gave her a quick hug, and headed towards the bathroom.

After I got it together, I was on my way to the bar to get a bottled water when I heard someone call my name. I turned around, and it was John. Fuck.

"Alizé? You okay? It looks like you were bawling."

That asshole knew exactly what the fuck was wrong with me, but he had to rub it in my face.

"Nah, I'm cool. I hit some purple in the dressing room."

"Oh, okay because I thought maybe you were boo-hooing over Tony."

"You're funny. I'll talk to you later. I'm getting ready to get out of here."

"Tony told me what happened. That was some dramatic shit huh?"

"It was drama."

"I'm surprised that Camille didn't try to knock you out! She might be little, but she's scrappy!"

I was already fucked up, and it seemed like he was just hoping to get a reaction out of me, so I gave him what he wanted.

"What the fuck do you want from me?"

"Damn baby! Why you tripping? I was going to ask if you want to dance for my boy's bachelor party in a couple of weeks."

"Nah, I'm cool."

"Why you running off?"

John grabbed my hand when I turned around to leave. This nigga was trying to fuck.

"John, don't grab me. I'm leaving."

"Tony's going to be at the party. He's the one that told me to get you."

Just when I thought my night couldn't get any worse, it had. Now Tony was tricking me out to his friends? He knew that fucking went down at those parties, so I guess he really was over me. I knew that my mouth must have been wide open, so I quickly started speaking, trying to hide my shock and disappointment.

"I'm busy."

I walked to the bar, and stood silently as one single tear fell down my cheek. Tammy walked over, and the only word that I could force from my lips was *water*, no please or thank you would come. I gulped the entire bottle, and turned to find that John had left. Hypnotiq walked over to me with street clothes on.

"You ready girl?"

"Yeah, give me two minutes to put my clothes on."

I walked past her, and made a bee line for the locker room, my safe haven. I felt like everyone at the bar had been staring at me, and I couldn't take the spotlight. I changed into my street clothes, and met Hypnotiq in the kitchen. She drove my car to her apartment, and I wondered why we didn't go to my house. She gave me a towel, and told me to get in the shower. She turned the water on, and I stayed in there for what seemed like forever, but when I got out I felt brand new. We laid on Hypnotiq's bed, and I told her what John had said to me by the bar. She said that it didn't sound true, and to not let it bother me.

"Can I call him to find out?"

"Girl, are you going to call him every time you hear something? You're never going to have any peace."

"I know you're right, but this is killing me. I just want to know if every thing we had was bullshit. Did he really care about me, or was I just something to do?"

I felt comfortable talking to Hypnotiq because she was fucking with a married man, and she knew what I was going through. Brandy and I talked very briefly about Tony. She never said *I told you so*, and I appreciated that, but she had never been in a situation like this, so she really didn't know what to say to me. She tried, but she just couldn't help.

"He cared about you, but he wasn't giving up his wife and kids, but you knew that...right?"

"Of course. I just need to hear him say what I actually meant to him."

"In your heart, you know how he felt about you. Nobody knows better than you. You don't need him to tell you anything because you already know."

Hypnotiq's words were dead on; she had no idea what she was doing for my battered soul.

"Girl, listen to me. It's only been a couple of weeks. You need to really give yourself time to work through your feelings, and find the peace you need to move on. Everybody will tell you to just move on, but you can't do that without truly moving through all the feelings that you are going to face. Anger, hurt, resentment, stupidity...all of that. Let yourself feel every bit of it, and then you can grow emotionally strong. You have to go through every single negative feeling to get to the other side. This is my advice. I'm telling you this because I have done the same thing, and I know it helps the healing process. You cannot talk to or see Tony for awhile. There is no specific time frame, but you need to give yourself time to live without him. If you call him, and you get the voicemail, you're going to be consumed with the thought of him calling back. If you call, and he answers, you'll wonder when he's going to call again, and you're going to allow yourself to think that the feelings are still there because he accepted your call. If you see him face to face, forget about it! It's a vicious trap, so don't allow yourself to get sucked into it."

"Yeah, you're right. I just feel like shit right now!"

"Of course you do! Don't even be ashamed of that!"

"I feel like a stupid bitch because I caught feelings for somebody that I could never have. And the thing that makes it worse is the fact that I never could've meant anything to him even if he was single because I'm a stripper. The last couple of weeks have forced me to recognize my job, my lifestyle, and my future. Hypnotiq, I don't like what I see. You feel me?"

"Yeah, girl. That's a whole other topic, but you can work on both at the same time. You wanna get out of the game? This life isn't for everybody. What else do you want to do?"

"Girl, I don't know."

"Well, you don't have to figure everything out right this minute. Just go to bed, and write some things down tomorrow. You should start keeping a journal of your feelings, dreams, and goals. I have one, and it really helps me to keep my thoughts together."

"Hypnotiq, I don't know what to say..." I leaned over, and gave her a big hug.

"Please. You want some hot tea?"

"No, I need to just lie down."

I started to get under the covers, and my cell phone started ringing. It was Tony. I must have looked like I had seen a ghost because Hypnotiq grabbed my phone.

"You answering it?"

"No. Let's go to bed."

Hypnotiq was right. Just the fact that he called, and I didn't answer made me feel powerful. I would've felt weak and pitiful if I answered his call. That one phone call shifted my whole mood. I felt like I could conquer the world! Hypnotiq turned off the lights, and we snuggled into her cozy bed. I pulled the covers up to my nose, and shut my eyes.

I never would've thought that that person would be Hypnotiq. I thought she was the most beautiful woman I had ever met, but I had no idea that she would be such a good friend. I trusted her, and she allowed me to cry on her shoulder without being a know-it-all or telling me what to do. She gave me advice, but she wasn't pushy. If it wasn't for her, I think I would've lost my mind. I started to drift off to sleep until the voicemail indicator went off. I pressed the cancel button, and decided that I would listen to the voicemail in the morning. I was out of it, and I knew that I would never be able to get back to sleep if I heard Tony's voice.

❦   ❦   ❦

The next morning, Hypnotiq and I woke up to somebody knocking on her front door. I was sleeping like a nigga fresh out of jail, so I was a little irritated when I heard all that loud banging. Hypnotiq dragged herself out of bed, and apologized for Jason. I guess he had called her to say he was on the way. I stayed in the bed. I fell asleep again, but I woke up when I smelled steak and grilled onions.

I got up, and threw on some clothes. I walked into Hypnotiq's bathroom, washed up, and yanked my hair into a ponytail. Before I could even say good morning, I looked at Hypnotiq and her man. They were in the kitchen just holding each other. Her head lay on his shoulder, and his arms were resting right above her ass. A lump grew in my throat, and tears formed in the corners of my eyes. That was what I longed for, a man that would be there for me, and love my dirty drawls like Jason.

"Hey girl."

They saw me. I had hoped that my face didn't look terribly tragic as they turned to look at me. I hoped that the tears hadn't welled up, and skated down my face. I hoped that my mouth wasn't contorted from the lump in my throat. I hoped that I didn't look like I felt.

"Hey! Something is smelling up in here!"

"My baby is making us some steak, eggs, and potatoes. Want some orange juice, coffee, tea?"

"I'll have some coffee. Thanks girl. You guys need any help?"

Jason spoke up.

"Nah, I got this. You guys just relax. Renee, can you turn the game on?"

Hypnotiq and I walked to the living room, and she turned the game on. We sat down, and she asked me how I was doing. I told her that I was doing much better, and thanked her again. As soon as we focused on the game, the commentator reminded viewers that the Los Angeles Sunshine would be playing in the second half of the double header. Great! Hypnotiq just told me last night that I needed to steer clear of Tony for a while for the sake of healing, but I couldn't escape him! Jason wanted to watch the game. What was I supposed to do? Stomp out of the room like a third grader? No, I was going to be mature about the situation, but now I remembered that he not only called last night, but also left me a voicemail.

"I'm going to go make your bed." I needed a reason to get out of the room.

"Girl please. I'll do it after we eat. There is no rush!"

"That's okay. You know I don't feel right just sitting around when you and Jason are cooking!"

As I was talking, I just started walking towards her bedroom, so that she couldn't stop me. When I got in her room, I shut the door, and pulled my phone out of my bag. I turned it on, but it was chirping "low battery." I quickly called my voicemail, but I had to skip through a couple of messages to get to Tony's. All I heard was "Mia…" and the phone cut off! My mobile charger was in my car outside of Hypnotiq's apartment, but that was doing a lot. For some reason, I felt like I had to sneak and listen to Tony's message. I didn't have any reason to hide. I was going outside to charge my phone in the car!

"Hyp-no, I'm going to charge my phone. I'll be right back."

"Okay, but hurry 'cause the food will be ready in a few minutes."

"O.K."

I grabbed my keys, and walked out feeling more like an adult because I decided not to slink out of the house like I was doing something wrong. I put the phone on the charger, and called the voicemail.

"Mia, I need to talk to you, so call me when you get the message."

I gripped my chest, and pressed 1 to repeat more times than I can remember. Why didn't he say more? Talk about what? I wondered what my next move would be…tell Hypnotiq, call him? I felt like a hostage. I left the phone on the charger, and went back in the house.

"You ready to eat?"

Hypnotiq was such a genuine person, and I didn't want to keep secrets from her, so I decided to tell her about the voicemail after we ate.

"I'm starving!"

Jason made a steak that would cost about $45 in a restaurant. It was so tender that I didn't even need a knife; I just took my fork and pulled bite-sized pieces off of the steak and popped it into my mouth. He seasoned the meat so well that the sides of my jaw began to water as soon as the steak hit my tongue. Jason grilled onions, and slow-cooked the steak to the point where we didn't even need A-1 sauce. The flavorful hash brown potatoes were sautéed with onions to a golden brown. Jason's scrambled eggs were full of cheese and onions, and the smell had to piss her neighbors off.

I didn't talk much as I ate because I wanted to focus on the food in front of me. I did pause to compliment Jason every now and then, but those were the only words out of my mouth. By the time I finished my plate, I had to roll out of my chair. Not only was Jason the #1 boyfriend, but he cooked like a chef in a famous restaurant.

I had to fight the #1 couple to load the dishwasher, but I was successful. I finished in the kitchen, and sat down to watch the rest of the game with them. When I started to feel sleepy, I told them I was going home to sleep it off. They teased me about being a typical Negro, and we all laughed. Hypnotiq told me that she would be at my apartment to get me for the show, so she would call me later.

When I got home, I turned my phone off, and flopped on my bed. Out of nowhere, I thought about calling Tony because I knew he couldn't answer his phone. He was either having a meeting, or he was practicing, but either way, he was busy. I didn't have a chance to talk to Hypnotiq about the voicemail since Jason was there, so I decided to just be cool. I closed my eyes, and it was a wrap.

CHAPTER 18

✧

I was in a deep coma-like sleep when my house phone snatched me up. I grabbed the phone to stop that irritating, loud ringing noise from penetrating my brain.

"Did I wake you up?" It was Tony. I had no warning, Hypnotiq wasn't there, and I was half-sleep!

"Hey…can I…call you back…in a minute?" Good! Get yourself together!

"The game is going to start soon. I just wanted to see if I could come by after I leave here."

How did he always seem to capture my authority from me? I told him I would call him later, and now he's not only keeping me on the phone, but he's trying to come over? I had to be strong.

"I'm busy tonight."

"What you got going?"

"I have a party." Questioning? Wow he never did that before.

"Where?"

"*The Fish Bowl.*" Was he showing up? He was killing me.

"Okay, I'm going to call you later."

"Tony, what do you want? We're done." I found my balls.

"I don't have time to get into all that. I'm going to talk to you later."

The only thing that I could squeeze out was a sheepish "bye" before he hung up. I talked big and bad until I heard his voice, and then I turned into jelly. I had given up way too much information, and for what? Now I would be looking across the room all night, wondering if Tony would really show up at the club. This was exactly what I didn't want to happen. I had to call Hypnotiq. I barely let her say hello before I started in about Tony.

"What did he say?"

"Girl, he didn't say anything! He had left a voicemail last night just saying that he wanted to talk, but I didn't call him back, so he called my house."

"Well, he may show up tonight. Are you ready for that?"

"Hell no, but I'm going to act cool though. Never let them see you sweat!"

"Well, I'll be there at 10, and we can talk some more."

We hung up, and I got out of bed. I cleaned up, washed clothes, and packed my bag for later. I still wasn't hungry after that big breakfast, but I called Brandy to see if she wanted to go to the mall. I went by her house, and picked her up. Lorenzo walked her outside, and I didn't know how much more I could take of all of the loving couples around me before I overdosed on intimacy. We walked around The Grove, and I ended up buying an outfit and some shoes. I also bought some makeup and a new purse. Brandy bought some makeup and some shoes, and we left. On the way home, we stopped and got ice cream. We talked, but I avoided the Tony conversation. I just told her that I hadn't talked to him. I was going to tell her to meet me at the club tonight, but since Tony *might* have shown up, I revoked her invitation. I dropped her off, and got home just in time to meet Hypnotiq.

We pulled up to the club, and there was already a line outside. There were a few limos in front, and security guards were running around making sure people got out of the way. Hypnotiq and I walked in the front door, and ran into the club manager, Michelle. She was a stud, and her girl was a bartender. Michelle was cool, but she was as jealous as a dude, and she was always getting into with other cats when she was faded when they flirted with her girl too much. She wore one long braid down her back, and she dressed like a man. She was actually a pretty girl, but she wasn't soft or feminine at all, and I'm sure that she never got play because brothas could look at her, and see how she got down. I never understood why the lipstick lesbians loved studs because they treated them just like niggas did: cheating, whooping their ass, and basically acting like clueless, selfish assholes. If I was going to deal with all the regular bullshit, there had to be, at the very least, a real dick between their legs.

"Hi ladies."

"Hey Michelle!" Hypnotiq and I were talking in unison.

"You guys know where to change right? It's going to be big tonight. We got a couple of celebs in the house."

"Yeah, we saw the limos outside."

"Okay, well I'll let you guys go. Let me know if you need anything. Did you tell the DJ what you wanted to hear?"

"No, we just walked in."

"Just let him know."

"Cool."

We walked to the bar and got two Remy Martins, then walked to the back. The dressing room was a big empty room with mirrors all over the walls. There were a couple of other girls in there, but they looked like waitresses. I didn't feel like being polite and having a thoughtless conversation, so I just said hi and kept it moving. Hypnotiq and I found a corner, and just started laying our stuff out. She went and told the DJ what we wanted to hear, and stopped by the bar again. I plugged in my hot curler, and took out my makeup. I had to put some thick foundation on my bikini area because I got waxed after I dropped Brandy at home, and I still looked irritated. I brought a couple of outfits, but I didn't know what I was wearing. Hypnotiq wanted us to look similar. I didn't care. She could've put a clown outfit, nappy wig, and a red nose on me, and that would've been cool. I wasn't feeling it. I was only there because she invited me, and I wanted to stay distracted.

Hypnotiq came back, and we sipped on our new drinks. She looked at my outfits compared with what she had brought, and she decided on two sexy things that we had in common. Whenever she saw me drift into a different place, she would come over and tell me to snap out of it. I didn't even realize that I was fading in and out of the conversation, and staring into space when people were talking to me.

After we had been in the back getting dressed, drinking, and hanging out for over an hour, it was time to go on stage. Michelle came in and told us the club was packed, and they were ready for us. By the time we walked out, the club was filled with mostly bitches, but niggas too, both gay and straight. The DJ was bumping, and we strutted out like we were the shit. The lights dimmed, and a spotlight hit us dead in the eyes. We hopped in front of the stage, and jumped on all fours. I was pumping my ass hella hard until I felt a sharp pinch in my right knee. The pinch turned into a stinging sensation, and then I felt warm, sticky liquid oozing from the prickly pain. I thought I had put my knee in some liquor, but I looked down to see that I had cut my knee on a jagged piece of glass. Blood was trickling down my leg, but I didn't freak out because I was a professional. I kept my ass facing the audience, but I took it down to a slow grind. The audience was hollering like it was hot, but I had to relieve some of the pressure off of that knee. With one quick movement, I wiped the blood away that was forming into a clot. There was money all over the floor, and a couple of the bills stuck to the blood on my leg. My knee was throbbing, the music was getting louder, and the lights were blinding. I tried to work it out, but I started feeling dizzy and weak. I was lightheaded. The DJ was yelling trying to get the crowd to break us off, but I just wanted the set to end. I looked at Hypnotiq, and she was looking at my knee. I didn't know if the audience peeped it or not, but I didn't stop dancing.

When the song started fading, I slowly moved off the stage, and let Hypnotiq finish without me. I could feel the blood oozing down my leg, and I knew that it was quite visible by now. I trotted in the bathroom, and the sight of all that blood freaked me the fuck out! The front of my right leg was covered in crimson from my knee to my ankle. I leaned on the wall for support, and rested my right foot on the counter. I could barely see the cut because it was swollen and there were blood clots covering it. I grabbed some paper towels, and shoved them under the running water. Michelle must have seen the drama because she came in the bathroom to check on me.

"Damn, girl, you okay?"

She looked nervous, not because I had cut myself, but maybe because she was afraid I would ask for some bread.

"I cut my shit on some glass."

"Let me go see if we have a first aid kit behind the bar, or maybe in the office."

Michelle ran out, and I slowly and carefully rubbed the blood off of my leg. I had wiped up most of the blood when I realized that my knee was not only swollen, but very tender. There was an exaggerated bump a few centimeters to the right of the cut, I still had glass in my knee. The cut was deep, and white flesh was poking out from underneath the skin. As soon as I wiped the blood away, it began to bead again. Michelle returned with a bartender and a first aid kit. They soaked a piece of gauze with antiseptic, and the bartender gingerly cleaned the cut. Michelle wrapped me with plenty of bandages like we were at the emergency room at Cedars-Sinai. They took care of me. I looked a hot mess, and the pain was kicking. My whole leg was throbbing. I had to turn around and sit my ass on the counter.

"Did everybody see the blood?"

"Not at first, but then it was pretty obvious, but shit happens. Don't trip. What happened anyway?"

"I don't know. I was working it out, and I felt the glass slice my knee."

"Somebody must have dropped a glass. I really want to apologize for that. Let me give you another $200 so you can go to the doctor, and make sure the glass is out. You may need stitches."

"Thanks, Michelle. I'm going to the doctor tomorrow because it looks like the glass is still in there."

"No problem. If the $200 doesn't cover it, just come back with the receipt, and I'll take care of it for you.

"That's cool. How's Hypnotiq doing?"

"She's working it out! No offense, but girl they forgot about all the blood. You know them bitches love her!"

She was funny and I thought about the fact that I really was happy that I ended up in the bathroom instead of onstage, but I could've done without the cut, the blood, and the drama. We hobbled into the back room with me using the two of them like crutches. I was limping around taking my clothes off when I heard the waitresses talking to each other.

"Girl, I saw a couple of the Sunshine players in here!"

"Shut up! Bitch where? I got to find me a baller tonight! I'm tired of working!"

"You a fool for that one!"

"Bitch, you think I'm playing! I'm sick of all these broke ass niggas. Shit, I'm trying to get mine! Show me where these niggas is at!"

They laughed as they walked back onto the floor. Tony was there. I was a bloody, hot mess, and Tony was there. I couldn't put my jeans back on because my knee was on fire. I looked through my bag, and found a mini skirt, so I threw that on with the top I had on when I got there. I dabbed the oil and sweat off of my face, checked my hair and makeup, and strolled my handicapped ass out to the floor. I wouldn't look for Tony; I would wait for him to approach me. I didn't want to look overeager. I looked down at my bandages on my knee, and laughed out loud. I looked ridiculous, and I was in pain. I had to put my slides on, and they made me feel sloppy. Heels made me feel tall and sexy, I felt like a housewife with the flip flops on.

As I walked through the crowd, I could hear people whispering and pointing at me. They were acting like I got shot or something. My girl was still dancing. Hypnotiq was at the end of her third song, and I had hoped it was her last. I felt an enormous amount of guilt as I watched the sweat pouring down her face, and chest. She was a bad bitch, and the audience was captivated by her beauty, her body, and her exotic moves.

Luckily, they were watching Hypnotiq, and not Bloody Mary walking through the crowd. I was making my way to the bar when I saw two of Tony's teammates. My heart began to pound, and I frantically looked around for Tony because I couldn't stand to be surprised by him coming up to me from behind.

The anticipation was killing me as I looked for the tallest figures in the house. None of them were Tony. Within a few minutes, I had scanned the entire room, and I didn't see him. Maybe he didn't show up after all, but why would he tell me that he needed to talk to me, ask where I'm going to be, and then not show up? Cocksucker.

I stepped towards the bar, and it was as if the waters parted because I had a clear path to the bartender right in front of me. It was the same one that had helped me in the bathroom. She had mopped up the blood from all over my leg, and I didn't even know her name. I was sure that she knew that I was in shock, and perhaps had forgotten about niceties. I thanked her again for playing Florence Nightingale, and asked her name. Cara. She asked what I wanted, and quickly prepared a drink for me at no charge. Maybe the blood and bandage thing was working to my advantage.

Hypnotiq finally staggered off the dance floor after four songs. The entire stage was covered with money in all denominations. Two bouncers with large trash bags scooped it all up, and followed behind Hypnotiq. She made a beeline for the back room, and I was right behind her with a drink.

"Girl, are you okay? I saw your knee!"

She grabbed a clean, white bar towel and carefully dabbed her face and neck, so that she didn't smear her makeup. She was flawless.

"I'm okay. I cut myself on some glass."

"You may need stitches. How does it feel?"

"It's swollen, and it wouldn't stop bleeding. I think the glass is still in there."

"You want go to the emergency room?"

"Nah. Michelle gave me $200, and I'll just go to the clinic tomorrow."

"Well, if you want to go tonight just let me know."

Hypnotiq was more than supportive. She started undressing, and I took a seat on the floor. I propped my leg up, and didn't care that my panties were showing. Nobody should've been looking between my legs. That was their bad.

"Did Mr. Man show up? I saw some of his boys."

"No."

Hypnotiq could tell by my response that I was disappointed, and didn't really feel like talking, so the conversation ended there. She put on her street clothes, and we cruised the club. Beauty and the Beast.

I was standing in the middle of a crowd surrounded by more than a hundred people, but I had never felt so lonely. I could've been sitting on my couch in a robe, eating ice cream, watching a talk show, and I wouldn't have felt any lonelier than I felt at that moment. I could see people and hear music, but I couldn't feel it. People talked at me and walked through me because I wasn't there. I was consumed with thoughts of Tony, and I realized right then that Hypnotiq knew her shit. She told me that it would be easier on my spirit to go cold turkey, and not have any contact with Tony. He had called my house, and implied that he was showing up to the club, but he never really said that he was. Just the *thought* of him walking into the club had me fucked up.

I was geeked when Tony called me last night and left a voicemail, but I didn't feel like shit until I talked to him, and he tricked me into believing that I was going to see him. When I heard his voicemail, my heart beat a little faster. I was nervous, and my stomach felt queasy like when I drank too much, and was afraid that I would throw up in my girl's car.

Ironically, that was a comforting feeling, the thought of him, the sound of his voice, and the notion that he missed me. He had me on a hook, and he reeled me in when he got me on the phone. I wanted to shout, "Leave me the fuck alone and stop fucking with my feelings!"…but I couldn't. Hella weak! Not only did I tell him where I would be, but my stupid ass actually looked for him all night. I fucked my whole night off by answering the phone this morning. I allowed him to manipulate my emotions. I put myself back at square one. I never really knew how much I really cared about Tony, and how much he affected my life until he was out of it.

As Hypnotiq and I walked through the club, we got play from both guys and girls. Even though it was a lesbian spot, all types showed up. There were celebrities, athletes, gay men, lesbians, bisexuals, and others. That kind of a mix meant more security because there was always at least one guaranteed fight. When the studs pulled a female from a straight man, there was always drama because their manhood was threatened. The studs didn't mind fighting brothas either. There were girls walking around the club looking just like dudes. They had close fades, baseball caps, 3X white tees, sagging jeans, and Jordans. They walked like niggas, and it was hard to tell who was what.

Sometimes the flaming homosexuals would hit on straight cats, and that was almost always a fight when liquor was involved. A lot of cats on the down-low hung out at these kinds of clubs because they could hook up with other secretly gay men. Swinging couples either came to find a third, or a whole other couple to swap with them. The voyeurs came to find a man for their girl-friend or wife to fuck while they watched. Some freaky shit popped off at these kinds of clubs.

I wanted to sit down, so I pulled Hypnotiq towards the VIP section. The bouncer lifted the red velvet rope, and welcomed us inside. We sat down on one of the couches, and the waitress came right over with a bottle of Dom P and two glasses on ice. The music was loud, so she pointed to two guys leaning on the bar. Fuck. They were Tony's teammates. Before I could say anything, Hypnotiq motioned for them to come over. I yanked her sleeve, and told her who they were, but it was too late.

They came over, and shook our hands. We thanked them for the champagne and introduced ourselves. I was as nervous a pretty boy in lockup. I didn't know if they knew about me or not, but I gave them my dance name. I noticed that the point guard was paying a lot of attention to Hypnotiq, which left me with the center. He was being cool, but I think we both knew that he was playing wingman. I'm sure that I probably looked cuter than I felt, but with my knee and the slides, I didn't feel sexy. Not to mention the fact that these were Tony's boys. I was making polite conversation when I saw Hypnotiq exchanging numbers. They stood up, and my dude said that it was nice to meet me, but he didn't ask for my number. I didn't want him to, but I was a little offended that he didn't at least ask.

As soon as they walked away, Hypnotiq and I chopped it up. I told her that I was a nervous wreck because I didn't know what they knew, or if they knew about me at all. She said her dude didn't say anything. She said he was cool, and they were supposed to go to lunch in the next day or two. He was single. I told her to do her thing. Tony knew Hypnotiq, and I knew that when his teammate got to practice the next day, he would be running his mouth about the fine stripper he met at *The Fish Bowl* the night before, and Tony would pick up the phone and call me.

We stayed in VIP for a little while, but it was time to call it a night when the inevitable fight broke out. Michelle had given us our money right before it popped off, so we just ducked out before the club shut down. Hypnotiq made over $1,100 in tips, and she surprised me by still giving me half. I told her that I didn't earn it, but she said that it wasn't my fault that I got slashed, and she was pretty sure that the audience threw some sympathy money up there for me. We laughed so hard that tears started to come down, and she just hugged me without saying a word.

The next day Hypnotiq and I went to the urgent care clinic. The doctor took an X-ray, and I definitely had a piece of glass lodged in my knee. They had to slice my knee open, remove the glass, and stitch me up. It hurt like hell, but my knee actually felt a lot less tender after the minor surgery. The nurses put a bandage on me, and sent me out the door. Everything cost $305, so I called Michelle, and she agreed to give me the rest of the money. She knew that I could push the issue, and she didn't want that. The floor should've been thoroughly swept for glass before we performed, and there was no way around it. It was the responsibility of the club, but it didn't have to get ugly because Michelle took care of it. She ended up giving me $350 and buying us lunch that same day.

CHAPTER 19

Tony had called me the next day to ask me if I had told anybody about us because he had heard some shit. I told him no, but he lingered on the phone. I didn't bail him out, and after a few seconds of silence, I told him that I had another call. We said goodbye, and I hung up. That phone call pissed me off because he must have thought he was a boss asking me if I told anybody about him. Who the fuck was he? His wife must have been sweating him over something she heard. I didn't care anymore. He never called again, and I didn't call him. One day turned into two, and one week turned into two. I figured that was it. I tripped the first few days, but as the days slowly kept passing by, I began to move on. I really did miss him, but it helped that we didn't talk or see each other.

Hypnotiq went to lunch with the basketball player, but she stopped taking his calls after he straight out told her that he wanted a threesome with her and another stripper. She said that he made her feel nasty, and she wasn't fucking with him. That wasn't anything new; a lot of athletes were straight freaks. Regular, straight up sex wasn't good enough for them, and their sexual appetites were off the hook. Hypnotiq had body everywhere, and he asked for a second girl right off the bat? That's hella disrespectful. They hadn't even kicked it yet, and after he showed his ass, they never would.

Unfortunately, dancers get little to no respect. Niggas expected you to be down for whatever. They talked to you like I all you did was sit around and fuck all day. They think you will suck any dick, take it in the ass, and fuck them and their friends with your stripper friends. When a stripper said no, they just couldn't believe it. After all, brothas went to strippers for the things that their wives and girlfriends wouldn't do, so when we said no they lost all hope in the sex industry.

Hypnotiq got Big D to set me up with one of his boys, even though I told her that I was cool. I was not in the mood for bullshit. I told Hypnotiq to tell Big D that he could tell his boy that I was a dancer, but that it wasn't that kind of party. I didn't mind meeting a new friend, and just having somebody to hang out with sometime, but I didn't want him to think it was a jump off. Big D was a nice guy, and I knew that his friend probably would be too. I had asked Hypnotiq if it was one of the guys from the party we did a few months ago, and she said he wasn't there. She didn't know anything about him, but Big D said he was a good dude.

I never talked to my blind date on the phone, so this date was extra blind. We set everything up between Hypnotiq and Big D. We decided to meet for dinner at Houston's on a Friday night. I decided to look stylish, yet sophisticated, so I wore some dark gray slacks and a sheer black blouse. I slid on my black high heel sandals, and wore minimal makeup. I was sexy, but reserved. I took one last look in the mirror, hopped in my car, and drove to the restaurant. When I got there, and started looking around the bar, I realized that I didn't even know what he looked like! I guess that proved that I wasn't looking for my true love on this date. I didn't even stop to ask how he looked, if he was cute, or any of the other questions that people ask when they're being set up. Just as I was looking around the room like a lost puppy, my cell phone rang. It was Hypnotiq.

"Girl, I am standing in the restaurant, and I don't even know what my date looks like!"

"I just hung up with Big D, and he conveniently forgot to mention that his boy is white!" I was silent as I scanned the room again looking for cute white boys.

"Shut up!"

"Yeah girl, but fuck it! Have a good time. Nobody said to marry him!"

"You're right, okay I see a white man staring at me. I think it's him."

"His name is Brent. Go get him!"

We hung up, and I slid my phone back in my purse. That was him. He started making his way towards me, and I noticed that he was actually pretty cute. He was tall with a body that screamed to be touched. He wore chocolate slacks with a chocolate button down shirt. Prada shoes, chunky sterling silver bracelet, and hair shaped into the new Mohawk; he hadn't shaved in two days, but it looked good. He was very GQ, and I was pleasantly surprised.

"Mia?"

"Brent?"

"That's me. How are you?"

He extended his hand, and I took it in mine. His hands were soft like he had never worked a day of hard work in his whole life.

"I'm fine. You know I have to tell you I didn't know that you were white. My friend called just now to tell me who to look for. You may have seen the surprised look on my face."

"I did. Well, that must have been a shock. Thomas told me that you were black, but I guess you must date white guys all the time since they didn't tell you."

We both laughed, and I knew that he would be fun. In my mind, I had to put the story with the face. Hypnotiq told me that Brent worked for Def Jam Records, he was divorced, two kids, and had a fat pocket. He traveled a lot and worked long hours, so his wife got tired of a cold bed. She had been having an affair with her high school sweetheart, and when she confessed to Brent, he wanted a divorce. Her motivation for confessing was to have a fresh start, and encourage her husband to spend more time with her, but it backfired, and because she was an adulterer, she didn't get any alimony. Stupid bitch. I didn't know much about Brent yet, but he was fine *and* paid? Some females don't realize how good they really have it.

We talked about his job, movies, and dating, but the whole time I was wondering what his dick looked like. The white guys in pornos were hung like horses. But of course they were packing, or they wouldn't have been in movies. Brent was a regular guy, and I wondered what he was holding between his legs.

I knew that the black man-big dick stereotype was bullshit, so the white man-little dick stereotype had to be bullshit too. I don't know who started that rumor about brothas, but I wished that they would print a retraction on the front page of the Los Angeles Times. All niggas do NOT have big dicks! I have seen some little ones in my day, but nobody ever talks about that. If only these poor little white girls knew that it was just a myth, they wouldn't be fucking off their inheritances and trust funds for that black dick. I had fucked a couple of cats with dicks that looked like little brown thumbs that would slip out when I was on top bouncing up and down…

"So, Mia, Thomas told me that you're a dancer?"

"Yeah, I've been doing it for a couple of years now."

"How do you like it?"

"Honestly, it's just a job. I know that I don't want to do it forever."

"Really? What else do you want to do?"

"I'm going to start taking some classes soon."

"Education is always in the plus column. Do you know what you want to study?"

"I'm not sure yet. I'm actually interested in a lot of things."

"Well, college is the best place for you to figure it out. Good for you."

Brent's words were very encouraging. I never really had a man ask me about my goals, and actually supported my ideas. Most guys at the club assumed that I loved dancing, and that I didn't want to do anything else, so they never asked. If I did mention that I wanted to go back to school, a lot would say something discouraging without really knowing that they were subconsciously breaking my spirit. I had become more and more frustrated with the club, niggas, and hustling.

Brent and I ate a glorious dinner, and he was a perfect gentleman without being corny. He was cool, and I could tell that he hung out with brothas. He didn't use slang, or try to "act black", but he had a confident swagger. He didn't nervously ask me questions while trying to carefully ignore the fact that I was black. Brent held a conversation with me as I'm sure he does with anyone that he had just met. He asked me questions about myself, and looked me in the eyes when I answered. He seemed terribly interested in everything that I had to say.

As we shared a huge sundae, he was telling me work stories, and we laughed so hard that people kept looking at us. At first I wondered if they were looking because of our interracial date, but then I realized it was because we were laughing so loud. I had never been on a date with a white man, and I was having fun. When I went out with Tony, he was always nervously looking around to see if he knew anyone in the room. He constantly looked at his watch, and almost jumped out of his chair when his wife called. Brent was relaxed and gave me all of his attention. When his cell phone rang, he answered it, but politely said that he was on a date. I felt valuable.

After we finished eating, Brent asked me if I wanted to take a ride, and I told him that was cool. We drove to a dark baseball field, and I began to wonder just how well Big D knew him. It was as if he read my mind because he said that he wasn't trying to make out; he had something to show me. I told him what I was thinking, and we both found it very funny.

We parked right behind home base, and he told me that he played Little League baseball ever since he was eight years old, and in the middle of his third season, his mother and father broke up. His father promised him that he would never miss a game, but he never saw his son play another game after the divorce. He said that every time he stepped up to home plate, he would look over his shoulder to see if his father was pulling up just in time, but he never did.

For years, Brent would look over his shoulder before he took his first swing, and that became his trademark. All through high school, everyone thought that was his patented move, but he never shared his secret motivation with anyone until he had a son. After he divorced his wife, he promised his kids that he would always be there for every game, recital, play, or talent show, and he kept his word. Brent said that as hurt he was, his father's absence gave him everything he needed to be the best father in the world.

I was so touched by Brent's sensitivity and vulnerability. The moment was so sacred that I didn't want to disrespect it by verbally comforting him, so I just rubbed his hand, and looked straight ahead at home base.

🍁　　　🍁　　　🍁

I couldn't wait to get home and call Hypnotiq. I told her that Brent was a very special man, and she was so happy that we got along so well. When I told her about the baseball field, she gushed like a proud mother. I had to admit to her that I was excited about my new friend. While we were talking, Brent was clicking in, so I told her to hold on. He just wanted to make sure that I made it home safely. Hypnotiq and I stayed on the phone giggling like two eighth graders for over an hour.

The next morning, I opened my eyes and thought about Brent. I hadn't had that much fun on a date in an extremely long time. He made me laugh, he asked thoughtful questions about my life and my future, and he was sincere. Brent was a breath of fresh air. I didn't want to put too much stock in him so soon, but I had to take inventory of his inviting personality.

I had to recognize what I had been missing for so long. I thought Tony and I had some semblance of a relationship, but in reality, he was using me. I gave far more than I ever received, and the most disappointing aspect was that I thought that was cool. I had somehow convinced myself that he was worth it. I didn't get what I wanted out of that hook up, but I settled for what he gave me. My anger shifted from Tony to myself because I somehow didn't think that I deserved any better than that. It's not like I was getting ready to fall in love with Brent, but sometimes it takes a different perspective to recognize how fucked up things really were in another situation.

Brandy called, and wanted me to go with her to Costco to buy food for her Thanksgiving party at her job. Her boss gave her the money, and asked her to pick up the things they would need. I threw on some clothes, and ate some cereal while I waited for her to come scoop me. I went in my room, made up my bed, and straightened up the kitchen. Brandy called me when she was around the corner, and I put my tennis shoes on, and waited in front. I told her about Brent as we drove, and she was very pleased to hear that I had met an unattached man.

"Girl, I am so happy that you have found somebody nice that doesn't have somebody at home."

"Yeah, he seems like a fun person to kick it with."

"Do you think you could get serious with a white man?"

"Dang, are you going to buy a bridesmaid's dress today? I just met the man!"

"I know, but I'm just asking because if you don't see yourself getting serious with him, you shouldn't get too close."

"No worries."

That was the shit that irritated me about Brandy. She had a sobering effect on my high. She always had to be mature and thoughtful about everything instead of just saying fuck it sometimes. I had been on one date, and she was already asking if I could marry and have kids with the man. She would never consider just hanging out, or playing it by ear. Brandy wanted everything to fit in a neat little box, but life wasn't always neat and tidy, and it pissed me off that she always pushed her opinions on me. I know she didn't do it intentionally, but she did it nonetheless, and it drove me absolutely crazy. Most of the time, I had to bite my tongue and count to ten, or I would go postal on her ass. Brandy was the only one in my life that could get away with that shit, but she was still pushing it.

When we got to Costco, we grabbed a cart, and filled it up with everything on Brandy's list. She needed plastic cups, utensils, paper towels, and paper plates. We grabbed a turkey, vegetables, fruit, drinks, croissants, cheese, crackers, and everything else under the sun. I think we went down every aisle of that monstrous store, and I was ready to leave after the first half hour. Everybody on the west side of L.A. was in that store right then, and I began to feel like the concrete walls were shrinking. Brandy told me that I could throw in a couple of things that I needed for my apartment, but I just got some frozen egg rolls.

I noticed a few guilty weekend fathers indulging their children with whatever they asked for, and it made me think of Brent. No sooner than the thought of him had entered my mind did my cell phone ring, and it was him. I showed Brandy my phone, and quickly answered it since it was on the third ring. He said he was just calling to say hello, and thank me for such a wonderful evening. I couldn't wipe the goofy smile off of my face. He told me to call him when I left the store, and maybe we could get together. He really was a nice guy, but I just didn't know if I was emotionally available for anyone so soon after Tony.

Brandy and I finally reached the bottom of the grocery list, and proceeded to the checkout. We stopped for a slice of pizza, and as we were walking out, Tony's wife was walking in. I didn't notice her until she was almost out of sight, but she had seen me. By the time I looked up and saw her face, she was already staring at me. She had stopped pushing her cart, but I kept walking forward without giving her much attention. I tried to keep my composure, but I was completely surprised to see her. I didn't know if she was going to approach me or what. She followed me with her eyes until we turned the corner in the parking lot. She had the two kids with her, and the little girl kept saying, "Mommy, mommy" but she didn't answer her. I didn't tell Brandy, and she just chattered away about how nice the party was going to be.

All the way home, I thought about that awkward, uncomfortable moment, and wondered if I had ever been in the same room with her before, and just didn't know who she was. I had hoped that I wasn't going to be running into her all over L.A. I was done with Tony, and I didn't need any reminders of him, including his wife and kids. Brandy kept asking me if I was thinking about Brent because I was so deep in thought. I just told her yes, but if it were Hypnotiq, I would've told the truth. Brandy had a low tolerance for bullshit, and I didn't even want to open that can of worms. She would bash me for stressing over a married man, and tell me to just forget about him. Brandy would say it just like that, like it was easy.

Brandy was going to drop me at home, but I told her to just let me get my car, and I would help her unload all of the groceries. I got my car, and followed her home. We took all of the refrigerated and frozen food out, and left the paper items in her car. I was starting to get hungry, so I asked Brandy what she had to eat. We ended up eating some leftover fried Snapper, and I made some fries. After we ate, we put *Baby Boy* in, and fell asleep on the couch.

I woke up when Lorenzo called Brandy's phone. They were supposed to go bowling with his family, and he wanted to know what time she would be ready. Brandy invited me, but I told her I was going home to relax.

"Come on, girl, it will be fun."

"It sounds like it, but I got home late from my date last night. You guys go and have fun."

"I still think you should go. Why sit in the house alone?"

I couldn't help but think that she thought I would get lonely, and call Tony. I felt like I was taking part in an intervention.

"What time are you guys going?"

"8 o'clock! Oh, you're going to have so much fun!"

"Okay, well let me go run my errands, so that I'll be ready. What bowling alley are you guys going to?"

"We're going to Hollywood Bowl. Want us to come and get you?"

She was sweet, but more than that, she wanted to make sure that I wasn't flaking on her.

"You guys can come get me. That's cool."

"We'll be there at 7:30, so be ready. I'll call you around 7."

I got my stuff together, grabbed a soda on my way out the door, and hugged Brandy at my car. She expressed her delight in the fact that I was making positive changes in my life, and that she was always there for me.

"Mia, I know we don't always see eye to eye, but I only want what's best for you, and not necessarily what you want. Sometimes the things that we think we want are not good for us. I couldn't be your friend in good faith, and watch you keep bumping your head and not say anything."

"Awww…thank you girl! I'm a work in progress, so don't give up on me!"

"Just know that I love you, and I'm always here for you."

"Thanks sweetie!"

I was literally blown away by her thoughtful words as we embraced. Brandy was my friend and I loved her, but at times I felt like she was too idealistic and a tad bit judgmental about my life. She wasn't a hater like the girls at the club, and she never called me a home-wrecker, she was just being my friend. In the past, I had a tendency to shield her from some of the tawdry things in my life because I felt that she couldn't take it, and more importantly, I didn't think I could take it. I needed a friend, not my mother, so I didn't share a whole lot with her. I decided that I was going to be more patient with her, and remember that she wasn't a jaded stripper, so things that were everyday for me were shocking to her.

I left Brandy's and stopped at Target to buy tampons, razors, and laundry detergent, but I ended up spending $86. When I got home, I cleaned out my work bag, and washed a couple of loads. I was tired of looking at the same shit, so I pulled out new costumes and shoes. I threw away an empty eyelash case, body spray container, and a tampon wrapper. When the locker room got crowded, sometimes it was easier to throw trash in my bag instead of pushing my way through a locker room full of girls to the bathroom.

I found some phone numbers, bobby pins, safety pins, and a few dollar bills at the bottom of the bag. It smelled like smoke, liquor, sweat, throw-up, body spray, and burnt hair from the flat iron. The bag was through, so it went in the trash. I didn't want it to smell up the apartment, so I put it outside.

Walking downstairs to dump the trash, my knees made sounds like pecans in a nutcracker. I called them stripper knees. When I walked, my knees clacked and crunched, and if anyone was anywhere near me, they could hear the cartilage fighting a violent battle below the surface. My legs and feet used to be pretty, but now I had keloids and scars from scraping a nail, a piece of hard tile, and glass.

My feet had begun to spread like a pregnant woman, and my ankles became thicker. I got corns on my toes for squishing them through tight, strappy sandals and patent leather knee boots. Walking around on six-inch heels for eight and nine hours was bad on the knees, and pumping my ass up and down on all fours didn't help either. Sometimes my feet would just become numb or tingly in the middle of my shift, and I would have to take my shoes off and massage them.

The skin on the bottom of my feet had become tougher, and the skin was thicker. I had calluses, and if I didn't get a pedicure every week, my feet would look like I had walked barefoot from here to New York. I wasn't exactly sure of the damage that I had done, but I knew that I was extremely hard on my body. The knees were already vulnerable, and mine were injured almost as badly as a 350-pound linebacker, or a center on a basketball team. It came with the territory, and to make that money, you had to immerse yourself completely into the game, feet first...

CHAPTER 20

Brandy and Lorenzo came to pick me up at 7:45, and we headed towards the bowling alley. I had talked to Brent, and he had to attend a business dinner. He was in the middle of a contract negotiation, and the singer wanted to get some food in a nice sit-down restaurant. I hadn't heard of Shawna, but apparently she could sing, so the label was bending over backwards to sign her. A few other executives were joining them, and he expected to be gone for a few hours. I loved to hear him talk about work because he was proud, and it was better than talking about my line of work. I wasn't ashamed to be a dancer, but I wasn't exactly proud either.

We pulled up to the bowling alley, and Lorenzo saw some of his relatives in the parking lot. They hugged and kissed, talking and laughing loudly; I could tell they were a close, loving family. My family was pretty tight, but there was a lot of gossiping, hating, and competition. People talked behind each other's back like they weren't even related. It was sad really, and I preferred to hang out with my friend's families rather than my own. Lorenzo's family gave me and Brandy love, and we moved the party inside. Lorenzo had a really cute cousin, but he brought his girl that was just alright looking. They both were looking at me, and she knew like I knew that I could get him if I wanted to, but I was trying to turn over a new leaf. Lucky for her ass.

My bowling bag and shoes were at my mom's house, so I went up to the counter to get some rental shoes when I saw this chick staring at me. I didn't recognize her, but she was all in my shit. Somebody walked up and stood right next to her, it was Camille. I had just seen the bitch earlier at Costco, and now she was at the bowling alley? L.A. can't be that small. I kept handling my business, and walked over to Brandy.

"Girl, you're not going to believe this shit, but Tony's wife and her girl were mean-mugging me at the counter!"

"What? I can't believe she's here."

"I saw her earlier when we were leaving Costco, but it was for just a second. I'm just tripping that she's in here right now. What are the fucking odds?"

"Do you want us to take you home?"

"I'm not running from that bitch. I'm the one that did her the favor by telling her about her man. She should be thanking me!"

"Try to ignore them. Don't make eye contact."

"Shit, her and her girl were making eye contact with me!"

Brandy pulled my hand, and we went to the bathroom.

"Girl, just breathe. We're going to go back out there, and pretend they're not there."

"I'm not tripping. I know one thing, I am bloated, cramping, and irritable. Those bitches better leave me the fuck alone because I am not in the mood!"

We were checking our hair and makeup when the door opened, and there stood Camille and her girl. They walked behind us, and the friend started popping off.

"Is that the bitch?"

"That's her!"

My blood was boiling as I turned around to face my ex boyfriend's wife.

"Do you have something to say to me? I gave your husband back, so what's your fucking problem?"

"You fucking bitch!"

The friend lunged at me, and almost knocked Camille to the ground. She pulled my hair, and tried to swing me around the bathroom. Brandy got knocked into the sink and back of her head hit the mirror, shattering the glass sending sharp chunks crashing in the sink and on the floor. Brandy screamed, and ran to get security, but while she was gone, the two of them took turns punching and kicking the shit out of me. Camille started punching me in the stomach, and I dropped to my knees. I jumped to my feet and grabbed Camille, banged her up against the wall, and started squeezing the shit out of her neck. She was coughing and choking, squealing like a pig. The friend grabbed me from behind and wrestled me to the ground.

As I was lying on my back, the friend was holding my arms down on either side of me. Camille was calling me all kinds of bitches, and yelling that I was trying to kill her. She sat her big ass on my pelvis, and started slapping me in the face like a little girl. I gave her one good right to her dome, and she fell off of me. I scrambled to get up before the friend got at me.

Camille rose to her feet with the look of a mad woman. They had me hemmed up, but I was swinging on both of them. I hit one of them in the nose, and punched another in the stomach. One of them threw me against the stall door, and I fell on the toilet. Before she could come in, I jumped up and slammed the door in the friend's face, and she howled like a wolf as blood came pouring from her mouth

I flew out of the stall, and Camille jumped on my back, and dropped me to the ground. She spit in my face, and I tried to scratch her face off. We were wrestling around when security came in to break it up. Everybody was swinging, and there was blood and hair all over the floor. The mirror was broke, and the sink was full of shattered pieces. Brandy kept calling my name, but I was like a crazed animal; I wanted to kill them.

The security guards had called LAPD, and a few minutes after they dragged us out of the bathroom, I was sitting in the back of a squad car. Everybody in the bowling alley stopped what they were doing, and stared at us as we had walked through the lobby, handcuffed, bloody, scratched, swollen, clothes and hair fucked up. Brandy followed me out, but the cops wouldn't even listen to her. Camille asked them to call Tony, and he came speeding through the parking lot within minutes. Because the cops were on his dick, they asked Camille if she wanted to press charges against *me*, but she said no.

After about 30 minutes, the cops finally came over to ask me what happened. I told them that I was in the bathroom, the two females came in talking shit, and they whooped my ass, two on one. They asked if I wanted to press charges, and I said no. I got a couple of good licks in and the shit was over, I didn't give a fuck. The cops let me out of the car, and removed the handcuffs from my red, puffy hands.

When I looked at Tony, he dropped his head and wouldn't even look at me as I stepped out of the cop car. Camille was crying and holding onto Tony for dear life, no doubt her friend got her into some shit that she really wasn't down for. Her friend was a big mouth rat, and I couldn't imagine the two of them hanging out. They had probably known each other since high school, but the friend had no class. If Camille wanted to fight me, she had her chance at the gym. When we met that first time, she was calm and appreciative that I was honest with her, I allowed her to put her nagging mind to rest. Tonight, she wasn't that same humble woman, she was out for blood, but I think her messy girl got her juiced, and she got ahead of herself. She couldn't even fight, if she saw me one on one, I would've mopped her Chanel ass all over that pissy bowling alley bathroom floor. I was walking towards Lorenzo's car when Camille's friend yelled "bitch" across the parking lot. I yelled "fuck you" and kept it moving.

I apologized a million times to Lorenzo and his family, but I'm sure they still thought of me as a trouble-making stripper. How could Brandy explain...*she used to fuck with this married guy, and his wife was still tripping*...I had embarrassed Brandy, Lorenzo, his family, and myself. I came close to being arrested on two counts of assault all because I fucked with a married man.

As we were on the way back to my apartment, Brandy asked if I wanted her to come in, and help me clean myself up. I told her that I would be fine, but in the back of my mind, I already knew that I was calling Hypnotiq to calm my nerves. I could feel a speech on the tip of Brandy's tongue, and I wasn't in the mood for the motherly routine.

I walked in the door, and immediately went to look at the damage. Wow! I had thin, swollen cuts and red bruises on my face and neck, my hair was a ratty mess, and my sexy new top was ripped. When I saw the blood on my True Religion jeans, I snatched them off and threw them in the washer with cold water and a ton of Tide.

I had already decided when Tony refused to look at me in the parking lot that I was going to call him and tell him about his self. Maybe it was childish, but I had to tell him how fucked up that shit was; his wife and her girl double-teamed me when I didn't even say shit to them. He didn't answer the first time I called, but I hung up and called again. It went straight to voicemail. A few minutes later, he called me back.

"What the fuck was that?" I was heated.

"Look Mia, Camille told me she saw you at Costco and you were pointing and laughing at her with your girl. She said that when she saw you at the bowling alley, you were talking shit."

"Why would I do that? I fucked her husband! Why would *I* be mad?"

"Maybe because I stopped seeing you."

"Yeah, but I'm the one that told her what was really going on. If I was trying to hold onto you so bad, why would I admit to fucking you?"

"I can't answer that. I had to leave the house to call you. She's still pissed off, but she and Leanne are at the house cleaning up. When I got the call from LAPD, I was scared, but when I saw you guys, I wanted to laugh because the shit looked funny. All of you guys in separate police cars looking hella mad!"

He started laughing, and I thought about how we looked like a couple of high school girls fighting over the first string quarterback in the girl's locker room. It was funny, but I didn't feel like joining him in laughter. I wanted to keep my mad face for a little while longer.

"You need to check your wife though. If she steps to me again, it's on. She needs to check your ass. She's fucking with me when you're the one that she needs to be mad at."

"Like I said, she said that you were fucking with her."

"And you believed that shit? You were just a fuck, I don't need to play silly games with your wife. I don't get down like that."

I had almost convinced myself that I didn't care when in reality I cared a lot more than I wanted to.

"I don't know what to believe."

"Whatever."

"Do you miss me?"

"What the fuck are you talking about? I almost caught a case from fucking with you! Are you serious?"

"Tell me you don't, and I'll hang up." This nigga had done some reverse psychology on my ass, and it worked.

"Why are you fucking with me? You stopped seeing *me* remember?"

"I had to do that, but you still didn't answer my question."

"I don't miss you."

Of course I did, but fuck him. He hung up on me. My mouth was wide open when I closed my phone. I was sitting perfectly still in a state of shock when he called right back.

"I'm giving you one last chance…"

We both fell out laughing. That was what I missed the most about him. He was funny and he never took anything too seriously. I could never stay mad at him because he had a way of laughing everything off, even when I was seeing red, he always knew how to calm me down.

"You don't have no fucking sense!"

"That's what you like about me. So what up? You miss me or what?"

"A little."

"A little huh? I'm around the corner from your spot. Want me to stop by to check your wounds?"

"Wounds? You need to check their wounds. I was handling mine with two bitches! What?!"

"I'm getting ready to pass you up."

"Come on! Shit!"

That was the only time that I have ever been relieved that I was on my period. I knew that he would try to fuck and complicate shit even more, but I was safe. He was knocking at my door five minutes later. I opened the door, and he fell out laughing as soon as he saw me.

"Damn!"

"Fuck you. I bet those bitches look a lot worse. I'm hopping in the shower, so just sit down and watch t.v."

"Need any help?"

"I'm cool, and besides my Aunt Flo is visiting."

"I can still help you wash your back or something."

"I thought you were scared at the sight of a little blood."

Not only did Tony forget my name when I was on my period, but I wouldn't even fuck me if I was getting ready to start in the next day or two because he was afraid that it may come down. He also wouldn't fuck when I was just ending my period. He wanted everything nice and clean.

"Your back isn't bleeding is it?"

"Very funny, I'll call you when I'm ready."

I walked in the bathroom and started the shower water. I took off all my clothes, and tied my hair up in a ponytail. I snatched the old tampon out, and inserted a new one. It had only been in for two hours, but there was blood on the string. I grabbed the manicure scissors out of the cabinet, and cut the string off. My hair was fucked up, so I just stepped in without my shower cap. I stood under the warm water, and let it run all over my tender face. I washed my whole body, and called Tony in. He walked in, and pulled back the shower curtain. He stood outside of the tub looking me up and down. I told him to focus on my back.

I gave him the towel, and he rubbed it effortlessly over my back. His hand dipped to the small of my back, where he moved the towel in a small circular motion. Tony caressed my ass with the soapy, wet towel, one cheek and then the other. He poked between my legs until I opened up wide. He slowly dragged the towel along my pussy until I thought I would scream. He dropped the towel on the bottom of the tub, and turned me around to face him.

Water was running off of my nipples, and he took one of them in his mouth. He nibbled on my right nipple, and then the left. He squeezed my tits together and viciously sucked all over them, making loud slurping noises. Tony stepped into the shower, grabbed my face, and seductively jammed his limp, juicy tongue in my mouth. I tried to hold back at first, but then I gave in completely. He was fully dressed, and dripping wet standing underneath the shower head looking more sexy than he ever had.

"You feel like giving me some head?"

I instantly dropped to my knees, and fumbled with his belt buckle and zipper. I dropped his pants, and yanked his dick out of the top of his boxers. Just looking at his dick fucked me up. I pulled it kind of hard because he liked that. I fingered his balls, and put them in my mouth. I massaged his nuts with my tongue and jaws until he was squirming around like a newborn baby.

Tony loved for me to politely bite on his nipples, but tonight I put a little bit more tooth on them because after all, his wife did try to beat my ass. After his boxers were down around his ankles, I ran my mouth around his inner thighs and stomach until I felt that I had teased him enough. I put my entire mouth on his bulging dick, and he let out a loud moan. I slowly moved my tongue up and down the length of his manhood. I jacked him off with my mouth. He started thrusting his hips, and forcing his dick in my mouth to a rhythmic beat. Tony wanted to cum, so I quickly let his dick go.

"What you doing?" He was breathing hard, and his heart was beating through his chest.

"I want some dick."

"But...I thought you said you were on your period."

"I don't give a fuck. If you want to get off, I need that dick inside of me."

"When did you start?"

"Today is my last day. It's really light." Lying bitch.

"Where are we going to do it?"

"We can stay right here in the shower baby. You won't see anything. Turn your head."

He was not happy about it, but his dick was a sword, and he would've agreed to anything to get me to finish him off. I dug the tampon out of my pussy, and threw it in the toilet. Tony was fumbling through his pockets for a condom. Did he know he was coming over here for some pussy? Or did he have a condom for somebody else?

I took the condom from his hand, and ripped the top of the package off. I pulled out the condom, and slid it on his beautiful dick. I got up off my knees, and poked my ass out until I felt his dick poking me. I grabbed it, and stuck it in. He was moving around before it was even all the way in. After a couple thrusts, it was in, and we both were rocking our hips like we hadn't fucked in years. I wasn't going to cum like that, so I started rubbing my clit. Tony was fucking me like he was mad at me, mad for whooping his wife's ass, and I loved it.

"Yeah baby, I beat the shit out of your wife! Show me how mad you are!"

He was fucking me harder and harder, and I looked down and saw a crimson trail in the tub. I wanted to change his focus before he changed his mind. I stood up, and faced him. I leaned back towards the shower wall, and lifted my right leg to rest on the edge of the tub. I shoved his dick back inside of me, and it was in the right place to make me cum. I moved with him as our passion exploded together.

I put Tony's clothes in the dryer, and we sat down on the couch. He was wearing my pink terry cloth robe, and he turned me down cold when I said that I wanted a picture. He teased me about dropping more blood than I said I had in me. I told him I wanted some dick, so a girl's gotta do what a girl's gotta do! I was reaching for the remote when he grabbed my hand, and told me that he wanted to talk. I figured that he was going to tell me that we just had a one time deal, and nothing had changed.

"I wanted you to know that I didn't come over here to fuck you, and walk out of your life. I really have missed you."

"Have you?"

"Yes, I have. I was going to call you in the next day or two, but then this thing happened…"

"Good point. You want to get back with me *after* your wife and I have actually put hands on?"

"You guys had a fight. It's out of her system. If she sees you again, she probably wouldn't even say anything to you."

"What are we talking about?"

"I want us to have more of a one on one relationship than we had before. How does that sound?"

"We could barely go out in public before, it has to be even worse now, and you want to be closer?"

"I really wasn't careful the first time. When I was dealing with you before, I was dealing with other chicks, and all of that made Camille very suspicious. I cut everybody off, so it would be just me and you."

"And Camille."

"Well of course. I'm not trying to be messy, I just like hanging out with you. You're funny, and you like to have a good time. You're my friend plus I really like fucking you. *Really* like fucking you."

"So, let me get this straight. I fuck the best, so you got rid of the other chicks?"

"Yeah."

"If I was fucking you so good, why did you need those other bitches?"

"Come on now! You know how I get down. I'm not a one-woman man."

"You had your wife and, and you had me, so when did you ever have only one woman?"

"It was just something to do when I was with my boys. It didn't mean anything."

"Whatever Tony. Okay, so your wife gets all of the benefits, and I get what?"

"Well, I wanted to talk to you about that too. I want to help you out a little bit. If you want to stop dancing, I can get you a job at Ron's club."

If I wanted to ask for anything, now was the time or forever hold my peace. Now was the time because I had him right where I wanted him. There wouldn't be much room for negotiation after tonight.

"That might be cool. I need to think about all of this. A lot of shit popped off tonight. Besides, I just met someone." Oops, I didn't mean to be that honest.

"What? Who?"

"My friend set me up."

"You want to be with this nigga or what?" Nigga? Not quite.

"I just met him."

"Well, I'm not tripping if you got somebody on the side because I have a wife, but I would like you to be discreet. Don't mention my name to anybody at the club. If you jump off, you better use condoms." I felt like a teenager living in my mother's house all over again.

"Let's finish talking tomorrow. My face hurts. I need to take something so I can sleep."

"You need me to get you something?"

"I want some ice cream, but I think it's too cold for my face. Can you get me some Hennessey?"

"Yeah, I'll get it."

Tony was rummaging through my cabinets trying to find the glasses as I lay my head on one of the pillows. I was getting sleepy, but my head was pounding. Tony finally brought my drink, and I sat up to take a sip. He sat down, and I lay my head on his lap. He had offered me a relationship and a job just when I was trying to get him out of my system. I thought about the pros and cons until my face wore me out. I stretched out on the couch, and Tony stroked my hair and rubbed my back until I fell asleep with my head in his lap. He must have fell asleep too because an hour later, he carried me into my bed, and covered me up.

Tony lay in my bed next to me for what seemed like most of the night, even though I knew it wasn't. It felt really good to have a man in my bed without any fucking going on, I felt safe, secure, and cared for. Tony held me close to his body, and I felt his heartbeat beating on my back. I felt him kiss my cheek, and then he got up out of the bed. He covered me up, and let himself out of the front door.

CHAPTER 21

I had on dark shades, a baseball cap, and concealer on my bruises. My face felt twice as big as it looked, my whole body was sore and weary from the rumble that I took part in. I had been a stunt woman last night pulling, kicking, and punching my way out of the bowling alley bathroom. As I sat at our table at Jerry's Deli in mid-Wilshire telling Hypnotiq the story of last night's activities, her shocked expression was written all over her face. She couldn't believe that the three of us were actually fighting in the bathroom of a bowling alley. I told her that she better believe it because I had scars to prove it. When I told her about the second part of the story featuring Tony and a shower, she almost fainted.

"No you didn't!"

"I couldn't help it. I was gone once I talked to him on the phone. I thought I had moved on, but I guess not."

"So what are you going to do?"

Our food was ready. We ordered grilled chicken sandwiches with sliced avocado and Swiss cheese. I ordered a Neopolitan shake, she ordered a chocolate one, and we both got fries. I couldn't even remember the last time that I had eaten, and Jerry's was the perfect way to reintroduce myself to food.

"I'm going to continue fucking his ass!"

"Really? Just be careful okay? We now know that his wife and her friends are fucking crazy!"

"Well like he said last night, we just have to be more careful. Remember, all of this started because he called my house from his home phone? I don't know girl. There is a serious attraction there, and I guess I don't want to deny myself.

And to tell you the truth, his wife made this a competition. I guess I want to fuck her the same time I'm fucking him."

"So, her fighting you at the bowling alley made you want to fight for Tony?"

"Well not exactly, but it sweetens the pot a little. I was trying to do the right thing for her and myself because I didn't have to tell her shit at the gym that day. I felt sorry for her, and I thought that Tony was an asshole for cheating on her, especially after she had just had a baby, but then her and her girl want to gang up on me? She's fucking with the wrong bitch!"

"So, are you going to stop dancing or what?"

"Hell yeah! You know I've been talking about getting out of the game. Girl, I could be a manager or hostess or something. Maybe I can talk to him about getting you something! I want to have a good-bye party at the club in the next few weeks. I haven't even told Tony that I would agree to get back with him, and I'm planning farewell parties!"

"Well, we'll see. How about you get in the door first, and we'll take it from there. Girl, if this is what you want, I am happy for you. I will always have your back regardless. Have you talked to Brent?"

"He had left a message last night while I was in the back of the cop car, but I haven't called him back yet."

"What are you waiting for? Is it because of Tony?"

"I don't know what I'm doing. Brent is out of my league anyway. What does he want with a stripper? A black stripper at that. He ain't taking me home to mama!"

"Who knows where it could lead. Are you going out with him again?"

"Yeah, he's cool. I'm going to call him in a little bit. You happy now?"

"I'm not trying to force the situation, it's just that Brent is a good guy, and I think that you should at least give him a shot."

"I'm calling him! Now let's eat!"

We grubbed like we hadn't eaten the whole week. Brent called while I was walking to the restroom. I stood in the stall, locked the door behind me, and grabbed the phone.

"Hello?"

"Hey, this is Brent. How are you?"

"I'm good, and you?"

"Cool. I was getting ready to grab something to eat, and I wanted to see if you were hungry."

"That is so sweet, but Hypnotiq...uh Renee and I are at Jerry's Deli. Where are you going?"

"I was thinking about Mexican. I know you said that was one of your favorites."

He was already taking note of my favorites, and I was pleasantly surprised. Tony always chose the food when we ate together.

"Oh, if I hadn't just eaten I would've met you."

"Well, what are you doing when you leave there? Maybe we could catch a movie or something."

Within a few seconds, I had to figure out what I wanted from Brent. I fucked Tony last night, and we were talking about starting our relationship up again. I didn't want to lead Brent on because he had already been hurt by his ex-wife, and he really was a sweet person. I already knew that I was making a mistake.

"Yeah, we can do that. Call me after you get done eating."

"Okay, I'll call you in about an hour or so."

We hung up, and I threw the phone in my bag. I pulled my sweats down, and squatted over the toilet. There was blood all over my panties, and the pad was full, so I had to change it. Fucking Tony last night forced my trickle to come down like a flood. I was cramping, and I really just wanted to climb in my bed, and start the day over.

Hypnotiq and I parted ways, and I flew home. I turned off both of my phones, and lay in the bed. My stomach was full, and I fell asleep right away. When I woke up three hours later, I felt a little better. I checked my cell phone and saw that Brent and Tony had called me. I called Tony first just in case he wanted to hook up. His voicemail came on. *Family time.* I hung up without leaving a message. I called Brent, and he was at home. *Available.* He had already called the movies, and said he was just waiting on me. It was still light outside, and I didn't want Brent to see my face. I made up an excuse, so that we could go to a later show, and he was cool with it. Tony beeped in, and I told Brent that I had to call him back.

"What up Tyson? You cool?"

"Not really. My whole body is fucked up, my face is sore, and I have cramps."

"Damn! Anything else?"

"You asked!"

"We never finished our conversation from last night. You still fucking with me or what?"

"Why should I?"

"You know what I got!"

"You know I missed fucking with you."

"I know you did. You think you'll feel better in a couple of days?" What was he up to?

"I should be. Why?"

"We're playing up in the Bay Saturday, so I'm calling to see if you want to roll. We're staying the night too."

I felt a tingling sensation travel from the hair on my arms, across my chest causing my heart to beat wildly at the thought of having Tony all to myself for a whole day. His wife fucked up by bringing the drama to me because now it was on and popping. I played cool.

"When are you going?"

"We leave the day after tomorrow, and come back the next day. Are you still going to be dropping blood, or are you going to be cool?"

"I'll be cool."

"Ok, so let me call my travel agent so I can get your tickets, and I'll bring them by tonight or in the morning. Can you get one of your girls to drop you at the airport?"

"I'm sure Hypnotiq can."

"Ok cool. I'll call you before I come through."

We hung up, and the smile on my face was as bright as Hen-a-C's new gold diamond-cut grill. I ran in my room to pick out my clothes. I pulled out my sexiest, tightest jeans and tops, high heeled sandals, and threw them in my fake Louis Vuitton overnight bag with my new Nikes. As I took out a couple of g-strings and matching bras, I decided to bring along a piece of trampy lingerie.

Thank goodness I wasn't dropping as much blood as I was the day before. All I could think about was fucking the shit out of Tony in an anonymous, out-of-town hotel room, and I knew that he wasn't letting me get away with another night of blood-fucking. From the bathroom, I reached for the tooth-paste, toothbrush, mouth wash, floss, face soap, moisturizer, makeup, tampons, pads, pantiliners, body wash, body spray, deodorant, lotion, and a shower cap.

All of that went into my overnight bag, and I left it next to the sink so that I could use everything up until I left. I looked at my do rag in the drawer, but I wasn't wearing that in front of Tony, so I knew my hair would be a mess the next day. I would just have to work it out; it reminded me to take my flat iron out of my work bag, and put it in the carry-on.

Next, I had to hit the nail ship for a fill, pedicure, and waxing. Sitting in traffic on the 10, I called Hypnotiq to make sure that she could drop me off the next morning. She was shocked by the whole thing, but she said no problem. It was hard for both of us to believe that Tony was taking me out of town so soon after the championship bout.

All of a sudden this beautiful, black bitch was on the side of me in a black Bentley coupe. She was shocking. Her long, black hair was blowing in the wind. She he had on some white Christian Dior glasses and flawless makeup. Her hands were on top of the steering wheel, and the fat ring on her finger glistened as the light hit it. I looked at her, and smirked because that was what I thought Tony's wife would look like, but instead she looked like a basic house-wife. I expected sexy, but she was motherly, frumpy, self-sacrificing, boring. This bitch probably didn't have kids, she looked too sexy. She had a really good job, or a really good husband. I wanted what she had. The rules of the game had changed; I was going to get what I wanted from Tony this time around. Every move had to be thoughtful, and most of all deliberate.

I was instantly irritated when I walked into the nail shop because it was filled with people that didn't have anywhere special to go, and I had a timeline. After I told the woman what I needed, she whisked me to the back for the wax-ing. I pulled my sweats down, and hopped on the table. The wax lady walked in, and within minutes she was ripping hair from all over my body. Irritated, red, and oily, I went back to the chairs and waited for my other services.

Two young, black chicks were having a conversation about college classes and the cost of textbooks, and I became envious. I always wanted to go to col-lege, but I felt intimidated, even more so after I started dancing. No one would take me seriously, and the girls at the club would definitely hate. Anytime a girl started nursing or cosmetology classes, the haters would show their horns.

Misery loves company, and the girls that knew they couldn't do anything else but dance were so jealous of girls that had goals and dreams that didn't involve music videos, B movies, and chasing bachelor parties. Now that Tony was hooking me up with a legitimate job, maybe I would get my feet wet with a class or two at the junior college next semester.

The ladies wanted to do my pedicure first, and then give me a fill, but I told them I had somewhere to go and I would come back later, so they ended up reluctantly doing both at the same time. They were so full of shit. I watched a girl getting a fill, and I wondered why the owners didn't give customers the same surgical masks that the nail techs wore. Whatever poisons they were try-ing to keep out of their bodies were invading ours, but I guess they didn't care. I heard them speaking Vietnamese to each other, and I wondered what they were saying. They would get louder, and with all of them talking at the same time, I began to think they were probably wondering what each other was say-ing just like me.

Finally, I was back in my car. I stopped at a drug store on the way home to buy a douche; I had to get it because I hated that brownish-black blood and slight stinch that signaled the end of my period. They gave me birth control pills after the abortion, and I had been taking them so my period was lighter, and I didn't have to worry about the possibility of getting pregnant again. I didn't know if I was going to keep filling the prescription, but it was cool for the time being.

While I waited in line, Brent called my phone, but I let it go to voicemail. I had forgotten to call him back after Tony mentioned the away game. I didn't know what to say to him, and I didn't feel like lying standing in line with a vin-egar and water douche in my hand. I had planned on calling him before I went to bed to tell him that I took some medicine for the cramps, and woke up late. As I stood in line, I wondered what I was going to eat. Fish tacos came to mind, so I stopped at Rubio's for three tacos.

I went home and nuked them in the microwave for a minute. I got right up and finished packing, and then cleaned the apartment spotlessly. Brent came to mind, and I called to explain my predicament. Just as I had expected, he was forgiving and concerned. I almost felt guilty running out of town with my married boyfriend. I told him that I was going to be working a lot of hours over the next couple of days, but that I would call him soon. He asked me if I needed him to bring me anything, but I told him I was cool.

I called myself sitting on the couch for a second to catch my breath, but I fell asleep. I got up a few hours later, and dragged myself onto the bed. Just as I snuggled in, Tony called to say that he was bringing the tickets, but I couldn't bring myself to get all dolled up, so I threw on my robe, and waited on the couch for him to ring the bell. I was so sleepy, and kept fighting it until I finally heard his truck. I opened the door, and he made a smart comment about my homeless appearance, and we laughed. He gave me the tickets, and told me that he would see me in Oakland the day after tomorrow.

Tony said that he was sending a driver to get me, so to look for a guy near the baggage claim holding a sign with my name on it. He was going to drive me to the hotel, and Tony was going to meet me there. He was also going to bring the tickets to the game. I was the bitch in the Bentley. I gave him a hug and thanked him. I stuffed the tickets in my purse, and fell asleep in minutes.

The next day, I ran a couple of errands, worked out, and basically waited for the fun to begin.

CHAPTER 22

The plane trip was uneventful. When the flight attendant came by me to ask what I wanted to drink and hand me some peanuts, I was unconscious. I hated the take-off, so I always closed my eyes as if I could pretend that I was somewhere else. Something about the plane going from 0–200 miles an hour in a few seconds caused me to question my reoccurring decision to trust air travel amidst the rumors of drunken pilots in the cock pit. Whenever the nose of the plane started to climb, and my whole body felt like it was being pulled backwards by a tremendous force, I would say a quick prayer. The engines were loud, the plane always rocked slightly from side to side, and the ride wasn't fluid until we had reached about 10,000 feet. I guess the turbulence is greater the closer the plane is to the ground, but after about 25,000 feet you almost forgot you were literally flying above the clouds.

I had dozed off shortly after takeoff. I jumped and my eyes flew open when the person sitting next to me came back to his seat. I never understood the kind of people that ran to the bathroom as soon as the pilot turned the seat belt light off. Why didn't they use the bathroom in the airport? The bathrooms on planes were ridiculous; they were tight, cramped little areas with a stainless steel toilet filled with blue water. You couldn't even turn in a small circle without hitting the wall or counter. In my entire life, I have only been in about three airplane bathrooms, and that was only because I flew for five plus hours.

Since I was up, I took advantage of my window seat. As I stared straight out the window, the breathtaking horizon captured my attention. The clouds underneath the plane were fluffy and white; the sky was blue like a newborn baby boy's room. The sun was playful, skipping over the clouds with excitement. I felt peaceful and safe. My mind drifted over thoughts of Tony, the club, my new job, college, and a more secure future.

When I got back to L.A., I planned on setting some goals for myself, and taking hold of my life that had been spinning out of control. I don't think I ever felt like I deserved more, but suddenly I began to see the insecurities that had plagued my growth. All of a sudden, I felt the moment when the plane began to descend. It seemed as if the pilot was braking as the plane seemed to slow down, and then dip. I could imagine the nose of the plane pointing downward towards the surface of the earth. The engines got louder, and I could hear the wing flaps mechanically rising up. We quickly lost thousands of feet within about 10 minutes.

It only took about an hour to get to Oakland, but by the time I got there, I was ready to have fun. I planned on having a glorious time, and leaving the drama behind in the city of angels. I was in the Yay Area! When the plane landed, people jumped up trying to scramble for their overhead luggage, but they couldn't go anywhere. I always stayed in my seat until the line was actually moving. I got up when it was my turn, and I retrieved my bag from the compartment on top of my seat. I walked through the aisle, and the pilots and a flight attendant told me to have a wonderful day. I wished them the same.

I found my way down to the baggage claim, and spotted a tall white man holding a sign with my name on it. I wished that the bitch in the Bentley could see me now! I approached him, and he asked me if I was Mia. I followed him out of the doors, across the parking lot to the back door of a shiny, black Lincoln Continental with limo tint. He unlocked the doors, and opened my door for me. He put my bag in the trunk and scurried to the driver's door.

"How was your flight ma'am?"

"It was cool."

"So, I'm taking you to the Courtyard Marriott?"

"I'm not sure really." I felt like a ho, I didn't even know where I was being taken.

"I was just checking, but I have the directions written right here. I'll have you there in a minute."

I sat quietly looking out the window and just like he said, we were there in a minute. He pulled the car up to the front, and hopped out to open my door. I stepped out, and he glided to the trunk to get my bag. He ushered me into the lobby, and asked me where I wanted my bag. I thanked him and said that I would take it. He sort of lingered, and I realized he was silently begging for a tip. I reached in my purse and gave him $5. He seemed dejected, but he thanked me anyway. For all I knew, Tony had included his tip in the bill, so I wasn't tripping. He should've just been grateful for whatever he got; he only drove me one mile! I told the librarian at the front desk my name, she gave me my key, and pointed towards the elevator.

The room wasn't as glamorous as I had hoped or expected, but it was neat and clean. It wasn't Vegas. I called Brandy and Hypnotiq to tell them that I had made it safely. I put my bag in the closet, and pulled the comforter back on the bed. I never sat or slept under the first two blankets because my friend used to work in a hotel, and she said they never washed them because the management didn't want them to fade. Once they washed them a couple of times, they looked old and they had to throw them away. My girl told me that they would find wet cum stains, blood, spit, throw up…anything you could imagine on those blankets. I tell everybody I know to pull the blankets back, and sit on the sheets. That was the only layer of the bed that was washed every single time.

I turned the t.v. on, and pulled my phone out to call Tony.

"You made it? How was the flight?"

"It was cool. I just got to the room."

"I'm almost done with practice, and I'll be by there. Are you hungry?"

"Starving. I was sleep when they handed peanuts out on the plane."

"Okay, I'll grab some In N Out on the way over. I'll call you when I get there."

We hung up, and I flipped the channels until I found Jerry Springer. I listened to the tales of men cheating on their women with other men, mothers sleeping with their daughter's husbands, and sisters sleeping with their brothers. There were a couple of fights, and the audience members made cruel comments to the guests. I turned the channel before Jerry's final thoughts. I didn't see the point of him giving "thoughtful" advice after he just spent an hour laughing and making fun of the twisted lives of his guests. Jerry always ended the show with "Take care of yourself…and each other" but if people truly did that, there would be no Jerry Springer Show. No one would have secrets, dirt, and general messiness. People would honor their commitments, and be honest and respectful of themselves and others.

Tony called, and I told him what I wanted a #1 well done, animal style, fries, a root beer, and a Neopolitan shake. I put on more lip gloss, combed my hair, and used Raspberry body spray on my neck and clothes. Tony was knocking on the door within 20 minutes. I opened the door, and he looked especially handsome with bags of good-smelling food. I grabbed the sodas and shakes as he stepped into the room. He put the food down, and gave me a big hug. I let him hug me and I held onto him like I hadn't seen him in forever. I was happy to get out of L.A. Tony granted me the opportunity and the means to get out of town, and just kick it. I have never believed that things happened accidentally. I had to get in that fight the other night for me to be standing there in Tony's arms. He let his arms loosely drape around my waist, and he kissed me on my forehead. I was a young teenager again.

We snatched open the bags, and grubbed. We laughed and talked like no time had passed between the night he told me good-bye until now. It had been over a month, but the feelings I had for him were as fresh as they had ever been. I truly missed him and the chemistry that we had. We were like old friends when we got together, but I also loved fucking the shit out of him. I guess that was what a successful relationship looked like except my friend was married.

After we ate, we lounged on the bed with our stomachs poked out like pot belly pigs. I kept taking deep breaths because it felt like someone was sitting on my chest, but it was all that food that I had inhaled. Soon, we looked like a couple of drugged pigs lying across the bed in peculiar positions to appease the ache and fullness of our bellies. We had dozed off until Tony's phone went off. It was one of his teammates asking where he was because they were all heading towards the arena. He told him that he was straight, and they hung up.

"I need to get over to the arena. Let me give you your ticket. Now you know to be cool right? If anyone asks who you're with, don't say any names."

"I got it." I dropped from heaven to earth as soon as the words left his lips.

"I have a car coming to get you at 6:30, the game starts at 7:30. The arena is only a few minutes away."

"I'll be ready."

"One last thing, feel like giving me a little good luck head?"

I was paying for my plane ticket, driver, and hotel room. Oh, and burger and fries. A minute ago, I wanted to suck the skin off of his dick, but the don't-mention-my-name comment chased the sexy away. I had to pretend that I wasn't fucking irritated and offended because I was going to play this situation out with some thought.

"Yeah baby, let me break you off a little something."

He was so horny that he didn't even realize that I was faking it. Actually, he may have known, but didn't give a fuck. I dropped to my knees and yanked down his sweats. Tony was caught off guard, but he liked it. I rubbed my cheek on his dick through his boxers, and I felt it grow stiff. I pulled down his shorts, and slowly rolled my tongue around his belly button. My mouth followed the trail of hair from his stomach down to his dick, and I allowed my tongue to caress the head, leaving hot wetness on the tip. I relaxed the back of my mouth, and inserted his dick all the way back to the entry of my throat. I sucked it soft, and then harder. Tony was pushing the back of my head onto his dick, but it went back too far, and I gagged a little. I had to move my head back, or his dick was going to be drowning in burgers and fries. I let his dick slowly fall out of my mouth.

"You done?"

"You said you just wanted a little. Don't you have to go?"

"Yeah, I do. Damn, that was good."

"That was just a tease. I'll take care of you later."

I wiped the spit from my mouth with the back of my hand, and slowly stood up. Tony liked talking to me while he was standing over me with a mouth full of dick. I was getting good at playing blonde. I was going to stroke his ego, dick, and whatever else to get what I wanted.

Tony left, and I hopped in the shower. I put on my Versace jeans and a cute little top, high-heeled sandals, and put on dramatic makeup. My hair was flat-ironed, so I just had to unwrap it, and comb it out. I was ready when the front desk called me to say that my car was downstairs. I grabbed my purse and a coat, and jumped in the elevator.

When the doors opened, the driver was standing by the car right in front. He was an older black man, and very knowledgeable. On the 15 minute drive, he told me about all of the celebrities and athletes that he had picked up and dropped off. He knew who was cheating, who was gay, and who fucked in the back of chauffeured cars. He asked me who I was going to see, and I knew he wasn't the type that you could exactly lie to.

Here I was a single woman being picked up from a hotel, and being driven to a basketball game all by my lonesome. Earlier, I had told him that I was from L.A., so it didn't take a rocket scientist to figure out that I was flown-in pussy, but I didn't want him to add me to his list of who's who, so I said that my best friend was getting married to a player, and they flew me in for the wedding. I stuttered thinking of an unmarried player on the team, a wedding date, and a venue. He knew I was lying, but whatever.

The driver pulled up to the parking lot attendant, and told him that he was dropping me off. They allowed him to drive up close to the front, so that I didn't have far to walk. I thanked him, and gave him the same tip I gave the last guy. He was more grateful, and I thought about what he would say about me after I left his car. I walked up the stairs to the main entry, and fished the ticket out of my purse. A security woman wanted to look in my purse for weapons, and she let me walk in.

I didn't see any decent girls. I saw a lot of mothers with their sweatshirts, jerseys, and jeans pulled up to their ribs. They wore pontytails, tennis shoes, and no makeup. I knew that I looked good, but there was absolutely no competition. I found the section that my seat was in, and the view was not impressive. I wasn't surprised because I already prepared myself, players got the worse tickets, unless you were a wife, and then you had prime seating behind the bench.

I found my seat, and watched the guys warming up. Tony was so fine. He was practicing jumpers, free throws, and doing lay-ups. He moved like silk. His arms and legs were of steel. He was beautiful.

During half-time, I walked to the clubhouse for a drink. Tony's team was winning, and he was balling. I'd like to think he was showing off for me. When I stepped into the clubhouse, I saw a few attractive females, but most of them had too much, makeup, hats, extra accessories, and braids. The Bay Area was not L.A. The girls tried too hard, and ended up wearing too much shit.

A few of the guys had on country jean suits and do rags. They looked hot and greasy. Most of the young cats had dreads with the ends dipped in red dye, gold grillz, and tall white tees that reached their knees. I saw a couple of guys that I would fuck with, but just a couple. They were tall and cute with hip hop clothes and flossy jewelry, probably hustlers or D boys judging by their glistening diamonds and arrogant swagger. I sat at the bar and ordered an apple Martini. Niggas and bitches were staring because judging by my style and expensive tastes, I was an obvious outsider sitting alone in a bar; they had no choice but to assume that I was there with one of the players. One cat was bold enough to step to me, but I shut him down so tough his boys clowned him when he got back to his table. I finished my drink, and stopped at the bathroom before I went back to my seat.

Tony's team ended up winning the game at the buzzer. I stayed in my seat because I realized that we hadn't made plans for what was supposed to happen after the game. The crowds had started moving towards the door at the end of the fourth quarter, and by now the arena was near empty. A few stragglers were down near the floor, and the janitors were cleaning up ticket stubs, snack packages, and beer cups. After about 30 minutes, my cell phone rang. Tony was in the locker room, and he told me to meet him by the elevator at the end of the tunnel. I got up and walked over there. He came out and quickly ushered me over to the player parking lot. I figured it was because he didn't want an ambitious photographer to get a picture of us, but he later said it was because he had to catch up with his boys. I didn't believe it for a minute, but I kept my mouth shut.

Tony was freshly showered and the smell of Issey Miyake eased into my space as he walked towards me. He had on Evisu jeans and shirt, platinum and diamond necklace with a cross hanging from it, and a new pair of Jordans. He had a fresh cut, and his goatee was nicely trimmed. I wanted to eat him.

"You feel like going out?"

"Yeah, that's cool."

"A couple of my teammates are going to a club in San Francisco."

"I haven't been to San Francisco in years."

"Okay, let's go because we're following them over there."

Tony always walked a few paces ahead of me, and I assumed it was because he didn't want anyone to see him with any female that wasn't his wife. I wasn't happy about it, but that was one of the aspects of our relationship that I had to accept. We walked out of the same generic doors as the fans because there might have been photographers at the tunnel where the players came out for autographs. I was getting to the point where the secrecy and the hiding were no longer sexy, it was obvious and degrading.

After we got in the car, Tony talked about the game, his super stats for the night. When he asked if I was enjoying myself so far I lied. I tried my best to convince him that I was having a good time, but the truth was that I was actually kind of bored. I never would've told him that, but I wasn't having as much fun as I thought we would. I wished that I had one of my girls with me because I was basically alone, and I missed having someone to chill with. The game was cool, but I couldn't laugh, act silly, or talk shit about how the females looked a hot mess because I was by myself.

Tony called his boy, and he met us at a gas station by the arena. We followed him and a couple of other cars to the freeway. The Bay Bridge was a beautiful sight. The toll booth had a million lanes, and I felt like we were in New York. The lights on the bridge guided us towards the city. Within a few minutes we were on the other side of the bay, driving down a narrow one-way street. All of a sudden a club appeared in the middle of the dark, deserted alley. We left the cars with the valet and quickly moved through the VIP line outside of the club.

The club was popping, as soon as we walked in people were stepping aside for Tony and me. His boys were right behind us, but it seemed like Tony kept hesitating so they could catch up. We were treated like celebrities. The bouncer grabbed the club manager, and he swept us into the VIP area and brought out bottles of champagne. The DJ was bumping rap, and the crowd was mostly black with a few Asians, whites, and Hispanics sprinkled in. I was the only female in the group, and I noticed that Tony always put space between us, so that no one could really figure out who I was with. If word got back to his wife, he could easily say that one of his boys brought a female, but not him. I hadn't planned on saying anything about it to Tony, but I couldn't help but peep his game.

Tony didn't want to dance, and I'm sure it was because our bodies would be too close. He was out of town, but not on another planet. Some of his boys went to cruise the club, and females were falling all over themselves trying to get to them. At least some of the girls were a lot cuter than I had seen earlier. A couple of them had fake tits and weaves down their backs, and I felt like I was at home. They had on cute, short, tight outfits trying to meet their new ex boyfriend. Tony was looking but he was trying to be respectful and not too obvious. At one point, Tony told me that he would be right back, and I assumed he was going to call his wife, but I didn't trip. When he walked out of the VIP, I waited a few minutes, and walked out myself.

I went to the bathroom upstairs to check my hair and makeup. The DJ was playing reggaeton, and people were sweating on the dance floor. When I walked in the bathroom, I could hear two females in separate stalls having a conversation.

"Did you see all of those tall brothas in VIP?"

"Yes I did! They have to be in the NBA. There was a game tonight, and I saw the waiter taking champagne over there."

"Well, let's get down there before somebody else gets to them first!"

"I'm not worried because I have the skills to get any man I want."

"You're so nasty!"

They started laughing, and the toilets flushed. Two ditzy Barbie dolls popped out of the stalls. They both had platinum blonde hair, fake boobs, baby clothes, and five-inch heels. They wore dark pink lipliner to make their lips look fuller, and frosty light pink lipstick. They almost looked like twins. They looked at me like they had seen a ghost. Their private conversation had been infiltrated by the enemy.

"What skills do you have?" I rudely butted in the conversation, and took them completely by surprise. If they merely thought they saw a ghost before, the devil herself had just joined them in the ladies room.

"What do you mean?"

"Well, a minute ago you said you had skills, and I was just wondering in what."

"I…we…we were just playing around. I don't want any problems."

"Well, I do have a problem." I was going to use these unsuspecting dolls for my own pleasure.

"Why?"

They both had a surprised, frightened look on their face. They didn't want to talk to me, but because I was black, they figured they better indulge me in conversation.

"Why do you white bitches come to these black clubs looking for niggas? Are you trying to piss your rich daddies off? Or do you think all of those shiny black monkeys have dicks down to their knees? It's not true you know. Some of them have dicks like little brown thumbs. You need to stick with white boys because the niggas are going to treat you like shit because deep down they don't think they deserve to be with you, so they're going to disrespect you for being with them. Get it?"

"We just came to have fun. We don't want to fight with you."

"Why do you all think that black chicks want to fight you? We don't give a fuck about you white bitches sucking all that black dick in the men's room of nightclubs. Do your thing. They might break you off, they might even marry you, but they're using you for your whiteness. You make them feel accepted, but those niggas that you get to walk you down the aisle are still cheating with the sistas. We have something that can't be duplicated. You can't relate. Just remember one thing, you can never be me."

I said what I had to say and walked out the door. I felt like I had got a life-time of bullshit off of my chest, and it felt good. When I got back to the VIP, Tony was back.

"Where did you go?"

"I was in the bathroom."

A few minutes later, I saw the two dolls making their way around the club, and I smiled like the cat that ate the bird. I saw them stop at the bar where two of Tony's teammates were ordering drinks. In a few minutes the guys walked away without numbers being exchanged. The dolls dropped their fake smiles, shrugged their shoulders, and moved on.

We hung out a little while, and I got a buzz off the champagne. Tony slipped my hand onto his hard dick, and I told him to meet me in the men's room upstairs. I left first, and he was a few seconds behind me. I walked into the bathroom and the black guy at the urinal didn't look very shocked to see me.

He zipped his dick up and walked out. Tony walked in, and I pulled him into one of the stalls. My drunken tongue swallowed his dick and balls with one gulp. He was going crazy.

We took it to the room and fucked like rabbits for the next few hours. He had to leave me, and stay the night at the team's hotel. I wore his ass out and fell asleep as soon as he left. I didn't see him until I got back to L.A.

CHAPTER 23

The Bay Area was cool, but I couldn't wait to get back in my own bed on my own turf. Before I left L.A., I was looking forward to getting away and experiencing a change of scenery, but the truth is that the trip was pretty uneventful. Tony and I got to spend a little time alone, but it wasn't as much as I would've liked. Besides the time we spent in my hotel room, he was still acting like a married man tiptoeing around with his chick on the side. I guess I thought he would treat me more like wifey while we were out of town, but he didn't.

While we were in public, he didn't touch me, let alone stand close to me. I don't know exactly what I expected from him, but I wasn't completely satisfied with the way we existed together. I would've never told him that because he would probably just discount everything that I had to say, plus I didn't want him to stop inviting me. At some point, I had to get it through my head that Tony was a public figure, so he was always married, even when he was more than a few miles away from home.

When I checked out of my room, I thought about how many girls Tony had probably flown in for games, and questioned if they even stayed in the exact same hotel. I wondered if Tony had a file that contained a permanent imprint of his credit card. The front desk clerk was a homely white woman in her mid-40s; no doubt she had stories to top the limo driver's tales. I caught her shaking her gray-covered head in the reflection on the glass doors as I turned towards the exit.

The driver was waiting in front of the double doors as soon as I walked outside.

"Are you waiting for a car?"

"Yes I am. I have a flight to L.A. at 12:05."

"I'm Bob, and your chariot awaits."

The average-looking white man tipped his hat, and opened my door for me. Bob had a kind face, and he clearly loved his job. After I stepped in the car, he shut my door, jogged to the trunk with my luggage, and ran around to the driver's seat. Bob had to be in his early 50s, but he didn't seem to care that he looked like a failure pushing that car and shuffling around with other's people bags for a living. He was a white man; he should've been a CEO of something, anything other than a chauffeur. Within a few minutes into the ride, Bob displayed his whiteness.

"So, I heard you were visiting an NBA player. Anybody I'd know?"

"No, not me. I wish!"

I wanted to curse his nosey ass out, but I held my tongue. Who told him who I was there to see? The first driver? The librarian at the front desk? Even though I would never see him again, I wasn't going to let him think even for a split second that I was a groupie because I'm sure in his mind he thought every black, sexy chick that he picked up from a hotel and dropped at the airport was sucking some player's dick. They may very well have been groupies, but that was none of his business, he needed to drive more and talk less.

My flight was quick and dirty and Hypnotiq was there to pick me up from the curb. We grabbed lunch at The Burnt Tortilla and chopped up the trip. Hypnotiq was howling when I told her about what I did to the Barbie's in the club bathroom.

"Girl, you didn't?"

"Why didn't I? I get sick of them thinking they're all that!"

"You are stupid!"

"I know, but that's why you love me!"

"I wish I was there to see the look on their faces."

"It was priceless. The funny part was that I don't give a fuck about those white bitches. They can get all the black dick they want!"

I told Hypnotiq about how the trip wasn't popping like I thought it would be. We discussed my delusions of grandeur over cubed steak burritos and crispy beef tacos with extra cheese. After we couldn't eat another bite, we rolled out of the restaurant and into my apartment. Hypnotiq stayed for a little while, giving me the update on Big D, and their increasing love affair.

He had professed his love for her, but he still wasn't leaving his wife. He told Hypnotiq that he had never had a connection with any other woman like he had with her. Big D said that he couldn't leave his wife because he wanted to keep the family together plus see his kids everyday. He thought that if he left her, she would act a fool and keep the kids from him. Hypnotiq said that she never even initiated any conversation about him getting a divorce, he just brought it up one day that he really wished that she had a greater role in his life. She was satisfied with the way things were going because she still had Jason, so she wasn't alone, and Big D was spending money and taking her on trips. She had the best of both worlds.

As soon as Hypnotiq left, I took my clothes off, snuggled in my fluffy robe, and plopped down on the couch. Hypnotiq called and asked if I wanted to do a party with her, but I told her I was jet lagged. She clowned and said jet lag her ass because I hadn't even changed time zones! I just wanted to relax. Within the next half hour, the t.v. was watching me. I dragged my tired ass off the couch and got into bed.

The next morning, I thought about the fact that Tony never mentioned his proposition again, and I wanted to make sure he was still offering me a job before I threw a going-away party at the club and got my face cracked. I wanted to call him, but it was early, so I figured he was having family time. I waited until 11 to call, but his voicemail picked up, so I hung up. A couple of hours later, he returned my call, and I told him that we never finished the conversation about working at his boy's club. He told me he would come by in a little bit. I unpacked, washed clothes, and went to the mailbox. Tony called from around the corner. I threw on some shorts, a wife beater, and sandals.

We talked about the club, and he seemed a little hesitant. When I asked him what was up, he said that he didn't know if it would be a good idea because his wife showed up sometimes. If she saw me there, it would be all bad.

"Why didn't you think about that before you made the offer?"

I was clearly disappointed. I thought I finally had my chance to get out of the life, but then within a few minutes he had erased all of it.

"I'm sorry, it's just that I hadn't thought about that before I offered you the job."

"I need a new gig, and that would've been perfect for me."

"Look, I didn't say it was a wrap. I just need to think about it. Maybe I can try to get you a job in another club somewhere."

"Tony, I was already planning a farewell party at the club, and you know those hating bitches would love for me to walk in there and say I'm not going anywhere."

I lied. I hadn't even begun to plan the party, but I wanted to make him feel bad for running his mouth the other night.

"I hear you. Let me make some calls, and I'll let you know something in the next day or two. Is that cool?"

What was I supposed to say? I could tell that he already felt guilty, but I wanted to make him feel worse.

"I guess that's all I can do."

He started hugging on me, and trying to make me laugh. I was trying to hold back the laughter for as long as I could, and then I let it go. I didn't want to let him off the hook, but it was too late.

Tony called me later and said that he talked to one of his boys who knew someone that owned a club, and they said they needed a waitress, but I told him that wasn't enough money for me to leave the club. He got back on the phone. He called again with a hostess job, and I told him no. He realized that he had spoken to soon about working at his boy's club, but now he felt responsible.

Finally, he told me that he would allow me to work in Ron's club, but I had strict rules that I had to follow. Tony would talk to Ron about making me some kind of an assistant shift manager, but I would have to train and take my job very seriously. The most important rule was that I had to disappear if Camille ever showed up. He said that I had to immediately walk to the kitchen, and stay there until the coast was clear. I was a little offended, but I wanted the job, so I agreed to everything and jumped up and down with shocked happiness.

I called Hypnotiq with my news and she was genuinely delighted for me. I told her that we needed to plan my party at the club, and she was cool with it. I hadn't been that excited in a long time. I had never intended on dancing for over two years; it was supposed to be something that I was going to try, but it was never supposed to be a career. Stripping had changed me, and it wasn't for the good. I had wanted to get out of the club for awhile, but without skills, I would never make as much money as I did in the club.

After awhile, some of the girls had begun to hate the club because they felt chained to it, and the only thing they could do to break free was to get more education, but because they had been taking their clothes off for perfect strangers, their self-esteem was shot, and they were intimidated as hell. In relative terms, dancing was easy money, and the girls had a tendency to get lazy and less motivated about taking classes, studying, and sitting in a room full of people that they thought were smarter than they were. It was a vicious cycle, but I was determined to break it.

For the next few days, Hypnotiq and I shopped for costumes, decorations, and new work clothes for my new career. I discreetly told a couple of girls at the club that I was moving on, and let them spread it to everybody else. I told the important people: the owner, the managers, bartenders, and DJs. Meanwhile, Tony had been in contact with Ron, and he was cool with giving me a job. He wanted to meet with me too see what I was suited for. Tony was basically going to be funneling my paycheck from his own personal money into the business, so Ron didn't have anything to lose; he got an extra body at no cost.

I was so nervous the first time I met Ron. Tony had given him my number, and he called me to set up a time to meet. I wanted to impress Ron, so I tried on several different outfits to get the perfect look. I wanted to seem professional, yet sexy enough for a Saturday night on Sunset Boulevard amidst the working girls and three-piece suits.

When I walked in the club, I got excited as I looked around at the velvet couches, high tables, and silver beaded curtains separating the VIP area. There were different colored lights, an elongated, modern bar and humongous dance floor. This was where I needed to be. I met Ron at the bar, and we talked about the duties and responsibilities in the club, and what I would be qualified to do. I told him that I was willing to train, and anxious to get started.

He said that he enjoyed my enthusiasm, and that he would get back to me with the dates that I should report back for training. We decided that I would start as a hostess, and work my way up from there. I have to admit that I was reaching for higher heights, but since Tony had already told me that he was bankrolling my position, I gladly accepted the job.

A couple of days later Tony left tickets at will call for me, Hypnotiq and Brandy. We were going to celebrate my new job, and I was walking on water at the thought of leaving the club. After the game, everybody was meeting at a club in Hollywood. The day of the game, the girls and I spent the day at the nail shop and the mall. We took our clothes over Hypnotiq's apartment to get dressed and have cocktails.

We left at 6:30 in my car, and used the handicapped card that I bought from the hustle man at the club, and parked right near the walkway. After we stopped at will call, we headed for the inside of the arena. As usual, our seats were terrible, but I had my friends, so it was all good. We watched the game, but we also spent time looking in the stands, talking about people and the weak ass cheerleaders.

Their little dance moves were supposed to be hip hop, but they were so watered down and stiff. They looked a mess, and the only reason they were out there was to fuck with the players, even though that wasn't supposed to jump off. Tony told me that last season one of the players got caught getting boss from one of the dancers in the locker room during practice. She was fired, and they told him to cut it out.

For some reason, I looked near the player bench and locked in on Camille sitting in the spouse's section. My smile faded. I shuttered at the thought of seeing her as often as I had in the last few weeks. Some chicks may have got off on rubbing her face in it, and showing off the fact that they were sharing her husband, but I didn't. I didn't want to see her because ironically, that reminded me of the harsh reality that my boyfriend had a wife.

In my mind, I could pretend that we had a real relationship, and I was the only woman in his life, but to keep setting eyes on her forced me to see things as they really were. Realizing that I was sharing a man wasn't cool. I felt weak to his advances, and desperate to think that this was all that I deserved. I didn't say anything to the girls. When they noticed my change in mood, I told them that I was thinking about whether or not I locked my car.

At half-time we walked to get a drink, and carelessly flirted with some boys. After the game was over, we all hopped back in my car, and took off for The Cheesecake Factory. We munched on appetizers until our entrees came. Tony called to check in, and I told him we were finishing up, and then going back to Hypnotiq's. He was leaving the gym and going home to change, but I knew that he had to drop Camille off. He just didn't want to mention her, he had no idea that I had seen her in the stands. Tony didn't talk about her, and I didn't ask questions. He said that John, Lou, and a couple of his teammates were rolling too. I told him that we would meet them there in a couple of hours.

We slipped out of our jeans and into sexy dresses once we got to back to Hypnotiq's. I touched up my makeup and combed my hair. We sat around laughing and talking until it was time to go. I pulled up to the front of the club and the line was around the corner. I called Tony so that he could get us in, he was only a few minutes away. VIP was full, so I parked and we started walking towards the front. We met up with Tony and walked right through the red velvet rope into the club.

John and Lou were there normal goofy selves, strutting around with their chests puffed out making sure everyone saw them with Tony. I think he let them hang around because they inflated his ego. They were gophers; they did everything he asked them to do. He had them go to the bar and order our drinks, and they were happy to do it. We made our way to the VIP lounge. When John and Lou returned with the champagne and glasses, John whispered in the bouncer's ear standing in front of the lounge, and I could only imagine what they told him. "We're Tony's bitches, can we get in?"

Tony's phone rang, and his face lost color. It was his wife. He rushed out of the VIP answering the phone. Hypnotiq and Brandy gave me a supportive look, and I just shrugged my shoulders. I felt stupid. Tony came back and told John to follow him. At that point, I knew something was up. A few seconds later, John came over and whispered in my ear that we had to leave because Camille and her girls were on their way up there. I saw Tony walking towards the front of the club as he left John to do his dirty work. I got up and walked over to my girls and told them what was up.

"We gotta go."

Hypnotiq knew the deal, but Brandy looked clueless.

"Tony's wife decided to surprise him. Apparently, she's a few minutes away, so we gotta get ghost."

"Where's Tony? Did he just leave you here?" Brandy always had to ask stupid ass questions at the most fucked up time.

"He's checking his fucking game! Let's go!"

We left the VIP area, and started walking to the front door when John gently grabbed the top of my arm.

"You gotta leave out the back."

"What? That's a fire exit! Won't the alarm go off?"

"Tony talked to the owner, and they turned it off. They have a security guard at the door to let you guys out. Where did you park? I can walk you to the car."

"Fuck me! Not only am I sneaking me and my girls out of the club, but I'm tipping out the *back* of the fucking club?"

"Mia, you know how we get down. I know it looks fucked up, but what do you want him to do?"

How *we* get down? The flunky was trying to school me on how to creep. I was getting more irritated by the minute.

"John, don't say anything to me. As a matter of fact, you don't even have to walk us to the car. Thank you."

"You sure? Three women walking by themselves at night ain't cool."

"We're fine!"

I snatched both of their hands, busted the fire door open, and stomped down the street dragging my friends. My pride was sitting on the lovely velvet couches in the VIP, next to the bottle of bubbly and champagne flutes. Tony didn't even have the decency to tell me good-bye. My cell rang. It was him.

"What the fuck do you want?"

"Mia, I know you're upset, but I was calling to tell you that you left your purse."

I stormed out of there in such a huff that I left my purse with my wallet and keys. We couldn't have gone anywhere if we wanted to.

"How am I going to get my shit?"

"John is coming back out. Just stay where you are, and he'll catch up to you. Look, I'm sorry about what happened. I didn't know she was coming."

"You scurried out of the VIP like a rat! You couldn't even tell me to get the fuck out of the club yourself? You sent John over there, and you didn't even say a word to me!"

"Mia, Camille was already on her way. You guys just had a fight a couple of weeks ago. I just wanted to keep the peace."

"This was supposed to be my fucking night!"

"Mia, I'll make it up to you okay? Just go home and relax. I'll try to call you a little later."

"Go home? I'm going out! I'm celebrating tonight with or without you."

"Mia, I know you're mad, but what was I supposed to do?"

"Be a fucking man! Stop running! At some point, you're going to have to man up, and stop hiding behind your wife's apron! I'm so sick of this shit!"

"You trying to quit me now? It's one night. I'll take you out soon."

"It's always next time! I got my girls out and you have me looking real stupid right now!"

"What do you want me to say? I'm sorry."

"Don't say shit!"

I hung the phone up in his face as Hypnotiq and Brandy watched silently. John was coming up the block, and I just wanted to snatch my bag from his stupid hands and bounce. Hypnotiq must have read my mind because she offered to walk towards John and get the purse. Brandy started trying to put her arms around me, but that wasn't what I needed right then; I wasn't sad, I was pissed. She sensed me pulling back, so she left me alone.

"Mia, I'm sorry that I made you mad in there. I was just didn't know where Tony went."

"Brandy, when shit is popping off like that, don't ask me stupid ass questions, okay? That's all I ask."

"Well, you don't have to take it out on me."

"You're right. I'm on one right now. I'm sorry."

I reached over and gave her a hug. I felt bad because sometimes I forgot that Brandy wasn't used to the bullshit, and she asked Pollyanna questions because she didn't know any better. Hypnotiq was used to the cheating, the confrontations, and the fights so she knew how to react, when to talk, and when to console me. It wasn't Brandy's fault that she led an envied life.

I was talking that shit to Tony, but I didn't even feel like going anywhere else. I wanted to go home and climb in my bed. I dropped Brandy off first. Hypnotiq asked me if I wanted her to come and stay with me, but I told her I was cool. I didn't want to talk, I didn't want to cry, I just wanted to *be*.

I drove home and cried out of embarrassment and disappointment. Tony had a way of pumping me up, and letting me down. Our relationship hadn't always consisted of so many highs and lows, ups and downs. There used to be a time when we had careless encounters, fucking and joking. In time, things changed but because it was so unexpected, neither one of us knew how we were supposed to react. The more affection Tony showed me, the more I wanted.

I used to follow his lead, but then I got to the point where I wanted more, and had the nerve to get pissy if he went back to treating me more like work than a number two. I wasn't supposed to be a two because he was married, but it happened, which was all the more reason for him to hide what we had from his boys because he had broken the rules. The situation was becoming more complicated and convoluted. I couldn't help but wonder how much more I could take, how long it would last, and how it would eventually end.

CHAPTER 24

The morning light never let me down, it brought me peace and hopefulness. No matter the events of the previous night, the new day always met me with optimism and fresh perspective, but the morning after getting kicked out of the club, I didn't have the same bounce back. Most nights, Tony was the last thing I thought about before I went to bed, and as soon as I opened my eyes, I shook the morning fog and recalled how things ended between us the night before.

Last night was a mess. I had to search deep for solace. I looked at my phone, and Tony had called when the club let out, but I'm glad I was sleep because I may have answered it. I needed him to understand how hurt and embarrassed I was, and if I talked to him last night he was going to try and smooth everything over, and I would've caved.

Getting out of bed was extremely difficult. I didn't want to interact with anyone. I turned my phones off, and just lay in bed thinking about what I could've done to save face last night. I could've put my foot down instead of slinking out of the club, but that would've been the end of me and Tony. I hated feeling like someone else had control over me. Camille had power over Tony, and Tony had power over me. I didn't have power over anyone, not even me, and that was the problem. I realized that I was more angry with myself than I could ever be at Tony.

After a few hours, I finally dragged myself out of bed and into the shower. I turned my phone back on, and Brent had left a message. He said that he didn't know if he should call anymore; he felt like he was bugging me. He sounded sad, and I felt responsible. I called him, and he agreed to pick me up in an hour for lunch and a movie. I really wasn't in the mood, and I went back and forth in my mind whether or not I should actually go out with him, but I ultimately decided that Brent was sweet, plus I needed to get out of the house. I put some clothes on, but I wasn't as sexy as I would've been if I had been going out with Tony.

Our date was cool even though I wasn't there in spirit. I was preoccupied with Tony, even though Brent tried his best to change my frame of mind. It didn't improve much, but I never let Brent know what was really going on. I told him that I had worked late the night before, and the poor thing believed every word out of my mouth. I was so used to hanging around liars and thieves that I forgot what it was like to be around a guy that was so trusting.

Brent dropped me back home, and I returned a call from Hypnotiq. She had a party she wanted me to go to with her. She said that it was co-ed, and they were cashing us out. Tony had called me a couple of times, and I was ignoring him. It made it easier to do when I kept myself busy with other things. I told her to pick me up at 8.

Hypnotiq left out the fact that the couple was white until we were driving towards the valley. She said that Susie and Bob were a swinging couple that came into *Aces* together, but tonight they wanted some private entertainment for them and their friends in their home. She said they were well-dressed professionals that walked on the wild side after they left their high rise business offices for the night.

Hypnotiq had never done a party at their house before, but when they came in the club Susie would break bread for Bob's endless lap dances. She said that Susie would just sit right next to them, quietly smiling as she moved up and down Bob's lap. She was taking mental notes on how to drive her husband up the wall, like she was watching the exotic black whore wind him up for her to unwind when they got home. It sounded to me like they were trying to take it to the next level by inviting Hypnotiq to the house, they were tired of fucking around and wanted the real deal; she said she was down for whatever.

Hypnotiq and I were just chatting away, but when we pulled up to the mini mansion, I became speechless at the sight of the exotic car dealership in the driveway and along the curb. The Lamborghini and the Ferrari caught my attention first, but there were a couple of big body Mercedes and BMWs too. The party was looking up already. We grabbed our bags, and walked up to the estate situated in a neighborhood of manicured lawns, flood lights, and semicircular driveways.

The inside of the house was immaculate. The furnishings were ultra modern with hardwood floors, black leather couches with clean edges and a chaise lounge. There was a bookcase that covered an entire wall, gigantic silver-framed mirrors, large red vases, and African artifacts that symbolized their liberal, forward thinking philosophies.

All of the bold kitchen appliances were stainless steel, and as if it were a competition, the large red area rug shamelessly begged for attention. Susie took us to her bedroom upstairs, and gave each of us $500 and a Cosmopolitan. She said that she informed her friends to be generous with tips since we missed a night of work to drive all the way to the valley.

Susie was tall and slender with big boobs, no hips or ass. She was a fine white girl that wasn't the least bit intimidated by the two around the way girls standing in front of her. Her long blonde hair was straight and freshly trimmed. Her makeup was aggressively applied with heavy, dark eyelids and brazen red lips. Susie's clothes were sexy but sophisticated; she wore black slim-fit slacks paired with a black silk blouse proudly boasting her cleavage popping through the third unused buttonhole. She left us alone to get dressed.

Bob was an average-looking white man, and it was obvious that he married up by snagging Susie. He had a slight beer belly that he camouflaged well in his expensive, athletically cut suit and Italian leather loafers. His hair was styled like a movie star with mousse and little spikes. The fact that he had money made him look far more attractive than he was in reality.

Susie was the more assertive of the two, and Bob seemed to take the back seat and let her be the spokesperson for the both of them. He came upstairs to tell us that Susie was ready for us to start the show, but even then it was as if he was asking instead of telling us.

There were three other couples that were as well-dressed and liberal as their hosts. They were obviously nervous as they were drinking like fish. By the end of the first hour, they were starting to take their own clothes off, turning the music up louder, and dancing to the other beat. Hypnotiq and I were dancing, but they jumped up on the side of us doing their thing right next to us. We were laughing at them, not with them, but they were too faded to know the difference.

When the song ended, the two of us went upstairs to change, and I noticed that Susie was following us. She stood there while we changed costumes, and told us what she would like to see next. We told her what we had, and she looked over everything in our bag of tricks. For the next set, we brought out whips, paddles, and handcuffs at the request of Susie.

The men and women lined up for us to use our toys on them. For the most part, Susie kind of sat back and watched the others indulge in their hidden fantasies. Bob was having a wonderful time, but he kept glancing at Susie as if to get her approval for his desire to be spanked and whipped. I didn't know about Hypnotiq, but I was really tripping off of these rich white folks and the freaky shit they were in to. I didn't give a fuck though; I got to control the situation, dominate and beat them while getting paid.

In the middle of the madness, I saw Susie whispering in Hypnotiq's ear. Something told me that her thirst for the bizarre was about to get nastier, and I was right. When we went upstairs after dancing for two songs, Hypnotiq told me that Susie wanted her to fuck Bob in their living room in front of her and their friends. Innocently, I asked her if she was going to do it and she said that Susie was giving her another thousand dollars, she didn't have to say yes, I understood.

We both had already made a few hundred in tips, so Hypnotiq was leaving with at least about $2,000 for a few hours of work. Fucking Bob wasn't a big deal to her; she looked at it as strictly work. As we walked down the steps, I could see they had pulled a full-sized mattress onto the living room floor, dimmed the lights, lit a few candles, and changed the music selection from booty-popping to smooth jazz. All of the white people were sitting in a single row in front of the mattress as if it were an altar.

Hypnotiq grabbed Bob's hand and led him to the mattress. She kneeled down, and pulled him next to her. After she laid him down on his back, she removed his shoes and socks, unzipped his pants, and shimmied them down his legs. She stuck her hand in the slit in his boxers and pulled out a huge dick! My mouth dropped open, and my eyes widened. Hypnotiq was playing cool, but I knew she was tripping as hard as I was because Bob didn't act like he had a big dick, he was nice.

I envied Hypnotiq and I knew that she was going to have fun beyond just work. She tucked his dick back in, and slid his boxers down. I didn't see them before, but there was a little basket full of condoms near the mattress, and Hypnotiq grabbed one and ripped the top off. She slowly rolled the condom onto Bob's dick. She leaned over him to the point her titties were hanging right over his face. He licked them like a frog on a lily pad, timidly but fast. She grabbed his dick and threw her pussy on top of it. We had brought down some Astroglide out of my bag for her, but I knew she wouldn't need it with a dick like that. She was turned on, and didn't need the fake juice.

Hypnotiq moved up and down, sliding his dick in and out of her pussy. She would rise up to where only the head of his dick was still inside. She turned around and leaned her head over his knees. Bob sat up a little so that he could watch her pussy from behind. At first, it seemed like Bob was trying to hold back his excitement in order to preserve his wife's dignity, but after a few minutes he was all into it, regardless of who was watching.

Bob got bold and gently pushed Hypnotiq on all fours and stated fucking her from the back. She was authentically moaning and then she was screaming; Bob was giving her all of it and she was taking it. Susie was smiling, but did not move from her chair. The other couples had started fucking with each other, and I was standing there observing everybody.

Bob removed himself from Hypnotiq and told her to lie down. They were sweaty. He entered her again from the top, and she wrapped her legs around his back. They were moving together, faster and faster and then Hypnotiq started breathing harder and rotating her hips in tight circles. She yelled as she started to cum, and Bob was right behind her grunting in ecstasy.

When they were finished, Susie sat up and started clapping for them. The other couples were busy engaging in a full-out orgy, and were oblivious to Susie's overture. Hypnotiq, Bob, Susie, and I went upstairs together, and Susie told Hypnotiq she wanted her to join them in a threesome. When I left, Bob and Hypnotiq were cleaning up while Susie started taking her clothes off. I felt like chopped liver as I walked down the stairs alone.

The men and women were still fucking and sucking on each other. I didn't know who was married to who, and it was impossible to tell because everybody was connected by the mouth, dick or pussy.

I walked past them to the kitchen where I opened the refrigerator to get something to drink. I found some Hawaiian Punch as I snooped around. Tony called my phone, but by the time I got to it he had hung up. I hadn't talked to him since I cussed his ass out in front of the club. I was nowhere near my apartment, so it was safe to call him back. I was getting ready to call him back when Hypnotiq came down and said that one of the other couples wanted a threesome with me. I told her that I was going to make a call first. She walked over to the living room and told them I was coming over in a minute.

"Now you want to call me back?"

"What do you want Tony?"

"What you doing?"

"I'm at a party with Hypnotiq."

"Want me to come by?"

"No, we're in the valley with some white people."

"Oh, when are you coming back to town?"

"In about an hour. Why?"

"I wanted to come by with some ice cream."

He knew what he was doing including ice cream in his apology; just the mere mention of ice cream made me weak.

"I'll call you when I leave here."

I walked across the living room, and I saw the couple that wanted to fuck with me sitting on one of the couches as if they were watching the room spinning. The other two couples were planning on watching, they sat naked on the floor.

"You guys okay?"

They were so faded I thought they were getting ready to pass out from alcohol poisoning.

"We want to fuck you." They were giggling and touching all over each other. The whole scene looked like a scene from a movie.

"What do you guys want?"

"We both want to eat your pussy, and then Anthony is going to fuck you. Is that okay? We have a thousand dollars. Is that good enough?"

"Throw in another $500 and I'll suck his dick."

"You got a deal!"

I lay on the mattress, and the wife went to work eating my pussy. Anthony was trying to stick his dick in my mouth, but I turned my head and pointed at the basket o' condoms. He snatched one, and ripped the top off. He fumbled around until he got it on, and then he gently shoved his dick in my mouth. I wasn't as lucky as Hypnotiq. His dick was on the small side, but I made him feel like he was a grown man. The taste of the Noxynol-9 was disgusting, but I wasn't sucking him bare dick. I was moaning and flicking my tongue in and out of my mouth like he had the biggest, baddest dick in the world. I was an actress, but he was paying for the fantasy. He was loving it, and the wife was breaking me off proper, which gave me the motivation to show my appreciation.

Anthony pulled his dick out of my mouth, and got on his knees to eat my pussy. I sucked his wife's titties, and fucked with her pussy with my fingers. She was moving around and thrashing her hips side to side. I didn't want her to come on my fingers, so I moved my hands to her thighs. Anthony sat up and stuck his dick inside of me. He was pumping in and out like a teenager, but I wasn't tripping because that meant it would be over soon. I lifted my hips off the mattress and moved with him, but I stopped before I came because I was saving that for Tony. The wife was off to the side, but she was cool because she kept rubbing my arms and shoulders. Anthony was getting ready to cum; he was sweating and breathing hard like a track star. When he let loose, he yelled and I turned my head to get a look at his wife. She wasn't jealous, she was happy for him. White people were special.

🍁   🍁   🍁

On the way home, Hypnotiq told me what went down with the threesome. She said that Susie ate her pussy and licked her asshole. Susie started sucking Bob's dick while he ate Hypnotiq's pussy. Bob fucked Hypnotiq until he was almost ready to cum, and then he climbed inside of his wife. Hypnotiq said they were treating her like she was the queen bee and she didn't have to do anything. I told her what jumped off with me, and we both laughed about how racism is such a thing of the past!

I called Tony when I got in the apartment, and he said he would be there in a half hour. I was still mad, but not like last night. I threw my work bag in the back of the closet, and hopped in the shower. I douched to get the sweat, Noxynol-9, and body odor off of my pussy. I gargled with Listerine, flossed and brushed my teeth. After I was carefully sanitized, I threw on some clothes and waited for Tony.

He walked in with ice cream in his hand, and an apology on his lips. He went on and on about how he wanted to keep Camille from seeing me, and how he wasn't trying to disrespect me by sending John over. He just did what he thought was best at the time. Camille and her friends decided to go to the club at the last minute.

I told him that I knew that I was a secret, but he could've handled the situation a little better. He could've told me what was going on, said good-bye, and I would've slipped out quietly. I still wouldn't have been completely happy, but it would've been better than what took place. I told him that I didn't like John being his errand boy because he was all in my business, and I didn't like sneaking out the back door. It was embarrassing, plus I had my girls with me. He said that he didn't know what else he could've done when she could've been walking through the front door any minute.

I asked him if that was what it was going to be like when I worked at Ron's club, and he said pretty much. He didn't want me and Camille to have any contact, and if I couldn't handle it, I would have to forget the job. He explained rather assertively that he liked kicking it with me, but his family came first. I had to understand and accept that if I wanted to continue a relationship with him.

Tony was threatening me, basically telling me that I better get right or get left. As shameless as it sounded, I didn't want to live without him. After awhile, the conversation came to end as we agreed to disagree. I had become furious at Tony for treating me like a mistress, but that's what I was. The reality was that the truth hurts.

We changed the subject and Tony and I shared my ice cream while we watched a basketball game on t.v. He started kissing on my neck, and then he suddenly stopped.

"What exactly did you do tonight at the party?"

"Since when have you questioned what I do?"

"I'm getting ready to lick and suck all over you, so I'm asking."

"Tony, I just left a house party, but I'm clean."

"Don't get mad. I'm asking, but I'm also reminding you to protect the both of us."

"And I do. If you don't want to fuck me…"

I dropped my head back, rolling my eyes at the thought of him questioning my hygiene and the way I got down. If only he knew how I sanitized myself before he got there. I almost drew blood I scrubbed so hard. There wasn't a trace of anybody else on my body. Tony apologized, stood up, and grabbed my hand.

We went in my room, and didn't come out until we were dehydrated two hours later and in need of fluids.

CHAPTER 25

Ron called, and I spent a few afternoons a week in the club learning the business. I was so juiced that I went back during business hours to watch the employees interact with real customers and real issues. A couple of customers had forgotten their IDs at home, one man was so drunk the bartender had to cut him off, and a woman complained that there wasn't any toilet tissue in the restroom. Ron would come up to me every time something popped off just so that I could gauge the kinds of problems that came up night after night.

He would tell me what happened, and then he would say, "What would you do?" I answered as best as I could, and he would tell me what I should've said. Most of the time, my answers were cool, but he said I would learn more by doing. As the hostess, he said that I would be at the center of activity, and it was the best way for me to catch on. After about two weeks of training, Ron felt confident in putting me out on the floor as a hostess. I told him that I needed to tie up loose ends at *Aces,* and I would be ready in a week.

I quickly learned that the club had licks just like the strip club. Some of the females put me on, and told me how to take tips from impatient customers that wanted to jump the line, didn't have ID, or others that wanted to get in VIP. There was money to be made everywhere, and I was ready to make it. One of the other hostesses told me that Ron gave out drink tickets sometimes, but when she got a hold of them, she would sell them for half the price of the average drink, which was about $4 or $5. The girls told me that Ron was going to start paying R&B groups to come and perform, and they couldn't wait to meet their favorites singers, plus watch more money pour into the club.

Meanwhile, I put the finishing touches on my farewell party. The theme was Betty Boop, so the girls that I chose to dance with me were going to wear tightly-curled hair or Shirley Temple curls, sexy exaggerated makeup with blood-red lips, bustiers, feather boas and fishnet stockings. We were going to decorate the club with black and red balloons, streamers, and sheer curtains. I had paid for posters advertising my party, and placed them on the walls of the club two weeks ahead of time.

Brothas liked to come to parties because they got to look at new booty, well-thought out costumes, live DJs, and food. The cost of admission was a little higher on party nights, but it was worth it. There was a party at least once or twice a month for birthdays, anniversaries, baby and wedding showers, graduations, farewells and welcome backs.

On the afternoon of the party, Hypnotiq was picking up chicken wings, potato salad, and pasta salad. Brandy was getting the cake, plates, and eating utensils. A couple of the girls from the club were picking up tablecloths, and large trash bags for the money pick-up. Tony said that he and his boys would slide through, but he didn't know what time he could get out of the house because Camille was spending the day with her mother and sister, and he had the kids. I told him that I understood, but deep down I knew that I would be disappointed if he didn't make it. Tony was responsible for this, and I wanted him to share in my happiness.

This was a big night for me because it marked the end of one chapter and the beginning of the next. I danced at the club over two years, and for a normal job that wasn't that big of a deal, but two years at *Aces* was like four years anywhere else. I was so naïve and trusting when my foot first crossed the threshold, but in time I had become jaded and crafty.

I got to the club first, and people were hugging and congratulating me on getting up out of the club. For the first time in a long time, I felt proud. I went in the back to put my bag up, and I asked a couple of girls to walk to my car to get the rest of the decorations. We brought them in, and started hanging stuff up. Girls were dancing on stage, so I didn't get a chance to put anything up on the mirrors behind the stage, so I concentrated on the tables, chairs and the bar. Hypnotiq and Brandy walked in together. We set the food up, but kept everything covered or it would've been gone before the party started. It was about 8, and the party was starting at 9. The DJ got there, and set up his table right next to the stage.

Hypnotiq, the other girls, and I went to the back to start getting ready. Tonight was going to be big, so I put extra baby powder underneath my titties and deodorant in the crack of my ass. I put some Vaseline on my teeth, to keep my lips from getting stuck. Most of the girls were excited about me moving on, and kept asking me questions about my plans and if I would miss anything about the club. They said they would come see me at my new spot, and we would keep in touch.

The haters were quietly hating through the entire conversation, but I wasn't letting them spoil my night. We got dressed, put on makeup, and curled our hair in our cramped quarters, and I kept thinking about the fact that this was going to be the last time I ever got dressed in the smoky, stank, smothering locker room of *Aces*.

The DJ started playing our first song, and my heart began pounding so loud I thought the girls standing next to me could hear it. Beads of sweat formed on my top lip, my forehead and my armpits. Me and the girls had a Tequila shot before we started getting dressed, but it didn't calm my nerves the slightest bit. I hadn't been nervous about going on stage since the first night after the contest.

I had so many hopes, that everything went perfectly, that Tony was in the audience cashing me out on stage, and I hoped that I would never be back in that club.

Hypnotiq, Dream, and I walked on stage together, the crowd started yelling and throwing cash at us. We had a choreographed routine that had everybody on their feet. I tried to scan the room without looking terribly obvious, but with the dark lights, and packed house, I couldn't find Tony. At the end of the song we all dropped into the splits, and the men sitting at the edge of the stage dug deep in their pockets. We ran to the wings of the stage, and Brandy came up with trash bags to scoop the money up. It was a lot of money, and I wanted to avoid any sticky finger issues, so the money was grabbed after every song.

I came out to the next song by myself, and I was able to focus on the crowd better since my eyes had adjusted to the light. Tony wasn't in the club. He was so tall that I should've been able to find him, even if he was sitting down. I worked it out to the fast song, and went topless for the next slow jam. I took a short break and let the other girls in my show go up. I covered my ass and walked around in the audience.

All of my regulars were asking for dances, but I told them they had to wait until I finished on stage. Customers were just throwing money at me as I walked through. I was smiling as big as I stashed the cash in my little money bag. I was looking for Tony, and I couldn't find him. I was trying not to get disappointed and fuck my mood off, so I took another shot of Patron the bartender bought me, and went backstage to change for the next set.

My music started, and I walked back on stage, feeling the liquor piercing my blood vessels. I moved a little slower and nastier, hands on my knees rocking my hips up and down to the beat. I grabbed the pole, and twisted around at top speed. I leaned my back up against the pole and slowly rolled my pelvis towards the man in the front row. I didn't know if it was the tequila, or the absence of Tony, but a wave of emotion crashed down on me; I felt melancholy, sad even. A single tear fell from the corner of my eye, but I quickly wiped it away before anyone was the wiser.

All of a sudden, a tall figure on the other side of the stage caught my eye, it was Tony. I looked at him, and I wanted to run to him and jump in his arms, but I got control of myself. He was waving money in his hand, and I seductively walked towards him, carefully placing one foot in front of the other. When I reached Tony I got on all fours with my stomach facing up. I teased him with my pussy, and he hit me with wads of cash. I stayed in front of him for at least three minutes, with a mound of cash all around me. I was foggy, but I wasn't so faded that I didn't realize that Tony's move intimidated other niggas so they kept their ones in their pockets. It was cool though because Tony more than made up for what I was missing from everybody else.

The song ended, and I couldn't wait to get off stage and run into Tony's arms. I made my way through the crowd to the spot where he was standing, but when I got there, he was gone. I quickly turned around, but I didn't see him anywhere, and I couldn't stop the tears from forming in my eyes. I tried to take deep breaths, and blow the air out slowly, but it didn't help. The tears started running out of my eyes as if someone had turned the faucet on.

I couldn't wipe them away fast enough before new ones were created. Someone asked me if I was okay, and I said that I had an eyelash in my eye. I was making my way to the bathroom when I saw him. He was leaving the restroom, and I instantly felt like a silly drunk. Tony grabbed me and asked what was wrong, and I told him the same eyelash lie. He gave me a big hug as if he didn't believe me, and I was lost in his arms.

When I somewhat gained my composure, I thanked him for coming and cashing me out. He said that he could only stay for a little while because he got Camille's little sister to sit with the kids for an hour. I was just happy to see him, and I appreciated his effort. We talked for a minute, and I had to go back up. He said he would stay for the next set, but then he had to be out.

I watched Tony go through the velvet curtains after he threw another couple of hundred dollars on stage. The rest of the show was cool. Everybody ate, drank and wished me well. A couple of celebrities and athletes were in the house, and a director was there looking for dancers for an upcoming movie. He asked me for my number, and I gave it to him. For some reason, playing a dancer in a movie was a lot better than being one in real life.

At the end of the night, Brandy and I carried the trash bags in my apartment and counted it right then. I made $5,921 in one night, and that was after I tipped the bartender, DJ and Brandy. I only spent about $200 on decorations and food, so all of that was good money. Before I walked out of the club, I hugged everybody and told them that I wouldn't be a stranger. I knew that I needed some time to pass before I set foot back in the club. I needed to feel that I had truly moved on before I could revisit the past.

CHAPTER 26

Within a few weeks, I really began to feel like *Aces* wasn't a part of my life anymore. Before I officially left the club, I had taken a few days or a week off to get away, but it didn't feel like I was really gone until more time than that had passed. I spent my first few days at home unpacking work bags, washing costumes, and storing them in a box at the back of the closet; I didn't want to throw them away because I had spent a lot of money, and Hypnotiq or someone else may have wanted to borrow them.

I spent a lot of time at the mall shopping for new work clothes. I bought more slacks and blouses, skirts, and dresses. I wanted people to take me seriously, so I had to dress the part. I swore that I wasn't wearing anything that even breathed strip club, no short, skin tight, see through, booty out, massive cleavage type of clothes. I knew that I would see some guys that used to come in the club, but I wanted them to look at me differently in my new job, and hopefully treat me with more respect than I got at the club. When I was stripping, guys were always tapping or pinching my booty, flipping my titties, or hugging and grabbing me from behind. I would turn red when strangers would touch me, and I sure as hell wasn't going to put up with it at my new spot.

Ron started me off as a hostess during the weekdays when the club was slower; he wanted me to get my feet wet before I dove in the deep end. I mostly worked on Tuesday Salsa nights, Wednesday karaoke nights, and Thursday reggae nights. I was beginning to get the hang of what it took to run a club, anticipating potential issues, meeting the needs of the customers, and being Ron's eyes and ears when he wasn't there. He began to trust me, give me more responsibilities, and within five months, I was the assistant manager Thursday through Saturday night.

The transition was seamless, and I was ready to handle any situation thrown my way. Ron would still come in on the weekends, but he would mostly walk around, greeting customers, and shaking hands. For the most part, I was in charge, but occasionally Ron would ask me to do things like getting a barback to clean up broken glass or to alert security to a would-be fight on the dance floor. I worked harder than I ever had at hustling. I came in early, stayed late, and made myself available for anything that the club needed.

There were times when I had to run to Costco or Beverages and More before I came in because we ran out of liquor, cups, or napkins but we were days away from deliveries. When the toilet tissue or hand soap was completely out, I would refill it myself if I couldn't find the janitor.

At first, it was awkward giving out orders. When I was stripping, all of the dancers were pretty much on the same level, besides the fact that the OGs had the best shifts and more regular customers, but nobody was telling anybody else what to do. Now, I had to actually boss people around, and it was weird because they had been working at the club longer than me, and they had more experience. Most of the employees were cool, but I had heard that a few of the waitresses were talking shit, and starting rumors that the only reason I was promoted so quickly to Assistant Manager was because I was fucking my way to the top. I wasn't going to say shit to those hating bitches, but when I heard the Ron rumor, I had to say something because he was good to me *and* married. Once I checked the biggest mouth, the rumors stopped. Silly bitch was only half-right; I did fuck my way to the top, but not with Ron.

Ron trusted me with cash, bank deposits, and keys to the building. It took awhile for him to get to that point because he had to get to know me, and learn to trust me. After about just a few months, I became his right-hand; he knew that he could count on me.

Tony would come in the club a couple of times a month, and I felt proud when he watched me talk to bartenders about serving drinks without napkins, and checking the coat-check girl about smoking in the bathroom. Tony told me that Ron talked about how well I handled myself with customers, employees, and always went out of my way to make sure everybody had a good night. He said that Ron told him that I was an asset to the club, and he was happy that Tony brought me in.

A few of the girls from *Aces* came in the club, and most of them were impressed with my new job. They were screaming, jumping up and down, hugging me like proud mothers. Those were the ones that came to see me doing well, and genuinely congratulated me. Others came to the club to make sure that I wasn't lying about the whole thing, and to see if I was falling on my face. The haters came in quietly as if they were spying, and the look of disappointment on their faces when they saw I was big-timing was priceless. Killing them with kindness was the best revenge; I smiled in their faces, and made sure that I was just as pleasant as I could be. When I felt extremely evil, I would buy them a round of drinks.

Tony and my relationship stayed drama-free, but it also wasn't what it used to be. Because Camille and I had finally come to blows, there were no more movies or restaurants. We were spending most of our time in my apartment, and frankly it had gotten old, but of course Tony was cool with it. He was spending less money, getting his dick sucked, and all without the possibility of getting caught unless Camille followed him up to my front door. He had invited me to a couple of those wild barbecues, but I was over it. I didn't feel the need to flaunt my status with Tony, compete with other chicks, or impress his boys anymore. Because I worked most weekends, I didn't go on the road with him after that trip to the Bay Area.

I think I stayed with him out of comfort, memories of what used to be, and the fact that he talked a good game. My stupid ass believed him, even when I knew things would probably never change between us. He kept telling me that after time, we would be able to hang out a little more, but we had to be cool for awhile. I complained sometimes, but I never demanded more, and because I put up with it, he had no reason to do anything differently. I never thought that it could happen, but Tony's star had begun to lose its shine.

One Saturday afternoon, Tony called to tell me that he was coming in the club later on with some of his teammates. I arranged for a few bottles of Dom Perignon and chilled glasses to be delivered to the VIP lounge when they arrived. I was standing near the bar making sure everything was cool when Tony called my phone a little while later.

"I don't know if I'm going to be able to make it tonight."

"Why? Is something wrong?"

"Camille and her girls have been in Vegas since Thursday night. She was supposed to be home tonight before the game, but she just called to say that they didn't make their plane, so no telling when she will get here. I'm going to have the kids after the game because I already told the nanny she could have the night off."

"Well, call me if you're coming through."

I didn't argue with him because I could tell that he was already pissed off by the fact that she was being so fucking inconsiderate. I kept my thoughts to myself, but I wondered why they missed their plane, and if she was finally getting hers.

Tony was playing in the last game of the first round playoffs that night with the series dead even, and she wouldn't even be there to support him. If she was paying him back for fucking with me, she should've just left him alone when she busted us. She decided to stay with him, so she needed to get over herself and stop acting like a heartless bitch.

I had time to kill, so I left the club to get a pastrami sandwich from TOGO's and chill at the apartment until it was time to go back to work. Before I fell asleep, Tony's team was up by 17.

When I got to the club, I told the bartender that I wouldn't need the champagne anymore, and checked in with the DJ and the hostess. It was only 9, so we were still setting up and getting everything ready to open the doors at 10. Tonight was going to be big because Tony's team had won, and the town was going to be ready to celebrate. Hypnotiq and a couple of girls from the club were coming through too, so I hooked them up with passes.

The doors opened and the club filled up fast. Hypnotiq came early to keep me company, and I gave her some drink tickets. I told her about Tony and Camille, and she couldn't believe Camille's selfishness.

"What? She wasn't even there to see her man win the playoffs?"

"Nope, and he can't even celebrate with his teammates because he already gave the nanny the night off."

"Wow. That's off the hook. Well, I'll keep you company."

"Thanks girl, it's just that this is the kind of shit that pisses me off. Camille has it all, and she doesn't even appreciate it."

"I guess she's doing her this time around."

"Pretty much. I'm not mad but if she wants to fuck around we can get our shit out in the open!"

"Girl, you are crazy! She is not letting that paycheck go out the door, and especially not for you."

"Yeah, you're right."

I didn't want to argue the point because deep down I knew that she was right, but I just wanted Tony to myself. I was tired of sharing him, and there seemed to be no end in sight to the complication of our relationship. A part of me wished that I could leave him alone, and find a normal union but I didn't have the strength. He made me feel whole when we were together, and when we were apart I missed him more that I cared to admit, even to myself. I played Brent for so long that he finally stopped calling. Subconsciously, I think I wanted him to give up, so that I didn't have to be the one to hurt him.

Hypnotiq and I were having a drink at the bar when Tony called my phone.

"Hey, Camille finally showed up, and I need to get out of this house."

"What happened?"

"I don't want to get into it right now. I'll be down there in a little bit."

Hypnotiq walked with me to the kitchen to set up the champagne, and then we went to the front door to check out the crowd outside. There was a line down the block, and cars were steady pulling up. We saw a Phantom and a Ferrari pull up to the front; they had to be Tony's teammates. The groupies were trying to get in the VIP line, but I told the bouncer to tell them to get back in the "regular" line unless they had $50 each.

I was squirming around because I had waited too long to go to the bathroom, but they needed me at the ticket counter. Hypnotiq had walked inside with one of her customers from the club. I finally broke free after I dealt with a 37-year old man that forgot his ID. I let him in the club, and power-walked to the bathroom. I felt a little bit of pee start to come down as I tried to unsuccessfully squeeze my pelvis as I walked into the stall.

I pulled my dress up, and my G-string had a big wet spot in the crotch. I pulled my panties down, stepped out of them, and threw them in the silver container reserved for used tampons and pads. I walked in as a lady, and walked out as a commando in a sexy little black dress. I grabbed a couple of paper towels, shoved them under the warm water, and went back in the stall to wipe my pussy. I checked my makeup and hair, and then went back on the floor.

When I walked out into the dark club, I looked for Hypnotiq, but my eyes found Tony. I skipped over to him and gave him a great big hug. I didn't care about discretion and modesty; I was proud of his win, and I wanted him to know it.

"Congratulations baby!!"

"Hey Mia." I could tell by his tone that he was upset.

"You okay baby?"

"I'm fucking pissed, but I don't want to talk about it. You're at work."

"Baby, talk to me." I knew that it had something to do with Camille.

"Camille missed her plane because they were at a party at Ken's house the night before."

Ken played basketball for the Atlanta Eagles, and Tony didn't fuck with him. If the party was the night before, that probably meant that she stayed the night at his house. Hella disrespectful.

"What does that mean?" I was playing stupid, so that he would get even more pissed off by telling me the details, then it would be my job to calm him down.

"I told you that I don't fuck with that nigga, and not only did she go to his house, but her and her girls stayed the night too! She said they had got faded, and ended up passing out, so he let them stay in one of the guest rooms."

"You think she fucked him?" I secretly hoped that she had, so everybody could come out of the closet.

"She might as well have because it sure fucking looks like it! How the fuck am I supposed to show my face in the locker room when everybody thinks my wife is fucking this nigga?"

I wanted to be sympathetic, but I was starting to get jealous because he was acting jealous. I regretted making him tell me all of this.

"Well, I'm sure she didn't."

"Whatever."

"Did you guys argue about it when she got home?"

"She said she didn't fuck him, but she wasn't trying to apologize for going to his house. She didn't understand that that shit was completely out of pocket. I haven't talked to him ever since he started fucking one of my works. I didn't give a fuck about the bitch, but he was talking mad shit to the broad about me. He was telling her about my other little works, and basically running his mouth like a little bitch. He's married just like I am, so it's not like he was trying to make the female his woman. I don't claim no work; if he wanted to fuck the bitch, that's his business, but keep my name out of it!"

"Why did Camille think you and Ken were beefing?"

What I wanted to ask him was when all this shit popped off, and was I dealing with him when he had more work than he could handle, but I decided to address that later.

"I told her that he was talking a gang of shit on the court."

"She fell for that?"

"That's not the point. Look, let's talk about something else. I came out to get away from the drama."

"I thought you came to see me?"

"Of course I did."

Tony gave me a hug, but I could tell that he was still pissed. I walked him to the VIP lounge where he met up with some of his boys. Soon, they were laughing and reminiscing about their 3-pointers and slam dunks. I had spent too much time giving Tony marriage counseling, so I had to make my presence felt around the club.

I met up with Hypnotiq and filled her in as we walked around. Groupies of all shades were in full force. The club had never seen so many weaves, push up bras, and four inch heels. A few of them were hovering around the bouncer standing in front of the VIP velvet rope. They were flirting mercilessly, and even though our bouncers were immune to bouncing boobies and jiggling asses, the girls didn't move on the off chance that VIP would open up to commoners.

I peeped Tony leaving VIP, and my eyes followed him to the men's room, where he rushed in and nearly knocked a man down as he was coming out. I noticed the blue light on his phone attached to his ear. When he didn't come right out, I knew it had to be Camille. I almost walked right in the bathroom to tell him to fucking hang up the phone. I was tired of him whining about her kicking it at Ken's house, coupled with the fact that he was allowing her to ruin his big night. Hypnotiq tried to call me down, but the longer he stayed in the restroom, the more pissed off I got.

Finally, he emerged from the men's room, visibly upset. He started walking towards me, but it was like he didn't even see me. Tony walked right past me, and out the door. I followed him, but all he did was stand right outside the door to get some air. He looked deep in thought, and I wasn't going to disturb him because I knew that he had talked to Camille, and he needed some time alone.

She was the only person that could change his mood from playful and cool to fucked up and shitty in 15 seconds flat. He had just been laughing, kicking it with his friends before her disturbing phone call. Deep down, it bothered me that she had such an exclusive power over him, and the ability to manipulate his emotions even when they were apart. After a few minutes, he walked back in and headed for VIP while the females were tripping all over themselves to be seen by him, but they were shadows.

I snapped out of my trance when one of the bartenders came to tell me that they were out of Grey Goose Vodka, Hypnotiq, and White Zinfandel, so I walked to the locked storeroom to grab what they needed. One of the barbacks walked with me to help carry some of the bottles.

When we got back to the floor, I noticed a large group of people gathering near the VIP, and then there were security guards rushing ahead of the crowd. After I quickly dropped the liquor at the bar, I made my way towards VIP. I began to worry because Tony was in there, and he was upset. There was a tight semi-circle near the front of the velvet ropes, but one of the bouncers saw me, and cleared a path. None of them knew that I fucked with Tony; they let me in as the boss rather than the concerned "girlfriend".

The blood left my face when I saw Camille and Tony as they sat quietly yelling at each other on one of the couches. I didn't know what to do as I stood dead in my tracks. John wasn't there to show me to the back door, and I knew Tony must have been sweating bullets at the thought of me and Camille butting heads again.

Just as I was about to turn on my heels and go to the back office, I heard a female call my name. I turned to face the owner of the voice, and it was Camille. Now she was standing up, and my jaw had almost dropped to the floor. Camille had done a 360 degree makeover, and an overwhelming feeling of envy washed over me. She had lost all her baby weight, and she had on a pair of tight jeans and a little white top, with a chocolate bolero sweater on top. She had on chunky, turquoise-colored jewelry. Her hair was colored dirty blonde, and cut in long layers. Naturally, I didn't have any hatred towards her per se, but for her I represented all that was wrong with her world. Camille wasn't ghetto, but I brought out the worst in her.

"What the fuck is she doing here?"

"Camille…she…" I didn't know what Tony was going to say, but I stopped him before he allowed the lie to leave his lips.

"I work here."

"You what?"

"You heard me."

"Did you know she was here?"

Camille was looking to Tony for answers, but he was distracted by how this whole incident must have looked to his teammates, so he was trying to play cool. The fun had left the VIP, and all that was left were stunned looks, cracked faces, and panic.

"No, I didn't know she was here."

"Tony, tell the truth."

I felt so disrespected and humiliated in front of his boys, her friends, the bouncers, and the growing crowd.

"What the fuck is that supposed to mean, Tony?"

"I mean I saw her, but I didn't know she worked here."

"This is not the place for this conversation. Let's go back to the office."

I wanted them to get out of the ear shot of customers and employees, plus I was trying to salvage the dignity and respect that I had in the club.

"Oh, now we need to talk? Bitch, you can say whatever you have to say to me right here." Camille was heated, and she wasn't backing down for anything.

"As I said before, I work here, and I don't want any problems."

"I don't give a fuck about your job! What do you need to say to me?"

"Baby, let's not make a scene in Ron's club." Tony was pleading with a hushed voice and desperate, guilty eyes.

"You didn't give a fuck about Ron's club when you let him hire this bitch! What happened, she was tired of taking her clothes off for bread?"

"I'm not going to let you disrespect me in my place of business. Either you come to the back so that we can finish this discussion, or you'll have to leave."

"Oh, you're throwing me out?" Camille started to step closer to me.

"Tony, get her!"

I yelled at Tony for standing there trying to blend in with the crowd while his wife disrespected me, his boy's club, and him for allowing his wife to run her mouth about our personal business in front of his teammates and everybody else. If nobody knew that we were fucking before, they knew now.

"Camille, let's go."

"Get the fuck away from me! You still fucking this ho?"

"Who are you calling a ho? At least I didn't spend the night at some other nigga's house, and miss my husband's game!"

She had taken it a little too far, and I lost it. At that point, I didn't give a fuck about the job, I was about to whoop her ass.

"You told her my fucking business?"

Camille was looking at Tony with daggers in her eyes, and his fear prevented him from thinking clearly. He should have snatched her ass up, and dragged her out of the club kicking and screaming. She was making a fool of herself, and he should've been shutting her up instead of letting her embarrass the both of them.

"I was upset when I left the house…"

I could almost see Tony's balls leave his dick hanging there, and shrivel up into his abdomen like when he was in his mama's stomach.

"I don't give a fuck! Bitch you just won't go away, will you?"

"Ask your husband. He's the one that can't leave me alone."

"Oh really?"

She lunged towards me, and it was on. She pushed me back, and I fell on one of the couches, my dress was up around my hips with my freshly waxed pussy staring up at the crowd. The audience moaned as I yanked my dress down. Before Tony or security could stop me, I jumped up, cocked my fist back, and punched Camille dead in the eye, and she fell like a suicide jumper hitting a concrete mattress.

"Bitch, you got me fucked up!"

I was ready to go a few rounds with her, but the fight was over in the first. None of her friends jumped in like Leanne at the bowling alley, so she got dropped before she knew what hit her. She was just laying there like she was sleep.

"Camille!"

Tony ran to her side like a little bitch. He was calling her name, trying to revive her because she looked dead. One of the security guards went to get smelling salts from the office. My hand was numb at first, but then it was aching like it was sitting in a roaring fireplace. I shook it out, but the pain started kicking in. My knuckles were red, and had started to swell. Tony was glaring at me with a hot mixture of shock and anger as the security guards pulled me out of the VIP and escorted me to the back office.

As I sat in a blind fury in the big, rolling chair behind the desk with an ice pack on my fist, one of the security guards called Ron at home. He described the incident as "mild" because Tim was one of my boys, and he didn't want me to get fired, but the truth is that I knew there would be some repercussion to the fight that I was involved in, both with Ron and Tony.

I thanked Tim for making the call and having my back, and then he went to get Hypnotiq for me. She was on the other side of the club, and she didn't even know what had went down until Tim came and brought her in the office.

"Alizé! Girl, what happened? I was talking to Glenn from the club, and Tim came and told me you were in a fight!"

"Camille showed up. I didn't even know she was coming. She fucking pushed me down, so I dropped the bitch!"

"But Alizé, what about your job?"

"I don't know. Ron is on his way up here."

"What was Tony doing?"

"Acting like a bitch. He tried to lie and say that he didn't know I was working here and shit. I tried to get them back here to talk, but she was talking shit, so I clocked her. My fucking hand is killing me!"

"Girl, what are you going to do about Tony? You have this bomb-ass job because of him, but he's not leaving his wife, and you can't keep getting in fights with her. Not to mention the fact that this is your place of business now. This is not *Aces* where bitches whoop ass on a daily; this is a respectable club, so that strip club shit isn't going down here."

"You're right, but I don't know what the fuck I'm doing. I hope I still have a job. Do me a favor and go see if Camille came to. When they brought me back here she looked unconscious."

"I'll go see, but honey, do me a favor, and really think about this situation. When the shit hit the fan, Tony lied to protect his wife, and when the fight happened, he was by her side. He didn't come back here to check on you, and he probably won't. His loyalty is to her, and you need to figure out how much more you can take before you leave him alone. You know I love you, and I'm here for you anytime you want to talk, but it kills me to see you keep getting your heart stepped on."

"Thank you sweetie, but the situation has taken on a life of its own. I may not need to make any decisions because after tonight, Ron and Tony are probably done fucking with me."

Hypnotiq went to check on Camille, and came back to report. She said that they had moved her to the couch, and she was sitting up, but looking drowsy. Her eye was red and puffy, and Tony was holding an ice pack and her purse. One of Camille's friends was bringing the car around, so they could take her home.

The crowd had started to move on, but everybody was talking about the fight between the club manager and the basketball player's wife on playoff night. Ron got to the club within 30 minutes, and I told him my version of the truth. Tony had already called him before he got to the club to apologize for bringing drama to his spot. Ron made his punishment swift; I was suspended for a week, and he and I would talk before I could return to work.

Hypnotiq drove me home, and I tried to call Tony, but his phone went right to voicemail. I needed to let him know that I didn't appreciate him hanging me out to dry like that, letting me take all of Camille's heat. I just left a message saying to call me back as soon as possible. In my heart, I knew that calming Camille down was his first priority, so I wouldn't hear from him until the next day at least.

CHAPTER 27

Maybe it was fucked up for me to say it, but I have always thought that women had control over whether or not their men cheated on them. The only thing a female has to do is maintain everything she used to do when they very first met. Always looking sexy enough to eat, satisfying them sexually, and being a friend that supports them, listens to them, and laughs more than they complain.

I hadn't had a boyfriend since God was a child, and unfortunately I didn't have the knowledge then that I have now. What I have done is use my knowledge on other females' men, which I have learned is way too easy. I already had an advantage because I didn't have the responsibilities of a wife, or a reason to nag. I never felt guilty for hooking up with a married man because if he felt completely satisfied, supported, and respected he didn't *want* to go anywhere else. It is not true that all men cheat; there have been occasions when I would approach a guy, and he would flat out tell me that he had somebody at home. Of course there will always be some men who cheat *just because*, but for the most part there weren't being taken care of physically, emotionally or both.

In some way, Camille was not satisfying Tony, and he was wide open to meet someone else to fulfill his needs, and that was where I came in the picture. There were several females before me, and I was sure there would be plenty more after me. In other words, as special as I thought I was, deep down I realized that it wasn't so much me as it was Tony needing something other than his wife. I knew that without a doubt, if it wasn't me it would've been another female.

In my mind, I had gone over several scenarios that could play out the first time that I talked to Tony after last night. He would either quit me, or apologize for being a pussy. I would either quit him, or apologize for knocking his wife out. There really weren't many options in the complex, fucked up situation that we were in.

When my phone rang the next morning, I thought I was happy to see Tony's name on my caller ID because I hadn't quite figured out if I was pissed off, disappointed, or sorry for what happened last night.

"Tony…"

"No, this is his *wife!*"

"What?"

I couldn't believe that she had called my apartment after I had knocked her out in front of her husband, his teammates, and her friends, and I wondered if Tony was sitting right there listening to the absurd conversation that was just around the corner.

"For the last time, I want you to leave my husband alone. Your job at the club is a wrap, so you can go back to the strip club tonight."

Explosive feelings of shock and disappointment rushed over me, and sent chills through my bones. I sat stunned and silent for what seemed like forever. My new life had been snatched from me; everything that I had accomplished in the past few months had been utterly erased within seconds. All of the ideas and projects that I had started at the club would never be completed by me. What a difference a day makes, yesterday I woke up with the world at my fingertips, and today my reality had been altered…again.

I didn't give a fuck about Tony. That relationship had been sinking like a ship with holes in it, so I could've cared less about her husband, I just wanted my job back.

"Why are you calling me?"

I reached down deep to trap the tears that were trying to get to the surface. I wasn't going to show weakness while this bitch crushed my plans and took immense pleasure in it.

"I just wanted to know if it was that hard to find your own man?"

"No, it isn't hard. In fact, it was easy to get your husband's attention. If you took care of him the way a woman should, I couldn't have snatched him from you. I'm not the reason for Tony cheating, you are!" I wanted to hurt her feelings and make her feel as bad as I did.

"You would like to think that you did something spectacular to get Tony, but it's not that difficult; he's a pussy hound. You should have more respect for yourself, and get someone that can be all yours. Why would you settle for someone that just wants to fuck? He's not offering you anything because he doesn't want anything else from you."

"What do you care? Do you respect yourself? You were getting your freak on with Ken in Vegas!"

"No, even though Tony continually disrespects me, I would never disrespect *myself* and fuck one of his teammates. My name will never be mentioned in a locker room. Just leave my family alone so that we can live our lives."

"Why don't you tell your husband to leave me alone because he is the one coming after me. I left his ass alone after I saw you at the gym. He came over here and fucked me the same night I whooped your ass at the bowling alley."

"He what?" She couldn't hide the surprise in her voice.

"I said that your husband was over here fucking me when you were tending to your wounds."

"I'm not surprised really. I guess you think being married to Tony is really something special huh? Well let me tell you what, being involved with Tony isn't all that it's cracked up to be. Because he is a professional athlete, he is gone most of the year, and I have to raise our two kids by myself. I have to wipe the tears, and explain to my son why daddy can't make his school events and basketball games. And even when he is here, he's running with his boys half the time, or fucking around on me. Tony is a wonderful father, but he doesn't take of my needs. You're not the first girl, and you're not even the only one he's seeing right now. He's using you, he's using me. Tony is a very selfish man. He only thinks about what he wants. For the most part, I have a good life; I have a nanny, a cook, maids, cars, a beautiful home, and more money than I could ever spend, but that's the trade-off. There are times when I wish that I could give up all the money to have a man that truly believed that I was the only woman he needed."

For the first time in this whole bizarre conversation, I was speechless. Never before had I thought about the cross that Camille had to bear in exchange for her extravagant lifestyle. I didn't realize that she was lonely, shut-out, and a virtual single mother. Quite often I thought about the fact that Tony was basically using me, but I rationalized it by saying that I was getting something out of the relationship too. Camille had the validation of being his wife, the mother of his kids, and the woman of the house.

Truth be told, my delusions of grandeur allowed me to believe that I gave him something that his wife could not or would not give him, and I somehow held the key to his happiness. But in reality, I was a diversion for Tony, something to do, a reason to get out of the house, a way to escape his responsibilities, and not to mention someone that would let him use their body as his real-life blow-up doll.

Camille sensed that I didn't have much to say, but she told me to give her a call later because the baby had woken up from his nap. She realized that talking to me seriously and respectfully did more damage than fighting and calling me bitches. Everything that she said to me reverberated in my ears for hours later. I still hadn't talked to Tony, and I didn't know what I would've said to him anyway. I thought about what kind of a man he was to have it all, but still not satisfied. He was plain greedy, just like most of his friends, and females like me made it possible.

It was as if I talked him up because my cell phone rang while I was at the grocery store picking up the stuff to make tacos.

I had disgust in my voice and disappointment in my heart.

"What you doing?"

Tony had a way of believing that if you didn't mention something unpleasant, then it didn't really happen. He was so passive-aggressive, he never would've got right into what happened last night unless I did.

"Grocery shopping."

"I wanted to come by."

"For what Tony? Camille called me earlier, and we had a long talk."

"What? What did she call you for?"

"She wanted me to leave her family alone. She had a lot to say about what a ho you are, and how you're fucking with other females besides me."

"Look, call me when you're on the way home, and I'm coming over."

"Why? She also told me that I lost my job at the club. Was that a part of your deal to stay in the house, you had to fire me?"

"I'll come by when you get home."

He couldn't take the heat, and he needed to get off the phone, so that he could come up with a plan of action. I purposely dumped a lot on him all at once.

Both Hypnotiq and Brandy called me while I was in the store, and by the time I told the story three times, the employees and customers were ready to comment on my tragic life as I heard exaggerated sighs and witnessed slow, disapproving head-shaking.

When I got home, I unloaded the groceries with two trips up and down the stairs as the neighborhood kids sat on the top of the steps playing jacks. I turned the pot on, and cooked the ground beef and chopped onions. I popped the head of lettuce, and let it drain in the colander with the washed tomatoes. I grated the Monterey Jack and cheddar cheeses, and cut up the tomatoes. I cut up the avocado, and took the sour cream out of the fridge, so it wouldn't still be ice cold by the time I finished frying up the tacos. I chopped the lettuce last, so that most of the water was drained out. Tacos made me happy, and after last night *and* this afternoon, I needed a half dozen to get right. I took the oil, frying pan, and pie tin draped with two paper towels out on the counter, and waited for the tomato sauce to cook into the ground beef.

I sat on the couch, turned the t.v. on, and cradled my swollen, sore hand where I had punched Camille. Tony called again, and I dropped my head in my hands wondering how I got in the middle of his marriage when he was supposed to be someone to just have fun with. I answered the phone to find out if I had lost my job.

"You home yet?"

"I'm home, but I don't know what you need to come over here for. Say what you need to say over the phone. You ain't fucking, so there's no need in you driving over here."

"We don't need to fuck, but I'm not going to sit here and have this whole conversation on the phone. I'm around the corner from you. Go open the door."

"Tony, why are you pushing the issue? You need to focus on your wife and your family. Keep it funky, I don't mean shit to you and I never will."

"Why are you talking like this, because you talked to Camille? Of course she told you what she wanted you to hear. She was hella mad last night when she found out that you worked at Ron's, and that I told you about Vegas. She's not going anywhere."

"See, that's just the problem. I'm never going to be anything more than your little work, and I'm getting tired of bumping into your wife all over L.A., and now she's calling my phone. I just lost the best job I ever had, and it's about time I moved the fuck on."

"I'm outside your door, come open it."

"Tony...ugh!"

It really pissed me off how manipulative he could be. I'm trying to tell him how I feel, but he always had a way of discounting my feelings, and smoothing everything over as if I was seeing things that weren't really there.

I didn't have on makeup, hair was thrown up in a clip, and I had on basketball shorts and a big shirt; for the first time since I had met Tony, I didn't care how I looked.

I walked to the door, opened it, and there Tony stood with ice cream in his hands. I stood in the doorway with my arms folded over my chest in a fashion that should have told him that I wasn't feeling him or his ice cream, but he was oblivious so he persevered.

"I brought you some ice cream."

"Thank you."

No reason to waste good dessert. I walked to the kitchen to put it in the freezer. While I was in there I stirred the ground beef, and turned the heat off.

"Damn! What you cooking?"

"I'm making *myself* some tacos. What did you come over here to say?"

"Mia, I can't see you anymore. Camille understands me, and she knows that I'm not a one-woman man. You guys have had too many confrontations, so I have to be cool for now. My family is my first priority, so if I need to settle down for a little while, then that's what I have to do. Camille knows how I get down, but she doesn't like shit thrown up in her face, and I haven't been fair."

I couldn't believe the words that were coming out of his mouth, and if I didn't hear it for myself, I wouldn't have believed that a man could be that arrogant. After the last break up, I was heartbroken at the thought of living without Tony. At the time, I knew that I would miss hanging out with him. It was killing me that I was losing my friend more than anything else, but this time was different. There was an uncontrollable emotion that took over me, angry at how much time I had wasted nurturing a dead-end relationship. My feelings had changed; I didn't feel the same about Tony, like when I used to believe that the earth rotated around him, he was my light.

There were times when I wished that I could go back to the way I used to feel, when fucking and X-rated parties were enough. I had evolved to a point where that wasn't satisfying or even fun anymore. I began to think that Tony and his boys were just that…boys, and instead of having a half-ass relationship with a baller, I longed for a normal relationship with a square. Brent gave me a taste of that, and I didn't realize it until it was too late, but I hadn't been treated like a lady in a long time. Brent made me a priority during our short-lived union; he actually made plans with me instead of trying to hook up at the last minute all the time. He followed through, and made me feel special by giving me all of his attention, and not looking over his shoulder for potential snitches.

"Tony, that's cool. I've expected it, and I've had enough anyway. Ron suspended me from the club for a week, and I'm sure he's going to fire me as soon as I get back. He can't have that kind of drama in his club. I'm tired of being used by you, and Camille said that I'm not even the only one."

"Look Mia, you know how I get down…"

I had grown so very tired of that overused, pathetic phrase; I thought I would lose my mind if he said it one more time in a five minute period. It was so arrogant and grandiose.

"Damn nigga, you got it like that? You got a mistress for the mistress? You're the fucking man, but you know what, I'm out. The fact that you're fucking other bitches is just doing too much. Your wife and I have been in two fucking fights, I'm going through all this bullshit, and that still isn't enough for you."

I walked back to the door, and held it open for Tony to slide on out. I felt very sure of my actions although from last night to this morning, I wasn't sure of what I would say to Tony, but after the things that he had just said to me, I was convinced that this relationship was not only unhealthy, but toxic.

"You can bounce because there isn't shit else to talk about." Tony gave me a nonchalant look like he wasn't going anywhere, so I said it again.

"Please leave."

Tony walked over to me, and I thought he was going to finally get up out of my apartment, but he didn't walk out of the door, he shut it.

"Mia, don't be like that. You know I care about you, or I wouldn't even spend time with you. Do you know many chicks would *love* to be in your position?"

"Tony, when is the last time we went out to eat, or went to a movie? The *only* thing we do is FUCK! A whole bunch of bitches would put up with that shit for a minute, but that shit gets played out! I got a million niggas trying to lay at my feet! Nigga *what*?! Get the fuck the out of my house!"

All of a sudden, Tony yanked my shirt, and ripped it from my body. I wasn't wearing a bra, and he started licking and sucking all over my titties, while sinking his teeth in my nipples. I tried to shove him away, but he was stronger than me and very persistent. My pussy started heating up, but I tried to fight the feeling. I didn't want to give in to him; I had felt so strong just a few minutes before he started attacking my chastity. I kept my hurt hand by my side, but I tried to push his head off of one nipple, and then the other, but he wouldn't stop. My flesh was on fire, and I was become weaker as he left each erect nipple warm and moist from his agile tongue and sexy mouth.

"Tony…"

"Shhh…"

He pulled my shorts down, and pushed me on the couch. Tony ate the fuck out of my pussy, and I the battle continued between me and myself; I wanted to give in, but fuck him. I was squirming all over the couch, trying to break free. He slowly caressed my clit with his fat tongue, and then licked my pussy lips until it got nice and wet. He carried the moisture from my slit to my clit, and I had to bite my lip before I yelled out something stupid, like *I love you*. I was pushing his shoulders away from my body, and he sat up for a second. For a split second, I was afraid that he finally gave up, convinced that my hitting and fighting was for real. I was relieved when Tony slipped my shorts all the way off, spread my legs all the way open, and then pushed my legs up near my head so that he could shove his entire face in my pussy. I was moaning and rebelling against the way he made me feel, and then I was just moaning; he had won.

Tony finally let my legs go, and began to kiss me. I tasted myself as he made tiny circles in my mouth with his full tongue.

"Tony, I don't want to…"

He put his hands on either side of my face, and sucked on my bottom lip. He knew that drove me crazy; he wasn't playing fair. As much as I wanted him to stop, I wanted him to keep going because the thought of standing there with my morals and a throbbing pussy was immoral in itself.

He quickly pulled a condom out of his pocket, unbuckled his belt, and let his pants fall to his ankles. Tony unrolled that condom and slapped it on his dick faster than I could say *nigga please*. He slid his dick in me, and I arched my back to accommodate his voracious dick. He had never stuck his dick in me without me sucking it first; he was desperate to get that dick in there, blow my mind, and get back to life as he knew it. He sat up a little so that his dick rubbed nicely against my clit. I was rocking back and forth, taking it all. I came against my will, but it was earth-shattering. I saw stars and my dizzy head wobbled like a bobble head sitting on top of a pencil neck. Tony came hard, and we both sat on the couch in a silent daze.

He carefully pulled the condom off, and walked to the bathroom to flush it. I heard the water shooting out of the faucet at full force like a fire hydrant, and I knew he was using all of my soap washing every trace of me off his dick, while I still sat unmoved in a stupor. When I finally got up, I grabbed a towel out of the linen closet, wet it in the kitchen sink, and washed my swollen pussy. I didn't rinse want to rinse it out in the kitchen, so I just threw it in a grocery bag and threw it in the corner.

I told myself that nothing had changed, and we just got down one last time. Tony came back from the bathroom like he had just won a war.

"You making me some tacos?"

"How many do you want?"

"Make me like four, thanks."

Tony sat down on the couch, and started flipping channels like it was all good. He ignored the fact that we were done. Tony wanted to fuck, and that's what he did. My body was merely a vessel meant for his pleasure. I looked at him with different eyes as he watched the basketball game. He was selfish and greedy, and he didn't give a fuck about me or Camille because he was disrespecting her by being over here when he had just told her last night that he was done with me.

Silently, I fried his four tacos and gave him some grape soda. I was getting ready to sit down and eat mine, and he asked for one more. I rolled my eyes, and brought him one off of my plate, and made myself another one. I never would've felt irritated or annoyed by anything he would have said or done just a few weeks ago, but something in me had changed. Whether or not Camille was sincere or not, the things that she had said on the phone truly had an effect on me. Not to mention the fact that he walked in here like I should have been appreciative to him for allowing me to be in his presence. The sex was all of that, but I was tired of his shit. Let him find another mindless piece of ass; I was done.

I was supposed to talk to Ron the next day, but I didn't see the point of fighting for my job anymore. He was going to fire me, so I decided to save myself the humiliation. I was going to call him in the morning, and tell him that I wanted to come by and pick up my personal belongings in the office, and then I would be out of his hair for good.

When I was finally able to sit down and eat my food, there was a knock at the door. I looked in the peep hole, and Camille's face looked back at me.

"Open the fucking door! I know Tony's in there, I can see his truck!"

I turned my back on the door with my hands on my hips and a shitty look on my face. That was the final fucking straw. The bitch was knocking on my front door, waking up my neighbors, and putting everybody in my business.

"Tony, Camille is outside! Get your fucking bitch from banging on my shit!"

Tony dropped his food, scrambled into his jeans and shirt, slid his feet into his shoes and opened the door. He was trying to slide outside, but she bust the door open, walked in and slammed it behind her.

"What the fuck are you doing over here?"

"I had to drop something off…"

"Motherfucker, it smells like pussy, your condom wrapper is on the floor *and* you're eating tacos? Don't talk to me like I'm fucking stupid!"

Tony started reaching for his necklace that was lying on the table, and moving towards Camille. She snatched her arm away when he tried to touch her.

"Is it that hard for you to find a man of your own? Do you want to be his wife or something? You're cooking and shit?"

"While you're talking shit, you need to check your husband! He's over here at my fucking apartment after he told you it was over the last time! You need to focus on his ass, and not me! You have this situation fucked up!"

She turned around to look at him as if he would have an answer. Standing in front of his wife he was the biggest pussy.

"Baby I'm sorry. She left something at the club last night, and I was just bringing it to her."

"Tony, why don't you stop lying?? You came over here to break up with me *again*, and when I told you to get the fuck out, you started trying to fuck! Tell your wife the truth! We fucked! She didn't come all the way over here for nothing!"

"Mia shut up!"

"Shut up? Shut up? Why don't you *and* your wife get the fuck out of my house! I don't want his messy ass anyway! You can have him!"

Camille looked at Tony like he was the sorry consolation prize that he was. His busted ass kept trying to touch on her, and she kept moving out of dodge, all over my living room.

"Tony stop! Don't fucking touch me!"

"Baby…"

"I am so sick of your shit! I can't believe that I had to follow you over here like we're in high school! We're married and I have your kids! You are so fucking messy! How the fuck can you keep doing me like this?"

"Let's go home."

"Fuck that! We're going to talk right now! Does she fuck better than me? Is that it?"

"Camille that's not true. Can we go home and talk?"

"You have disrespected me in so many ways and I'm not putting up with your shit anymore. I look good, and I deserve a lot better than this. If you don't want me, I'm sure I can find somebody else that will!"

"You're talking crazy now. I love you and I want to keep our family together."

"I can't tell! We can end this right now! Do you want to keep fucking her?"

"Hell nah! I'm leaving with you. I'm done with her. It was nothing."

Nothing? I didn't even give a fuck! Her face relaxed and I could tell she wasn't going anywhere. He was pleading and simping, and I was getting tired of the whole pitiful scene. I just wanted them out of my fucking apartment. Tony kept trying to touch Camille and guide her towards the door, but she kept yanking and pulling away from him. I couldn't believe that he was jocking his wife like I wasn't even standing there. I was invisible; his one and only priority was getting his wife to stay with his sorry ass. A couple of months ago I would've been a bawling mess holding onto his legs, trying to get him to choose me, but now I was ready for them to take their shit out of my apartment. I moved towards the door and opened it for them to walk out. I was emotionless and mentally exhausted from the endless drama.

"Camille, I'm sorry for the part that I played in this bullshit. You don't have to worry about me anymore, so I would appreciate it if you never came back over here."

The look in her eyes told me that she believed what I was saying, but she knew in her heart of hearts that Tony would replace me in no time. My worries were over, but hers had just begun…again.

CHAPTER 28

I was a bundle of nerves when I picked up the phone to call Ron a week later. I didn't know what he was going to say to me, but I decided it was better to confront my fears, and get it over with then remain in the land of denial.

Ron sounded dry when he answered the phone, and even though he was generally a pretty quiet guy, he had definitely been friendlier than he was with me right then. He told me to come in the next afternoon to meet with him, but I stopped him mid-sentence.

"Look Ron, you gave me the position of assistant manager, and I was absolutely unprofessional. You don't have to say anything else. I will come by to get my things from your office…"

"You're right, but there's no need to jump the gun. Come in, and we'll talk then."

"Okay Ron."

I hung up the phone and tried to figure out what else he could possibly have to say to me. It was foreign to me, but it felt like I was being sent to the principal's office. When I worked at *Aces*, the atmosphere was business casual in the truest form of the word. Everybody hustled and handled their business, but at the same time, the environment was casual and informal. If the owner and managers had to chastise an employee, they said whatever they had to say in front of *whoever* happened to be standing near-by; there was no privacy, protocol, or hard-and-fast rules.

Strippers hit chicks over the head with beer bottles, yanked weaves out of each other's heads, and cussed niggas and bitches out in a heart beat, and while they may have been suspended for a couple of days, or even fired, they could always come back. Even though the managers talked a big game, there were no absolutes in the club, and that was the life that I had grown accustomed too, so I wasn't sure how seriously I should have taken the meeting with Ron. This was the real world, and I had never been so nervous to talk to my boss.

Brandy and Lorenzo were having a barbeque the next day, and she wanted me to go shopping with her. She came and picked me up, and we went by Smart and Final and Costco. Brandy bought a gang of chicken, sausages, sodas, buffalo wings, beer, liquor, and everything for hamburgers. As we walked through the stores, all of the families and couples began to surround me, and I remembered why I didn't like exposing myself to these kinds of places. It was filled with oversized quantities reminding single people like me, that we were losers for living alone without someone to love us. Picture-perfect kids begged for 12 pack boxes of Drumstick ice cream cones and dinosaur-shaped chicken nuggets while guilt-ridden parents obliged them. Baskets filled to the brim with the makings of family dinners, humongous coffee cans, and 48 pack containers of toilet tissue were intimidating. I felt like people were staring at me because I wasn't pushing a cart, I was merely standing next to someone pushing a cart.

Brandy's car was packed by the time we finished running errands. As we were pulling up to the house, she called Lorenzo, and he came out to help carry everything in.

Her man was fine; tall, chocolate brown with beautiful, slightly-slanted eyes, and a tight body. He had a close fade, smooth skin, a nice goatee, and a *Brandy* tattoo on his neck. Brandy and Zo were the perfect couple; she took care of his every need, and he was a faithful bad boy. He wore hip hop gear, and looked like he was down for whatever, but he never even looked at other women in a way that made them think that it could jump off. Ironically, females were even more turned on by Zo because he *wasn't* fucking. He told every one of them that he had a girl, and he wasn't looking for anything else, he was satisfied with what he had at home.

Zo had never cheated, and the best thing of all was that he placed Brandy above everything and everybody else. He scheduled real dates with her, took her on little trips out of town, and bought her sentimental gifts just because. His mother and father had been married for 20 years, but Zo was 17 when his mother died of cancer. Before she died, she would talk to Zo, and tell him how much she loved his father, and how they took care of each other every day of their lives. Zo's father showed him how to be a man by going to work everyday, coming home every night, taking care of his family, and treating his mother like she was the only woman in the world for him.

When Brandy tried to get the stuff out of the car, Zo told her to go in and sit down. He was a man.

As the two of them put the groceries up, I sat on the couch and contemplated my future. Ron was being vague over the phone, and I couldn't figure out why he couldn't just tell me that it was a wrap over the phone instead of cracking my face in person. What would my next plan be? I had my savings to live off of, which was over $20,000, and I could go back to school. I didn't even know what I would major in, but I could figure that out later.

"Hey girl, what are you so deep in thought about?"

"I have that meeting with Ron tomorrow."

"Well, now that you and Tony are done, do you think he'll still let you work there?"

"I doubt it. I don't even know if I would want to. Tony was paying me more than what my job was worth, so what would Ron do even *if* he wanted to keep me on? Pay me less?"

"I hear you. Well, I know you don't want to go back to the club."

"Hell no, I have my savings and I could take some classes."

"That sounds like a bomb plan! Let me know if I can help you choose classes, or if you need help with the financial aid application."

Brandy had always tried to get me to take classes with her when I first started dancing, but I always told her *not right now*. I couldn't wait to get out of high school, and the thought of continuing my education was always very unappealing to me. When she graduated from Cal State Northridge, and I sat in the audience watching her walk across the stage, I wished that I had taken her advice. She got a degree in Marketing, and slid right into her job on the Miracle Mile. She had job security, a 401k, and benefits, while I had bad knees, a shitty attitude, and a fucked up perspective on life.

"Well, after I talk to him, I'll know what I have to do."

"Do you want me to go with you?"

"Thanks girl, but I can handle it. I have no expectations, and if anything I have prepared myself for the worst."

"Have you heard from Tony?"

"Nope."

"I know it's only been a week, but do you miss him?"

"You know what? I thought I would, but I don't. When we stopped talking the last time, I missed him so much I couldn't see straight, but this time is different. The relationship had started to play itself out because all we did was stay in my apartment all the time. We didn't go anywhere or do anything besides fuck at one or two in the morning when his wife thought he was out with the boys. I was starting to feel like used, so it's cool that it ended. I should've let him go a few months ago, but I didn't know how, but his wife popping up at my house finally did it for me."

"I'm happy that situation didn't turn out as bad as it could have. She could've went crazy and brought a gun."

"I got heat too, but I hear what you're saying."

Brandy, Lorenzo, and I made hamburgers and watched *Any Given Sunday*. I ended up falling asleep on the couch. Brandy had thrown a blanket on me, and then her and Zo went in the bedroom; she pushed the door closed, and turned the lights off. An hour or so later, I had to go to the bathroom, so I wobbled threw the dark living room, and down the hallway. As I passed Brandy's room, I heard her moaning, so I peeked through the slit in her door.

She was on the bed lying on her stomach, and Lorenzo's face was between her bent legs. All I could see was the back of his head moving up and down, side to side in small circles. Brandy was grabbing at his head like she was getting ready to cum. She was calling his name, rocking and rolling her hips, and grabbing the blankets. Suddenly he stopped, and got in a 69 position, laying his body on top of hers. Lorenzo slid his dick in Brandy's mouth, and stuck his tongue back in her pussy. I opened the door a little, so I could see his dick. Brandy was trying her best to take it all, but she had to move her head to the side because it was probably going down too far. The room was dark, and if it wasn't for the street lights, I couldn't have seen a thing, but I saw that dick, and it was nice. They were going at it for a while, and I stood there lurking in the shadows with my flaming pussy. If it wasn't my best friend in the room, I would've asked to join in, but since it was I stuck my hand between my legs, and rubbed them together.

Lorenzo was on top, pumping his dick in and out of Brandy's mouth while his mouth was concentrated on her clit. They both started moving around faster until Lorenzo rolled Brandy on her side. He pulled his dick out of her mouth, and rolled her on her stomach where he entered her from behind. She wasn't very sexy, but she was taking it. Brandy was squealing like a pig, and Lorenzo let her off the hook, and she climbed on top. She was kind of boring, but then again she wasn't a stripper. She moved around on his dick while Lorenzo was pushing her hips down on his lap. Instead of her riding him, she was basically sitting on his dick, and he was doing all the work. Lorenzo was moaning and moving faster and faster. She wasn't very animated, but I think I saw her come. Lorenzo was pushing and pulling her hips up and down on him, and he finally came, yelling out like a wounded animal.

When I heard him offer to get Brandy some water, I ducked out of the hall, and dove on the couch. I pulled my shirt off, unhooked my bra, and threw them under the covers. I pushed my panties down my legs until they reached the tip of my toes. I rubbed the lips of my pussy, sliding my finger in and out, and transferring the moisture to my clit. I rubbed it slowly as the mental picture of what Lorenzo was doing to Brandy flashed across my mind like a porno.

A few minutes later, Lorenzo had thrown on some basketball shorts, and walked out of the door. He was on his way to the kitchen when he couldn't help but stop at the couch. I was playing with my pussy, staring at him, daring him to fuck me because I was much better than my best friend. His sweaty, naked chest was a well-chisled piece of steel; the smell of sex on his body made my pussy throb like a healthy heartbeat.

"I'm sorry. I was going to get some water."

Instead of me pretending that I didn't see him, and covering myself with the blanket, I sat there and let him watch me pleasure myself. He stood there for another second as if he couldn't believe what he was watching, and then he moved on to the kitchen. Instantly, I covered myself up with the blanket, so that by the time he came back through I looked more like his girlfriend's best friend lying on the couch. Any other cat would've jumped in my pussy face first, but Lorenzo really was a good dude. Ironically, the way that he played me made me want him even more.

Lorenzo nervously fumbled around in the kitchen until he came out with a 32 ounce Slurpee cup full of water. He clearly didn't know what he should say to me.

"Good night."

"Yeah, good night. I'm sorry if I made you feel uncomfortable before. I just needed to release some stress."

"I'm cool. Do your thing."

"See you in the morning."

"Okay…umm…night."

Lorenzo disappeared into the afterglow of the bedroom while I lay on the cold couch by myself. I probably took it too far, but I wanted him to get rough, grab me around my neck, and force his dick in my mouth like a savage, so that I could tell Brandy that he just took it, and I had no choice.

Those were the times when I thought: *You can take the girl out of the strip club, but you can't take the strip club out of the girl.* I was used to being an exhibitionist and pushing the envelope, but the truth is that I enjoyed embarrassing decent, faithful men. I loved the power and the way that they quickly forgot commitments, responsibility, and morals when pussy was staring at them in the face. Probably not a wise choice to push Lorenzo's buttons because he was my girl's man, but I wanted him, and I was used to getting what I wanted.

❦   ❦   ❦

The next morning, I got up before Brandy and Lorenzo, and ducked out of the apartment before they woke up. I knew that he hadn't said anything to her last night, but just in case he woke up with a conscious, I wanted to be gone when Brandy came looking for me.

I lounged around my place for a little while before it was time to meet Ron. I hadn't heard anything from Tony, and I honestly started to miss him a little. It's not that I missed all of the attention that he showered me with because Lord knows that wasn't it. I had grown comfortable with him, and if anything, I missed his friendship. In retrospect, we should've left our relationship the way it was in the beginning. Laughing and fucking. Everything got fucked up when we started hanging out and playing house, catching feelings.

After I got dressed, I drove to the club and saw Ron's car in the front. I pulled behind him, and walked to the back. Ron opened the door.

"Hey Mia, come on in."

"Thanks Ron. How you doing?"

"I'm good. You?"

"I'm fine. Thank you."

We hadn't been so formal since the first day we had met. I followed him into the office, and I took a seat on the other side of his desk. He looked like he was at a lost for words, but he finally began to speak.

"What happened the other night was unacceptable."

"I know, and I can't apologize enough. I will completely understand if you have to let me go, but I promise that nothing like that will ever happen again."

"Mia, I have to be honest with you. When Tony called me about hiring you, I warned him that something like this could happen, you and Camille meeting up. He said that he didn't think anything like that would ever happen, but now it has."

"I never thought it could happen either, Ron. I was minding my own business, but when she confronted me, I tried to get her in the office so that we could talk in private, but she pushed me down on the couch. I'm sure it doesn't matter to you, but I was only defending myself."

"No, it doesn't matter. I can't have my managers hitting anybody at any time."

"You're right."

"Well Mia, I talked to Tony. He told me that you guys aren't seeing each other anymore. I want to keep you, but only under the condition that you do not get in any more fights."

"I won't Ron, you can trust me. Thank you for believing in me!"

"Well now wait a minute. I know that Tony had agreed to pay your salary, but now that you guys are done, you're on payroll like everybody else. I don't exactly know how much Tony was paying you, but I can still give you $800 a week."

"Well, I figured that. Tony was giving me another $500 a week, but I'll take it."

"Okay, so if you agree to everything you can work tonight if you want to. If for any reason Camille comes back in here, you just go on about your business. If you get into it again with her, I'm going to have to let you go."

"I understand, and I just want to thank you for giving me another chance. Working here has been the best experience of my life, and I want to show you that I take my job very seriously."

"Well, if I didn't believe you, you wouldn't be here right now."

"Okay, well I'll be back later on tonight then."

I stood up, and shook Ron's hand. I knew that even if Ron didn't fire me, Tony's punk ass was going to take his money back, but that's cool. I wasn't broke when I took the job, and I was putting Tony's kickback in my freezer anyway, so working for the straight salary was cool. Even with the extra money, it was less than I made at *Aces*, so it didn't matter anyway. As long as I was able to pay my bills, I was happy to get out of the strip club.

On my way home, I called Hypnotiq to tell her my good news. Big D had taken her to New York early that morning, and she was shopping while he was in a meeting with one of the new rappers he had just signed with. Big D had given her $2,000 to go pick up a few things while he was handling business. She told Jason that she was going to see her mother, and he had been blowing up her phone asking a million questions about where she was and what she was doing.

Hypnotiq was in love with Big D, but she didn't have to tell me because I knew how she felt when I saw how she started playing Jason. Whenever Big D wanted to see her, she made herself available to him. Jason was a good dude, but he didn't have the money and power that Big D had.

While I was talking to Hypnotiq, Tony was clicking in. I told her to hold on, and clicked over.

"You told Ron you wanted to come back to the club?"

"Yeah why?"

"You know I'm not paying you that extra anymore."

"I know."

He was hoping that I was going to bail on the job without the extra money. He didn't want to be the bad guy by telling me not to go back, and he didn't want to straight out tell Ron to fire me, but he thought pulling the money away was going to make me quit. He was such a pussy, but I was going to play his game.

"I'm just surprised."

"Is there a problem?"

"Nah, it's just that I told Camille…well, I told her that you weren't going to work there anymore."

"What are you saying Tony? You want me to quit?"

"I guess if I don't go up there, Camille has no reason to be there. It's cool. How are you?"

"I'm fine Tony, but don't bullshit me. You were hoping that I would turn the job down weren't you? Keep it real. You don't want to be the bad guy, so you're trying to manipulate the situation."

"Look Mia, I'm sorry if it sounds fucked up, but I'm just tired of hearing Camille's mouth. You and I have been cool, but my first priority is to her and my kids."

Just then, I remembered why I didn't miss him all that much. His constant whining was too much for. I wanted to yell at the top of my lungs for him to shut the fuck up, but I simply told him that I had someone on the other line. I was walking on a thin line between a job and the unemployment line, so I wasn't going to do anything to push Tony over the edge, giving him the encouragement he needed to find his balls and fire my black ass. We hung up, but I knew that it would not be the last time that I would talk to him about my job at the club.

CHAPTER 29

Working at the club for the next few days helped to get my mind off of all the shit that had been going on in my twisted life. The club was loud, busy, and someone always needed something from me, I didn't have much time to think about me until I got home at night. Thank God it was usually close to three in the morning because my eyelids tended to fall shortly after I walked in the door. During the day, I worked out and spent a lot of time with Brandy and Hypnotiq.

Hypnotiq was like an investigative reporter giving me updates on the happenings at the club. Who was fucking who, who got in a fight, who was fired and who was rehired. A lot of my old customers had latched onto new dancers, but most of them called me first to make sure I wasn't coming back before they jumped ship. I kept in touch with a few of them, going to lunch and shopping. Hypnotiq gave me the dirt on who the new chosen ladies were, and most of them were the obvious choices. The vultures had always circled around my regulars because they saw me getting paid. Initially, I was pretty jealous at the thought of *my* money being spent on another bitch, but eventually I got over it; that was the game.

Brandy never said anything to me about masturbating in front of her man, so I began to think that maybe I could flip the good boyfriend. If he had no intention of fucking with me, he would've told Brandy that I was doing too much, disrespecting her in her own home. Could be that he didn't want to start any shit between best friends, and chalked it up to a stripper just showing off, harmlessly flirting, or just fucking around. Either way, quite was kept.

Tony stayed true to his word and didn't try to see me, or even contact me for that matter. There were times when I would still miss his friendship, like when

I was driving down Sunset Boulevard and passed *Dublin's* where he was hanging out with friends one night. He had called and told me to come up there, but he said to sit across from him, touching my pussy and rubbing on my titties. He didn't want me to actually talk to him; he just wanted a private peep show. Unbeknownst to anyone else, I performed for him right in the middle of the bar, and afterwards we laughed our asses off at the thought of other people watching the show.

Sweet memories would pop into my head and force me to remember the fun we used to have before the first time Camille and I ever set eyes on each other. The human brain is merciful, and mine allowed me to focus on everything that was sunny about our relationship, but I had to continually remind myself that our liaison produced mostly rain.

One Saturday evening about a week after I had returned from my suspension, I walked into the club early as I usually did, but I was surprised to find Ron there. His normal routine on Saturdays was to pop in about 11 or 12 midnight to play backup in case I needed him. Instead of him just casually walking around, waiting for me to show up, he was actually working.

"Hey Ron! What are you doing here?"

"Oh hey, I'm just checking on a few things. How are you?"

"I'm good. Is anything wrong?"

"Uh no, I was just going over some of the bills tonight instead of coming in tomorrow."

"Okay well, I'm going to check the liquor supply."

"Actually, I already had Sherry do that. She came in early too, so we gave you a hand."

"Oh, well…thank you. I'll just go in the office then."

"Okay."

Ron and I shared an uneasy, awkward moment that had my mind swirling. Call me paranoid, but I felt like I would be out of a job soon. Ron *never* came in early like that on a Saturday evening. It was *my* job to check the liquor supply, and take a trip to Costco or Beverages in More in case of shortages. Him showing up, coupled with the fact that Sherry was doing my work made me feel very insecure. I went to the office, sat down and tried to calm my nerves. My heart pumped gallons of blood through my chest, while I sat there holding my breath. As I tried to put two and two together, Ron sheepishly walked into the office.

"Ron, are you sure everything is cool? Something didn't feel right when I walked in."

"Look Mia, I never wanted it to come down to this…but…Tony called, and he wants me to let you go."

I can't say that I was completely shocked because I saw it coming. I just didn't think that Tony would end up being such a dick. I told him that I didn't want to fuck with him anymore, and even though he had to dump me anyway, I hurt his ego and he fired me.

"What? Why can't you tell him that you want me to stay?"

"Now Mia, you know I can't do that."

"You won't even stand up for me when I have come in early, worked late, and scrubbed fucking puke out of the urinal in a $200 dress because Paco had left for the night! I have been working hella hard in this fucking club and this is how you repay me?!"

"Mia, you were…are a very good employee, but my hands are tied. Tony was insistent that you can no longer work on the premises. Give him a call if you want, but the choice is up to him."

"Call him for what? Camille's the one that told him to fire me, and then he called and told you to fire me! I'm surrounding by a bunch of pussies! If anything, I need to call Camille. She's the one running your fucking club! Thanks a lot for everything you have done for me Ron!"

"Mia I know you're upset, and I wish there was something I could do for you."

"Fuck you Ron! I don't need your fucking sympathy! I need a job!"

I stormed out of the office, and slammed the door behind me. I drove my car down the 10 freeway on auto pilot. My greatest fear was finally realized. It wasn't a possibility anymore, it was a reality. I had to wrap my mind around the idea that my life had shifted again, and I was back at square one.

Brandy was so pleased when I told her that I thought about taking classes, but I think I just told her what she wanted to hear. I was never good at school, and the thought of college was intimidating to me. There weren't many subjects that I actually liked, and I didn't focus long enough to appreciate anything the teachers were trying to feed me. I never took school seriously; I cut classes, cheated on tests, and copied my friend's homework. Everything was boring to me, and the teachers got on my nerves preaching all the time. They used to say, "You may not understand the value of an education now, but you will someday." Well, I guess that day had come for me because I wouldn't have been in this situation if I had been taking classes instead of taking my clothes off, especially after I barely graduated from high school.

Tony answered his phone like he expected me to call.

"Well Ron did your dirty work for you. Why couldn't I keep my fucking job? I haven't bothered you or your wife!"

"Camille drove by the club last night and saw your car. I'm not going to be going through this bullshit every night I'm in town. I told her we stopped fucking around, but with you at the club *after* I told her you gone was just too much for her. She took the kids and went to her cousin's house for the weekend."

"Am I supposed to feel sorry for you? You should've told her in the beginning that I was still working there. Your slick ass is always lying! That's what she's tired of. Why don't you try being a true player, and tell her the truth. Only a bitch maid nigga lies to protect his ass. You're tired of hearing Camille's mouth, but I'm tired of hearing you bitching about your situation. I hope you have learned from all this bullshit and try being faithful to your wife for once in your life."

"You weren't saying all that when you were fucking with me."

"Yeah, but that was before all this fucking drama bumping into your wife all over L.A.! I don't have a job now! I should've kept my black ass at *Aces*! I should've known this shit was going to turn out all bad. My mother used to always say, 'However you start something is the way it will end.' I got my job because I was fucking you. I stopped fucking you, and I lost my job. If I would've got the job in a legit way, it wouldn't have ended because of personal bullshit. Easy come, easy go."

"You going back to dancing?"

"Why the fuck do you care? I gotta go."

"Mia, I wish things could be different, but I just can't risk…"

I slammed the phone down before he could finish that familiar phrase. If I heard it one more time I think I would've drove my car off of the nearest freeway overpass. Calling him had been pointless. If I wanted to make something happen, I should've called Camille. She had the balls in that family; Tony just made the money.

I called Hypnotiq after I woke up from my nap to see if she was going to the club.

"What's going on girl?"

"Shit! Everything and nothing. I'm out of a job."

"Girl, what happened?"

"Apparently Camille drove by the club last night, and saw my car out front. Tony's stupid ass had told her that he got rid of me, so she was pissed off. I don't even know why she was over there, probably checking on his lying ass."

"Damn girl. I'm sorry to hear that. Tony told you not to go up there anymore?"

"No, his punk ass told Ron to do it. I went in there earlier, and Ron was there doing my job, and he had the bartender do some of the other stuff that I used to do. I knew something was up, we talked, and he told me I couldn't come back. I called Tony for the details, but that was a waste of fucking time."

"I was really hoping that it was going to work out for you. What are you going to do now?"

"I've asked myself that question a million times. Even before tonight, I had been thinking about what I would do if the other shoe dropped, and now it has. I have some money saved up, but it won't last forever. If I have to walk back in that club, I will feel like a failure, and some of those bitches will be all too happy to point that shit out for me."

"You can't be worried about what other people will say; you have to handle your business. Is there anything else that you want to do?"

"Girl, I barely graduated high school, and I have never worked for more than minimum wage. Where would I go? What would I do? I will never find a job paying me even half of what I was making dancing. I feel stuck, like I don't have any other choices."

"You always have choices. It's about you deciding what you want, and possibly making sacrifices. If you don't want to go back to the club, find something else. What about going back to school?"

"Girl, I can't see it. I don't want to do hair or nursing like everybody else at the club. I never thought about a career when I was in high school, I just thought about a job and working. It's funny, but I never planned my future. I never had goals or dreams, I just wanted to make money. It used to drive my mom crazy because when I was a teenager, she would always ask me what I wanted to do, and I always said that I didn't know."

"Well I'm here if you need to talk. I'm getting ready to leave for the club now."

"I was trying to get you a job with me, but I guess it's a good thing you didn't leave because you would've lost your customers, and I would've felt like shit."

"Don't worry about me girl. I'll be at *Aces* until something or *someone* better comes along!"

I told Hypnotiq that I would meet her at the club just to hang out and we hung up.

❦   ❦   ❦

I had to be extra fine walking in the club because I hadn't been back since I left. I quit dancing for a better opportunity, so I had to look like it. I put on a sexy dress, high-heeled sandals, fierce hair and makeup.

When I walked in, everybody was hugging me and asking me how everything was. I took a page from Tony's book and lied my ass off, telling everybody that I was loving my new job, and bragging about how Ron trusted me with money and keys, and let me run the place by myself. I felt like a fraud at first, but after a couple of hours and plenty of drinks the lies came out fast and easy. It had been almost six months since my going away party, but nothing had changed except the music.

I imagined myself back up on the pole performing tricks, grinding on the laps of married men for $20, and subjecting myself to the mental bullshit associated with the strip game. I looked through the club with different eyes. Because I had been gone for so long, I noticed things that I had taken for granted before. Dark lights kept the club anonymous and mysterious, but it also concealed the seediness. The ancient ceiling had the old school white, micro-balled acoustic covering sprayed with fine glitter. There were hooks, staples, and pieces of colored balloon string hanging from the ceiling where dancers had parties and ripped the decorations down. The liquor-stained, gum smudged carpet was disgusting, and some of the dancers actually walked around barefooted after closing.

The mirror on the back of the stage was cracked, greasy, and full of fingerprints. The wooded stage floor was slick and covered with a dark gray film. The pole was covered with oil from the girls smothering their bodies before they went up. It was no doubt covered in bacteria and germs from the girls rubbing their pussy and ass all over it.

The club was still rocking old school big screens instead of plasmas or flat screens. All of the black pleather chairs and stools looked a hundred years old with cracked seats exposing the cheap, white polyester filling. The sticky, wood-like tables were crooked, and they rocked if you leaned on them. The kitchen was a hot mess, and the fire was a blessing. They should've stopped serving food long before the kitchen was partially burned by an out of control grease fire.

The cramped bathroom had one toilet with a seat that was as old as Margaret. There were empty beer bottles, shot glasses, and glasses holding melting pieces of ice on the sink, lined up along the floor, and on the back of the toilet tank. Ashes from weed and Swisher Sweets lined the top of the metal toilet tissue holder. Tampon wrappers, cut strings, and crimson-stained baby wipes filled the trash can. Margaret didn't even put in a new towel dispenser. She had one of those old school cotton towel machines where you had to pull down the nasty, wet, looped towel to wipe your hands. It wouldn't surprise me if the floors had never been thoroughly cleaned, and running a dirty mop across the urine and blood-spotted floor didn't count.

There was so much wrong with the club, and I never understood why Margaret didn't take better care of her investment. She had the money, but she refused to fix the place up. *Aces* was the filthiest, most popular strip club in L.A., and it had been my bread and butter for over two years. Against my better judgment, I asked the night manager about coming back.

"Hey Trish, can I talk to you for a minute?"

"Yeah what's going on?"

"Well, I know I have been away for a few months, but I want to come back."

"I thought you were working down at that club."

"I was, but it isn't working out."

"I'm sorry to hear about that. Well, you know you can always come back here. Customers are still asking where you went. When do you want to start?"

"I can start next week."

"See you then."

The conversation was quick and matter-of-factly because she had had this same discussion many times before when dancers trotted off to do something better, but came back with their tails between their legs begging for the job that they had washed their hands of.

She walked off, and I stood there feeling like I had signed a deal with the devil. I started dancing because I wanted to, I quit because I wanted to, but then I was in a situation where I had to go back because I felt like I couldn't do anything else. It almost felt like I was forced into shaking my ass at gunpoint. It's like the difference between fucking someone because you want to, and getting raped. You're fucking either way, but being forced to do it makes all the difference in the world.

In all actuality, I didn't have to go back to the club, but realistically my savings wouldn't last me forever, so instead of burning through all of it and then trying to figure out what to do next, I decided to take action first.

I went home, and pulled out the stripper box at the back of my closet. Looking through all of the costumes, shoes, and little purses, I thought about what I was going to tell those nosey, hating bitches that wouldn't release me from their clutches until they knew every detail about what brought me back to the club. I decided on something they would surely believe as all strippers were into green. I wasn't making enough money for all of the hard work that I did.

I dumped the box upside down, put all of the costumes in the drawer, lined the shoes up in the closet, and put the box by the trash can in the kitchen.

CHAPTER 30

✿

My first night in the club was like an episode of the *Surreal Life*. I had called all of my regulars to fill the club up, but I still felt like a fish out of water. There were so many new chicks that were walking around like they were the shit. They didn't know I was an old dancer at first, so they tried to talk down to me like I was a new jack, but I quickly put them in their place.

One of them was called Blaze. She was about 19 or 20 and hella pretty. She was tall with a thick body, stacked on the top and bottom. She had only been there a couple of weeks, but the men ate her up. Blaze had a tattoo with flames along the small of her back, and she wore some bomb costumes. She wore her own long hair, and she knew how to apply her makeup perfectly. She got along cool with everybody, and she stayed out of drama like Hypnotiq. She was trying to explain to me about how the locker situation worked in the dressing room as soon as I walked in.

"You have to use the bottom locker since you just got here."

"Excuse me, do I know you?"

"I'm Blaze, and you are…?" She extended her hand, and I reluctantly shook it.

"I'm Alizé, and I'm not new."

"Oh, I'm sorry. It's just that I have never seen you before. How long have you worked here?"

"Over two years. I took a break for a little while."

Two of my biggest haters snickered, but I didn't care because they weren't worth the energy it would take to beat their asses, plus I was focused on my new competition.

"That's cool. I've only been here for a couple of weeks. I used to dance downtown. Who are you going on stage with?"

"I just got here, so I haven't hooked up with anybody yet."

"How about you and me?"

This situation could've played out two different ways: either I dance with her, and show that I'm not threatened by her crazy beauty, or I tell her no and look like a punk.

"That's cool. When are you up?"

"Next set. I chose Jamie Foxx's *Sex* song, and Black Eyed Peas' *My Hump*. Is that cool with you?"

"I can fuck with anything by Jamie."

When I had left the club, Jamie was just a comedian, and when I returned he had become a real actor with an Oscar and a multi-platinum album. Time changes everything.

"Okay?! I'll go tell Elgin we're going up together."

"I'll go on the outside first."

"Cool."

I told her that I wanted to go outside first because that meant that I got to walk around the edge of the stage, and she had to go topless to the fast song, which was always funny-looking to me. I fumbled through my bag trying to find the sexiest, most revealing costume in my bag. If Blaze danced half as good as she looked, I was in trouble. I should've practiced my dance moves at home before my first night back, but it was too late now. I had hoped that I was still limber enough to hit splits, and put my legs behind my head.

Hypnotiq was my only partner, but she had already planned on going out of town with Big D, so I was on my own. I got dressed like it was senior prom all over again, making sure that everything was perfect. I had never got dressed so fast, but I had to dance with Blaze because she was bad, and it was always best to dance with a strong girl. I never danced with fat, ugly bitches because she basically came up off of me. I would fuck with ugly or fat, but not both. Cats would still tip a girl with a bad body and fucked up face, and the same for girls with a pretty face, but no body.

Blaze had been walking around while I was getting dressed, but she flew in the back when the DJ started yelling our names.

"Alright fellas, show Miracle and Coco your appreciation by putting your hands together. Coming up next we got Alizé and Blaze. Alizé took a little break, but she couldn't leave us alone, so she's back in the house."

"You ready?"

"Let's go!" I was as ready as I would ever be. I wasn't nervous at all.

Blaze let me walk out first out of respect. I heard the applause before we got all the way out of the curtain, and I felt appreciated. I put extra on it to the point I almost through my hip bone out of the socket. I walked to the outside of the stage, while Blaze strolled into the middle. As I tried to get back in my old groove, I was straining my neck to see what Blaze was up to. She was working it for a fast song. I always thought it was corny trying to be sexy with your titties out on a fast song. It was much easier to be seductive with a slow song, but Blaze was a champ. She had teardrop C cups, and she knew how to work it. She wasn't doing too much, but she was sexy, and I shuddered to think about what she was going to do during the slow song. I was wrapping my legs around the pole, flipping, twisting and twirling to the Black Eyed Peas. Balled-up money was hitting me on my legs and ass. It was flying everywhere, and some of it was making its way all the way back to where Blaze was.

"Clap your hands for Alizé and Blaze. They got one more coming up."

Blaze grabbed her top off the floor, and slowly walked behind the curtain. I followed her in. Sweat was beading on her forehead and the space between her tits.

"Damn girl, you worked it out! It was like you never left!"

"Like riding a bike…"

Jamie Foxx's sexy voice floated up over the ceiling, and beckoned me to bring it. I seductively walked in the middle of the stage, while Blaze followed me and stepped on the outside of the stage. I closed my eyes and let the song guide me. *Sex. Stronger than any drug, even love…*I imagined myself standing in front of my couch while I teased a fine nigga sitting in my apartment. I rolled my hips, touching my legs and inner thighs. I slowly untied my top, and threw it against the back mirror. I rubbed my titties and squeezed my nipples with my thumb and index fingers until they turned red. I dropped my hands near my pussy and spread my fingers across my pelvis, grabbing and pulling at my thong, carefully so that my lips didn't pop out.

I fell to my knees, and motioned my mouth and hands like I was sucking dick, in and out. I got on all fours and walked as smoothly as a panther until I reached the horizontal bar in front. I straddled the pole, and acted like I was riding a dick, moving my hips slower, then faster. I got up on my squatted legs, and bounced my ass up and down with my back to the audience. The money started hitting my ass like rain as I isolated the muscles, moving one cheek at a time. I did a somersault and flipped into the splits, bouncing my pussy up and down with my hands to the side.

Jamie was done, and so was I. I snapped out of the trance that he had me under, grabbed my top, and skipped to the back. I was so caught up that I barely paid attention to what Blaze was doing; she was cool, but she wasn't me.

"That was cool. You were on one!"

"It was Jamie."

"Whatever it was, you were good."

"Thanks." I moved past Blaze to the dressing room, and she followed me, steadily talking.

"Maybe we can become partners."

"Thanks, but I used to dance with Hypnotiq. She's out of town tonight."

"Oh, well whenever she's gone?"

"We'll see."

For her to be so pretty, she was too eager, but I guess she was still fresh-faced, and hadn't been jaded quite yet.

My regulars let me give them table dances, bought me drinks, and talked about what brought me back to the club. Besides Hypnotiq, I didn't tell anyone that I fucked my way into the job, so everybody believed whatever I told them, or at least they believed me to my face. What they said after I walked away is whatever.

Blaze came up to me towards the end of the night, and asked if I wanted to go get some food after the club closed. I told her that was cool, and we decided on Fatburger. After last call, I started getting dressed and told Blaze that I would wait for her at the bar. She was still giving a table dance, so I talked to Hypnotiq in the kitchen.

"How was your first night back? I wish I could've been there, but Big D had already planned this trip."

"I understand. I wish I had somewhere to go. It was cool. I ended up dancing with Blaze."

"She's fine huh? She gets her money too."

"We're going to get food after we leave here. When are you coming home?"

"I never want to leave Vegas, but we're leaving tomorrow night."

"Where do you be telling Jason that you're going? I know he's going crazy."

"Girl, he was tripping. He was blowing up my phone as usual. I had to turn it off. I told him I was going to Vegas with a couple of girls."

"What are you going to do with him, and what's up with you and Big D? You guys are always going somewhere."

"I'm thinking about letting Jason go. I'm hurting him, and I know it isn't fair. I wouldn't be doing it for Big D because he's married. I just realized that what I've been doing is changing Jason. We don't even have fun anymore because he is so suspicious, jealous, and mad all the time."

"Well, think about it first. We'll talk when you get back. I'll be there like you have always been there for me."

"Speaking of, have you talked to Tony?"

"I haven't, and I'm cool with that. I saw a side of him that that really turned me off. He was a punk. I miss having regular dick though. I want some of Brandy's."

"Have you lost your mind? Stop looking at him with impure eyes before you get yourself in trouble! Well, let me get off this phone. I'm standing at the crap tables and people are staring at me."

"Want me to pick you up from the airport?"

"Jason is picking me up, and I think we're going to talk when we get back to my place."

"I'm nervous, and it's not even my business. Want me to come over after?"

"Yeah, I'm sure I'll need a shoulder to cry on."

"Okay girl, I'm out."

"Peace."

Hypnotiq hung up just as Blaze was walking into the kitchen.

"You ready? I'll drive."

"Okay, let me put my bag in the car."

Blaze followed me to my car, so that I could drop my bag off. Some guys were getting blazed behind a car, and they jumped when they saw us. We giggled, and kept walking.

Blaze and I ate, talked, and got to know each other a little better. She was a junior at UCLA, and she was dancing to pay her tuition. Her parents didn't have the money to pay all of her expenses, so she started dancing at a club downtown where one of her classmates was working. She said the clientele consisted of mostly older white men and Mexicans, but not too many brothas. Blaze found out about *Aces* from someone on campus, so she decided to try Amateur Night, and she just kept coming back. She said that her parents disapproved of her stripping, but they didn't disown her; she told them she was only doing it until she was done with school. She was studying to be an architect, and the more we talked the more I thought she was somebody that I could hang out with. She was a stripper, but she wasn't living the life. She had parents, a boyfriend, and didn't hang out with the other dancers.

While we talked, I kept thinking about dick. Jamie's song did something to me, so as Blaze was telling me about her life, I was thinking about who I could call. The only person who kept popping up on my wish list was Brandy's boy-friend, Lorenzo. I had always thought he was fine as fuck, but after my steady dick walked out the door, and I saw him putting in work at Brandy's, I couldn't stop thinking about him. He had a body that wouldn't quit, and the fact that he was a good man turned me on even more. I hadn't had a good man since…since…a long time ago.

Blaze dropped me off at my car, and we exchanged phone numbers. She wanted to go to the mall the next day, and I told her that was cool. I decided to call Brandy and stir some shit up.

"Did I wake you and Lorenzo up?" I wanted to see if he was there before I drove all the way over to her apartment.

"I'm in the bed. He just came over from playing cards at his boy's house. I think he's in there watching a movie."

"I wanted to crash on your couch. I'm a little faded, and I'm closer to your spot."

"Yeah, come on. I'll tell Lorenzo to open the door."

"Thanks girl."

Poor thing, she was so incredibly vulnerable. I raced over there before Lorenzo finished his movie, and got in the bed. I hopped out of my car, and ran up the stairs. He opened the door looking like a chocolate statue.

"What you still doing up Lorenzo?"

"Just watching a movie. Brandy's still in the bed."

"I know. She told me I could crash."

"Well, I'll get out of here so you can get some sleep." He started moving towards the hallway, but I stepped in front of him. He looked like he had seen a ghost.

"No, don't let me run you off. Sit and talk to me."

"Okay." He was scared shitless.

Lorenzo walked back to the couch, and nervously sat down. He eyes were pointed towards the t.v., but he wasn't watching it, too busy waiting for me to do something to embarrass him again. I didn't say or do anything for a few minutes, just so that I could watch him squirm. The tension in the room could've been cut with a knife. Finally, I put him out of his misery.

"So, Brandy said you were playing cards at a friend's house?"

"Yeah, I was at my boy Mike's house."

"Did anybody get naked?"

"Nah, it was just me and my boys."

"That's boring. If there were girls there, would you play stripping games?"

"Nah, I'm cool."

"You wouldn't at least take your shirt off? Let me see your chest."

"Why?"

"I just wanna see. Don't be shy."

Lorenzo was acting shy, and if he wasn't black, he would've turned red. He lifted his Jordan shirt to reveal the muscled chest and arms that I had been dreaming about.

"Nice. Now why would you hesitate to show that off?"

"It's not about that. My shirt isn't that big of a deal, but I'm just not taking my pants off."

"What are you hiding down there?"

"Nothing."

"Let me see. Take down your pants."

"What? You're tripping."

I moved over next to Lorenzo, so that my whole left side was touching his whole right side. He scooched over a little, and I scooched right after him. He leaned over, and rested his head on his hand. Lorenzo looked like hip hop, but he acted like easy listening. He wasn't taking my flirting seriously at all, so I had to step my game up before he scurried down the hallway into Brandy's bed.

"I saw you the other night."

"What?"

"When you were fucking Brandy." His eyes got big, and then he just started shaking his head and laughing to himself.

"How did you...where were you?"

"I was peeking through the slit in the door. So, I already saw what you had. I just want to see it again."

"That's your girl in the other room you know."

"She's my girl, but I don't want to fuck *her*. Take it out. Let me just kiss it a little."

"Kiss it? You're funny." He was looking at me like he didn't believe me, but he wanted to believe me. He wanted to pull his dick out so bad, but he couldn't just whip it out; he wanted me to take it, so I did.

I slid off the couch, dropped to my knees, and starting putting my teeth on his dick right through his jeans. It went from soft to rock hard in five seconds flat. I kept biting at it until the front of his jeans were damp with the spit from my mouth.

"Are you going to take your pants down, or do you want me to bite through your jeans?"

He was turned on, but he wasn't ready to completely give in. The devilish angel sat back stunned, waiting for me to hold his hand, and walk him through the whole thing.

"I guess I'm going to have to do everything tonight huh?"

I unzipped his jeans, stuck my hand in, and pulled his voracious dick through the fly of his boxers and his zippers. It wasn't huge, but it was nice. It had more girth than anything, and the head was big. I loved heads; they were soft and sensitive. I loved when niggas slowly pulled the head in and out of my pussy and my mouth because I could feel the rim, and it drove me up the wall.

Lorenzo wanted me to stop and keep going all at once. He didn't want to be a bad boyfriend, but at the same time, he knew that I was a stripper and I was going to give him something that Brandy, as hard as she tried, couldn't give him. I felt so powerful hovering over his dick, I wanted to fuck with him a little bit more before I took him to heaven.

"You want me to stop?" I was holding his dick firmly in my head, with my breath caressing it as I spoke.

"I mean…shit, it's out now."

"I can put it back."

I started trying to stuff his dick back through his zipper, and he pulled my hand away. I had him.

"What do you want me to do?"

"You're playing now."

"I just don't want to force you to do something that you don't want to do."

I guess I had taken him to the edge because he grabbed my face with one hand and shoved his dick in my mouth with the other. I took my hand off his dick, and sucked the head gently and slowly. Lorenzo was moaning, quietly of course as I put more pressure on his rod. I started sucking it harder and harder, forcing the whole thing down my throat. He started getting louder and louder, so I took my mouth off and started licking the head with the tip of my tongue. I gave him full boss again, and he started raising his hips off the couch, keeping rhythm with my thrusts. Lorenzo put his hands on the side of my head near my ears, and pushed my head down firmly on his lap. I could tell he was ready to cum, so I quickly released my jaws; I wanted some dick, and if he came it wasn't going to happen because once he got a nut off, his right mind would've returned.

"What are you doing?"

"I want some dick. Take your pants off."

He yanked his pants down in one fall swoop, and I lifted my skirt up to my waist. I had taken my panties off in the car before I came in. As Lorenzo sat back down on the couch, I sat on his lap, and sucked his nipples and the rest of his stunning chest.

"Do you have a condom?"

"They're in the room. You don't have any?"

"No. Go get yours."

"What if she wakes up?"

"Just be careful."

I got off of Lorenzo's lap, and he tiptoed into the bedroom where Brandy was sleeping like a baby. He came back in a few minutes with two condoms. He had pulled his jeans up over his stiff wood, and he looked funny walking back from the room. It looked like a tent.

He pulled his jeans back down, ripped the condom wrapper, and slid it on his dick. I was impressed that it stayed hard for that long. He was so sexy. I straddled his lap, and stuck my tongue in his mouth, forming small circles in warm, Heineken mouth. Once my pussy got nice and wet, I sat on his dick and slowly slid down on the pole. It felt so good, and it was worth every bit of the guilt and shame that I would feel as soon as I got up. Lorenzo was sucking on my titties, and kissing on my neck. It was hot and forbidden. I was arching my back, taking every piece of that dick, humping, winding, and rolling my hips. Lorenzo was rocking and sweating, grabbing and pulling. Just as we were beginning to reach our climax together, I heard a shrill cry.

"What the fuck…?!"

Brandy was standing in the doorway of her bedroom with her mouth wide open, watching her best friend riding the fuck out of her man.

"Baby, let me explain." Lorenzo was trying to push me off of him, so that he could pull up his pants.

"Brandy, I'm so sorry." I almost melted when I saw the look in her eye.

"I trusted you! How could you do this to me? I have been by your side through all of your bullshit, and you fuck my man? Get the fuck out of my house!"

I got off of Lorenzo, pulled my skirt down, and grabbed my purse.

"Brandy, it was a mistake. Please let me talk to you."

"I have nothing to say to you! But then again, I shouldn't be surprised because you've been fucking other people's men for a long time, it's just that my stupid ass never thought you would fuck mine!"

"Brandy, I didn't mean for this to happen!"

"Why did you want to come over when I told you I was in the bed? Why didn't you come get in the bed with me? You're sitting on the couch with that fucking baby skirt on with your ass all out? I think you knew exactly what you were doing!"

I ran out of apologies and excuses, Brandy was my best friend, and she knew my tricks well. When I wanted something, I went and got it. There was nothing left for me to say so I sat there and took everything she wanted to give me.

"You fucking bitch! I have been there for you when your own mother didn't want to have anything to do with you! How could you rip my heart out like this? You are a greedy, selfish stripper and I want you to get the fuck out of my house! Don't ever call me because I am through fucking with you!"

"Brandy, I fucked up but you don't mean it."

"Why don't I? Get the fuck out! Get out!"

Brandy started coming towards me waving her fists, and Lorenzo got up to get between us. She was going to fight me, and if she would've made contact I wouldn't have touched her. I deserved an ass beating for breaking my best friend's heart. I wanted to fuck Lorenzo and I never considered Brandy's feelings. I was jealous of her, and the kind of man that she had. More than wanting to fuck him, I think I wanted to *be* Brandy for a short time and make love to her boyfriend.

"Lorenzo, get your fucking hands off of me! Get your shit too! You can go home with that ho!"

"Baby, I'm sorry…I…it was an accident."

"Accident? She slipped and fell on your dick? You are hella weak! Shut up and get out before I call the police!"

Brandy looked at me with pain, not anger, in her eyes. I had betrayed her; she was more upset with me than Lorenzo because she knew niggas weren't shit, but she never expected to be fucked by her best friend. We walked out of the apartment single file like school children on a field trip, but there were no words. He didn't even walk me to my car at nearly three in the morning. I went home, washed my pussy in the bathroom sink, and gargled with Listerine. I cried for the rest of the morning after Brandy ignored my eight phone calls and desperate messages. She never called me back, and I finally drifted off to sleep in a pool of tears and snotty tissues. In my mind, I thought that I would get a little from Lorenzo, and none would be the wiser, but he must have been in there slamming dresser drawers because Brandy was in the living room within a few minutes of him leaving the bedroom.

I had hurt my best friend in the whole world out of envy, greed, and lust, I had committed three of the seven deadly sins in one night.

CHAPTER 31

❀

Hypnotiq wasn't picking up her phone. I called her a couple of times, and then I finally just left a voicemail. I figured her and Big D were in the casino or something, so I just waited patiently for her to call me back. Everything rushed back when I opened my eyes that morning. I was fucking my best friend's man on her couch in the middle of the night while she was sleeping in the next room. I tried to call, but she wasn't feeling me, and I understood it, but I still wanted to plead my case. I had temporarily lost my sanity when I thought it would be cool to mount him. I needed Brandy in my life, and I had to make her understand that I was tripping and I was truly sorry, that she found out. I just wanted to fuck him once so that I could get him out of my head. I never wanted Brandy to know.

Hypnotiq finally called me back.

"Now you know if I call you that many times that something is wrong in my twisted little world."

"What did you do now?"

"I was fucking Lorenzo on Brandy's couch, and she walked in and caught us."

"Shut up! What the fuck were you thinking? Didn't I tell you to leave him alone? I know she is hot as fish grease!"

"You know what is truly fucked up? She was more hurt than mad. She kicked both of us out, and she isn't answering my calls."

"Well, you should've expected that. She's hot."

"Hurry up and get home, I'm running out of friends!"

"Why don't you go and fuck Jason, so I can have a reason to leave his ass alone!"

- 245 -

"That's hella fucked up! Now I'm a ho for hire?"

We laughed, and for a second I forgot about the shit that I had just stirred up in my own backyard.

"Look ho, I'll call you when I get back in town."

"Fuck you!"

We hung up, and I lay back down on the bed until Blaze called. She wanted to know when I would be ready to go to the mall. There was no way that I was going to share the events of the previous night with a perfect stranger. I couldn't tell her that I needed to wallow around the house in self-pity for a little while longer before I could get it together long enough to get dressed and look presentable to the outside world. I told her to give me an hour.

I went in the kitchen and ate a bowl of cereal while I sat on the couch watching t.v. I put the bowl in the sink, and stood inside of my closet. I grabbed some jeans and a little top, and lay them on my bed, where the covers and sheets were strewn everywhere. I didn't feel like making the bed, so I didn't. I got in the shower, washed up, brushed my teeth, and washed my face. I got dressed, and put on lots of makeup to cheer me up, but it didn't help. All of the makeup at the MAC counter couldn't color me guilt-free.

I gave Blaze directions, and she came by and picked me up. On the way to mall, she asked me questions about the club and stripping. Little did she know, I was not in the mood for all of the chit chat. I thought I would feel better by getting out of the house, but because I didn't really know Blaze, I should've known that was going to mean more discussion. If Hypnotiq and I had been driving to the mall, there would have been silence. She would've known that I felt like shit and she would respect that. The only time something might've been said would be if she saw a man walking down La Cienega dressed in red from head to toe, or if I saw a woman standing at the corner picking her underwear out of her ass.

The more that Blaze talked, the more I missed Hypnotiq. We knew each other so well that we didn't need words to communicate. We gave each other a look, a pinch, a nudge, or giggled, and the other knew exactly what was going on. With Brandy, I always felt that I had to prove that I was worthy of her friendship, trying to make her understand why I took my clothes off for money, and why I needed her to accept me for who I was, and not what she wanted me to be.

I could truly be myself with Hypnotiq without having to explain or apologize. She understood the strip game, and why we did what we had to do. She was a free spirit, but within reason. She was my shoulder when I needed it, like when I had just called to tell her that I had done the unthinkable, she ended up making a joke out of it. I know I was wrong, and she knew I was wrong, but no since in beating a dead horse; as my friend, it was her job was to check me, and then keep it moving.

As Blaze was going on and on about who she danced for last night, I decided that when Hypnotiq got home later that night, we would make tacos at her house and convalesce together. I couldn't wait to see her because at the present time I was friendless, and Blaze didn't count because I didn't even know her government name yet. For the time being, she was just another dancer to me.

We finally got to the mall after what seemed like three days. We walked around, and we both bought a few things. Blaze wanted to eat at the Hard Rock Café, so we walked over there, and waited for a table. The good thing about not knowing her was that she couldn't tell that something was terribly wrong with me, so I thankfully avoided her saying, "What's wrong?" a million times. I was much more quiet than normal because I was thinking about Brandy, Lorenzo, and Hypnotiq. We ate, and Blaze mercifully dropped me back at home. I was so happy to get out of her chatty car, and inside my silent walls.

I walked to the kitchen to get some water when I saw the light flashing on my answering machine. I pressed play, and it was a male voice.

"Hi Mia, this is Jason. Please call me when you get the message."

At first, I was confused by his call, but then I remembered Hypnotiq telling me that she told him she was going to Vegas with her girls. I wasn't about to help him bust my girl out, so I didn't call him back. He also knew where I lived, so if he had the balls to come to my front door, I wasn't answering it. I called Hypnotiq to warn her about him calling me, but I went right to voicemail. I left a message, and turned the t.v. on quietly.

I ended up falling asleep on the couch since I only slept for about three hours after all the drama from last night. I woke up to a loudly ringing phone; I was hoping it was Brandy, but it was Jason again. He didn't leave a message. I was starting to get worried, so I called Hypnotiq again. I figured that she was probably in the air, but I left a message anyway because I didn't want Jason to try and trip her up.

I got in the car, and ran to the grocery store to get everything for tacos. On the last message, I told Hypnotiq that I was going to cook for her, so don't eat anything after she got home. I left the food in the car when I got home, but I took the things out that were for me, like the peanut butter and my Spicy Doritos.

I waited for Hypnotiq to call me up until midnight, and her phone was still turned off. I was already worried because Jason had already called my house twice, not to mention the fact that he was already suspicious, and she was breaking up with him after he picked her up from the airport. I hopped in my car, and raced to her house, concerned but not panicked.

When I got to her apartment, there were lots of police cars, a fire truck, and an ambulance in front of her parking place, flashing red and blue lights, gurneys, and cops milling around like a colony of ants. I think my heart stopped beating for a few seconds as I drove towards the confusion, and parked as close to Hypnotiq's apartment as I could. I couldn't breathe; my chest was shrinking and my ribs were squeezing my lungs so tightly that I started sweating, gasping for breath.

I was barely able to stand, let alone walk as I approached the middle of the chaos: police giving other cops orders, paramedics grabbing things off the bus and running around, and millions of nosey neighbors. An 18-wheeler came out of nowhere and knocked me half a block when I followed the paramedic's enthusiastic path into Hypnotiq's door. I tried to charge the staircase, but three cops stopped me like I had run into a brick wall. I reached deep for strength, broke through their barricade, and galloped up the stairs two at a time.

The apartment was full of cops and detectives hovering over Jason. He was sitting on the couch covered in blood, looking as stressed as anyone I had ever seen; his head was in his hands, and he was sobbing uncontrollably and shouting that he was sorry. I looked through the kitchen and living room, and I didn't see Hypnotiq. I ran into the bedroom, and ran into a sea of blue EMT uniforms and medical equipment. In the center of it all was Hypnotiq lying slanted across her bed with her long legs dangling off the edge, and her head near her pillow. I leaned in closer to see my beautiful sister lying on her back with her chest covered in blood. Her stunning eyes were wide open, and she had an oxygen mask hanging near her chin instead of wrapped around her lovely face.

The paramedics weren't working on her, so I screamed at them at the top of my lungs.

"What the fuck are you doing? Save her! Do something!"

Before then, they didn't know that anyone else was in the room. A short, blonde woman came over to shoo me out of the room, but I put up a fight.

"Why isn't anyone helping her?"

Another woman joined the first, and they were grabbing on my arms, gently shoving me out of the room.

"Miss, are you related to the deceased?"

Deceased? Oh God no! Jason killed her after she ended the relationship. He picked her up from the airport, she dumped him, and he killed her!

"NOOOOOOO! She's not dead! She can't be!! Hell no!! Keep trying! Pleeeeease!"

They continued to nudge me out of the room, but I was thrashing around like a bull until I broke free from their restraints.

As I ran to Hypnotiq, I noticed the blood on the wall, the comforter, and the floor. It looked like someone had dumped buckets of blood all over the room. When I had first walked in, I was so absorbed with Hypnotiq that I didn't see the enormous bloodshed.

I kneeled by her side, and the rest of the paramedics backed away from us. I reached down and hugged her, and the tears just ran down my face. I rocked her, and cried so hard that my eyes burned from the sweat, blood and tears. I had to keep blinking so that I could see my sister as she lay motionless and silent. The stench of blood traveled through my nose, and pierced my lungs like a thousand swords. The odor was heavy like concrete. She smelled like a butcher shop, my stunning, magnificent sister.

"Sweetie, what happened to you? Who did this to you? You can't leave me! Please come back, Renee! Please come back! I love you sweetie, please wake up!"

As I was pleading and crying, screaming at the top of my lungs, gently shaking her to wake up, two of the detectives from the living room walked in the bedroom.

"Ma'am, how do you know the victim?"

"She's my fucking best friend! Did that muthafucka in there do this to her?"

Before they could answer, I took off for the living room. They were running behind me, but not quick enough. I pounced on top of Jason's lap, and started beating the shit out of him with my balled-up fists. I punched him in the head, the stomach, the chest, wherever I could make contact. He didn't fight back. He just put up his arms to defend himself and he cried deeper with every blow. He began trying to grab my flailing arms and hands, and then he just started holding me, and crying on my chest. I pushed him off, and my shirt became soaked with a fusion of his tears, my tears, and Hypnotiq's blood.

"What the fuck did you do Jason?"

"I couldn't live without her!"

"Oh my God! You selfish bastard!"

"Mia, I'm sorry! Please forgive me! I love her so much!"

"You sick son of a bitch! You took her from all of us! I hope you rot in hell!"

My hands were sore from punching his head, and I had scratches on my arms from Jason trying to stop me from pummeling him to death.

The detectives started pulling me off of him as the Coroner was rolling Hypnotiq out of the room on a gurney in a black body bag stamped with Los Angeles County Coroner's Office.

"Where are you taking her?! Wait!!"

The Coroner paused as I staggered towards the gurney.

"Can you please unzip the bag, so that I can say good-bye?"

The two men looked at each other, and then one of them slowly unzipped the top of the bag and stepped back.

Hypnotiq lay there looking as pretty as she ever did. Her beautiful, long black hair was streaked with blood, and her makeup was still nearly perfect except for the blood smudges on her cheeks. Her face was angelic and serene. Even in death, she was perfect.

"I don't know how I'm ever going to live without you in this fucked up world." I looked deep in her face for a sign, an answer, but she lay perfectly still.

"Rest in peace my sister. I love you." I leaned in, and kissed her softly on the lips.

I slowly backed up, and the Coroner gently zipped the bag, pushed the gurney through the living room, and out the front door. Jason sat on the couch in awe as his girlfriend of almost three years rolled out of her apartment for the last time.

All of a sudden he hopped up, grabbed one of the cop's guns off of his holster, placed the gun in his mouth, and pulled the trigger. His body dropped like a ton of bricks. His brain was splattered on the silver-framed mirror behind Hypnotiq's couch, and I sighed a breath of relief because I didn't have to call my boys to take care of him. I wanted him dead. It wasn't fair for him to breathe after he had plucked the most regal human being on God's green earth from her subjects.

The paramedics and detectives ran over to assess the situation, and I walked back to Hypnotiq's room. I ransacked her jewelry case, and found her diamond necklace that Big D had bought her a couple of months ago. She loved it, but she couldn't wear it very often because Jason would've been suspicious. The diamond heart was exquisite, and she told me that it cost almost $4,000. I slipped it into my pants pocket, and grabbed the picture of us in Vegas that was on her dresser mirror. I looked around her room one last time, and headed towards the living room where Jason's limp body hung halfway off of the couch. Part of his head was blown off, and his mother would have to have a closed casket.

One of the detectives said that he wanted to ask me some questions. I told him how long Hypnotiq and Jason had been together, the nature of their relationship, and gave him an account of the last few days. Hypnotiq was cheating on him with a married man, and went to Vegas with the other guy. Jason had been growing suspicious for quite a while, and she was planning on breaking up with him after he picked her up from the airport that night.

Turnaround is fair play, so the detective filled me in on some information. The neighbors said that there was screaming, several gunshots, and a loud thump about an hour ago, and someone called 911. Hypnotiq must have begging for her life; it was my only hope that she died quickly. Jason told the officers that he borrowed a gun from one of his friends by telling him that he wanted to kill his mother's sick dog. Jason had went to her apartment yesterday after she stopped taking his calls, and he found an itinerary for Mr. and Mrs. Bines only, none of her friend's names were listed as fellow passengers. He had planned on killing her after he called the hotel where she was staying, and a man answered the phone. When the police got there, she was already dead, and he was leaning over the body crying.

I was mentally exhausted, and barely able to walk to my car. One of the detectives asked me if I wanted a ride home, but I told him that I was okay, I was going to a friend's house.

I sat in my car, and called Brandy, but naturally she didn't answer her phone. I drove to her apartment, and banged on the door.

"Brandy, please open the door! Something terrible has happened! I need to talk to you!"

Nothing. She wouldn't open the door, and I knew that she could hear me. The dearly departed at the cemetery across the freeway heard me.

"Brandy...Hypnotiq is...dead! Please!!"

Finally, I heard the lock click, and the doorknob turned. Brandy appeared at the door without any expression on her face.

"Brandy, can I come in? I need to speak to you."

"What did you say about Hypnotiq? What's wrong? Why are you covered in blood?"

"Are you going to let me in?"

She reluctantly stepped back, and pushed the door open. I took her hand, and sat her down on the couch. It was almost three in the morning, and I had only slept about four hours in the last 24 hours.

"Brandy, I have some bad news. Hypnotiq…Jason shot her."

"What?! How is she?"

"Sweetie, she's gone."

"How…I don't…what happened?" The tears started rolling down her cheeks.

"She was breaking up with him, and I guess he couldn't take it."

"I just can't believe it! When did this happen?"

"Just a couple of hours ago. I just left her apartment."

"You were there?"

"Not when it happened. She was supposed to call me after her and Jason talked, and I was going to come over. She hadn't called by midnight, and I had begun to worry because Jason had called my apartment twice today. Her phone was turned off, so I drove over there. There were cop cars, a fire truck, and an ambulance, and I knew something was wrong."

"Did you get to see her?"

"Yes, she was in her room covered in blood. She was already gone when I got there. Jason was still in the living room. He shot himself in the head right in front of me!"

"Mia, are you okay? He didn't hurt you did he?" She was shockingly glaring at my shirt saturated in blood.

"No, he probably just wanted to be with Hypnotiq." I dropped my head, and the tears dropped again like a thunderstorm on my face.

"I can't believe this! Do you want to stay here tonight?" She grabbed my hand, and held it in hers.

"Brandy, about the other night…"

I felt the need to make amends, and hold onto my only living friend with both battered fists.

"Not now. Why don't you get in the shower, and I'll get you some clothes to put on."

I undressed, and stepped into the warm shower. Brandy came behind me, and through the clear shower curtain I watched her dump the bloody clothes in a large garbage bag. She sprayed Clorox bleach cleaner on the floor, got on her hands and knees, and scrubbed the last piece of Hypnotiq off of the bathroom floor.

I didn't think about it until I lay my head on the pillow that night, but Jason could've just as easily shot me before he shot himself. After all, I had covered for Hypnotiq, and lied to Jason when she was with Big D. And I was whooping on him when I saw what he had done. I was so consumed with my sister that I never even stopped to think about my safety.

I don't know what I would've done if Brandy didn't open that door, but I was grateful, and I would do everything in my power to make things right between us.

CHAPTER 32

I had to call Big D as soon as I opened my eyes the following day. He had to know that his angel was in heaven.

"Big D?"

"Yeah, who's this?"

"It's Alizé, Hypnotiq's friend."

"Oh yeah. Good morning."

I had rehearsed several times before I even picked up the phone because I didn't know how I would ever explain to him that his girl was gone. He had just taken her to Vegas for them to spend time together, they took a flight home together, and I was sure they had kissed each other good bye before they entered the baggage claim area where Jason or his wife may have been waiting for them.

"D, I don't know how to tell you this…"

"What's wrong? Is Hypnotiq okay?"

"No, she isn't."

"What happened?" His voice was getting louder as he was growing more impatient and more fearful.

"She tried to break up with Jason…he…she's gone D."

"Wait a fucking minute! You're telling me that this nigga killed her?"

"I'm sorry D. I hate that I have to tell you this over the phone, but…yes he did."

"Is this a fucking joke?? You gotta be fucking with me!!"

"No…I wish I was. Did she tell you that she was breaking up with him?"

"No, she didn't tell me. I know he kept calling her phone in Vegas, and she was getting frustrated, so I told her to just turn it off!"

"She told me that she was going to do it after he picked her up from the air-port. She was supposed to call me after he left last night. She never called, so I went over there. That's when I saw the cops and the ambulance. She was dead when I got there."

The tears were welling up as I retold the story of last night's events.

"Where is he? Did he run?"

"No, he shot himself in the head after I got to the apartment. He's dead."

Big D was silent for a few seconds, and I could hear him sniffing, and trying to gain his composure.

"I don't know what to say. Can I see her?"

"The Coroner took her early this morning. Maybe you can go to the morgue. It had just happened right before I got there. She had blood in her hair, and blood on her cheeks, but she was still so beautiful. I miss her so much…"

I broke down in tears all over again, and Big D sounded like he was quietly sobbing right along with me. I knew that he was going to miss her more than even he knew. Tragically, he had to hide his grief and his tears from the world. He had to suffer in silence. He couldn't bear to revisit the argument he had had with his wife over Hypnotiq. He didn't want to taint her memory with yelling and vicious accusations, which is what Big D thought would happen if he even attempted to explain his broken heart to his wife.

The next few weeks were a blur. I stopped by the club about a week after because Trish called and told me that Hypnotiq had a few things she had left there. When I walked in, it was business as usual. A few of the girls came up and hugged me, and asked me how I was doing, but everything was popping as usual. Hypnotiq had been dancing there for over 3 years, and the girls had hella respect for her, so they did hang a few pictures of her up in the locker room and in the kitchen, but they continued making money.

I wasn't surprised or even offended because death wasn't a stranger to the club. Not a month went by where someone associated with the club didn't end up dead. Drug dealers were set up, robbed, and killed. There were home inva-sions, drug overdoses, and fatal attractions type murders. Pimps and hookers were shot, snitches came up missing, and J Cats that turned state's evidence were permanently silenced before they could appear in court. There was always a new obituary on the cork board in the kitchen. When the dancers saw them hanging up there, they discussed the circumstances of the death, but no one ever became over-emotionally because they were desensitized to death and dying, not to mention the fact that it was so prevalent. It was the life, fast money, slanging, and hustling, risky business.

Big D paid for the entire funeral and internment, with her mother's permission, and the service was fit for a princess with the church covered in pink roses, an expensive pink casket, and a white horse and carriage to carry her body to the mausoleum.

Jason's funeral was threatened with retaliation, so LAPD was there, and the whole ordeal was on the news and in the paper for days. UPS released a statement that Jason was a "consistent" employee, and they had never witnessed "irregular" or dangerous behavior.

Tony called and gave me his condolences after he saw Hypnotiq's picture in the paper. He told me to call him if I needed anything at all. The next day, I received a gigantic flower arrangement and a $500 gift card for Ralph's Market. I thought it was odd, but when I called to thank him, he said that I could order groceries, toiletries, and cleaning supplies online, and they would deliver to my home. He said that he knew that I didn't feel like leaving the house. I thanked him from the bottom of my heart for his generosity and thoughtfulness. He said that he never wanted there to be any bad blood between us, and through a flood of tears, I assured him that there wouldn't be. I was genuinely touched by his kind gesture.

Blaze and Brandy had been coming by bringing me food and reminding me that Hypnotiq would want me to keep living, but I couldn't snap out of it. I was so deeply moved by her death that I was stuck; I didn't want to do anything, but wallow in grief. I didn't go to work, and I only showered when someone ran the water, stripped my clothes off, and pulled me under the water.

I lost about 15 pounds because I didn't want to eat. I didn't have a taste for anything, and even when I did eat, the food was tasteless and odorless. For brief moments, I was slightly functional until something would draw me into a memory of Hypnotiq. Sometimes it was watching a movie like *Scarface* or driving past the Beverly Center that would set me back on the road to recovery.

Most of the time, I felt like I had a hole in my soul. I felt empty. I had a permanent knot in my throat and in my stomach. The tears were never ending, and my eyes stayed red and swollen for days. Nothing interested me, I was depressed, and I was so lost. I felt like I was fumbling through a large, dark room searching for the light switch, tripping and stumbling over tables, couches, and potted plants. I was withering away, and if it weren't for Blaze and Brandy, I don't know what would have happened to me.

After a couple of weeks, I began to pull myself together, and find the strength that I needed to move on from the agony of losing my girl. I found comfort in visiting Hypnotiq's tomb to talk with her. She was the one that I looked to for advice, and without her it was hard for me to know which way to go. I swore that I could feel her spirit urging me to go on. I would tell her that I needed her guidance, and because I knew her so well, and had counted on her so many times in the past, I knew what she would want me to do.

Eventually I started eating, taking long walks at the beach, and going back to the gym. The day after Hypnotiq's death, Brandy bought me a pink journal, and on that same day I began to write down the emotions that I was feeling and all of the questions that couldn't be answered because the only two people that were in the apartment that night were both gone. I remembered that Hypnotiq had told me to get a journal and write down what I was feeling, what I wanted, and goals for the future. She told met hat she kept one, and it helped to sort her feelings out. I wondered where her journal was, and if her mother found it when they went to clean her apartment out. I couldn't bring myself to go back over there.

The journal from Brandy was the most precious gift that she could give me because I was able to write down things that I didn't want to share with anybody else, like the fact that I had loved Hypnotiq more than a friend. I thought I had a crush on her earlier on in our relationship, but I realized that it was not as trivial as that. I was in love with her, but without a sexual affinity.

I didn't have to touch or kiss her romantically; I just wanted to be in the same room with her. Having such a close relationship with her made me feel lucky, like I was more special than anybody else because I had the opportunity to spend almost three years with someone that cleared up rainy days with her smile alone. I admired her in so many ways: she was as thoughtful and wise as a mother of three, but as funny and goofy as a youngster on the last day of school. She never had a negative word to say about anybody and her eternal optimism was infectious. Hypnotiq's energy and spirit were gifts to all those who knew her. She made you want to be better than you were the day before, and I only wished that I could have done more to make her proud.

I recalled the last conversation that we had was about me fucking my best friend's man, and my last words to her being *fuck you* when she called me a ho. We were joking, but I had to live with the thought of my selfish and disrespectful behavior being the last picture that she envisioned of me before she slipped away.

I wrote in my journal that I wished I had driven to her place earlier that night, or that I had insisted on picking her up from the airport. A part of me blamed myself because I should've done more when Jason had called my house twice. He never called me, and I should've known that something was wrong. Hypnotiq told me that she was going to quit him, and although I didn't know he was crazy, I shouldn't have left her alone with him when she told him. I could've stayed in the living room while they talked in the bedroom. I beat myself up for days because I felt like I could've saved her. She needed me, and I didn't come through for her.

I couldn't shake those feelings for awhile, and I knew that it was unhealthy, but writing became therapeutic for me. I was able to let go of the anger that I attributed to God for allowing this to happen to one of his most precious angels. It took me awhile to call it, but perhaps God wanted Hypnotiq for himself because He missed her more than I did. I finally evolved into a place where I relinquished my selfishness, and recognized that it was better for her to be with God instead of living in hell here on earth.

Within just a couple of weeks, I had filled up the first journal, so I went to the bookstore and bought two more. I almost became addicted to writing because I needed it for my sanity. When I would have a particularly gloomy day, I would pick up my journal and find solace in adorning the blank sheets with my feelings and memories of my sister. I began buying different color pens, and making random sketches of butterflies, hearts, and rainbows on the pages.

In school, I never liked writing. I couldn't spell very well, and teachers always gave me bad grades in English, but I found that writing about what I was feeling was the only thing that got me through the tough days. Sometimes, I would go back and read past entries dated weeks before, and I was amazed at how I could transform myself back just from reading from the pages. The entries were so descriptive and heart wrenching that I could actually relive exactly how I felt at the time that I wrote it.

On some of the pages, I wrote actual letters to Hypnotiq. I specifically talked to her about that night when I hugged her lifeless body, how lost I was, and how she was the one that actually pulled me out of the shadows. Communicating with her in my journal made me feel like I hadn't completely lost her. I even asked her advice on how to approach Brandy. I had been trying to begin a conversation with her, but she didn't want to talk about the night I betrayed her. Somehow Hypnotiq's answer floated up from the pages, and I knew what I needed to do.

I was moved to the point that I thought I should write Brandy a letter. Our relationship had been functional at best, but I missed the comfort of the friendship that we once had. Brandy had taken care of me, and let me use her for the healing process, and handling my grief, but things weren't the same. I thought a letter would be perfect because then she couldn't deny me, ignore me, or give me a blank stare as I apologized profusely. I knew that she was still upset with me, but I think the loss of our friend put things into perspective for her; although, I still needed to clear my conscience.

In the letter, I told Brandy that I was selfish, and that I had made a huge mistake. I told her that I took her friendship for granted because I knew that if she found out, she would forgive me. I told her that I looked up to her, and I was never as good a friend to her as she was to me. I treasured and loved her, and would never hurt her again. I poured my heart out into that letter, and I slipped into her purse when she came over to visit one afternoon about a month after Hypnotiq had been gone.

For days after Brandy had walked in on me and Lorenzo, he called her four or five times a day, but he had a new relationship with the female voice on her voicemail prompt because she refused to answer his calls, not out of spite, but because she really didn't think she would ever talk to him again. She had always told herself that she could never continue a relationship with a cheater.

Brandy was the most traditional twenty-something that I knew, she believed in old school values, so it was never a question what she would do if her man ever tasted the nectar of another woman's fruit. Brandy had high standards, and a code of ethics and morals; I was the only part of her life that was unclean and sinful.

Lorenzo didn't give up easily. He was out of his mind with guilt, keeping the local florist in business sending her flowers every other day. Poor Brandy was crying for Hypnotiq and the loss of the loving relationship that she thought she had, and she was fucked because she didn't really have anybody to talk to because her best friend was also the enemy. She told her mom and sister what happened, but it wasn't the same as talking to your best friend.

Launching a full assault, Lorenzo showed up one day in the lobby of Brandy's office, quietly but insistently begging her to speak to him in front of the building. Out of fear and the pure threat of embarrassment, Brandy agreed to talk to him outside. They didn't get five feet from the double doors before Lorenzo began pleading his case.

"Brandy, please talk to me."

"Don't come to my job like this!"

"I'm sorry, but you haven't been returning my calls, and I need to talk to you."

Lorenzo's distressed face was covered with beads of sweat. He had it bad; he would've put on a pink dress and hopped on one foot singing *The American Anthem* if Brandy told him to.

"Baby, I'm sorry. I'll do whatever it takes to make this right. I love you and I miss you."

"Were you loving me when Mia was perched on top of your dick??" Brandy's tongue was dipped in vinegar.

"Baby, she was all over me and I..."

"That's what you came here to do? Make excuses?? You're a grown ass man! Are you telling me that she took advantage of you? She just took the dick from you?? When she dropped to her knees and you knew she was going to put her mouth on your dick, why didn't you get up?? Do not belittle my fucking intelligence! You are not the victim in this situation!"

"No...I...I fucked up!!"

"You're got damn right you did! It's bad enough that you fucked my girl, but in my house?? That is hella disrespectful! You couldn't have fucked up any worse than that. I take that back, you could've told me to roll over, and fucked her in my bed!"

"Baby, come on now..."

This was not what Lorenzo had expected when he decided to take his show on the road. Brandy was actually becoming more and more agitated, and if he was smart, he would've ended the conversation, but he didn't know if he would ever have a chance to talk to her again. He sat there and took it because he knew he had to if he ever wanted to get back on Brandy's team.

"What can I do to make it up to you? I need you in my life baby."

"Fuck you Lorenzo! You should've thought about that when you fucked my best friend on *my* couch!"

She was so hurt that she couldn't look at him without thinking about his stinging betrayal. Brandy had put Lorenzo up on a pedestal, and it was too painful for her to think that he was a normal man with selfish thoughts and forbidden, lustful desires. She was stripped naked in the middle of Wilshire Boulevard during rush hour.

Lorenzo hung his head in shame before the tear began its journey into the unknown features of his face. He made one heartfelt plea before he left her.

"I know you need to get back to work, but can you pick up your phone later?"

Brandy didn't answer him, but the look on her face told him that she would, even though she was careful to not look overly eager. She wanted him to wonder a little, and suffer more.

Eventually, Brandy's anger and disappointment began to ease out of her way, and allowed her to have conversations with Lorenzo that weren't bitter or toxic. Brandy allowed Lorenzo to get some things off of his chest as she listened with one ear, and then with two. Her body was tense and unforgiving, her stiffness urging him to give up, but he ignored the rigid stance, and vowed to love her exclusively for the rest of his life if she would have him.

Within a few days, Lorenzo had succeeded in tearing down the monuments that had stood been between them. Although it was against her will, Brandy had to confront the feelings that she still had for Lorenzo when he pressed her to tell him if she wanted him to walk out of the door forever.

When the sour taste of infidelity finally freed itself from Brandy's mouth, she was able to bring herself to tell Lorenzo of the tragedy that had taken place.

He was shocked and saddened by Hypnotiq's death, even though he had only seen her a couple of times when everybody got together, he couldn't believe that she was gone. Lorenzo reached out to console Brandy as she began to relive the tremendous loss, and it was hard for her to hold onto lingering contempt and righteousness while death was staring her in the face. Things that seemed so vitally important the day before were quickly trivialized in the face of death.

CHAPTER 33

During my worst days when I couldn't get out of bed, eat, or speak to anyone, Blaze would bring me food, clean my house, and braid my nappy, matted hair. When Hallmark commercials caused me to burst into tears, she would rub my back as I lay on my bed sobbing uncontrollably. She listened to me reminisce about Hypnotiq and the memories that we shared, the laughter and the tears. On so many occasions, I questioned why I did not follow my intuition, my gut feeling that whispered to me that night and said that something wasn't quite right. I was not only grieving for my friend, but I was consumed with remorse, continually going over what I could've done to change the outcome of that night's catastrophic events.

Instead of letting me beat myself up, Blaze reassured me that there was nothing that I could've done to change any part of what happened because it had been God's will. She told me that Hypnotiq, and Jason for that matter, were meant to die that day, and I had absolutely no control over the situation or their final destiny. Blaze said that it was their time to go, and they were destined to leave the earth that day, be it by a fatal car accident on the way home or a devastating earthquake when they got back to Hypnotiq's apartment. She had a holistic way of accepting death, and it was comforting to me because I was finally able to make sense of why it had to happen.

The point that she kept trying to drive home was just that, there was no *why*, things happened in life that we may never understand, but it wasn't meant for us to understand. She told me that no matter your religion, everyone should have faith that a higher being has the power to make things happen that are part of a master plan, unbeknownst to us, so it was pointless to question unexplainable, horrific events.

Although the concept was vague and terribly deep, it brought me relief and allowed me to lay down my burdens, and release the tremendous amount of guilt that weighed so heavily on my heart.

Besides writing in my journal and with the occasional help of Brandy, Blaze brought me back to life. She went out of her way to babysit me, hold my hand, and become my replacement friend. Brandy took some time off of work to sit with me, but eventually she had to go back to work, and Blaze stepped in, never missing a single beat. She was determined to never leave me alone. I guess a part of her knew that my sorrow multiplied in times of solitude and extreme loneliness, so she did everything she could to ease my pain and misery. She even missed some classes just to sit at my feet, even though I urged her to go to school. In time, I had truly begun to rely on her support and couldn't imagine how I would've got through the rough patches without her.

In addition to playing nurse maid, Blaze continued to work at the club part-time. She would come back and tell me how everybody was asking about me, how I was doing, and when I was coming back. Blaze thought it would be a good idea for me to get back in the club with the niggas, the loud music, and other distractions, so that I could get my mind off of things, but I couldn't bring myself to go back there yet. It seemed disrespectful to shake my ass and drink cocktails in the place where my sister's spirit had dwelled for over 3 years. The seediness of the club drew ghosts and evil spirits, and I couldn't be surrounded by negativity and lawlessness while my heart was still healing. Truth be told, I didn't know if and when I would *ever* return to the club.

Sometimes Blaze would come by and pick my brain about the strip game and the club. She was very inquisitive, relentless in asking me a million questions about the tricks of the trade. She said that she wanted to learn everything that she could, so that she could make her money and get out. She gave herself another six months to get her hustle on, and then she was going to focus more on her education and getting prepared to be a successful architect. We talked about her family, and the fact that they put a lot of pressure on her to quit the business. Her boyfriend, Ray, was at UCLA also, and he wasn't happy about her stripping either, so they argued about it a lot. Blaze didn't hang out with other dancers because she said she didn't trust them, they were messy, and she wasn't trying to have her business all through the club. She said that she didn't drink or smoke, and kept her mind clear of bullshit.

It was cool talking to Blaze because she was a lot like Hypnotiq in certain ways. She didn't talk a lot of shit about people, and she was optimistic with a positive energy. Like Hypnotiq, a beautiful girl whose personality was even more impressive than her stunning looks. Blaze was confident in her ways, but never arrogant. She was assertive, and always spoke her mind, but not in a way that was overbearing or intimidating. At the club, she seemed to get along with most of the dancers, and the men loved her. Blaze was always giving somebody a table dance, and onstage she got tips like some of the pros even though she had only been there for a little less than a month. She was making her money, but she wanted the stability of regular customers. Everybody knew that you didn't have to work quite as hard when you established a relationship with the men that continually contributed to your treasure chest.

Blaze would ask me about my regulars and what kind of money could be made. I told her how to find regulars and how to keep them. I told her to never discriminate against any man that walked in the door. Don't judge men by their clothes and jewelry or assume that you know what he's holding. The man in the light-blue postal uniform might make more money than the guy in the hip hop gear with the diamond-studded Rolex watch.

If a guy keeps trying to holler at you, go see what's up. Never play anybody or feel like you're too good to sit down and have a chat. Nobody is going to throw money at a chick that just stops by to say hello and keeps it moving. You have to sit and talk with them, tell them some things about yourself, and ask them some thoughtful questions. You have to give them your full attention, stroke their ego while you are speaking with them. You make them feel special and ultimately exchange numbers with them. Once you establish a relationship they will always seek you out first in the club, tip you onstage, and let you dance for them. That's what makes them a regular.

I told her how to schedule specific times for them to meet you at the club, so that other chicks wouldn't try to steal them when she wasn't there. I told her that she could make a lot of money doing parties, but to turn most of them down because they could be dangerous. Blaze listened intently like her life depended on it.

"So, how do you approach the guys that you want to be your regulars?"

"It doesn't work like that. You don't choose them, they choose you. You have to pay attention. When a nigga is breaking you off, he just chose you to be *his* regular. Obviously, the guy that is giving you three or four table dances is feeling you, but pay close attention to the nigga that is throwing money when you're onstage. That way, when you get off stage, you go up to him, rub your titties on his shoulder, and thank him for his generous donation *if* it was gener- ous. Niggas that throw less than $5 just get a "thank you baby." Anything over

$10 deserves some attention, and anything over $20 deserves the dumb blonde."

"The what?"

"You know. Either you sit on his lap, or you sit in a chair right next to him, and you laugh at his stupid jokes, compliment him, rub his head, and basically stroke his ego like a dumb blonde would."

"Oh, okay."

"Remember, men are in strip clubs to get what they don't receive at home. Either their girlfriends or wives don't appreciate them. They bitch, whine, and complain all the time, so they come to us to feel like a king. We're gorgeous, sexy, and attentive, so you want him to keep thinking about that shit when you're giving him a dance, or you're up onstage. When you make a man feel like he is the only man in the world, he will give you everything in his wallet *and* use the ATM by the DJ booth when they run out!"

"I got it. Now, how do you negotiate on how much money they give you?"

"Negotiate? Girl, this is the strip game, not the shopping district downtown! You get whatever they give you over the actual cost of a dance. Say you give them three dances, which is $60, but they give you $70, that's extra and you thank them with a big smile on your face because even though it was only a $10 tip, he didn't have to give you that, and if you want him to give you more, you better act like it was cool. If you don't look happy with it, some guys will give you more, but most won't, so be safe and just play along. Niggas hate arrogant dancers because after all, you are just taking your clothes off, and bouncing your ass up and down; this is not a difficult job."

"Dances are always $20 right?"

"Never dance for less than $20. Low-budget dancers might charge $10 or $15 just so they can get some dances, but it is never that serious. Once you start tricking yourself off like that, it will be nearly impossible for you to get back to the real money. Don't sell yourself short, even on slow days. It's better if you call it a night and go home before you start accepting less than you're worth."

"I hear you. You know, I've only made a couple thousand so far, but what do I do when I start making serious money?"

"Save it. You always need a cushion."

"Right. I know that, but I mean where do I put it, in the bank? Do they ask questions when you make huge deposits or what? I mean, we don't exactly have pay stubs."

"No banks. But if you insist on having an account, you can only keep a couple thousand in there, like three or four. Anytime you deposit $10,000 or more in cash, the bank has to fill out an IRS form, so you don't want that. You don't have a job! We're basically working under the table because we're not paying taxes on the shit we make."

"You've been in the club for a minute, so where do you put the rest of your money?"

"A lot of girls keep it in the house, or they take it to their mom's house, but it definitely has to be somebody you trust because once it's gone, it's gone. Most girls don't have a lot of stash though because they spend it before they even have it good in their hand. I don't know if you peeped game yet, but most of those bitches love to look like a million bucks, but they don't have shit to show for it. I spend some too, but I have a lot more put up."

"Really? That's what I want to do because I'm on a fast track. I have nothing against dancing, it's just that I know this is a temporary thing to pay for my education How much do you think I can make in another six months or so."

"It all depends on your hustle. I make money because I'm focused. I don't hang out with those bitches in the club. They love going to clubs, flying out of town to strip in Vegas and Atlanta, spending crazy money. I mean that shit was cool when I first got in the game, but then I realized that I barely broke even on those trips because I was spending as much as I was making, so I might as well keep my happy ass here in L.A. and keep all the money. Parties are cool, but be choosy. You can make as much as you want, but if you don't mind fucking or getting your pussy ate, you can make more. I have been fortunate to save up quite a bit."

"How much money have you been able to save?" Her eyes were wide with wonder, looking at me as if she was the student and I was the teacher.

"Well…I…"

"I'm sorry for being so nosey. That was a very personal question, and I understand if…"

The excitement in Blaze's face quickly lost its luster; she looked deflated as she leaned back on the couch in nervous discomfort.

"Over $20,000."

"Shut up!"

"Like I said, anything is possible."

"So, you keep yours in your mom's house?"

"Nah, I like to keep my money close to me, so I can smell it whenever I want to!"

She was laughing at me like I was Mike Epps. We kept talking about the club while I started getting dressed. As we talked about dancing and hustling, I thought about my own eagerness when I first started dancing. Hypnotiq was the one that put me on. She was patient with me when I asked her a million questions just as I had been with Blaze. Now, it was my turn to share the knowledge that I had gained over the last couple of years. The girls change, but the game remained the same.

We were starving, so we went to go get some Chinese food before Blaze went to work. I had deprived my taste buds for so long that they were genuinely appreciative of anything other than chicken soup. I ate shrimp-fried rice, chicken chow mein, kung pao chicken, and fried prawns. My stomach bulged out like a potbelly pig almost instantly, but I couldn't stop eating.

Blaze said that she understood why I wasn't going back to work, but she missed me at the club.

"When do you think you'll come back?"

"I can't right now. I have come a long way, but going back there right now will set me back, and I don't think I can handle that."

"I hear you girl. I don't want to rush you. Take all the time you need, it's just that I miss you honey!"

Blaze came on my side of the table and hugged me tightly. She was a sweet girl with a heart of gold.

"Thank you! I have thought about going back, but sometimes I sometimes I see myself in another club."

"Another club? Where would you go?"

"I think I might take a crack at *Timmy's*."

"*Timmy's*? Where is that?"

"White club in Orange County. I feel like making a change. Too many ghosts at *Aces*."

"I knew that it would be hard for you to be in the club without Hypnotiq, but I didn't know that you were talking about leaving all together!"

"I'm just talking, I haven't done anything yet. It's just a thought, but who knows. It would be a fresh start without anybody asking me how I'm doing, no memories of Hypnotiq in every corner, and basically an opportunity to move on."

"Well if you go, take me with you!"

I nodded my head. Everything was delicious, and when I became in serious danger of exploding, I packed the rest of the food to go. Blaze dropped me back at home, and she took off for work.

When I got back in my apartment, I began to seriously think about next steps. *Timmy's* was an all-white club in Orange County where a lot of the girls from the club wanted to dance, but couldn't make the cut. It's not that the girls from *Aces* were running from the brothas, everybody needed a change of scenery sometimes. Often when jealous wives and miscellaneous drama began to be too much, the girls would try to get out of town for a little while to a place where they could get out of dodge and anonymously make their money.

I had always heard about how hard it was to dance for white clubs because of the vast cultural differences in what was considered the most desirable physical qualities, but I was determined to try. My big, natural titties, voluptuous ass, and little waist were going to make me look quite exotic in a sea of slender Barbie dolls, and I thought it would be to my advantage.

Before I lay my head down that night, I made a decision that I was going to the O.C. the following week. I wrote a letter to Hypnotiq, telling her what I was planning on doing, and I explained to her that I wasn't ignoring her presence in *Aces*, I just needed more time to be able to work there *without* her. Her fingerprints were still on the wall mirror on stage, her name was still on a locker that the girls had decorated with flowers and little stuffed animals. The images were too fresh, and I wasn't sure that I could function when her passing was still so recent. I told her that I hoped that she understood that I was doing what I needed to do to get right.

Auditions were Tuesday, and I had to be there by 3:00 to get my name on the list. The audition was completely different than what I was used to, there was no audience participation at all. Danny, the manager, watched the girls dance onstage one by one in an empty club, if he was feeling you, you got the job, and if he wasn't, he showed you the door. So there was no true competition, no money thrown onstage, and no energy or eye contact from the customers. The dancers had to get up there cold, without the warmth or the love of the club. Danny put the CD in the old school, beat up mini boom box sitting at the front of the stage, sat down, and watched each performance with a critical, economic eye.

I was number two on the list. I flat-ironed my hair bone straight and added some long weave extensions because I knew that was what the white guys liked. I wore one of my sexiest costumes under my street clothes because I wasn't going to be standing in the dressing room getting dressed when I needed to be in the club watching all of the "amateurs".

The first girl up was "Buffy", super white, with platinum blonde, straight hair with extensions down to her butt. She had silicon titties, and a tiny little waist, but I couldn't tell where her back stopped and her ass started. Buffy looked like a life sized bottle of Pepto Bismo; pink costume, pink makeup, and pink nipples. Her performance was typical, a lot of stiff gyrations and flowery, dirty ballet moves. The combination of flowing arms and graceful, pointy toes looked more like a performance art exhibit instead of a raunchy strip club audition. It wasn't nasty or perverted at all.

Black strippers were much grimier than that. Black chicks took pride in the sweat that poured from their faces and arm pits as a badge of honor, pumping their asses hard and fast like the motor in a Ferrari. Black dancers rubbed, squeezed, and licked their nipples. White chicks couldn't even move those silicon mountains on their chests. We liked performing tricks and showing up the next bitch, and niggas received the benefit of all of it. They loved watching fat asses and thick thighs rolling in a rhythmic beat like ocean waves, booty cheeks spreading, and then clapping together like two gigantic hands. Pole tricks, somersaults, and head stands were standard for the stage. The danger and level of difficulty determined the flow of money that was showered on each dancer.

After Buffy left the stage, it was my turn, and from that point on, all eyes were on me. Jay-Z's *Big Pimpin'* was my song of choice. When I got up out of my seat to give the manager the CD, my swagger said that I had already won the contest. I slipped out of my clothes right there at the bottom of the stage. I walked up the stairs and stood at the front of the stage waiting for the music as I tweaked the thong in my ass, and adjusted the tiny triangles over my nipples.

Danny took his seat, and I started the kind of show he had never seen before. In my mind, the club was packed with nonchalant cats that had seen every trick I had ever done, I had to pull some tricks out of my ass. I looked the man dead in the eyes, and he couldn't hide his anticipation for my first move, he was on the edge of his chair, mesmerized with my hips, thighs, ass, and shakable titties. I wound my hips and pelvis in large circles while he looked me up and down like a shiny new car. I was twisting, turning and pumping my ass, and I caught the other girls looking as I turned around to face the front of the stage. A couple of them were whispering jealous whispers, which only gave me the confidence that I needed to try some things I hadn't done since my extended vacation.

By the time the song was going off, I had slid into the splits completely covered in sweat. Danny looked like he had been holding his breath the entire time.

"Uh, thank you…" was all that he could force from his lips. The next two white girls did their thing, and then he talked to us one at a time. He came up to me last.

"Alizé?"

"Yeah?"

"When can you start?"

"Friday night?"

"Well the girls have assigned shifts here, and since you're new you have to work in the daytime. How does that work for you?"

"That's cool…for now…because I know you'll put me on nights very soon."

"We'll see."

He delivered a half laugh, and handed me a job application that was sitting on the table where he was sitting. "Go ahead and fill this out."

"No problem, but can I get a bar towel first. I'm a little wet."

Danny walked behind the bar and grabbed a couple of towels, and tossed me one. I wiped my face and neck, under my arms and titties, and between my legs. Again, the white girls were looking at me. I guess they had never taken ho baths before, but they were about to get a full education after I started working.

Eventually, the white girls came up to me to make nice and pick my brain. They had names like Buffy, Kat, and Simone. When they introduced themselves, I had to pinch myself, so that I didn't laugh right in their faces, and ruin any chance of a pleasant working environment. The girls at *Aces* were fond of liquor labels, myself included: Alizé, Hypnotiq, Hena-C, Courvoiser, Remy, Dom P, Cris-tal, Tangueray, Moet, and Bombay Sapphire.

The two worlds were so dramatically different, but my mission was to make my money for being just that, unlike anything they had ever seen at the club. I called Blaze to tell her the good news, and she said we had to celebrate me breaking down walls. After we hung up, I asked where the bathroom was.

The dressing room was about the size of my apartment! There were individual vanity tables that had mirrors with big Hollywood lights around the frame. The couches and flat screen t.v. were tight, but the thing that absolutely blew my mind was the stand-up shower in the bathroom! I tried to contain my wild-eyed excitement, but it was difficult at best. No wonder the girls would give up their first born to work at these clubs; they actually treated the dancers like entertainers. I was glad that I didn't get dressed back there because I would've been even more ambitious, and probably thrown my back out trying to do some outrageous shit just to get a chance to take a shower in the locker room!

❦   ❦   ❦

That night, Blaze and I celebrated over crispy beef tacos and rolled tacos with guacamole and cheese from Benito's. I called it Benny's, and because the taco shop was open 24 hours with two different locations, it had fast become my favorite hole in the wall. We sat on the raggedy picnic tables in front of the ordering window on a busy L.A. street. I drowned my food in the lovely, tongue-tingling hot sauce and drifted into heaven after the first bite. Everybody called me a Mexican, but I took it as a compliment. On most occasions, I'd rather eat Mexican over soul food, which left a lot of my friends bothered and bewildered.

Blaze couldn't believe everything that I told her about the Orange County club. She wanted every detail, and after hearing about all of the perks, like the preferred parking lot, she asked when she should go audition. Blaze was a good dancer, but she wasn't as good as me, and I thought Danny would probably say that he didn't need two of *us*. I wound up telling her to let me break down the door first and make way for her. She was cool with that because with her classes, she wouldn't be able to drive out to the O.C. even a couple of times a week.

We finished our food, and Blaze suggested going to the movies. She called the movie listings and we headed towards the Marina.

"Girl, I am so glad that you are getting back into your groove, and having the courage to try new things. I know those white girls were tripping off of you."

"Hell yeah they were, but it was cool"

I got a little serious as I thought about Hypnotiq, and the promise that the two of us had made to audition for a white club before the summer ended, and even though she was gone, I had kept my part of the promise. Blaze noticed my suddenly somber mood.

"You okay girl?"

"I'm cool, it's just that Hypnotiq and I were supposed to do this together."

"You worked it out for the both of you, and she was watching." Blaze reached over and rubbed my arm the way Hypnotiq used to do.

"Thanks girl."

After the movies, Blaze asked if she could stay the night because she had an early class in the morning. When we got to my house, I took a shower, threw on some sweats, and fell asleep on the couch while we watched t.v. I was knocked out when Blaze nudged me to go get in the bed. She followed me in the room and climbed onto the other side of my bed. I fell out on my side, and slept like a baby.

CHAPTER 34

The next morning, Blaze must have crept out of the apartment because I didn't hear a peep. I was in a thick fog when I climbed out of the bed, made my way to the bathroom, and almost took my knee off when I banged it into the cabinet door under the sink. I desperately held onto the sink, grabbed my knee at the source of the agony, and cursed at the air. That shit hurt, and the pain was relentless, steady throbbing like the flashing light at a railroad crossing.

I got it together, and quickly sat down on the toilet before my full bladder flooded my brand new bathroom rugs. The warm liquid rushed out of the lower part of my body like a fire hydrant in the Bronx on a summer day. I wiped myself, pulled up my sweats, and washed my hands. After I wobbled back into the bedroom, I lay in my bed until the sound of my phone knocked me out of my sleep.

"Hey girl. Did I wake you up?" I was too sleepy to look at the caller ID, but I could tell that it was Blaze on the other line.

"No. Aren't you in class?"

"I'm getting ready to walk back in now. I had to change my tampon, so I thought I would call you before I went back to class. I just talked to Ray, and we want you to come out with us and one of his boys on Friday night."

"I don't know. I'm not trying to meet anybody."

"Come on girl, it'll be fun."

"I'll think about it."

"Okay, well go lay back down and I'll call you later."

We hung up, and I got back in the bed for a couple more hours. When I got up, I remembered my knee and the conversation that I had had with Blaze earlier. She had to change her tampon, so maybe that's why she was under my sink. I skipped to the bathroom, opened the cabinet, and pulled out my tampon box. I quickly rifled through the super tampons, and found my money in tact. I trusted her, but I just wanted to make sure that everything was everything. Besides, I knew that if she was going to steal from me, she would've done that a long time ago. I had been leaving money out everywhere almost since the beginning, and there was never even a missing quarter.

I put on some workout gear, and drove towards the gym. Brandy called me on the way.

"How are you feeling?"

"I'm okay. I got that job at *Timmy's*. I start on Friday."

"Well I know you wanted to work in a new club, but are you ready to go back?"

"I won't really know that until I get to work. We'll see."

"Okay. How is everything else?"

"Blaze called a little while ago. She wants me to go to dinner with her and her friends on Friday night."

"Are you going?"

"I'm really not feeling it, but maybe I need to get out of the house. Do you want to come?"

"Thanks, but I have to stay in the office late tonight. I have an important meeting tomorrow, and I have some work I need to do. By Friday, I'm going to be ready to fall out!"

"That's cool."

"So I'm calling because I read the letter that you slipped into my purse the other day."

"You got it?"

"I did. You know, you didn't have to do that. I was hella pissed about what happened, but after Hypnotiq…I just wasn't tripping as hard. I told you that we didn't have to talk about it. It's over. I love you, and I forgive you."

Her words dripped like hot fudge on a triple-scoop sundae. I had been feeling so badly about what I had done, and but before then there was no closure.

"Thank you, Brandy. I was wrong, and I have no excuse for what I did. It was me. He didn't want to do it, I came onto him. I am so sorry. I can't lose another friend, and I need you in my life. I will *never* hurt you again."

"I know you won't, and we don't have to talk about it anymore. What's done is done, but we just have to move on. Well, let me get back to work. I'll check on you later."

The heavy burden had been lifted and the awkwardness had disappeared. Brandy had been there for me unconditionally, but I didn't feel completely comfortable because we never got the chance to resolve our issues. Just because it wasn't brought up or discussed didn't mean that it was over for me. Especially after Hypnotiq, it was hard to be around Brandy without throwing myself at her feet, begging for forgiveness. The heavy silence was killing me, and the guilt that I felt behind Hypnotiq and Brandy was unbearable. I had written the letter as an attempt to begin the conversation, and she finally read it and put me out of my misery.

After I left the gym, I went to the mall to walk around. I had gotten so used to Blaze and Brandy being around me all the time that I felt exceptionally lonely when I was by myself. The mall was a different experience than it had been in the past because the things that brought me so much pleasure before were trivial and demeaning. I had lost my sister, and nothing would ever be the same.

I walked around for awhile looking at clothes and stuff, but everything looked similarly familiar. Vibrant colors and beautiful things seemed muted, and I felt like I was walking in a dizzy circle. I looked over the things that once moved me, but then I began to see them with different eyes. After awhile, I decided to leave because the mall just wasn't as thrilling as it used to be.

Blaze called when I got home to make sure that I was rolling, so I told her that I would hang. We hung up, and I went to my closet to see what I would wear on Friday. I tried on several pairs of jeans, and they were all hanging off of me. I hadn't put all my weight back on, but I didn't feel like buying new clothes either. Nothing fit right, and I gave up.

I cleaned up the apartment a little bit, and ate the Mrs. Field's chocolate chip cookie that I bought from the mall earlier. I relaxed on the couch until I began to feel sleepy. Before Hypnotiq left, I never really cared about getting enough sleep, I stayed out late, worked late, and ate late, but eventually I got to the point where I valued and looked forward to sleep. Sleep was the only time that I could see Hypnotiq, talk to her, and touch her. Sometimes it felt like I was talking to her when she was still alive, and at other times, I could sense that she was already gone, but still available to me in my dreams. I felt comfortable and easy when I woke up, as if her presence in my dreams would sustain me until I closed my eyes again.

❦   ❦   ❦

Friday finally came, and my first day at *Timmy's* was off the hook. I felt like it was my first day in the strip game because everything that I knew was irrelevant when I stepped from the dressing room onto the dance floor. I was in a foreign land with different customs and a different language, especially when it came to the rules about getting paid. The first time I was on stage, I was shocked and more than disappointed when I didn't feel one single dollar hit me in the ass.

After I got off stage, just as I was about to hang up my stilettos for good, Buffy came up and asked why didn't go pick my money up. She saw the confused look on my face, and explained that I needed to quickly make my way around the club to get my tips. The confusion grew on my face like the algae in the bottom of the pond at my apartment complex, so she grabbed my hand and walked me through every inch of the club. I had to grab the money from each and every man's hand, and personally thank him for the tip. The guys that didn't want to tip didn't make eye contact, and I realized that I could either try extra hard to milk him, or just move on. I was new, so I moved on.

After our gigantic lap around the club, I thanked Buffy and tried to give her some of the money, but she happily declined, and it was a good thing because I only made $56. She told me that it was considered disrespectful to literally throw money on the stage while a girl was dancing. It was cheap and demeaning, it would appear that the men were treating her like a prostitute or something. Some guys would sit close to the stage, hold money out, and wait for the girl to come get it, but they never threw it at them. The only time niggas put money in your hand at *Aces* was for a table dance. Other than that, they balled it up as tight as a spit wad, and chucked it at the females onstage like a third baseman throwing home. Nobody asked me for a dance, but Buffy tried her best to cheer me up by convincing me that they were either shy or intimidated by new blood; they had to get to know me first, so I didn't even try to push the issue by soliciting dances.

All in all, it was a harsh night. I had called some of my regulars to meet me up there, but they either had to work, or they didn't feel like sitting in all that traffic on the 405. I was all alone, and after watching the other girls prancing around collecting a couple of hundred dollars, and giving table dances every other song, I began to feel like I wasn't even in the room. When I was at *Aces,* I made all the money, and now I was starting from the bottom all over again. My money wasn't right, and I wasn't right. I felt completely out of place, kind of like a hooker sitting in the first pew.

❁   ❁   ❁

I was so defeated and ready to leave that I didn't even partake in the infamous shower. When I got home, I stepped in my humdrum shower, lathered up, and washed my hair. I ended up wearing the jeans that used to be the tightest in my closet. I put on a little makeup, and brushed my hair into a ponytail. Normally, I would've never left my apartment with a ponytail in my hair, but things were different now. It wasn't important.

Blaze called as I was sitting on the couch writing in my journal about my conversation with Brandy and my first night in a new club.

"You ready?"

"I'm ready."

"How was the club?"

"We'll talk when I see you."

"That bad?"

"Hell yeah!"

"Okay, we'll be there in 20 minutes. Girl, Ray's boy is fine!"

"I told you that I didn't want to meet anybody. I'm just hanging out."

"Okay, but you'll see."

They were at my house in 15 minutes, and I met them at the parking lot. Ray's boy was hella fine, but I still wasn't hooking up with him. We drove to Chili's, and Shawn tried to make small talk with me as we waited for our table. As he spoke very softly and chose his words very carefully, I knew that he had been warned about my "situation".

Dinner was cool, but I didn't say much. I wasn't in the mood to socialize, and I began to regret that I even left my apartment. They were strangers, and I didn't even know Blaze as well as them, so I just sat quietly and let them talk. I couldn't help but think about Hypnotiq, and how she would've ordered hot wings and the grilled steak and shrimp.

Bottles of beer and cocktails were flying everywhere, and after a few drinks I began to warm up to my tablemates. Ray and Shawn were already faded and acting goofy, and I tried to catch up. The liquor helped me relax, and be in the moment. I was loose and talkative. Before I started drinking, I felt like I was having an out of body experience; people were talking, I could see and hear them, but I felt like I was hovering in the air above, watching myself, but not actively participating in the conversations and laughter.

My appetite wasn't all the way back, plus I was full of mixed drinks so I had barely finished my chicken quesadillas when they started eating brownie fudge sundaes. Everyone finally finished, and it was time to get the hell out of there. The guys wanted to go play pool, but I told them to drop me off first. I leaned on Blaze as I wobbled out of the restaurant and into the car. I thought the drinks would help me forget the sadness that had embraced me for weeks, but instead it magnified and illuminated my suffering. On the way home, memories of Hypnotiq held me hostage for the entire ride, and I quietly let the tears do their thing.

When we got to my apartment, I thanked them for dinner and started walking towards my front door. Ray hopped out of the driver's seat, and asked if he could use my bathroom before they headed home. I told him that was cool, so Blaze and Shawn got out of the car and followed him in my place to wait.

Ray went in the bathroom while the other two sat down on the couch. I went in my room to yank my clothes off, so as soon as they left I could crawl in the bed. My buzz was starting to wear off, and I was exhausted from the club and the drinks. I threw a big robe over my naked body, and went back in the living room to turn the t.v. on.

"Here's the remote. You guys can turn to whatever you want."

"I don't care. Do you have a bottled water?" Blaze followed me into the kitchen.

"Shawn, do you want anything?"

"Nah I'm cool."

He was fidgeting, looking at his watch and the bathroom door, like he wanted to go in and pull Ray out of there. He must've had a girl waiting for him. Shit I didn't care. We had fun, but he was too young and broke for me. He was looking all silly when the bill came but I had no problem paying for my portion. That was cool because he wasn't getting no ass.

All of a sudden, the bathroom door flung open, and Ray ran out screaming with an evil look on his face, and a gun in his hand. I never saw it coming.

"All right bitch, give it up!"

He was aiming the gun at my face, taking long energetic strides to get to me. I was frozen.

"Bitch, did you fucking hear me? I said break bread!"

"Oh, you're going to rob me? I just lost my best friend, and you want to come in here and take my shit?"

"Bitch shut the fuck up! Where's the loot?"

"I don't keep my shit in the house!"

"Alizé, that's not what you told me…"

That bitch set this whole thing up. I was vulnerable and weak after Hypnotiq's death, and she used that to her advantage. Blaze used me from day one. She had been questioning me for weeks, setting me up so they could rob me. It was a month to the day that Hypnotiq was shot, and now it was my turn.

Ray stepped to me, pushed me into my bedroom, and threw me on the bed, landing on my stomach. Ray placed the gun to my temple, and Shawn pulled some handcuffs out of his pocket, and slapped them on my wrists. Blaze was guarding my bedroom door to prevent me from escaping.

"Bitch, if I have to ask you again, you're going to join your friend! Where the fuck is the money?"

A couple of weeks ago, I would've told him to just pull the trigger because I didn't care if I lived or died. But now I wasn't ready to go. I couldn't leave the world like this, not today.

He was pressing the gun against my temple so hard that my head was beating like a '64 Impala. My heart was in my throat, and my whole body was shaking. I trusted Blaze too soon; out of loneliness and grief I needed a friend. I told her too much of my business, brought these strangers to my house, and then I had a gun to my head. I could see her face as I turned my head towards the door, and she was emotionless. I wanted to whoop that bitch's ass if it was the last thing I ever did.

"In the freezer."

"Go look in the freezer y'all!"

"Can you take the fucking gun from my head? I just told you where it was!"

"Shut up! You better not be lying!"

The longer the gun stayed on my head, the more petrified I became; the gun could have went off accidentally if he got nervous, or let his finger slip. I didn't want to give him a reason, so I didn't move, I barely breathed. Every minute felt like an hour.

I heard them rustling through my freezer, opening boxes and bags, throwing shit around, screaming at each other about where to look. Then, I heard laughing and yelling. They found it.

"Jackpot!!" They both were running towards my room like they won the Easter egg hunt.

"Y'all get it?"

Ray was straining his neck to look down the hall, and the gun was moving around on my temple. My body remained still, I closed my eyes tight and held my breath.

"Hell yeah! This has to be about 8 or 9 Gs!"

"Is that it?!" Ray showered my face as he screamed at the top of his lungs.

"That's it! You got it all!"

"I will blow your fucking head off!"

"I don't have anything else!!"

"Look under the bed, the closet, and the dresser! I don't believe this bitch!"

I knew that no one would ever look in the kitchen or the bathroom, and that's why I hid $8,000 in the freezer, and $14,000 under the super plus tampons in the box under the sink.

Blaze and Shawn were tossing my apartment looking for more money, and I nervously waited for them to give up. They were opening and slamming drawers, throwing clothes and hangers out of the closet, and kicking my shoes around. All of a sudden I felt the mattress move, and they were tilting it up while the gun was still to my head. I had never been so scared in my life, and I didn't move an inch as they lifted each corner of the bed, one at a time.

Ray leaned in and whispered in my ear.

"You pretty thick, nice titties, big ass. Is it true what they say about strippers?"

He used his free hand to run up my robe to grip my ass. I flinched as his hands touched my bare skin.

"What do they say?"

"Y'all know how to put it down."

"Ask your girlfriend."

"That's not my girl, that's my partner. She's not even a dancer. She's on the grind."

"Does she even go to UCLA?"

"Hell nah! She goes to the school of hard knocks!" I had been so stupid. All of it was a lie, and I believed her on the strength.

"There's nothing else here." Blaze was as comfortable as if she was robbing the owner of a 7–11.

"Yeah, let's go." Shawn joined in the conversation.

"I think I need to get me a sample before we leave. Y'all go wait in the other room."

Ray had taken the gun down, and I could already feel the bruise on the side of my head. Blaze and Shawn walked out of the room, and then I heard the front door close.

"Ray, please don't do this! You got the money! Please let me go!"

"Nah, I don't think I'm ready to let you go just yet."

I watched him lay the gun on the nightstand, and then he pulled his jeans down to his ankles. By the time he was pulling his boxers down, his dick was already hard.

"I know you got some K-Y."

I didn't want him to fuck me, but he was going to do it, so I begged him to be safe.

"Look in the nightstand, and please get a condom out of there too. Can I go to the bathroom first." My bladder was full from all the drinks, but he wouldn't let me move.

"Nah."

He fumbled around in the drawer, and pulled out the Astroglide and a Magnum XL condom, but I knew it wasn't going to fit. Ray left me on my stomach and shoved my robe up near my back. I heard him rip the top off the condom, and throw it on the nightstand. He slapped the baggy condom on, and squirted some lube on the top. I just prayed that he didn't hurt me, and the condom didn't slide off.

All of a sudden I felt his hands on my ass. He was spreading my legs, and placing his wet finger in my ass. He was going to fuck me in the ass! My hands were still handcuffed, and I couldn't brace myself or move at all. He moved his finger around in a circle, and then he added another finger inside.

"You're going to like this."

"Ray, please don't do this!! Ray, I can't move!! Please Ray!!"

I spoke softly because I didn't want to piss him off, but my voice was serious. I was pleading and begging, using his name to remind him that he was a human being and not a rapist, but it didn't help.

He climbed between my legs, and started shoving his dick in my ass. I screamed, but he wouldn't stop. He kept working it until it was finally in. My asshole was on fire, and when he started thrusting in and out, I thought I would die. I was crying, yelling, and moving as much as I could but he wouldn't stop. He was huffing, puffing, and sweating all over my back. The lube was gone, and the condom was dry. I felt my asshole ripping open, tearing and bleeding.

"No!! Please stop!! Ray, you're hurting me please!! Stop!!"

He kept pulling his dick in and out for what seemed like forever, and then he started going faster. I tried to pull my cheeks together, bearing my pelvis down on the bed, holding the comforter as tightly as I could, but he grabbed hold of my hips, and rammed it in even harder.

"Fuck!! Ray please stop!! You're killing me!! Please!"

I didn't have my hands to hold myself up, or to push him back, I tried to push my stomach as far into the bed as I could. My bladder bulged like a heavy water balloon. I couldn't hold it any longer and peed right there on myself, on him.

"What the fuck?!"

The entire bottom portion of his body was covered in my hot piss. I prayed a five second prayer that he would get up off of me, but he didn't. I begged him to stop, but he kept fucking me hard and relentlessly, and yelled proudly as he came.

"Damn girl! That shit was good!"

Ray climbed his nasty ass off of me, and pulled my robe down.

"Can I please go to the bathroom?"

My face was wet with tears, I was soaked in piss, my wrists were sore from the cuffs, and I didn't even know if I could stand on my feet.

"Hold on."

He took the key from his pant pocket, and unlocked the cuffs. When my hands were free, I rubbed both of them where they were red and swollen.

"You got a towel?"

This nigga was talking like we had just had consensual sex. I wanted to grab the gun off of the table and blow his head off, but I didn't have the strength.

I limped to the linen closet, and gave him a washcloth. I went back in my room, but I couldn't even sit down because my whole ass was on fire, burning from the inside out. I leaned on the wall and quietly sobbed while Ray washed up in the bathroom.

I never let my guard down, but I did for the first time in a long time, and I got jacked and raped. I carefully walked to the living room to get my phone and call Hypnotiq…it all rushed back at once that Hypnotiq was gone. A heavy cloud of anguish hurried over my bleak existence, and I crumbled like a bag of chips. I fainted from pure exhaustion and weariness. My body hit the floor like a sack of potatoes. The room went dark. I heard the whole thing, and I felt my body falling, but I couldn't stop it, and I couldn't move.

❋   ❋   ❋

When I came to, I was laying on the side of my bed with my face nearly under the bed and my robe up near my waist. I was groggy at first, and I didn't know why I was on the floor. Then, I felt pulsating pain from my asshole, my wrists, and the side of my head, and it all came back to me. I didn't know what to do. I didn't even know how long I had been down there.

I summoned up some strength, and walked to the front door. It was wide open. I looked down the stairs to see if their car was gone, and it was. I shut and locked the door, and walked all around the apartment to make sure they weren't still there. They threw all my shit out of the freezer. Frozen waffles, hot wings, and ice cubes were strewn all over the floor. My room was a fucking mess with clothes, shoes, hangers, and boxes everywhere. My bed was all fucked up, and the comforter was pissy.

The bathroom was spotless, except for the soap and water all over the sink from Ray washing his little dick. He left the condom in the toilet, and I don't know why I did it, but I grabbed it, and put it in a Ziploc bag in the freezer. After I washed my hands, I looked under the sink for my tampon box. I pulled it out, opened it, and looked down at a bunch of tampons. The money was gone.

My mouth fell open, and I started throwing everything out of the cabinet. I was like a crazed animal tearing at anything that touched my fingertips, tossing everything at the counter, the mirror, and the floor. Fuck me! I didn't know how they found it because I never said a word to Blaze. Maybe they found it after I passed out. Maybe they found it after they found the money in the freezer and asked me if there was anymore. I just went from over $22,000 to nothing. My savings, my rainy day fund, my backup plan, it was all gone, and I was broke.

I called Brandy, and told her to come over. I didn't tell her why because I didn't want her to crash the car, but I told her it was all bad.

CHAPTER 35

My legs were concrete pillars and my body was heavy and loaded down as if I had sandbags piled up to my neck. I was frozen with fear, excruciating pain, and overwhelming sadness. In just a few hours, my reality had changed once again. The night's activities were surreal and incomprehensible. My apartment looked like a scene from a movie, the aftermath of a sensationalized earthquake. The silence was deafening.

Food was thrown all over the kitchen, the couches were sitting on their side, pillows, frames, and candles were all over the floor in the living room, and my bedroom looked like a garage sale. My journals were sprawled across the carpet in front of my other nightstand where I kept them. I shuddered when I thought about the fact that they could've read my most intimate thoughts and feelings. I had to block it from my thoughts because it was too much to even consider. The Astroglide and the condom wrapper on the nightstand remained as evidence of the horrific pain and ultimate violation that had just taken place. It was all too much to absorb at once.

Sudden panic rushed over me, and my mind was racing like a computer, calculating exactly what had happened, why, how, and who those people were that I allowed in my home. As hard as I tried, I couldn't comprehend the things that I just witnessed and had been a part of. My head wouldn't allow me to receive the messages that my body was sending, as if protecting me from the horribleness of it all. I looked around, and I knew that something terrible had happened, my body was aching like I had been hit by a Mack truck, but I couldn't go back to the exact moment when things started to spiral out of control, and I was helpless to their terror.

I was sitting in a dazed stupor when Brandy finally knocked on my door, coming to rescue me from myself. She ended up letting herself in because my butt was nailed to the chair.

"Mia, oh my god what happened?"

I didn't speak. I couldn't find the words to form the thoughts that were in my head, then suddenly they took shape and I was able to pull the letters out of the stale air.

"You need to sit down."

There was no way I could tell her the chilling details of my night while she stood up. The news would rip the strength from her legs and whack her off of her feet.

She quickly looked around the apartment with wide eyed amazement, craning her neck to see in the kitchen and bedroom without moving from the designated spot on the floor. It was as if she didn't want to contaminate the evidence by moving or touching anything, so she stood perfectly still with a shocked, confused look on her face.

"You're scaring me, what's going on? Were you robbed?"

"Blaze."

"What about her? Where is she?"

"The bitch set me up."

"What?!"

Gradually, I was able to articulate everything that I wanted to tell Brandy about Blaze, the guys, and what they savagely took from me.

"The four of us went to dinner, and they bought me hella drinks. They were dropping me off in the parking lot when Blaze's dude asked to go to the bathroom. We all walked up the stairs and waited in the living room. All of a sudden, he came out of the bathroom with his gun blazing. He pointed it at my head, and they handcuffed me while they tore my shit up looking for the loot. They got the money from the freezer, and under my sink. They got me for over $20,000! I'm broke, Brandy! They took everything I had!"

"I can't believe it!"

"One of the niggas fucked me in the ass!"

"Mia, we have to take you to the emergency room right now!"

"Oh, and the Blaze character was a lie. She isn't in college, and she isn't even a real stripper! She was on the grind with those cats. The one guy wasn't even her real boyfriend! The whole thing was a fucking set up!"

"Mia, we need to call the police."

"The police? I'm a stripper! They're not going to believe shit I have to say or care. That money is gone! The police would start questioning me about having all that money in the house. They would probably think I was slanging or something. Anyway, I fainted, and when I woke up they were gone. They could be anywhere by now! I'll tell you one thing, they left L.A."

"How do you know that?"

"You can't rob somebody from the club, and then get up on stage the next night! Plus, they probably weren't even from out here in the first place. I never met anybody from her family, I never went to her apartment, and I never even knew her real name. A lot of dancers never told anybody their real name because they wanted to keep their private life private, so I never pushed. If I really sit and think about it, I didn't know shit about her, and I had her all in my spot, around my friends, and all in my business. Well they got what they wanted, and they moved on to their next hustle."

"I still think we need to call the police. You could be preventing them from doing it to somebody else."

"Brandy you're not listening to me, this is the life. There is no honor among thieves. I've never put a gun to somebody's head, but I have lied, cheated, and stole from niggas. They never called the police because they were married, or they had me sticking dildos up their ass, and they wanted to keep that shit on the low. I'm in the strip game, and we live by different rules. Blaze and her niggas are going to rob somebody else before the money runs out. What else are they going to do, get jobs? I know one thing, I will never see Blaze, or whatever the fuck her name is, again. What I would do to them is way more fucked up than what the court system would do. She will never show her face again because she may not get out alive."

"What would happen if she came back?"

"Torture. Death. I'm not saying that I would kill her, but if I told some of my people, they would do it for me, but trust and believe that I would get in on the torture. If she was paying attention while she was in the club, she knows that it's a wrap. That's why you try to get as much money as you can because you have to survive on that until the next hustle."

"What are you going to do now?"

"I don't know. I'm so mentally exhausted that I can't think straight. You know what I'm more disappointed about?"

"What?"

"Blaze knew that I was fucked up behind Hypnotiq. She let me cry on her shoulder, and talk about my girl until I was blue in the face. She knew that I was grieving, but she sat with those niggas night after night planning how to rob me! And when the one said he wanted to rape me, she left the apartment. I mean she already had the money in her hand, but she didn't even try to stop that motherfucker!"

"I am so sorry Mia. What can I do for you? Do you need anything?"

"I want to get in the hot shower. That's what I need more than anything."

"Are you sure that you don't want to call the police because you're going to wash off all the evidence."

"I'm sure. He left his condom in the toilet, and I put it in the freezer."

"Good thinking. Let me take pictures of you and your place before you get in."

Brandy grabbed my digital camera out of my closet, and started snapping pictures of me. She got the bruise on my face above my eyebrow where he stuck the gun, the redness from the cuffs on my wrists, and the fingerprint impressions on my ass and thighs from when he was fucking me. Brandy ran around the apartment taking pictures of all the damage all through the apartment. I was sore from head to toe, so I wasn't much help. It was almost two in the morning, and my eyes were bloodshot and swollen. When Brandy was done, she turned the water on for me, and started cleaning up.

I allowed my blood-stained, lubricated robe fall to the bathroom floor as I stepped in the shower very carefully. I had to brace myself and hold my breath just to rub the soapy rag over my tender body. I turned my back to the faucet, gingerly placed my hands on my cheeks, and spread my ass so the warm water could run through it. At first, the pain was unbearable, but the longer I stood under the forgiving water pellets, the more relaxed I began to feel.

It was incomprehensible, but Blaze had betrayed me when I was the most vulnerable. She would've never been able to get away with her lies and mysterious life if I hadn't been in such a deep funk. She nursed me back to health, mentally and physically. She had been my rock for the last few weeks, and I trusted her. If I could speak to her only once, I would only have one question. *When did she decide to rob me?* I couldn't ask her, so I had to rationalize it by myself.

When she got the tampon from my cabinet, she may have seen the money, and decided to rob me right then, or maybe the plan was already in action when she kept questioning me, asking me how much money I made, and where I hid it and shit. Maybe she was pretending to be my friend from day one.

Besides Brandy, Blaze had been the closest person to me lately. I didn't even know her real name. I didn't trust any of those broads at the club, but for some reason, I trusted her, and let her get way too close to me and my life.

After the dust settled, all I had was Brandy, and try as hard as she may, she would never understand my life of the last three years. She knew me before the game, and it was hard for her to appreciate the fact that I had changed. I could never resume a normal life after being immersed in the subculture of stripping. Everything was a hustle or a come-up to me. I was always looking for the next lick, making fast money for little to no work. It used to be that I would look at a man as a potential friend or boyfriend, but after I started stripping, I looked at a man as a breathing, walking ATM machine, and besides his dick I didn't want anything from him.

My mother had become increasingly fed up with me, and I could never tell her what had happened to me. She was only able to live with my decision to strip because I told her that it was temporary while I saved up money for college. I knew it was a lie, and she probably did too, but I needed to pacify her unwillingness to accept my choice. Months turned into years, and not only was I a bonified stripper, but I had adopted the accompanying lifestyle: drinking, drugs, absence of morality, and paid sex.

What was I going to do now? After Hypnotiq, I thought that dancing at a white club was going to be the answer to all of my prayers. I thought I had a chance to get away from everything evil and start off fresh, but the reality of the situation was that I wasn't going to make the same bread at the white club. I was brand new, I didn't have any regulars yet, and the men didn't even know if they were even feeling me yet. I took one step forward, and four back. I was dead broke, Hypnotiq and Tony were gone, I was raped, and betrayed by someone that I thought truly cared about me.

Up until that time, I had lived my life day by day. I had saved money, but never had a plan of how I was going to use it in the best way possible. I never had goals or aspirations to do anything but make money, and now that energy was a fucking waste of time because I had nothing to show for my long nights, parties, table dances, and for fucking niggas that I wouldn't even eat lunch with.

As I stood under the water, I could see the steam pouring out of the shower, but I couldn't feel the heat. I was numb. I felt like an empty shell. I had been stripped of everything, my life as I used to know it. My heart had been snatched from my chest far too many times, and I didn't have the strength to get it back. I didn't want to fight anymore. I won the battle after Hypnotiq's death, after watching Jason do himself right in front of me, and after the subsequent meltdown from not listening to my instincts and saving my girl, but not again.

As if it a spotlight came out of nowhere, the razor in the corner of my shower next to the shaving gel shook me, and grabbed my attention. I never understood how life could get so fucked up that people would shoot themselves in the head, jump out of windows, or step in front of trains, but now I knew exactly what they felt. I was wrapped in a blanket of hopelessness, and I had absolutely nothing to look forward to. I had nothing before last night, and now I had less than zero. There was nothing good or decent in my pitiful life. If I removed myself from this so-called life, I could see Hypnotiq again, everyday would be Sunday, and the sun would never go down. I wouldn't hurt anymore, and I wouldn't have to make difficult decisions or face my grim future.

A sinister smile grew across my face as I slowly bent down to pick up the razor and held it in my hand. I was shaking as I broke the plastic casing to reveal the small, extra sharp razor blade. It was as if I was waiting for the blade to speak to me, and tell me what to do. I just stared at it as the water continued to run over me. Watching the blade gave me the strength that I could never find before. I felt a burst of energy, and the crippling pain that prevented me from moving just 20 minutes ago had subsided. The sparkle from the blade made me feel relaxed and peaceful. After I stared at the blade long enough, it spoke to me. It said that if I wanted to feel that kind of contentment forever, I had to succumb to it.

I listened to the blade because it was the only thing that I had heard in a long time that brought me security and a sense of relief. With the blade in my trembling fingers, I ran it horizontally across my left wrist, right beneath the puffy redness from the handcuffs. A stinging, scintillating joy came from underneath the blade, and it beckoned me to press on, harder and faster. My eyes were closed as I applied more pressure to the plump, greenish veins peaking below my brown skin. The blade sliced through the bullshit, the dejection, and the melancholy that I had been plagued with for so long.

Breathing, thinking, and moving everyday had become cumbersome and time-consuming, the thought of planning and readjusting nerve-wracking, but the blade told me that I didn't have to do any of that anymore; the blade would take care of me. The euphoria increased as the drops of blood held hands and formed a modest trickle that mixed with water, and ran down my arm in a dark red stream. I wasn't scared, and the pain became overwhelmed by the tranquility of the upcoming painlessness.

Just as I was becoming fascinated and seduced by the slender piece of silver, Brandy walked into the bathroom, interrupting my chance to meet Death.

"Hey girl. I just wanted to check on you. Do you need me to help you wash up?"

I grudgingly snapped out of the spell that I was under to respond to my friend that was snatching me back into hell just as I was trying to rid myself of the noose around my neck. I released the pressure from my wrist, and rested the blade in the corner of the shower. The sharp pain rushed back with full force, I felt betrayed by the blade's spitefulness.

"No…umm…I got it. I'm just letting the hot water run over me. I'll be out in a minute."

"Okay, call me if you need anything."

"Thanks girl. By the way…I love you and I don't know what I would've done without you."

"You're tripping! Where else would I be?"

Little did she know, but she had saved my life. I did have a friend, and the best kind. She was a decent, loving person with a heart too big for her chest, and if anyone could pull me out of this disparity, it was Brandy.

I took inventory of the mutilation of my wrist, and it was marginal at best. I thought that I was on the very cusp of heaven and hell, but I wasn't even close. After I held my arm under the water, and wiped away the blood, I was embarrassed to find that I had scratched my wrist like a jealous girl who took a key to her cheating boyfriend's car, thin but deep.

Somehow my failed suicide attempt gave me the courage that I was willing to buy. Even though I was on the brink of death, I pulled myself back. I took Brandy's interruption as a sign; I wasn't meant to die that night.

I washed up, rinsed off, and stepped out of the shower. Undoubtedly, I felt renewed and rejuvenated, blessed with the opportunity to come back and make things right in my life.

"You out?"

"Yeah, I'm getting ready to throw some sweats on and lay down."

"Can I bring you anything?"

"How about some Hennessey?"

"Don't you think some milk would be better?"

"Brandy sweetie, I'm in pain right now. Back in the day, they rubbed liquor on the gums of teething babies before Orajel was created. Hook a sister up!"

"Okay, I'll get it."

Brandy meant well, but she had no idea of the pain that I felt, especially in my ass. My whole body was bent over as I shuffled to my bedroom. Ray, or whatever, had torn my asshole, and it was burning like a raging fire. I remembered that I had Preparation H in my cabinet to dry out the occasional red zit on my face. I turned around and went back in the bathroom to get the gel.

When I made it back to the room, I bent over my bed with my ass in the air. I unscrewed the top, squeezed a gang of gel on my right middle finger, and gently spread my cheeks apart. It hurt like hell, but I couldn't stop. I rubbed the gel on and around my booty hole, and the pain began to lessen instantly.

After I washed my hands, I saw my journals laying on the floor on the other side of my bed, carefully placed them in the nightstand, stepped into the baggiest sweats in my closet, threw on a shirt and socks, and crawled into the bed. I looked at my wrist for the first time since I got out of the shower. I almost laughed because I hadn't done shit. I couldn't even kill myself the right way. The cut was so meaningless that it stopped bleeding right after I stopped delicately butchering my wrist, so I didn't even need a band-aid. That was going to be my souvenir, my badge of courage, to remind me that things are never as bad as they seem.

I was never a terribly religious person, but I remember my mom always telling me, *Whatever doesn't kill you makes you stronger* and *God doesn't give you more than you can handle.* I don't know why those random phrases popped into my head, but they were right on time.

It was almost three in the morning, and I was finally sleepy. Brandy kept saying that she couldn't find the Hennessey, but she kept "looking" until I had fallen fast asleep. Her slick ass didn't want me to drink, and she knew I wasn't coming in there to get it. I always thought of her as the innocent one, but maybe she had the most game.

CHAPTER 36

Brandy didn't want to leave after I fell asleep, so she got in the bed with me sometime during the wee hours of the morning. She would've lost it if she knew that it was touch and go for a minute. I had performed a delicate tight-rope act, teetering between life and death high atop the gigantic circus tent of life. For the short time that I balanced myself, carefully putting one foot in front of the other, pure happiness washed over me that I hadn't felt in a very long time. I felt a sense of peace and comfort on the rope, even as I started to lean forward towards my impending fall into the darkness below.

My foot almost slipped, pulling me down off of the rope entirely, but Brandy caught me with her grace and mercy. I know that I didn't have the strength to pull myself up, I had the weight of the world on my shoulders, and I didn't want the responsibility of living anymore, I didn't want to make decisions and figure out how to do the right thing when I only knew how to do the wrong thing. Brandy's interruption was the sign that I wasn't looking for, but it found me. There was no sense in telling Brandy what *almost* happened; the point was that I was here, and I wanted to live.

I was in such pain that I woke up several times before I finally dismissed the notion of getting a good rest. I lay very still in my bed listening to the kids playing outside. It was a Saturday morning before the end of the school year, and they were intoxicated by the sun and the commencement of summer break. When I was there age, I felt exactly the same way. Three months of 9 o'clock sunsets, no school, no shoes, and daily ice cream man fixes were better than Christmas day.

Even as I got older, summer was always my favorite time of the year: Venice Beach, topless cars, baby shorts, and strappy sandals. Anything was possible during the summer. It was a time of pure, unadulterated fun, new beginnings, and eternal sunshine.

The welcoming sun was smiling at me through the newly bent mini-blind in my bedroom, daring me to get up and enjoy the remarkable day. I sat up slowly in the bed so that I didn't wake Brandy up. She was sleeping like a baby, and after being my lifesaver yet again, I didn't have the nerve to disturb her. I braced my arms on either side of me, and gradually lifted myself from the mattress, careful not to agitate Brandy or my asshole. The pulsating tenderness turned into a muffled pain. Last night, I didn't think I would ever sit comfortably again, but today I felt a glimmer of hope that everything would be alright. My mission was to get my journal and attempt to scribe my feelings about everything that happened last night. I sat at the foot of my bed and wrote for about 15 minutes until I felt an enormous amount of pressure in my stomach.

I hobbled into the bathroom and took as much time as I needed to sit on the toilet seat with care. My lower body tensed up as the trickle of pee was released from my bladder. Sitting on the toilet made my booty hole open up, and it felt like my intestines were going to squeeze out of the gaping hole if I didn't squeeze my ass tightly. I felt the enormous gas in my abdomen, and suddenly the parade of farts began to release successively from my butt. Relief and agony were all rolled in one as a toxic mixture of gas and slimy poop fell out of my ass. I sat on the toilet for what seemed like a half hour as I rid myself of all evidence of Ray, or whatever his name was. It took me another half hour to meticulously wipe my ass with a combination of toilet tissue and baby wipes.

The messiness of it all prompted me to get in the shower instead of standing at the sink for another lifetime. I was in and out before Brandy even woke up. As I walked through my spotless apartment, there was no evidence to prove that a crime had taken place not even 10 hours earlier. Brandy must have stayed up for hours; the kitchen, living room, bathroom, and bedroom were immaculate. I went in the kitchen to get that shot of Hennessey that Brandy had denied me a few hours ago. When I opened the freezer for ice, I had a nightmarish flashback of Blaze tossing my fridge looking for my money. It was all gone, all of the empty bags of veggies and boxes of frozen dinners. She took everything down to the last dollar. My freezer hadn't been that empty since I first started dancing. I drank a double, and left the busted kitchen.

I was still tired, so I went back in my room, lay on my stomach, and drifted back to sleep until I awoke to my cell phone an hour or so later. Brandy jumped too. It was one of the girls from the club, but I cancelled the call.

"I'm sorry."

"That's okay girl, it's not your fault. How did you sleep?"

"Terrible. I kept waking up."

"You poor baby. How do you feel?"

"Like shit."

"What would make you feel better? Anything?"

"At first I felt like just staying in the house, but the sun is so beautiful out-side."

"It really is. Do you want to grab some sandwiches and eat them in the park or something? That would be nice."

"I think I can handle that."

I thought about putting the top down on my BMW and soaking in the sun on the way to the park, when all of a sudden, I panicked wondering if Blaze took that too. My keys should've been on the counter, but I didn't remember seeing them when I went to make my drink.

"Brandy, did you see my car keys?"

"No. Where were they, in your purse?"

"When I got home last night, I left them on the counter before everything went bad. Oh gosh, please don't tell me they drove my shit away! Please don't tell me that!"

Pain or no pain, I ran to the bar where I always laid my keys when I walked in the apartment, and they weren't there. My heart was beating fast, and the tears began to form when Brandy yelled from the bedroom.

"Mia, your keys are in your purse, but let me make sure your car is outside."

I breathed a semi sigh of relief, I wouldn't be completely satisfied until she came back up the stairs and told me that my BMW was outside in one piece. Brandy ran past me and down the stairs like lightning. I didn't even get a chance to tell her to hurry. I crossed my fingers and said a quick prayer because you could never have enough good luck.

"Mia!"

I ran to the living room window that looked down on the street below. Mia was standing on the grass yelling like a fool.

"Mia, your car is fine girl!!"

"Thank you!!"

I smiled like I had won the lottery, and tears of joy and relief flew out of my eyes. I dropped to my knees and said a better prayer thanking God for letting me live last night, and for looking out for me this morning.

I was scared shitless; I had a tight whip sitting on 20s, and I just knew they had got me, but after I thought about it, they couldn't do anything with my car.

Because they probably moved around a lot, they didn't know of a chop shop, and if they took the car, I would've reported it stolen and they would've went to jail, so they were better off splitting the cash and buying a bucket for them to share.

Mia came bounding up the stairs and we hugged as if the cash was also lying in the back seat with a big red bow around it. At least I had a car, I didn't know how I was going to pay the note next month, but I had a car.

"Let's put clothes on and celebrate."

"Celebrate? Are you serious?"

"Mia, you have to celebrate the little victories as well as the big ones. If your car wasn't outside, things would've been much worse, wouldn't you agree?"

"You're right."

That was the thing that I loved about Brandy the most. She was eternally optimistic, grateful, and humble. After everything that happened last night, she wanted to celebrate my car being spared. Brandy was admirable and I appreciated her thoughtfulness.

We threw clothes on, and walked out to my car. Brandy hopped in the driver's seat, literally, and drove towards TOGO's. We ordered two small pastramis on white with everything plus Provolone cheese, Lay's chips, and sodas. Brandy drove to Echo Park, we ate under a tree, and talked about my future.

"I know we have talked about school a million times, but do you think you're ready to really talk about it now?"

"I've been thinking about it for a couple of weeks now, and I really thought about it last night and this morning. I'm busted, and my new job isn't going to pay me what I am used to getting."

"What's wrong with the club?"

"They do things differently over there. The manager started me on days, plus you have to walk around and literally take your money from the hands of every man in the spot. They call it disrespectful to throw money at a lady. For one, we're not fucking ladies, and for two, it's too much work, and since I'm new they're not fucking with me on dances yet. Eventually, I would come up, but it's going to take a minute to get there. I don't have that kind of time. I'm starting from square one."

"You're right girl. So, what do you think? What are you interested in?"

"I told you that I never liked school. I don't know what I would major in."

"Don't think of it like high school. Most of high school was bullshit. What do you like to do?"

"You know, I had been writing in that journal you gave me until I couldn't write anymore, so I went and bought me a couple more, and they're almost all the way filled up too. I wrote about Hypnotiq, and I found that it helped me get through the especially tough days. I wrote letters to her in there too. I didn't realize it until you gave me that journal, but writing helped me express the things that I couldn't say, and it helped release my anger and my guilt. On the days when I couldn't even get out of bed, I could write. I know it sounds silly, but my writing actually made me feel stronger."

"That doesn't sound silly at all! I am so proud of you! You have found your passion!"

"Passion?"

"Yes, I believe that everyone has a passion for doing something. For some people, it's painting, playing guitar or making model airplanes. Yours is writing!"

"It is? How do you know?"

"Can you live without it?"

"Well I have up to now, but since I have discovered it, I don't think I can."

"Nobody knows what their passion is until they discover it for the first time, and you have found it! Not to mention the fact that it is a very easy one. You can major in English, English Literature, British Literature, Creative Writing, etc."

"I can major in writing?"

"Well there is Journalism for people that want to be reporters or columnists for the paper. There are so many things you can do. On Monday, I'll take off work and we can go down to Santa Monica College to get you in summer school. The classes are only a couple of weeks, and you can get your feet wet before the fall semester. What do you think?"

Brandy was more enthusiastic about my future than I was, and I couldn't bear to disappoint her.

"Monday sounds good."

"You'll see Mia, this will be a whole new start. I'm behind you 100%!"

I couldn't tell her that I was *almost* convinced, so I smiled and lowered my head instead.

"I know we can get you a fee waiver for your tuition, but you might have to buy your own books. Do you want to start off with one or two classes?"

"I'm thinking one. I'm not back in one piece yet so you have to be careful with me."

I smiled at Brandy and pulled at her arm like a kid begging for candy at the checkout lane in the grocery store.

"Okay, I'm sure one class will be fine for now. What time of day do you want to go?"

"What do you mean?"

"Well do you want to go in the morning, afternoon, or evening? Morning is probably best. I know you don't want to wake up too early, but the tenured professors usually have earlier classes."

"Tenured?"

"You know, professors that have been around for awhile. They get first dibs at the schedule, and most of them teach from like 8 to 11 in the morning. Tenured professors are easier to get along with because they don't have anything to prove like the new instructors. They don't assign hella work or count absences and tardies against you. They're usually more laid back, you just have to get there hella early."

"That's *hella* early!"

"Well we'll look at the schedule on Monday, so don't stress. Let's just enjoy the weekend, and take care of you."

"I can't thank you enough for everything you have done for me. We're sitting here laughing, eating, and planning my life, but just a few hours ago I had a gun to my head and…"

"I know sweetie, but you're here now, and you're going to be okay. What do you want to do now?"

"I would say a movie, but I don't know if I want to sit on my ass for two more hours." I started laughing out loud until my body reminded me that I was still very sore. Maybe I need to go home and lay on my stomach for a little while."

"Instead of going to your house, let's go to mine. You really should call your apartment manager and see if he can change those locks today."

"I hadn't thought about it, but that's a good idea. I'll call him."

Brandy's phone rang, and I could tell that it was probably Lorenzo because she had a funny look on her face. She answered it, but spoke in whispery, coded responses. She felt bad for talking to her boyfriend in front of me when I was the tramp that should've been feeling bad.

After she hung up, we hopped in the car and headed towards her place. I figured that Lorenzo was supposed to come over, but she told him that I was coming, and he volunteered to stay at home. We didn't talk about him, but I assumed that they were back together and trying to work things out. At some point, we would be able to mention his name.

On the way to her house, Brandy went on and on about college, classes, books etc. It was driving me a little crazy, but I didn't have the heart to tell her to shut the fuck up. Although I appreciated Brandy's excitement and assistance, I felt so completely overwhelmed by my world spinning out of control. I had no control over my life and stood by helplessly watching my life happening to me, without the power of choice.

Brandy wanted me to jump into college as if it were a baptism, cleansing me of my sins. I believed her when she said she was behind me, and I knew that she would be there for me from start to finish encouraging and supporting me along the way, I just didn't know if I was up for the challenge.

Brandy made plans for us to go to the campus on Monday. She was going to take me to the Registrar's office, the Bursar's office, the financial aid office, and the bookstore. It sounded like we were going to visit every office on campus, and as she rattled off the itinerary for the day, I began to feel slightly overwhelmed, but I knew that Brandy would take care of me. She said that she would make sure that she got me in the right classes to ease my transition into college courses, so that I didn't feel weighed down. That morning, she was going to pick me up and we would ride to the campus together.

As anxious as I was to start my life over, the absence of money was like a splinter in my toe. Relatively speaking, the splinter was small, but the impact was big, and I couldn't stop thinking about it. I had a couple thousand dollars in the bank, but I was going to run through that in a couple of weeks when the rent and my car note were due. Forget trips to the mall; groceries, utilities, and car insurance would eat up whatever I had left. I felt desperate with no relief in sight. I had to keep reminding myself that I had my life, and with Brandy as my #1 cheerleader, I was blessed.

The issue of money gnawed at me for the rest of the day like when you couldn't remember if you turned the iron off after you left the house. I felt nervous and uneasy when my money was funny, and I didn't know how I would even concentrate in a classroom while my past due bills were sitting on my kitchen counter. I didn't know much about college, but I knew that financial aid took a couple of months to kick in, and I didn't think I could wait that long.

I had been financially comfortable for so long that it was unbearable to even think about living paycheck to paycheck, clipping coupons, and driving past the mall altogether, instead of stopping in and buying whatever I wanted. I went to Cheesecake Factory, Houston's, and Stinking Rose; I didn't eat at places where the employees wore greasy polyester shirts, and asked if I wanted fries with my order. As they say, I was accustomed to living a certain lifestyle, and I was in it knee deep with the car, the clothes, the shoes, the shades, and designer handbags. The bottom line was that even without the luxuries, I still couldn't pay my bills.

Before I drifted off to sleep at Brandy's, I thought about how life used to be so simple and uncomplicated right after high school, full of happiness and normalcy. Brandy and I worked at the mall, and we thought we were big time in our Guess jeans, Jordans and bamboo gold earrings. We went to the movies, the skating rink, and double dates with clean cut squares. I never drank, smoke, or even thought about kicking it with somebody that already had a female, no matter how cute he was. Smiles were abundant and the world was a beautiful place full of possibilities. No need for serious planning because my job at the mall was cool, and my discount alone was worth staying. I was a good kid that worked hard and had the utmost respect for myself.

If I knew then what I know now, I never would've stepped foot in a strip club. Within a few months, I was doing everything I swore that I would never do: drinking, drugs, lying, and cheating. Stripping itself was like a drug because none of the girls were ever satisfied with the money they made, always wanting more. First you start stripping, and then you're doing table dances, next its parties, touching and fondling, and then fucking and sucking for loot. After doing all that, for some girls moving up to pornos was the logical next step.

Basically, the line became blurred between what was decent and what you were willing to do for money. The longer a girl stripped, the longer she would remain there because after you start making serious money, you know you will never make a quarter of that working a straight job, so you begin to feel like you have to stay in the club. So, if a girl wanted to get out, she had to do it within the first six months to a year, but definitely no longer than a year or you became a slave to the club and the life.

There should've been a revolving door at the front for all the girls that would leave and come right back with shattered dreams, like when directors came in and plucked girls out of the club for B movies and rap videos. The pay was ridiculous, but the girls thought they were going to become Hollywood stars; the harsh reality was that most of the movies were straight to video. The rap videos were mostly uncut and didn't require much acting. The scripts called for titties and ass, no speaking lines just pole tricks, booty clapping, and the splits.

Some of the girls came back and told us stories about how they fucked some of the rappers and actors on the set for extra money. They took them to the trailers, and for $150 they would boss them up between takes. Most of the girls were just extras, so they didn't make much money. They would work from 9am to three or four the next morning for a few hundred dollars. It was peanuts, but they liked to come back to the club and brag about who they met. I wasn't above bossing a rapper, but there wasn't enough money to make me sit on a set for 18 or 19 hours for chump change. Every girl at the club had a different hustle, but my hustle was money. I didn't turn much down that had real money behind it.

Brandy must have thought I was sleep because I heard Lorenzo come in. I didn't dare leave her bedroom and cause either one of them to be embarrassed anymore than they already had been. I looked at the sliver on my wrist, and the secret that I held. To share it with anyone would give it life, and I didn't want to exploit the desperation that I felt at the moment when I couldn't see life beyond the moon and stars of that horrendous night. A demon had put blinders over my eyes that wouldn't allow me to see the hopeful sun just over the horizon, waiting to bring me sunshine and warmth. Tears had begun to dampen the pillowcase as a flood of emotions took hold of my lungs and seized my breath, quietly whimpering like a puppy separated from his mother.

My manager changed the locks Sunday, and I was able to sleep in my own apartment that night. In a fleeting moment of clarity, I took all of my stripper clothes, shoes, and bags out of my closet and put them in boxes and carried them down to the trunk of my car like a recovering drug addict removes syringes, spoons, and cotton balls from the medicine cabinet. I didn't know where I was taking them, but I didn't want them in my closet anymore. The memories were too fresh and haunting. The clothes reminded me of Hypnotiq, getting robbed, having a gun to my head, being raped, and all the money I broke my back to make, but no longer had. I locked the ghosts in the car, and started back upstairs.

As I got to the top, I heard my cell phone ringing. It was Brandy checking up on me. I wasn't 100%, but I was feeling much better than I did just the day before.

"Hey girl. Just checking on you. How are you?"

"I'm cool. I was just cleaning out my closet."

"Really?"

"Yeah, I took all of the stripper clothes out and put them in my trunk."

"What are you going to do with them now?"

"I have no idea, but I wanted to get them up out of here. They're hard to look at because every gruesome thing that has happened to me lately has some connection to the club. Hypnotiq, Blaze, the robbery, the rape, and the fact that I am now dead broke. The club laced me with all that money, but then it snatched it right out of my hand with no fucking warning."

Brandy could tell that I was getting agitated and frustrated, and she swooped in with her positive thoughts and well wishes.

"Maybe it was a good idea to get rid of everything. You don't need any negative reminders around you. I'm going to work half a day, and then I'll be right over about 12:30. Is that cool?"

"Yeah."

"You sound sad. Do you want me to come over?"

"Brandy, I'm not sad, I'm broke. College is cool, but what am I supposed to live on?"

"I can try to help you as much as I can, and you'll get financial aid by September."

"Are you serious? That's three fucking months away!"

"I know you're used to big money, but this is the real world, and you have to crawl before you can walk."

If I thought I was straddling the fence before, I knew I was sitting dead on top of it after my conversation with Brandy. She was right, fast money only applied to stripping, ho-ing, robbing, stealing, and hustling. Legit money was slow, and even when you did get it, it was nothing compared to what I was used to. Before I went to bed, I thought about legit jobs that I could get with my high school education, and I went to bed depressed.

The next morning, I got up and ate a bowl of cereal while I watched Jerry Springer. It was 10, and Brandy was going to be there in a couple of hours. I got in the shower, threw on some clothes and waited on the couch. I looked in my purse for some gum and realized that I didn't have any cash on me. I wanted to take Brandy to a cool little lunch in appreciation for everything she had done for me, so I grabbed my keys and went to the bank.

When I got to the parking lot, I searched for my ATM card and couldn't find it, so I walked inside to get cash from the teller. When it was my turn in line, I gave the teller the withdrawal slip for $500, but after she pulled up my account, the look on her face said it all. She looked confused, tapping buttons, nervously checking the screen over and over. When she fixed her lips to tell me that my balance was $14.20, I had hoped that Ashton Kutcher and the Punk'd crew was going to show up with a camera in my face, but they never came. Blaze and her boys had stolen my ATM card and hit up my account over the last two weeks for $3,000. For six days, she withdrew $500 a day while she was spending hours at my house, patting my back, and telling me that everything was going to be okay.

Well, my question had been answered; Blaze knew that she was going to rob me way before she reached in that tampon box that morning. I always had cash so I never needed my ATM card. I had no idea that she had stolen my card and was robbing me blind. The nerve of that bitch to be in my face, knowing that she was fucking me up against the wall.

When I told to the branch manager that someone had committed fraud against me, he politely explained that they would investigate, but that I should have filed a claim sooner. He said that I probably wouldn't recover the money because I didn't report the card stolen and because I had given the PIN number to Blaze. I had given it to her when she offered to go to the bank, get some cash and pay some bills for me a couple of weeks ago. The teller gave me a ten dollar bill, four ones, two dimes, a receipt, and told me to have a nice day.

When I got to the comfort of my own car, I let the tears out that had been fighting a battle with me inside the bank. I had truly hit bottom. I was already stressed out by the fact that I only had bill money for the next month or so, but then the teller twisted the knife that was already protruding from my chest.

I started the engine and took off down the freeway. I didn't know where I was going, but I had to get away. I drove for what seemed like forever and then I just stopped and turned the car off. I sat in my car, looking at the tiny little scabs on my wrist where a permanent scar would grow, and contemplated my fragile situation. After I sat there for awhile, I had an epiphany.

I knew what I had to do to escape the maze of constant agony and depression. My weaknesses were whispering to me, louder and louder until I finally acknowledged the voice. Something was telling me that I couldn't live like this anymore, not another day, not another hour. I couldn't go back to my childhood fears of having no money or food. I couldn't bear to feel the loneliness and insecurity that I felt as a kid. I had been violated by a man…again. I couldn't relive those nightmares again.

Suddenly, the hazy fog burned off, the tears dried up, and my face slowly became void of any expression. I knew what I had to do. I closed my eyes, and leaned my head back on the headrest. I couldn't feel anything anymore; I was numb to the tenderness of my wounds, the costly betrayals, death, and the long journey that I had to take to get to this place. Unexpectedly, I began to float out of my window, hovering above my car. I was looking down at myself sitting in the driver's seat no longer shedding tears, confused and disoriented. There was no more pain or stress, and a sense of calm peacefulness and comfort blanketed me.

My cell phone interrupted my final thoughts, yanking me from the clouds and throwing me back in the driver's seat. I looked down to see that it was Brandy calling. No doubt she was at my apartment wondering where I was, but I couldn't answer the phone because she would try to stop me from doing what I had to do. She would probably yell and scream, beg and cry, and tell me that she would be right there to save me from myself. I stepped out of my car alone and walked towards my destiny.

"Alizé? Damn girl, we haven't seen you in a minute! You back?"
"Yeah, I'm back."

Ultimately, I reacted no differently from anyone else under the same circumstances. Creatures of habit often return to their comfort zone in times of despair. The reality of my desperate situation was that I needed the club to get back on my feet. I hated the club with every fiber of my being, for changing me and tricking me into believing that I didn't deserve any better. I hated the club for allowing me to believe that I was there of my own free will, deceiving me into believing that I had power and control over my life when I had none. I hated the club for turning me out, creating a haven for prostitution, addiction and adultery. I hated the club for dragging me back into the pits of hell, forcing me to chase shadows that I wasn't yet ready to face.

In the end, *Aces* had become both my sanctuary and my cross to bear.

www.myspace.com/racylee

978-0-595-40020-1
0-595-40020-5

Printed in the United States
104076LV00005B/111/A